Patriot Apprentice

The Second Novel in the Hollister Series

RICHARD MODLIN

HARTSIDE PUBLISHING
OWENS CROSS ROADS, AL

-

The Second Novel in the Hollister Series

Copyright © Richard Modlin, 2015
Hartside Publishing
Owens Cross Roads, AL 35763

For further information please contact
richard@richardmodlin.com.

Printed in the United States of America.

ISBN-10: 0980047382
ISBN-13: 9780980047387
Library of Congress Control Number: 2014923025
Hartside Publishing, Owens Cross Roads, AL 35763

ACKNOWLEDGMENTS

The editorial comments, suggestions, and encouragement of my wife, author and photographer Marian Moore Lewis, as well as those of other members of my writers group—Rusty Bynum, William Case, Dr. William Goodson, and Sara McDaris—enhanced the quality of *Patriot Apprentice*. I would also like to recognize editors and magazine publishers Bob Berta of *County Wide* and G. Pierre Dumont of *Paper Talks Magazine*, both from Washington County, Maine, for enthusiastically promoting my books. The Porter Memorial Library in Machias, Maine, provided historical information and data on and maps of eighteenth-century Maine.

CHAPTER 1

Aknot tightened in Jack Hollister's stomach as he walked past freight wagons and groups of stevedores who were milling about to a shadowed corner of the wharf. He reached into his waistcoat pocket, removed his watch, and checked it. It was four o'clock in the afternoon. He continued down the wharf. Finding an inconspicuous place at a dock's edge, he looked across the water and saw what had brought him to the wharves. Not far ahead, the lines of the *Clara H*, the new Hollister brigantine, were being cast off. He lowered his head, rubbed his temples, and then looked up and watched the vessel. *Why did I come here?* From his hidden location, he scanned the vessel's deck. The hawser secured the brig to shore, and its trailing end swung free and hit the hull with a clap like the slap of a cat-o'-nine-tails. He thought of what Ian, his brother, had experienced last winter as a conscripted sailor aboard the HMS *Buzzard* and shivered. *He is going home to safety, but he's upset about my decision to stay in the colonies and as uncertain of my future as I am.*

A month had passed since Jack had concluded his position in the family business was superfluous and decided not to return to England with the Hollisters' Boston household. Though he knew remaining in America would be hazardous and unpredictable, he wanted to join the colonials in their quest for freedom. He wanted to be a part of this movement. However, with the British in charge of Boston, the city was not safe for any English person who avowed joining the rebelling colonials.

Jack's mind drifted back to the evening he had to refuse Ian's invitation to the family dinner. The reflection made him sad. To remain, however, he had to return to the Blue Goat Inn—a tavern and lodge where patriots could secretly meet. General George Washington had arranged for Nathan Hale, an undercover lieutenant in the Continental army, to sneak Jack into Boston. Washington had insisted Hale return to Cambridge in four days. That evening was the night of the fourth day. If Jack were to stay, he had to meet Nathan. Hale's connections would allow him safe passage out of Boston, across the Charles River, and to Washington's headquarters at the Vassall House in Cambridge.

Washington's desire to learn how the people in Boston were coping under the blockade necessitated Jack and Nathan's present visit to the city. The two men had returned to lodge at the Blue Goat Inn two nights before. While there Jack learned the *Clara H* was about to sail. Missing his relatives and still uncertain about his decision to remain in the colonies, Jack went to the wharf to see the vessel off.

Jack straightened and watched as the last hawser was hauled aboard. *Wonder what delayed Uncle Edgar's departure. Worrying about meeting a winter storm at sea perhaps made Uncle anxious. He wanted to leave at the beginning of September.*

That gave everyone two weeks to prepare to leave for England, but he probably did not realize it took longer than that to close and pack up the business. Jack tightened his coat about himself. *September is half over. My God. So is 1775.*

Jack noticed a lone figure leaning against the rail near the vessel's bow and recognized the MacAdam butler, Auggy. The butler's presence exacerbated Jack's uncertainties. *Been on this continent for over a year,* Jack thought and scratched his head. *Did I make the right decision to stay?*

Auggy raised his cap and waved.

Did he see me? Or is he waving good-bye to Boston?

Trying to avoid being noticed, Jack sidestepped behind a group of opulent-looking men. Auggy stopped waving for a moment and slowly moved his head about as if attempting to focus on where Jack had once stood. The butler searched the wharf while he advanced along the rail. He stopped as if he noticed something, leaned forward, and hoisted his arm. Jack could almost hear Auggy's cap fluttering as the butler shook it in his direction. "Damn! I have been spotted," Jack grumbled. He slunk lower and tried to remain hidden.

"Did you say something, young man?" one of the men said condescendingly.

A banker or merchant, Jack thought, and he sneered. *Pompous.* When he raised his eyes, the man's glare dumbfounded him. It was as if the rotund fellow, festooned in a black riding coat and lacy white shirt, read his thoughts. "Answer me, boy."

"No. Not to you, my good man."

"Slinking around like you are suggests you might be known to those aboard the English vessel." The merchant looked toward Jack, grinned at his partners, and puffed out his chest. This forced the lace on the shirt into his chin. He stuck his thumbs into his belt and turned to his friends while continuing to converse with Jack. "Well, if you know them..." He chuckled. "You have missed them. If you don't know them, you should be happy. What you are seeing, lad, are the bloody loyalists running for cover. Soon they'll all be gone, and we'll have our city back."

Two of the men removed their tricornes and fanned them at the *Clara H.*

"Aye, and good riddance," one grunted.

"May their voyage be as tormented as they made our lives," the other said.

"Now, what about you, lad?" the puffed fellow questioned. "Are ye friend or foe?"

Jack looked down. He moved his head back and forth. He parted his lips and tried to speak, but his words would not come forth. Instead he nodded and backed away. Finally he took a deep breath and mumbled, "I'm losing some people...I may never again see." He gasped and felt as if someone was squeezing his stomach.

"Come. Join us for an ale," the merchant said.

Jack shook his head. "Thank you, but I must meet someone very soon."

Nodding toward the man, he turned and plodded off to the far side of the wharf. He seated himself on a bollard. His eyes focused on the *Clara H.* Its bow rotated toward the channel. He could see Auggy now standing at the stern rail. With him were Ian, Uncle Edgar, and his cousins Clyde and Adair MacAdam. They all faced the wharf, but because of the distance to the vessel, he was unable to see their expressions. However, by the way Uncle Edgar gesticulated at the vessel's captain, Jack knew his uncle was angry. *Perhaps he wants the* Clara H *to return to the wharf and collect me.*

A wave of depression enveloped Jack as he watched the wind billow the square sails and tighten them against the halyards and sheets. The *Clara H* entered King's Road, and the Hollister brig headed for the Atlantic. A tear slid down Jack's cheek. *I may be on my own, but I will survive. I have disappointed them. I know that. If I ever see them again, I will try to explain.*

The bell atop Christ Church sounded. Jack lowered his head, slipped off the bollard, and began walking.

*　•　◆　•　*

Professor Morton, proprietor of the Blue Goat Inn, handed Lieutenant Hale another mug of coffee. "Jack just walked in," he said, "and he's looking a bit down in the mouth."

Hale grinned, picked up the second mug, strolled to a table in a dim corner of the inn, and motioned for Jack to join him. Jack walked over. The chair scraped against the floor as he pulled it away from the table and plopped himself down. "Thank you," he said and wrapped his hands around the mug. "The weather is turning cold."

Nathan nodded. "You went to the wharf. Did you meet with Ian? Or Uncle Edgar? Or anyone from the Hollister Exchange?"

"No." Jack shook his head. "But I did see them—Ian, Uncle Edgar, and their butler standing along the stern rail. The *Clara H* was already pointing for the Atlantic." He cupped his face in his hands and then raised his head. "Auggy spotted me. I think Uncle Edgar tried to have the captain return the brig to the wharf." Jack shrugged. "But it was too late."

"Seems that made you feel sad."

Jack sat back in the chair and took a long drink from the mug. "I really did not want them to see me," he said after swallowing. "Now they're on their way to Plymouth." He scratched his head and lowered it. "Probably never see them again."

"Not so," Nathan interrupted. "You are a Hollister—a well-connected British gentleman—but at this time, you are a lost soul. You do have a possible way to get back home if you still want to go there." Hale sipped his coffee and grinned. "The Royal Navy returned Ian when they learned he was a Hollister. Now you are in Boston, but the admiralty does not know that. By all rights you are still lost in the great northern fir forests. All you have to do is go to Admiral Graves's office and announce who you are. Being a Hollister and a friend of Lord North, the ol' boy will put you on the next vessel sailing for England."

Jack clasped his hands together and looked down. "Uncle Edgar appeared upset when the *Clara H*'s captain would not return." Linking his fingers and twisting his thumbs over each other, Jack took a deep breath. "Seeing them off like that without saying good-bye. I am feeling lost." He paused, sighed, and shook his head. He lowered his chin to his chest but kept his eyes closed.

The scheme Nathan proposed finally jelled in Jack's brain. *What Nathan says is true. Admiral Graves knows about Ian, but he doesn't know about me—that I am in Boston. It's a perfect way out if I want it.* Jack pursed his lips and nodded. *I'm here. This is where I want to be. I'm staying.*

Sitting up and straightening his shoulders, he clenched his fists and pounded them on the table. "You know that is not what I want. I admire your desire for freedom, and I want to be a part of this country's endeavor."

Nathan placed both his hands on the table's edge, smiled, and nodded. He rocked himself back against the wall. "Morton, my friend," he called out, "a tot of rum for me and our new patriot apprentice." Nathan's cheeks contorted into a satisfied smile.

Professor Morton rushed to the table holding two beakers of rum. He bent close to Nathan and flicked his head inconspicuously toward a table near the door. "Please remember where you are, my friends," he whispered. "There are many ears."

Glancing over Nathan's shoulder, Jack saw three British soldiers enjoying their drinks. They seemed oblivious to him and Nathan. "Aye," Nathan whispered. We need not be conspicuous." He nodded at Morton and let two coins roll out of his hand. "For you, my friend."

When the coins hit the tabletop, they clanged and caused one of the soldiers to look over at them. He stirred as if trying to stand. The chair scratched against the floor as the redcoat shoved back from the table. After a moment of shifting, the corporal relaxed and remained seated.

"Phew," Jack whispered. He and Nathan sat quietly for a few minutes and drank their rum. "Perhaps those redcoats are nervous. On the wharf I felt hostility toward redcoats and loyalists. I heard stevedores threaten to cut British throats. Then while I watched the *Clara H* depart, I overheard a group of well-dressed merchants say disparaging words about my family's business. 'Happy to be rid of them,' they said. Worse than that, though, they cursed their trip."

"Yes, Jack. Loyalist companies, such as the Hollister Exchange and others who trade with the military, are not taxed the way colonial merchants are. Now with the blockade, only goods from Britain are allowed in, and it's more costly compared with commodities and wares from the Netherlands, Spain, or the Virgin Islands. Colonials cannot make a profit."

Jack clasped his mug, took a drink, and spoke. "The people of Machias badly needed basic food supplies. The British Army needed lumber to build and improve barracks here in Boston. Machias had an abundance of wood, but they did not want to support Britain. So they did not trade. Instead they revolted."

"You took part in that fight, did you not?" Nathan grinned. "Did you enjoy fighting against your own countrymen?"

Jack pondered for a moment, narrowed his eyes, and answered. "Nay." He then measured his words. "I fought against an oppressor with little respect for his colonial subjects. I fought with people who have toiled to create a democracy they believe functions for them. A people who would serve Britain as a protectorate if allowed their freedom to become so, but no. Instead the king and parliament taxed them and lorded over them as if the colonials were nothing but criminals and ignorant serfs. King George and those tomfools create intolerable laws and know very little of the progress the Americans have made."

"And you, Jack, by your words are a special Englishman." Nathan chuckled and raised his mug. "I do believe I should toast you, you decrier of British rule. Huzzah, my friend!"

The two men drank, raised their mugs, and gulped again. Jack's mug made a slight thump when he set it back on the table. He wiped his mouth with his sleeve. Nathan swigged down his coffee, looked at Jack, and laughed. Though his hilarity continued, his facial features sobered. He bit his lip, stared over Jack's shoulder, and whispered. "I do believe it is time to leave. We have attracted some attention." Nathan shoved back his chair and rose. "Time to return to our accounts. Don't you think?" he said loudly enough for others to hear. "We stay any longer, the numbers will begin looking like a mandarin puzzle."

"Aye, amigo." Jack stood, walked around the table, and slapped Nathan on the back.

"So you have finally learned a little Spanish," Nathan said.

"My uncle believes we might trade with them again someday."

"Aye." Nathan put his arm across Jack's shoulders, and the two started for the door.

The corporal from the table of redcoats stood and blocked their way. "Gentlemen, may I ask your business?" He scowled at the two.

"We're accountants," Jack said and grinned. "We've overstayed our lunch. My uncle will be fuming when we return. Too much drink I believe. Don't you think, Nate?"

"Aye," Nathan answered. "Uncle Edgar will be angry and for good reason. We were also late yesterday."

"And where might your accounting be?" the corporal asked.

"Hollister Exchange and Transport, my friend," Jack said. "My uncle is Edgar Hollister."

The corporal nodded, pulled his chair to the side, and seated himself. "My mistake, gentlemen." He slid himself back among his comrades. "These days one never knows who is friend or foe."

The corporal took a drink of his ale while his comrades mumbled among themselves. Jack looked at Nathan and twitched his head toward Professor Morton, who stood behind the bar and looked nervous. Nathan nodded.

"Mr. Morton," Jack called out. "Would you be so kind as to provide these fine soldiers with a round of their favorite beverages?" Turning to the redcoats, he put his hand on the shoulder of the nearest. "We'll be leaving now. Continue doing such a fine job rooting out those disloyal rebels."

The corporal and several others gestured a thank-you. Jack and Nathan strolled out of the Blue Goat Inn.

———•◦•———

Exiting the Blue Goat Inn onto Sudbury Street, Jack and Nathan rounded the corner and hoofed down Hiller Lane to Green Lane. From there they walked fast and made a left onto Chamber Street. They turned into the first alleyway that terminated at the salt marsh edging the Charles River and came to rest against a building. They were gasping and laughing.

Jack bent over, grabbed his knees, and held the position for a moment. He straightened and saw Nathan flattened against the blackening red bricks. Nathan's head rolled skyward. "Are you all right?" Jack asked.

"Yes!" Nathan took a deep breath, coughed, and choked out a couple more laughs. He lowered his head and relaxed. "Yes. I am good. Whoa. That was some trot. We covered the distance in about fifteen minutes."

"Aye. We did." Jack nodded and inhaled and exhaled normally.

"And that fool corporal believed you," Nathan said and chuckled. "Quick thinking."

Jack sat down next to the building's side. With a glint in his eyes, he raised his brow. "We could not have told them we were students. Everyone knows Harvard is a hotbed of rebels. We would be sitting is some dungeon right now and trying to explain."

Nathan became more serious. "Aye. But what if those redcoats had known about the Hollisters?"

"Their eyes were sleepy and tired. Looked as if they had spent the day searching the streets and taverns for rebels. They were common soldiers not assigned to the wharf."

"Yes. And in each tavern they inspect, they enjoy a brew or two—free. Tapsters gain favors that way. They *were* aware of the Hollister name and the clout it carried with Great Britain, though."

"Aye. Sometimes being known is good, but the Hollister name does ring with the loyalists."

Nathan nodded. While the two young men talked, the sky darkened from evening twilight to black. Emerging from its new phase, the moon hung behind them as a thin crescent. It emitted very little light.

"Jack," Nathan said, "our ferry across the Charles will be arriving shortly. We need to get to the river."

"Hey, I cannot see you." Jack extended his hand and felt Nathan's coat. "Yes. Let us go."

With their fingers sliding along the building's bricks and feeling the cobblestones beneath their boots, the two young men moved down the pitch-dark alleyway. A short distance past the building's edge, the alley gave way to a smooth trail of shell and sand. They continued to walk, and soon their footsteps began to squish.

"We have reached the edge of the salt marsh," Jack whispered. He felt blades of cordgrass switching against his boots. "Do you know what the tide is doing?"

Nathan touched Jack's shoulder. "It should be flooding. Let us wait here. The coxswain will uncover and raise the lantern when the longboat's bow kisses the sand. Watch. Only a momentary flash we will see."

A chill, salty breeze whisked around them as they stood. Jack shivered, pulled the collar of his coat up, and tightened it around his neck. "I hope we did not jeopardize Professor Morton."

"Not him, I believe," Nathan said, "but we will have to be more cautious. We might have compromised our gathering place."

The subdued sound of gurgling water drifted toward them. Then there was a crunch, and the orangish light of a candle flame flashed.

"Grab my hand," Nathan said. "We will go it together."

After a few moments of sloshing forward, cold water from the Charles River flowed over the tops of Jack's and Nathan's boots. They took hold of the longboat when the water reached midway up their thighs. The lantern glowed at the coxswain's feet, and five pairs of legs were visible. Jack heard men wheezing and occasionally spitting.

"Push us off," someone said.

In a moment the bow was free of the sand, and the longboat slid back.

"Hurry. Get aboard," the coxswain mumbled.

Jack felt several strong hands grab onto him and haul him aboard. He fell onto a thwart between two oarsmen. Water poured out of his boots and off his britches. When he reached down to pull off his boots, he could feel Nathan seated forward of him. Before any other sound was made, someone issued a command. "Back away together!"

While the inertia shifted everyone back and forth with each pull of the oars, stomping feet echoed from the alleyway. Torches lit the edge of the salt marsh.

"A redcoat patrol," Nathan grunted.

"Dig for your lives," the coxswain shouted. The longboat sped backward for some yards. River water sloshed over the transom. The coxswain shoved the tiller hard to larboard. "Keep the pace, boys!" To allow the longboat to rotate around, the coxswain yelled, "Pull together, me lads."

With the bow pointed upriver, the boat slid forward. As the longboat moved parallel along the shore, several musket balls zinged overhead. Jack could see the torches being moved about. They showed clouds of musket exhaust twirling and dissipating. The soldiers fired several more shots. They splashed into the water before Jack felt the longboat lurch around ninety degrees. The bow now faced the middle of the river. *We're headed for the opposite shore.* Though the muskets kept firing, he could see the shots were striking the Charles River some yards behind the stern.

Within five minutes the longboat entered a drifting fogbank. Except for the gurgling and surging of the oars, everything else was silent for the next twenty minutes. The crunch finally came when the longboat beached itself on the shore of Plupp's Farm.

On the morning two days after he and Nathan had returned from Boston, Jack crawled out of his bunk. Billy,

Washington's personal valet; two other black servants; and a black boy entered the officer's barracks. Dressed in a long muslin nightgown, Jack stood yawning and running his fingers through his disheveled brownish-blond hair. Disregarding his condition, the entourage marched across the room past several other officers in various stages of consciousness and halted at the foot of Jack's cot.

"His Excellency would like you in proper dress when you present yourself at the luncheon," Billy announced. "You are expected there in two hours."

Washington's valet swung his arm over the cot and motioned for the servants to lay out what appeared to be a military uniform. Jack watched. His eyes scanned the apparel—knee-length pants with blue and gold stripes along the seam of each leg and a light-blue waistcoat that had two broad white stripes on each lapel. One originated at shoulder level and the other at the hip, and both tended toward the middle. When the waistcoat was buttoned, the stripes connected to form an X. A white, collarless muslin jumper with blousy sleeves partially covered the waistcoat. To Jack this shirt appeared like something his pirate friend, Dunkin, would wear. *What country do these clothes represent? I don't even recognize the service.*

Jack lifted his head and slightly twisted it to the side when one of the servants laid a dark-blue, long-tailed coat on his cot. Though golden spheres tacked down its epaulets, he could see where other official ornamental stripes and buttons had been removed. *Appears to be a British naval officer's coat.*

The servant boy set a pair of black, polished, calf-length leather boots on the floor. Above them and on the cot's edge, he placed a felt bicorne. Then he unhitched a wide leather belt from which hung a scabbard that contained a plain-handled cutlass. Lastly the boy laid the sword belt meticulously on the bundled blanket behind the bicorne.

The commotion around Jack attracted the other four officers who occupied the room to his cot. All stood around in their nightgowns and perused the apparel being so officially displayed for Jack's benefit. The oldest officer, George Washington's secretary, held his chin and began to grin. "His Excellency wants you to have a uniform representative of your assignment and service. Since the Continental army does not have a naval unit, I had to create a uniform for an officer of the lowest naval rank. So, my dear Master Hollister, or should I say Midshipman Hollister?" Washington's secretary paused and glared down at Jack. "Don't mention what I just said to you. His Excellency wants you to be surprised." He smiled. "To use a nautical term, it'll blow the wind out of his sails. So please act surprised. He plans to inform you at dinner." Washington's secretary stepped around the servants, bent over, and lifted the coat off the bed. Holding it up in front of him, he said, "British tailored, but I sew on American buttons." Then he laid the coat back on the cot. "Before you, Master Hollister, lies an eclectic combination of pieces that will comprise the uniform of our country's first midshipmen in General Washington's navy."

Jack stood with his mouth open. The servants remained stoic, and the other officers snickered.

"Wear it in good stead, Jack." The secretary motioned for the others to leave. "We also need to prepare ourselves for the ceremony. So we will leave you to clothe yourself. Billy will stay to help. Make sure you look proper."

Jack stood astounded. His mouth opened as if to say something, but words would not come. All he could do was nod as the others returned to their cots.

———•◦•———

Amid boisterous conversation, chiding, laughing, and coughing after Washington's staff officers had finished the noonday dinner, the servants cleared away food-dirtied dishes; platters containing bits and pieces of roasted fowl and vegetables; and partially filled and empty cruets, mugs, and bowls. Billy carried two bottles of Madeira to where General Washington sat. Not wearing his dark coat diminished Washington's tallness. The mixture of dim sunlight shining through the windows and candlelight colored the general's powdered white hair a dull gold but darkened his rosy cheeks.

Two servants followed the valet. Each balanced a tray of wineglasses. The first glass was placed in front of Washington. Then they turned and continued along the table. One servant was on each side, and each placed a glass in front of the other diners. Billy followed and filled the glasses with the after-dinner wine.

The general raised his hand. "Gentlemen, please bring yourselves to order. I have several announcements."

While the servants removed the remaining forks and knives, the room quieted. Feeling uncomfortable in the ill-fitting makeshift uniform, Jack shifted in his chair, tugged at his coat, ticked and adjusted buttons, and brushed crumbs off his pants. Seated midway down the table, he grasped his wineglass as George Washington pushed back his chair and stood.

"Gentlemen," Washington began, "as some of you might already know—since confidential information around these parts is not as private as I would like—I have empowered Colonel John Glover of Marblehead, Massachusetts, to charter several vessels to replace the *Hanna*—the only naval vessel we have. Though she has been quite successful, the *Hanna* is aging and needs to be returned to her owner.

"Colonel Glover has sent word he has procured a usually rigged schooner. It has the addition of a short third mast stepped over the rudder. Though it is sturdy and just shy of one hundred thirty feet in length. It is from a Mr. Thomas Stevens also of Marblehead. Glover says an angler used it, and the little after-sail provided slow headway while working."

"Aye, sir," one of the officers said. "Called a mizzen."

"Yes. So it is," Washington continued. "The colonel has contracted with a shipyard in Beverly to refit and arm this schooner as a naval vessel." Washington paused, his brows furrowed, and he straightened his stance. "Officially, gentlemen, we do not have a Continental navy. Though I am working to rectify that."

Jack looked at the other officers who began mumbling among themselves. His eyes connected with Nathan, who sat diagonally across from him. Nathan wore a smile.

"I would like to introduce Mr. Jack Hollister to those of you who have not yet met him." Washington nodded at Jack and continued. "Jack has come into our midst from the coast of Maine where he ennobled himself during the naval battle at Machias. I believe he is a true patriot, and I would like to distinguish his sailing abilities by awarding him the rank of midshipman in our as yet unformed navy." Washington faced Jack. "Please stand, Mr. Hollister." The general raised his glass of Madeira as Jack moved to stand. "A toast, gentlemen, to our first midshipman. Your past actions have shown you to be a patriot of this country as has your desire for independence. A midshipman is a seagoing apprentice. While at sea in this rank, you will develop a mastery of seamanship and gain confidence."

Chairs scraped against the floor as the people at the table stood, and in a chorus of deep voices, they proclaimed, "To Midshipman Jack." They lifted their glasses to their mouths and drank. Then the officers began to shout, "Huzzah! Huzzah!" Their hardy chant resounded through the room.

Straightening and tightening his muscles, he allowed a smile to form on his face. Words tumbled from his mouth. "It…it's an honor…sir."

"Yes, yes, Mr. Hollister," Washington said. "I'd like to welcome you to my staff of officers." Returning the wineglass to the table, the general sat down. "Please take your seats, gentlemen."

Again the chairs grated against the floor as the people settled into the chairs and adjusted themselves.

"Mr. Hollister, I am assigning you to the refurbished schooner as my liaison. You will travel to Beverly, Massachusetts, in the company of a small regiment I am sending there. Captain Thomas Morris, whom I have commissioned to master our new naval vessel, is expecting you. Mr. Morris wants you to arrive before he puts to sea. He intends to sail within a week. Incidentally the schooner has been renamed the *Piper*."

Jack nodded. "Thank you, sir. I will happily do my duty."

"Yes." Washington glanced over at Nathan Hale. "Lieutenant Hale." Nathan's head snapped up. "Lieutenant, your assignment has a bit of danger. I am sending you to New York City. Intelligence coming from that city is erratic, unpredictable, and mostly untrustworthy."

"Your Excellency, the city is under the loyalists' control," Nathan said. His eyes widened and glazed with misgiving. "With British regiments fortified on Staten Island and the loyalists in control of the city, patriots are having an ungodly time of it."

"I am counting on your cunning. The time you spent with those loyalists at Yale College should have given you the experience to deal with those crown-following New Yorkers. With what you know, Nathan, you should be able to integrate into their culture and gain their confidence. I need you to become one of them. Learn what those damn loyalists and redcoats are doing and thinking. Long

Island and New York City are strategic in many ways to our efforts."

"Aye, sir." Nathan clasped his hand. Beads of sweat appeared on his forehead. He nodded slightly. "An undercover agent, huh?" Nathan lifted his head. A sheepish smile covered his face. "We all know they imprison rebels and hang traitors without question."

"Yes," the general said. The others around the table stared at Nathan. He had raised his right arm and caused his shadow to appear as if the grim reaper stood behind him. "I need credible intelligence if our operations are to be successful. If we lose our quest for independence, we will all be facing the noose." Washington paused and drank some water. "You will have to pocket your jesting attitude. Watch your backside. You will need caution and care to bring you through this affair, Lieutenant."

"Begging your pardon, sir," Jack said. "Perhaps I should accompany Mr. Hale to New York."

"No, Mr. Hollister. Perhaps one day but not now. You have your orders and will be leaving for Beverly as soon as the caravan is loaded and the regiment mustered." The general straightened. "Thank you, gentlemen. Dinner is over."

<hr />

Outside the Vassall House, the officers stood in a scattered group. Their faces were sober or covered in half smiles. Several strolled over to Jack, shook his hand, patted him on the back, and wished him well.

Jack looked toward Nathan, who stood about ten feet away. He was conversing with an officer Jack had previously seen with Nathan but to whom he had not been introduced. Their conversation seemed amicable. Jack watched as this officer placed his arm across Nathan's shoulders. *He must be the fellow Nathan mentioned who had just returned from a mission to Long Island,* Jack thought. *Perhaps he's to be Nathan's contact in New York.*

CHAPTER 2

Sitting in a small Cambridge pub, Jack stared down at the tabletop and pondered. His eyes locked on the mug of ale he pushed from hand to hand. Nathan sat across from him. "Thinking of your future?" Nathan asked. He glanced at Jack, lifted his mug, and drank.

"I have an uncomfortable concern," Jack said and raised his head. Clutching the mug in both hands, he sighed. "I would feel better if I were going with you to New York. You need someone to look out for you. We did well in Boston."

"Thank you, Jack. Aye. We are a team, but clandestine missions are best done alone." Nathan sat back. A relaxed smile spread across his face. "I will not be going to New York until spring. Colonel Charles Webb asked that I return with him to Stamford, Connecticut, and help organize the Connecticut Regiment."

"Colonel Webb will be your contact in New York? Was he the one talking to you earlier?"

"No. That was Lieutenant Arian Brace. He says he knew me at Yale College." Nathan shook his head. "I do not recall him, but he told me he comes from the town of Jamaica on Long Island. Says he is well acquainted with Manhattan Island. Then he said he would be my contact in the city when the time came." Nathan raised his eyebrows and downed another gulp of ale. "I really do not believe I know this Lieutenant Brace fellow. Before I put any confidence in him, I will find out more about him."

"When you talked, you two seemed comfortable."

"Aye. The lieutenant's approach was definitely congenial, but he spoke fast like a salesman. I could not get a word in edgeways." Nathan finished his beer, set his mug down, and attempted to attract the barmaid's attention. "Let us have a tot of rum to celebrate your assignment, promotion, and future."

Jack nodded. "I am still concerned for your safety. I have heard matters are not well in the city for those who have aligned themselves with the American cause."

"Yes, Jack, but let us not dwell. Your assignment to the *Piper* seems full of excitement. Is this not what you wanted?"

"Aye."

As the barmaid approached their table, Nathan shouted out, "Bring us two tots of your best rum, m'lady."

"I will be leaving on the morrow, and we might not meet again for some time," Jack said. He stretched his arms toward the middle of the table and clasped his hands together.

"Not so. His Excellency General Washington has taken a liking to you. I believe he will reassign or promote you when the campaign here in Boston is complete."

The barmaid returned and set two small glasses of rum in front of Jack and Nathan.

"And the Boston campaign will be successful," Nathan continued. "There is discussion of acquiring cannons for emplacement around Boston." Nathan shook his head and rolled his eyes. "One of the general's colonels, a bookseller named Henry Knox, has this insane idea of bringing all the guns from Fort Ticonderoga to Cambridge. Three hundred miles. They weigh tons. The man's crazy. Who knows though?" Nathan raised his glass. "To Jack and the schooner *Piper*. May your campaign be successful."

The two men looked at each other, smiled, and shot down their drinks.

———•◦•———

Shortly after finishing his noon meal the next day, Jack received word the militia unit assigned to escort the convoy to Beverly had assembled and was ready to move out within the hour. He looked at the puffy clouds cruising across the deep blue overhead. *A pleasant day for a trip*, he thought.

Returning to the barracks, he collected his pack and headed for the yard in front of the Vassall House. When he arrived, Jack saw three flatbed wagons. Each had a team of horses attached and a unit of about twenty militiamen and their mounts. Tarpaulins covered whatever cargo the wagons carried. Jack wondered what the freight might be to warrant such a large number of guards. *Weapons? Powder? Perhaps currency to pay for the schooner?*

As he approached, a swarthy man adjusted the bridle on the lead horse of the first wagon and yelled out, "Hey, amigo! You ride with me. I have a clean seat."

"Captain Diaz," Jack answered and walked toward him. "It has been six weeks. I hope they have been good for you."

"Aye, *mi chico*. Life has been good." Diaz stopped what he was doing. He reached up and pushed some long, black strands of hair dangling down his face under the edge of his red Phrygian cap. Then his arms shot forward.

Jack gasped as the chubby, warty-faced man wrapped him in a bear hug. "From whom did you steal that liberty cap, my friend?"

"No steal. French friends on the Saint Lawrence give me one."

"A tribute to a fellow pirate no doubt." Jack chuckled and then coughed and tried to suck air back into his lungs.

"*Sí*, amigo." Diaz puffed out his chest.

In a high-pitched voice, words came from a wiry dwarf who appeared at the back of the wagon. "Master Jack, my man."

Behind the dwarf stood a man who was robust and two heads taller than the smaller fellow. He had a blacksmith's physique.

"Wondered where your henchmen were, Captain Diaz." Jack turned and faced the two newly arrived people. He offered his hand to the little man. "Shaver, it is good to see you," he said as they shook hands. Jack felt the big man's strength when he grasped his shoulder. "And you too, Mr. Duff."

"Aye, Master Jack," Duff said. "I have ordered lodging with God for any redcoats who get in our way."

"I believe you, Mr. Duff. Thank you."

A shout came from the sergeant in charge of the guard to mount up. Jack and Captain Diaz climbed onto the driver's seat of the wagon they stood next to. Shaver took charge of the middle wagon, and Duff took the third. With the command to move out, the column of militiamen started down the road. When they were about a hundred feet ahead of the wagons, Diaz snapped the reins, and the wagons began to move.

———•◦•———

Nathan ran out the door of the barracks. By the time he reached Vassall House yard, the convoy was turning off Brattle Street to the one that passed to the west of Winter Hill. This was where General Israel Putnam's troops camped and held the fortifications. "God be with you, Jack," he yelled, but no one in the wagons made any response.

"Your friend did not hear you," Lieutenant Arian Brace said. He was relaxing against the trunk of a massive oak. Nathan exhaled and nodded. "Stayed for that extra drink at lunch, did you not, Nathan?" Arian straightened and walked to where Nathan stood watching the transom of the last wagon disappear behind the cover of a small clump of trees.

"No. Just got delayed talking to several of His Excellency's staff members," Nathan said. His eyes were still trained on the distant trees. He turned and faced Arian. "I will see Jack when he returns in spring."

"Perhaps." Brace smirked. "Beverly is not far away, but much can happen in that short distance. I heard the convoy is carrying muskets, powder, and shot...but also a strong-box containing shillings General Washington expects to use to pay for the *Piper*'s lease."

Nathan's eyes widened. "How did you know about the strongbox? That is supposed to be a secret."

"There are ways of gaining information," Lieutenant Brace said, and he grinned defiantly. "And I know how to use them."

Nathan chewed his cheek and stared hard at Lieutenant Brace. "I only learned of the convoy's cargo moments ago," he said and furrowed his brow. "Washington's two staff officers detained me after lunch and told me when they learned of my concern for Jack's safety. I was then sworn to secrecy." A questioning expression crossed Nathan's face. "Those aboard the convoy were not even told of the strongbox. How did you find out?"

Arian pursed his lips and looked into the distance. He breathed softly and answered. "As I mentioned, I have ways of learning what others want to keep secret." Nathan started to step closer to Brace, but the lieutenant began to move away. "You will eventually learn, my inquisitive friend, that surreptitious knowledge can be both an advantage and at times lucrative." Arian turned and strolled off in the direction the convoy had gone.

———•◦•———

A few miles from the Mystic River Bridge, the road to Beverly paralleled the waterway on the right. To the left it ran alongside Winter Hill. General Putnam's troops occupied the redoubts down this face's mound and ensured the safety of colonial travelers from harassment by bandits and redcoat patrols. When the convoy neared these fortifications, a colonial officer led five horsemen and galloped toward them. Jack recognized the officer as the lieutenant who had delayed Captain Diaz and him two months earlier on their way to Cambridge.

The lieutenant and his sentries stopped at the head of the column and conversed with the sergeant of the escorting cavalry. When the two finished exchanging words, the lieutenant and his people pulled their reins, twisted in their saddles, and galloped toward the wagons. As they neared, the lieutenant raised his arm in recognition and yelled, "Good journey!"

Jack waved in reply. Clods of dirt and dust blasted from the horse hooves when General Putnam's sentries passed and continued south toward Cambridge.

Loud cranking, crunching, and clopping sounds vibrated from the bed of the bridge when the militia column and wagons crossed. The noise disturbed several slovenly dressed minutemen who were supposedly guarding the bridge from their hideouts in the bushes. They raised their muskets but lowered them when they spotted the militia's uniforms. Several whistled, shook their weapons, and disappeared back into the brush.

"Should be the last of Putnam's troops, amigo," Captain Diaz said. "We are now in open territory." He turned control of the horses over to Jack, reached under the seat, pulled out a musket, ran his hand down its barrel, and set the gun against the seat. "I keep it near in case trouble shows its face." Diaz again reached under the seat and brought up another musket and the caches of powder and shot. He set the second weapon next to Jack. "One for you, too, amigo. We be ready." Diaz placed the ammunition pouches on the seat, relaxed, yawned, and crossed his arms against his chest.

Staring ahead Jack saw the sergeant raise his arm and sling it forward. "Command to accelerate," he mumbled and snapped the reins.

The wagon sped up but kept its designated distance behind the military escort. With the sun low on the horizon, no one in the convoy noticed a band of riders approaching across a meadow from the west until several musket reports rattled the air. Immediately the escorting cavalry spread out to the east, jumped from their mounts, and took cover behind boulders and bushes.

Jack slapped the reins hard against the horses' backs and caused the lead one to rear. He pulled the straps taut and brought the team under control. The horses snorted, lurched forward, and began to gallop. Jack swung his head back and forth and tried to find Shaver and Duff. He saw the other two wagons had moved off the road and were pulling to his side. Shaver was on the right, and Duff was on the left. They came bounding over rocks and furrows, threw up dust, and ripped through knee-high brush.

"Head for the forest!" Captain Diaz yelled. He tried to grab his bouncing musket and simultaneously stay seated. With the gun's barrel clasped in his right hand, the captain flipped himself over the seat, sprawled onto the load of cargo, took aim over the transom, and shouted, "Try to go smooth! I shoot."

Steadying his jolting upper arm, he fired. The musket's report caused Jack to twist in the seat and look back. In the distance he saw a horse buck and throw its rider, but his eyes widened when he espied the right-front rim on Shaver's wagon hit a rock and splinter. He heard Shaver yell and jump off. He watched the wagon's left side lift as if in slow motion. The tarpaulin flapped. The casks of gunpowder flew into the air, flipped end over end, hit the ground, and tumbled along with Shaver into a gully. Two kegs burst upon impact and spurted thick clouds of charcoal-colored dust. The powder settled in clumps and piles that led toward the unbroken kegs rolling into the depression.

Jack watched as the scene behind him shrank away. Shaver was grabbing grass and bushes and struggling up the slope's side. He appeared injured.

Several musket balls whizzed over Jack's head. The militia was shooting at the apparent bandits, and they were returning fire. Jack twisted back and saw the renegades were about one hundred yards from the gully and riding hard.

"Shaver!" Diaz shouted.

Jack instinctively yanked the reins to the left. This caused the team to whirl into a turn and the freight wagon to hike to starboard. When the right wheels left the ground, Diaz was tossed to the opposite side of the wagon. The captain grabbed the tarpaulin before he flipped off. He held on until Jack stabilized the wagon after it had turned 180 degrees. Diaz then clawed his way to the seat, turned on his side, and crawled over the back and onto the bench.

Jack handed him the reins as the wagon moved to where Shaver was stumbling along. "I will get him," Jack yelled and jumped off the wagon.

Jack hit the ground and pitched over several low bushes. He jumped up, dashed to Shaver's side, and grabbed his collar.

"My ankle, Master Jack." Shaver winced.

"Later!" Jack looked at the dwarf's face. "Have you your pistol?" Diaz had again brought the wagon around and was racing back toward them. "Have you your pistol, man?"

Shaver groped at his waist. "Aye."

Shaver stumbled along as Jack pulled him. Jack was running toward the road, and Shaver yanked the gun from his belt. Shaver waved it in front of Jack's face.

With his free hand, Jack seized the gun. "Is it loaded?"

"Aye."

Jack cock the hammer as the wagon slipped next to them. "Grab hold, man," Jack yelled. "Pull yourself aboard. I'm right behind you."

Grappling the wagon's side as he ran next to it, Jack approached a pile of gunpowder. Across the gully he heard hooves pounding. Twisting low to his side and holding tight to the wagon's sideboard, he fired the pistol when he ran past the pile of powder.

The gunpowder erupted in a ball of sparks and flame that rapidly grew. The burst sputtered down the powder trail toward several intact kegs lying at the gully's bottom. Within an instant came the deafening whoosh and boom.

Amid the chaotic sounds of horses' hooves crunching against the ground and of horses snorting and whinnying, people screamed and shouted. Jack swung himself aboard the wagon. White and black smoke laced the heat from a rapidly distending orange ball. It singed the back of his clothes, neck, and hair.

The freight wagon raced ahead of the diminishing mushroom and toward the forest. Jack lay in the wagon bed next to a tarpaulin that covered a chest. His body was jarred as the wheels bounced over stones and through ruts. Beyond he heard the cavalry shouting, "Huzzah. Huzzah." He lifted himself and saw the escorting militia mount their horses, spur them to gallops, and follow the wagons into the forest.

Once inside the cover of trees, the convoy halted and began to regroup. The sergeant trotted up next to where Diaz, Jack, and Shaver rested. Duff had his wagon team fall in behind the captain's wagon. "All intact, Captain Diaz," the sergeant said, "except the wagon and ten kegs of powder."

"Aye, Sergeant," Diaz grumbled, "but the loss came to good use."

The last of the four cavalry rode in and joined the group. Between them were two restrained prisoners. "Caught these bastards," one of the riders said. "They are redcoats."

"Rather ragged uniforms they have," Diaz interrupted.

"Wanted us to think they are renegades, Captain. Asked to be treated as prisoners of war."

"Who they answering to?" the captain said.

The badly burned, bleeding prisoner was barely able to keep his balance, but he spoke up. "Our Tory commander in Boston, sir. Lieutenant Bra—"

"Hold your tongue, you damn fool," the other prisoner grumbled. "We don't have to answer their questions."

It startled Jack to hear what the wounded man had said, but before he could say anything, Diaz said, "Mr. Duff, take charge of these prisoners of war."

"Aye, sir." Duff held his musket and jumped from the wagon he was driving. He walked to the prisoners and hit the uninjured one in the side with the musket butt. The man cried out and grabbed his side. "Help your friend and follow me." Duff stalked off into the forest.

"Where is he taking them, Captain Diaz? Jack asked.

"To a better place."

Jack watched Duff and the prisoners disappear into the tangle of vegetation. After a few moments, two muffled musket blasts broke his stare.

———•◦•———

About twenty minutes after Duff returned and climbed onto the bench of his freight wagon, the convoy continued its journey toward Beverly. The sun lay on the horizon. When the column exited the forest, the sky glowed in twilight. Nearly ten degrees above the horizon and facing them was an almost full moon hanging in the eastern sky.

The sergeant signaled a halt to rest and sup. "We will continue after dark," he yelled.

The cavalry reined up and dismounted. Four duty soldiers stationed themselves around the perimeter as lookouts. Two rode back a short way into the forest and took positions in the brush on each side of the road. Diaz and Duff circled the wagons into the meadow. Jack crawled over the cargo and maneuvered a cask of water to the back of the wagon. He then grabbed the pouches containing fruit, cheese, and bread and slid off the bed of the lead wagon. Shaver followed. Once on the ground, he leaned on Jack's shoulder. The two hobbled to a small hillock between the wagons.

No fires were started. Everyone ate in silence for some minutes. Sitting next to Diaz, Jack eventually said in a low voice, "Wish Duff had not shot those men."

"You know that is my way," Diaz answered. "My people are ordered to kill redcoats." He crunched a bite from an apple and chewed for a moment. "What would you do with prisoners, amigo? We have no place for them."

"I heard the injured man mention a name before his comrade interrupted him. It sounded like the name of the officer who considers himself Lieutenant Hale's friend and superior."

"Duff said the injured man collapsed and died on his own before he reached the place of execution. To make sure he was dead, Duff's first shot was a coup de grâce. With his second he dispatched the other redcoat." Diaz continued to eat the apple. He coughed and said, "Aye. The dying one did start to say a name; 'e could have been saying Lieutenant Brace." Diaz shrugged and threw the core into the grass. "Alas, we will never know."

"Lieutenant Hale never introduced me to this Brace fellow, but what he said about the man makes me worry about Nathan's safety. Perhaps we should send a report of our encounter back to Cambridge. Nathan is my friend, and I would feel better if he were more cautious."

"Aye, Jack. Since you are the educated one, you scratch the report. I will have the sergeant deliver it when the cavalry returns to Cambridge."

Jack chewed on his lip and nodded. The cavalry sergeant called out the command for all to mount up and proceed on to Beverly. The moon and starlight illuminated the scape and cast the convoy into a collection of eerie shadows and silvery phantoms. The chill air, exhalations of gyrating horses, and wisps of fog rising from the earth made the scene even more ghostly.

———•◦•———

About ten o'clock in the evening, the convoy arrived in Beverly and made its way to the waterfront. The sergeant of the guard assigned two men to take charge of the wagons. "We will take them down the road to the militia barracks," he told Diaz. "It will be easier to watch over them."

Jack, Diaz, Shaver, and Duff found lodging at a nearby inn. Since little food remained after the hours of the evening meal, the group had to contend with leftovers washed down with full mugs of ale. The innkeeper served these in the barroom. Though late, several stevedores were seated at a nearby table.

"Aye, Henry," Jack overheard one of the gruff-looking men say. "Remember this day, my man. The twenty-sixth day of October in the year of our Lord 1775 is when they slid the schooner *Piper* down the roads."

"She's an ol' girl and didn't even sink when they put all those cannons aboard her," one of the other men said.

"Aye. Big for her design," another said. "Got three masts. First schooner I sees totin' a mizzenmast."

The three laughed and slurped down their beer.

"Captain Diaz, they are talking about the vessel I am to be aboard," Jack said.

"Aye, mate," Diaz said.

"I wonder where the *Piper* is docked."

"Ask, amigo. They will say...if they still have minds to remember."

Jack stood and walked to the stevedore. "I overheard you mention the schooner *Piper*. It would please me to know where she is docked."

"And who's askin'?"

"The name is Jack Hollister. I am to be the midshipman aboard her."

"Hollister," the gruff man said. "Hollister. Heard that name. Cannot seem to recall."

As he took a swig of his beer, his comrade said, "Was not that the fellow Charles Bowden's been talkin' about?"

"Aye," said the gruff stevedore. "Do ye know Mr. Bowden, lad?"

"Aye, I do. Is Mr. Bowden about?

The stevedore looked at his friends and sneered. Then he scanned the barroom. "Does not appear so,

Mr. Hollister. But he's around. Seen 'im earlier at the launching. He seems to be of importance to that vessel. You can find him tomorrow. Comes here for breakfast." The stevedore's head fell forward, but he quickly snapped it back up.

"Thank you, sir. I will find him on the morrow." About to turn and step back to his table, Jack stopped. "Begging your pardon, sir, but you have not told me where the *Piper* is docked."

One of the other dockworkers wobbled his head and strained his eyes open. "She's…tied to Steven's Dock." He slowly lifted his right arm and pointed to the inn's far wall. "'Bout a quarter mile down the road."

"Many thanks, sir." Jack returned to his friend's table.

"Workers during the day," Diaz said. "Drunkards at night."

"Perhaps so, but I learned what I wanted and also found out our friend Charles Bowden might be involved with the schooner." Jack remained standing, picked up his mug, and drank what beer was left. "I am off to bed. Tomorrow looks to be a big day."

"Aye, Midshipman Hollister," Diaz said with a grin. "It will indeed be." The Spanish pirate looked at Duff and Shaver and then up at Jack. "*Buenas noches,* amigo."

Jack awoke the next morning, rubbed his eyes, and stared out the window. Droplets hitting the room's windowpane distorted the scene beyond. Outside, the slow-falling rain momentarily puddled in the irregularities of the window glass and then spilled out to form vertical rivulets. Jack tried to focus on the glistening wetness while several hanging, transient droplets let loose and streaked down the misty background. He could smell the dreary damp, cold air forcing its way through the cracks and chinks along the frame edges.

Jack pulled the cloths and blankets of the shakedown upon which he slept around him. *Waterfront inns*, he thought and shivered. *Wretched places. A drunkard or whore's paradise.* After lying for some minutes and staring at a faded picture, he kicked off the covers, leaped up, and threw on his clothes. He continued to feel the wet coldness flitter around him. After stuffing his belongings into his pack, he scurried out the door. At the head of the stairs, he felt and smelled the warmth wafting from the hearth below.

His stomach grumbled as he descended the staircase to the public room. The aroma of wood smoke, bacon, and coffee overpowered the lingering odors of last evening's beer drinking.

Though the hour was early, the public room was half full of people breakfasting. Jack looked about but recognized no one. *Charles Bowden's not here. Diaz? Duff? Shaver? Still sleeping, I'm sure. Bundled in their shakedowns.*

Dressed in workaday clothing instead of his issued makeshift uniform, Jack did not attract any attention. He seated himself alone at a table near the fireplace. The savory smell of bacon lingered after he finished his breakfast. With a remaining piece of johnnycake, he swabbed the grease and bits of egg from the plate. Relishing this last tasty tidbit, he was about to wash it down with dark coffee when Diaz appeared at the table.

"*Buenos días,* amigo," the captain mumbled. "Much too much merriment. Not enough sleep."

Though Diaz continued to mumble, the grumbling din of a multitude of conversations ongoing in the room drowned his words. All Jack heard was, "No breakfast. Must go to militia barracks…seal deal on cargo." Nodding as if he understood what the captain was saying, Jack drank his coffee while Diaz kept talking.

"You must report to schooner *Piper.* Maybe we meet again someday." Diaz turned and began to leave but leaned back toward Jack. His head came within inches of the young man. He whispered, "You go to sea. Good luck, and may God be with you, amigo."

"And with you, my friend," Jack said and extended his hand, but Diaz had straightened and was already headed for the door.

Jack exhaled to clear Diaz's stale breath that hung near his nose, set down the coffee mug, and sat back in the chair. *Aye. I, too, need to be on my way*, he thought and stood. Tightening his coat about himself, he grabbed the drawstrings of his pack and walked toward the exit.

Jack felt an immediate chill when he stepped onto the sidewalk. The cold drizzle continued. He tightened the scarf around his neck. Across the street were the wharves and docks of Beverly, Massachusetts. *Somewhere is the schooner* Piper, he thought. To his right there were no vessels, but to the left and a quarter mile away, a tangle of masts and yardarms dissected the misty, gray sky. *It must be tied among them.*

Pulling the front of his tricorne down, Jack lowered his head and started walking. The mist moistened his face, and in a few minutes, an intermittent stream of rainwater dribbled off the tricorne's beak.

He walked fast toward the collection of vessels and saw only the sidewalk and the toes of his boots. The drizzle turned to rain. He pulled his shoulders forward and tightened his back and chest muscles. On two occasions he almost collided with other walkers. When he encountered a third group of people, he asked if they knew where the *Piper* was docked.

One of the men raised his arm and pointed down the street. "The vessel tied to Steven's Dock. On larboard. Third vessel."

"Many thanks," Jack replied.

He wiped the water off his face, crossed to the quay, and continued.

Jack tightened his coat around himself. Though the rain had slackened to a fine mist, a chilling, offshore wind gusted about him. Ahead a six-foot-wide deck of rain-soaked, heavy timbers bridged a gap between the quay and dock. Though the dock appeared substantial, rain had blackened and made slippery its bedding. Deep grooves and missing, splintered, and broken timbers scarred it. A sign identified this pier as Steven's Dock. It jutted several hundred feet out into the harbor.

Jack breathed deeply and tasted the salty rot that flavored his nose and mouth. Crossing the bridge, he

watched his steps in an attempt to balance himself on the
rickety, narrow planking. He could see through the spaces
between boards over what the bridge spanned. Below, a
tangle of flotsam and dark water swirled, rose, and fell
with each ocean swell. It moved around boulders, driftwood, and broken decking. He shivered when he stepped
onto Steven's Dock.

Not much more secure, he thought. He looked up and
carefully started walking down the middle of the dock. In
the misty grayness, it looked like the deck of a ghost ship
with its wet, dripping crew running about helter-skelter.
He moved cautiously and tried to avoid colliding with the
confusion of stevedores who were rolling casks, carrying
bundles and chests, and pushing empty and loaded carts
between the four large brigantines tied against the pier—
two on each side. Beyond, Jack saw a group of militiamen
milling about a wagon. Tied at the head of the dock was
the midsection of the hull and masts of a small schooner.
The massive cargo vessels Jack walked between hid its bow
and stern. Jack approached the wagon and recognized the
sergeant of the guard who had escorted Diaz, his crew, and
him to Beverly. He nodded as he neared. *Cargo we brought
from Cambridge was for the* Piper.

"Step lively, crew!" Jack heard the sergeant command.

Two soldiers in the wagon pushed a large chest to
a couple men standing behind the wagon's transom.
They reached for the chest's handles, caught them, and
pulled the ornate box back. It scraped toward them and
threw the fellows pushing the chest off-balance. One
fell onto the wagon bed and cursed loudly. The other

stumbled forward but righted himself. He, too, shouted cuss words at those who had yanked the chest to the wagon's edge. The men in the wagon collected themselves, jumped off, helped lift the chest off the vehicle, and set it on the ground.

Jack smiled at this crew's ineptness. The sergeant motioned for the four men to carry the box aboard the schooner. They followed several others who carried muskets, bundles, and pouches.

"Master Jack," the sergeant said, "you have found your vessel. The first officer has been asking of your whereabouts. You should board and present yourself."

"A good day to you, sir. Though it appears not to be so." Jack walked next to the wagon and nodded to the sergeant. "Your men seem to be in wretched moods."

"Too long at the tavern last evening they were."

Before Jack could comment, a tall, well-built man rose through the schooner's after hatch and stepped to the rail. "Midshipman Hollister, it is about time you made your appearance. I hope your ration of rum or this coastal weather did not slow your progress."

Jack looked up. The man on deck speaking to him had a disheveled crop of dusty hair and a scar down his cheek. A grin creased his handsome, ruddy face and belied his fierce comments.

Jack sighed comfortably, but felt his heart tremble. "Mr. Bowden," he yelled. Composing himself, he came to attention and saluted the schooner *Piper*'s first officer. "Midshipman Jack Hollister, requesting permission to come aboard, sir!"

Bowden returned the salute and said, "Permission granted, Midshipman." He then turned and strolled to the head of the gangway.

Without any faltering steps, Jack trod up the plank. The two men shook hands but then embraced in a welcome hug.

CHAPTER 3

Due to the overcast sky, night came early. The drizzle had finally stopped, and only an uncomfortable, cool, damp breeze blew off the water. After reminiscing for a time, Jack and Bowden quieted. The activity on the quay captured their attention. Though the pier next to the *Piper* was deserted, the two men stood against the starboard rail. They were mesmerized watching the liveliness occurring where the oil lamps illuminated the upper end of the pier. Jack broke the silence. "Night brings out the revelers."

"Aye, Jack." Bowden turned, faced Jack for a moment, and then scanned the stern of the freighter tied across the pier. "They have supped, and now they go to drink."

Jack shrugged and patted his belly. "'Twas a good supper cook made of ham and corn cakes this evening. Better than the gruel General Washington's men in the field must tolerate."

Bowden removed two cigars from a pocket inside his coat and offered one to Jack. "Life aboard a military vessel can be somewhat better. Captain Diaz stopped by last evening before his crew departed for Cambridge." He rotated and compressed the dense roll of aromatic tobacco between his thumb and forefinger. "These are from Cuba."

Jack accepted with a smile. The two moved to the gangway lantern and lit the cigars. Each exhaled a cloud of acrid smoke. "Where's Captain Morris?" Jack asked. "He and most of the crew were absent this evening."

"They are ashore. You'll meet Captain Morris tomorrow. Since he plans to sail on the morning tide, he wanted to spend the night at his home. So, too, it is with the crew. Most have wives, children, and livestock nearby. With the two men on deck watch, the cook, and two others below, we are alone on the schooner."

Jack's face contorted as he chewed on the cigar. "Is it wise to have so few aboard to guard the payment Colonel Glover is to collect in the morning?"

"It will be fine, Jack. No one knows the chest contains a strongbox."

As Jack cocked his head to the side, an angry neigh and the crashing sounds of an overturning wagon snapped their attention back to the distant quay. It was obvious something had caused a horse to rear and fall to the pavement. From their distant perspective, the accident seemed to cause merriment rather than confusion among the strollers. Jack and Bowden laughed. For a few moments, men yelled and scurried about chaotically. Some dashed out of sight as if chasing someone. Then the horse and wagon were righted, and the scene quieted.

Bowden shook his head and blew another cloud of cigar smoke. It mingled with the curling fog drifting across the schooner's deck. Before he could take another draw on the Cuban tobacco, the misty air enveloped the *Piper.*

Everything surrounding the men chilled and became vaporous and hazy.

"The warmth of rum would do us well," Jack said. He shivered. With his cigar clenched between his teeth, he pulled up his coat collar.

"Cook has a bottle," Bowden said, "but he's probably drunk most of it by now. I will go below and try to rescue us a tot."

"Aye," Jack said, "bring a mugful. Every deck guard could also use a bit of a kick."

Bowden smiled and nodded. "You have the compassion of a budding officer, my friend." He descended down the aft hatchway.

Jack awaited Bowden's return and continued to gaze toward the quay. The horse and wagon had been removed, and the revelers had dwindled to a few strollers. A light gust cleared the fog, but within moments the misty cloud recompressed and obscured everything. All Jack could see was the dim orangish glow the distant oil lamps created. He put his hands on the rail, set his right foot on the stringer above the waterway, leaned forward, and stretched his back. A dull thud against the larboard side of the hull startled him. He quickly jumped back and turned. His hand grabbed the handle of the pistol stuffed in the belt around his waist.

"Not so fast, me hearty," grumbled a large bearded face darkened by the sizeable brim of the tricorne pulled low in front.

Jack's right hand eased away from the pistol's stock. The dilated pupils of his eyes focused on the blackened muzzle inches from his nose. "It behooves the master to kneel and put his hands on the rail," the robust mucker growled, and he fanned the pistol toward the deck.

Jack cringed from the fetid stench that emanated from the ruffian's mouth and buckskin. He knelt.

"Aye. Now that's a fine fellow, doin' as he's ord—"

A musket blast from a short distance away ended the bearded man's statement. His forehead exploded and showered Jack with torn felt and bloody shrapnel. The man's arms flung upward, and he fell hard against the side of the deckhouse, slid to the deck, and rolled into a heap. Jack yanked his pistol from his belt, dropped to the deck, and slipped behind the cover of the deckhouse. A second, louder shot cracked.

A musket. From the bow, Jack surmised. Resting the muzzle of the pistol on the edge of the deckhouse roof, he popped up; peeked over; and saw the deck guard double over, drop his weapon, and fall back against the bulwarks. Jack fired toward the bow as two other muskets barked behind him.

"Damn it, Jack! What is happening?" Bowden called out.

Two sailors who had followed Bowden up on deck dropped down next to Jack and started to reload their guns. Jack had his ready to shoot again. Peering above the deckhouse, he spotted two figures crawling along the larboard bulwarks. He fired. The ball ricocheted and splintered the rail above one of the intruders.

A split second after, Bowden's weapon blasted. Its charge tore through the behind of the other purloiner.

This fellow yelled in pain and splayed himself on the deck. His accomplice jumped up and dived over the rail.

Jack saw movement near the capstan and pointed. The sailor next to him leveled his musket on the crouching shadow and fired. His shot missed and imbedded itself in the chest containing the strongbox the fellow was trying to pull across the deck. The crack of the musket ball's impact compelled the thief to release the chest's handle. He scampered to the rail and jumped overboard.

Jack, Bowden, and the sailors dashed to the larboard rail. Bowden and the sailors leveled their muskets at the two men rapidly swimming toward their longboat, which bobbed about forty feet forward of the *Piper*'s bow. Those aboard the *Piper* could not get their shots off. The rogues had already grabbed the gunwale, cut the tether, and pulled themselves to protection on the far side of the longboat. One sailor fired, but his shot hit the longboat's hull as it drifted into the cover of darkness.

Bowden snapped around to face Jack and the sailor. "Tend to the wounded," Bowden barked.

Jack dashed across the deck to the starboard side where the deck guard who destroyed the bearded man had fallen. Jack rounded the deckhouse and saw the second guard sitting on the deck and cradling the head of the other in his lap. Loud, distant voices distracted Jack. Some men on the sterns of other freighters tied to the dock were yelling questions toward him, but Jack waved them off. He turned his attention back to the boy sitting on deck.

"He's dead, sir," the second guard said.

Jack stood over him and watched as the sailor raised his head. *My God, this guard is only a boy,* he thought. *His musket is longer than he is tall.*

Tears filled the boy's eyes when he looked up. "He's my older brother," the little guard bawled.

A knot tightened in Jack's stomach. Ian's image flitted through his mind. Jack leaned down and placed his hand on the boy's shoulder. "I'm so sorry, lad."

"We have the bastard I shot," Bowden said as he came up to Jack and the crying guard. "Threatened to shoot him if he didn't inform on his partners." He looked down at the crying boy. "What have we here?"

The little guard looked up and garbled some words.

"Goddamn it, Toby, they shot your brother." Bowden clenched his free hand into a fist and gripped his musket in the other. He straightened, turned, and stomped off to the opposite side of the schooner where the injured mucker lay on his side and moaned. As Bowden was leaving, Jack overheard him growl, "That son of a bitch is a dead man. Killed one of my boys."

Amidships another sailor interrupted Bowden's traverse. The first officer slammed the butt of his musket hard onto the deck. "Aye, sailor," he said gruffly. "Go. It would be best to inform Captain Morris of this affair. While you are ashore, find and send a surgeon aboard. Our wounded prisoner will need looking to. I will have him questioned thoroughly. Then I will kill him."

Bowden paused as the sailor ran off the schooner and up the pier. The first officer returned to Toby, who was crying over his dead brother. "Midshipman Hollister, please help Seaman Toby lay his brother's body out on the deck-house roof. I will arrange for transport to take him home." Bowden saw the body of the scoundrel Toby's brother had shot lying in a heap forward from where everyone stood. "Toss that one on the pier for the scavengers," he said. "What remains, the embalmers can have."

———•◦•———

The sailor who went for Captain Morris, six of the *Piper*'s crew, and Captain Morris came running up the gangplank as the eastern horizon brightened. "What the hell happened here last night?" Morris yelled at Bowden, who was gesticulating while talking with Jack and the local constable.

"Thieves, sir!" Jack said. "Four of them boarded us while Mr. Bowden and I were reminiscing. After the strong-box they were."

"So I have been told. Did we lose anyone?"

"Aye. Josh McConnell." Jack's face looked drawn. "His brother, Toby, and two policemen have taken his body home."

"Damn! Josh was a fine, upcoming seaman. The loss will break his father's heart. Ol' Man McConnell lost his wife last winter. Now his eldest son is gone. There will be hell to pay!" Morris clenched his fists and then relaxed and shook hands with the constable. "Good to see you, William. Did anyone capture the scoundrels?"

"One dead. Josh shot him. Another took a ball in the arse." Jack pointed toward the mainmast. "We have him tied over there, sir. The other two got away."

"Why are you here, William?" Morris said. "This is a military matter. Why are the local police involved?"

"Disturbance on the quay last night. Some rascals stole a longboat," the constable said. "My men were on the quay when Mr. Bowden's messenger came running off the pier. He told them what had happened on the *Piper.* My men came to the schooner to assist. I arrived a short time ago because I suspected those thieves who stole the boat were the blackguards who raided your vessel."

"Thank you, William." Captain Morris turned to Bowden. "Is the bastard tied to the mast talking? Or do we have to persuade him a bit before he is hauled off to the gallows?"

"Aye," Bowden said. "Might have to prod him a bit, sir."

Morris faced Jack. "And who are you, sir?"

"Our new midshipman, Captain," Bowden said, and he put his hand on Jack's shoulder, "an old friend. Jack Hollister's his name. Aided in the capture of the *Margaretta.* A patriot he is, sir."

"Welcome aboard, Mr. Hollister." Captain Morris extended his right hand. "Sorry for the bit of turmoil that greeted your arrival. Not an unusual event when there is money lying about a ship's deck. Mr. Bowden, get the deck in order. Colonel Glover will be arriving soon."

Captain Morris took off to where the prisoner was tied. The constable motioned to two of his policemen to join him and followed behind the captain. Jack and Bowden did likewise. When they approached amidships, they saw the prisoner squirming against the large pole. He was trying to move his hands down to the wound the musket ball had created in the right cheek of his bottom.

When he spotted the men coming toward him, he yelled out. "Would be kind of you to tend to my wound 'fore I dies instead of running your mouths."

He glared at the group and tugged at his bonds. The blood on his pants appeared dried and blackened, and the wound was no longer bleeding.

"Spirited bastard," Morris said, and then he directed his comments to the angry prisoner. "That shot only tore out some fat. We will be getting you a hangman—not a doctor. But first the constable wants to know the names of the other scoundrels with you."

"Not tellin' you nothing till I get my wound treated."

"Your yellin' isn't helpin'. Wharf rats easily survive flesh wounds," Morris said while smirking. "Especially when they catch balls in the fat of their asses."

Everyone around the prisoner started to chuckle, but this only infuriated the man bound to the mast. "As I tol' you, I ain't a tellin' you nothing." The prisoner gritted his teeth, and then his face softened. He looked resignedly at Captain Morris. "Can't tell you anything 'cause I don't know those other gents. Was caught up in the fracas when youse were all shootin'."

"Balderdash!" Captain Morris crossed his arms against his chest and straightened his stance. He turned to the constable. "Call up your hangman. Since this son of a bitch is not talking, we have no use for him. We'll swing him from the yardarm to atone for Josh's killing. We need to hurry because I do not want to miss the tide.

Have your men escort the prisoner aft. I have a block and tackle arranged that will take care of this problem."

"Captain Morris, sir," Constable William said, "I don't believe justice will be served if this man is hung without an investigation and trial." William's voice cracked as he spoke.

"Need I remind you the shooting took place aboard this vessel? Whether we are tied to the dock or at sea, I am in command. Now if you do not want your people involved, I will have my crew take care of this situation. This scoundrel was shot while trying to escape after he and his miscreants enacted a misdeed upon my crew and vessel. In naval service murder is a hanging offense. Executive Officer Bowden and Midshipman Hollister, take the prisoner aft."

"Beggin' your pardon," the prisoner whimpered, "if the good captain will give me a moment..."

"For what, you bilge rat? The tide is making, and you are like a canker that needs to be removed before this vessel can get under way."

"A moment, sir. I have a wife and six chil'ren, sir, and I did not shoot your man. If I tells you what I know, will you commute my punishment to the Beverly Jail?"

"Speak, man." Captain Morris stiffened his stance, threw his arms down, and clasped his hands behind him. Glaring at the man tied to the mast, he paced to the starboard, to the larboard, and back again.

The prisoner took a breath and cocked his head toward Captain Morris. "As I tol' ye, I did not shoot the sailor. 'Twas a man named Partridge. That's all I know of him. Met him in the tavern two nights ago. He's offered me and my friend Rob Darby twenty quid each. Said he'd give it to us if we help him steal a chest off your deck. Needin' some extra money, so we agreed. Now Rob's o'er there lyin' on the dock. Your guard killed him." The prisoner butted his head against the mast. "Damn it, sir. This Partridge said it would be an easy steal." His head fell forward. "Ol' Robby's dead, an' I'm gonna hang."

"Did Partridge tell you what was in the chest?" Captain Morris's voice blared directly into the prisoner's face.

"Nay, sir. Except what he said made me an' Robby think there was something important in the box."

"Why? What did this man say?"

"That a Continental army lieutenant tol' him there were important papers in the box. This lieutenant said the British were willing to pay well for the papers." The prisoner pulled himself up and stopped whimpering. "Can I now be spared the noose, Captain?"

"Not just yet. I need the name of this lieutenant."

"Don't know it, sir. Only know he's come from a regiment barracked in Cambridge, sir, with General Washington's troops."

"Aye." Captain Morris squinted and nodded.

Startled by the prisoner's words, Jack blurted out, "Captain, this sounds like the same account one of the bandits told Jose Diaz's men. They captured the bandit after our patrol and wagons were chased and fired upon. We were transporting the very chest from Cambridge those rascals tried to steal last night. Before Diaz's man executed him, this bandit informed him of a lieutenant in the Continental army who told of the riches the strongbox contained."

"Aye." Morris stepped away from the prisoner, removed a handkerchief from his coat, and wiped it across his forehead. "The lieutenant these scoundrels have been mentioning is a blackguard himself. A British spy. We need his name."

"I have a suspicion, sir, but no evidence," Jack said. "It's only a feeling."

"And who might this person be?"

"A Lieutenant Arian Brace, sir. We have never been introduced, but he seems to know my friend Lieutenant Nathan Hale of the Connecticut Regiment. Lieutenant Hale said he was uncertain of Brace and could not recall him—despite Brace insisting they were acquainted. Brace's cavalier behavior with privy information caused Nathan concern. This worries me. General Washington assigned Lieutenant Hale to New York City in the spring to gather information on conditions there. Lieutenant Brace is to be his contact in the city."

"Aye, Jack." Captain Morris shuffled about and wrung his hands. "I will note your concern in my report to General Washington that there might be a British informer within his company. Colonel Glover will post it to Cambridge after we sail. Now, however, back to this goddamn prisoner." He bent toward the man tied to the mast and growled, "What does this Partridge look like? I am sure the constable wants to inform his men and our militia. That way they can be on the lookout for this culprit."

The prisoner squirmed at the bindings. "He's a woodsman, sir, who smelled of burned wood and skunk. All I knows is he'd kill anyone who barred his way."

"Aye. Like most of the worms that come from rot." The captain straightened and stepped away from the mast and prisoner. "Constable, have your men take this slime off my vessel. You may do with him as you like. The tide is about to turn, and I need to make for the sea. There are prizes out there I plan to collect."

———•◦•———

Two hours remained in the flooding tide before it reached its pinnacle. For now, though, the current flushing between the hull and pilings gushed so strongly, it caused the schooner to pull tight against its moorings and lurch about its lines. Though the distance from the vessel's deck to the dock was about eight feet, Constable William had to tread cautiously because the gangway moved side to side and up and down. The policemen surrounding the complaining, shackled prisoner slipped, and their left hands clenched along the safety line as they staggered along the plank.

Jack watched these men weave and stumble off the *Piper*. He expected the prisoner to be taken off in a stretcher because of his wound. Instead he was forced to limp down the plank with the aid of two police officers. Jack watched him and winced. *That ball in the arse must be causing him great pain.*

Jack noticed a tall, robust man in his fifties dressed like a gentleman waiting on the dock. He wore a long dark coat, black leather gloves, polished boots, and a beaver tricorne. The curls of his white wig hung low and covered his ears. A white silk cravat bulged at the neck from the opening in his coat. With him were four sturdy young men of the Beverly militia. Each carried a musket and had a pistol holstered at the waist. Jack saw the gentleman glance at the prisoner and grin.

"Colonel Glover, please come aboard," Captain Morris yelled, "and bring your guards."

As soon as Constable William and his entourage cleared the gangplank, Colonel John Glover stepped forward. He nodded at the constable as he passed. Glover puffed out his chest and walked up the plank without floundering. Each of his steps clacked solidly against the gangway planking as if the heels of his boots were contacting stable ground.

The colonel's militiamen stumbled aboard.

"Very good to see you, John," Captain Morris said, and he shook the colonel's hand. "Now I can rid myself of that damn strongbox."

"Aye. Seems it has brought you a bit of grief." Colonel Glover laughed.

Morris nodded but kept a somber face. He looked at Bowden and said, "First Officer Charles Bowden." He turned to Jack. "And Midshipman Jack Hollister."

"Pleasure to make your acquaintance, gentlemen."

To Captain Morris's surprise, he heard Jack ask, "Colonel Glover, did you recognize the prisoner? I observed you smile at him. It was as if you knew him."

"Aye, lad. He is a vagrant and petty thief. I am surprised he has attempted to thieve a prize from a vessel. That shot in the behind will dampen his stealing for a time."

"Poor fellow."

Captain Morris interrupted Jack. "He is not a poor fellow. I would have hung the blackguard had I had time."

"I just feel sorry for his wife and children." Jack ran his hand through his hair. "Says he has six young ones to feed."

Colonel Glover broke out in a coughing laugh. "The devil have that man. He uses the same story every time he is caught. That vagrant might have a few urchins he has sired, but he has no wife. He is usually in the company of one of the whores from a local bordello. By and by one of those witches will lay claim to him and stop by the jail. He is no one to fuss over."

"Sorry, sirs, for the outburst. Not knowing the truth, I felt a bit of compassion for the man."

"Aye, Jack. Let that be a lesson to ye," Morris said and turned to Glover. "Let us retire to my quarters. Mr. Hollister can supervise the transfer of the chest to your guards. I will inform you of what happened last evening and prepare a message for our esteemed commander. Mr. Bowden, please accompany us."

While Captain Morris, Colonel Glover, and Mr. Bowden disappeared down the after hatchway, Jack led the militia guards to the forward deck. As they neared the chest, Jack noticed it had been cut free of its lashings and moved close to the larboard gunwale. *Those crooks planned to throw it overboard,* he thought. *Wonder if it would have floated.* He got his answer when one of the militiamen grabbed the chest's side handles and tried to lift it.

"Bloody hell!" the soldier yelled and dropped the chest to the deck. He snapped himself straight, bent backward, and slapped his hand against the small of his back. "Blamed box woulda busted my back." The man recomposed himself. "Forgot the damn chest was loaded with ballast in case anyone attempted to steal it."

Jack remembered. It had taken four of Diaz's people to haul the chest aboard the schooner. It would take as many to carry it to the wagon waiting on the pier.

"Wonder what the strongbox in the chest contains that is so valuable," another militiaman said.

"Lord only knows," the other grunted. "Cannot be gold 'cause this ol' scow is old and not trustworthy. Though ol' man Stevens had it renovated."

"Two thousand pounds sterling," Glover called out as he came toward the party. He rolled up a parchment as he walked. "A proper sum for a Marblehead schooner. Now get your backs to it, and take that chest to the wagon. Careful. Do not drop it into the harbor."

Jack had two seamen string lanyards through the chest's handles. Two militiamen led, and two followed. They took hold of the lines, laid them over their shoulders, bent forward, and pulled the ropes taut. Holding the ropes tight, they straightened. The chest lifted off the deck and was suspended fore and aft between the pairs of militiamen. They marched off toward the gangplank.

The tidal current was nearing high tide and had slackened. The schooner's movements had stilled. The men were able to negotiate the bridge between the deck and dock without incident—except for a few grunts. Jack looked to see if the money box was secured on the wagon.

He then heard Captain Morris call out. "Good riddance. Now the gold is your problem, Colonel Glover."

Morris, Colonel Thompson, and Bowden returned to the deck. Glover chuckled and shook hands with the captain.

"Now I can tend to sailing this vessel," Morris said. "We will be ready to get under way so the tide can carry us out."

"Aye, you old sea dog," the colonel said, and he descended the gangway. "Fair winds, my friends. May God be with you."

CHAPTER 4

To maintain the schooner's stability and to aid steering, Captain Morris had only the mainsail raised. Its canvas looked dirty gray in the weak daylight filtering through the heavy cloud cover. Though the offshore breeze was light, this was the only sail hoisted. Slight puffs of wind and the tidal current carried the *Piper* out of the harbor and into the estuary. With the bow pointed toward the Atlantic, the helmsman adjusted to the northeast, and the vessel headed up the coast. After about two hours, Captain Morris called out to strike the mainsail, bring the vessel about, and drop the anchors.

Morris was standing behind the helm with Jack and Bowden, and Morris said, "We will lay off Tuck Point tonight and make for the Atlantic and the shipping lanes on the morning tide. This will give the crew time to become familiar with this vessel. Midshipman Hollister, you will be in charge of the gun crews. Four 4-pounders, two 20-pounders, and ten swivels equip our craft. Work with the crew. They are good men. Several are familiar with these guns and will teach you what you need to know."

Jack smiled and nodded. "Aye, sir."

Jack took a deep breath, adjusted his tricorne, and strolled off to amidships where the cannons were stored.

"Mr. Bowden, take charge of the deck. I will be in my quarters."

A gaunt-faced, middle-aged sailor lingered in the opening of the after hatchway. He snapped to attention as the captain approached. "Beggin' your pardon, sir. Just gettin' some air 'fore I go below to stoke the stove," he said, and his head disappeared below the cowling.

Morris laughed. "Cook is going to provide us a proper meal to celebrate our maiden voyage," he yelled and started down the ladder.

———•◦•———

Aromas of woodsmoke, fried onions, and roasting meat tickled Jack's nose as he inspected the schooner *Piper*'s armaments. His mouth watered and stomach grumbled. *Smells finer than the poorly cooked slop and gruel I have been living on*, he thought.

The tantalizing flavors also stimulated other crew members. "*Très bon*," said a sturdy, dark-complexioned man standing nearby. "Cook, he makes fine meal." The man directed his comment toward Jack. "*Je m'appelle* Gaspar Arno." He held his large hand out to Jack. "I help bring leg o' *boeuf* aboard for cook. Hope he not burn it too much."

Jack's mouth curled into a smile. He accepted Gaspar's hand. "I am Midshipman Hollister. Mr. Bowden says you know cannons."

"*Oui*, Monsieur Midshipman." Gaspar nodded. "Is so. I know cannon. Eight years I am prisoner sailor on man-o'-war. British dogs train me well. I teach you."

"Thank you, Gaspar. After dinner I will ask Mr. Bowden to assign a gun crew and you as my master gunner."

Looking proud and pleased, the stout little man smiled. "*Oui*, M. Hollister. I make good gunner."

The ship's bell chimed eight times to signify the beginning of the dog watches. Crew members going off watch left their positions on deck and in the rigging, and others scurried about to replace them.

"It is four o'clock, Gaspar," Jack said. "We can eat in about two hours. Enough time to enjoy the cook's celebratory repast."

"*Oui*. For now, though, I must leave and take my post at the bow." The Frenchman started to walk off but yelled back. "I have Mr. Bowden find replacement for my station. Then I shall return."

———•◦•———

The officers and crew of the schooner *Piper* numbered twenty-four, and living space aboard the ninety-five-ton vessel was scant. Nevertheless, the captain, first and second officers, and two midshipmen segregated themselves into a small wardroom at the very rear of the vessel. This room also doubled as the captain's cabin. The other officers shared two small compartments forward of the wardroom. Midshipmen were on the larboard side, and Bowden and the second officer were to starboard.

Shortly after hearing eight bells, Jack dropped down the after hatchway, which led to the officer quarters. He walked into the wardroom. Captain Morris and Mr.

Bowden were already seated at the centrally located table. It was suspended from the overhead beam and secured to the deck to keep it from swinging. When not in use, the table could be released from the deck, raised, and secured to the ceiling.

Though dishes and silverware were set in place, the cook had not yet served the food. Following Captain Morris's directive, the cook and his assistant were to first provide meals to the crew and then the officers.

The long crew's mess was located below the weather deck in the forward half of the vessel, which was accessible via the amidships hatchways. The berths were forward and beyond the bulkhead of the chain locker.

A portion of the crew's quarters was used for storage. Casks of gunpowder, shot, and larger items were housed amidships in the space between the crew's mess and officer quarters.

"Good afternoon, Jack," said Captain Morris. "I hope you found the *Piper*'s weaponry satisfactory. A small vessel such as ours can only handle small cannons."

"Aye, sir. I did. I also met Gaspar Arno. His experience has impressed me. I would like to request he be made my master gunner."

Both Bowden and Morris nodded.

"Aye. He is a fine fellow," said Bowden. "Several years ago Mr. Smoke and I rescued him after he escaped from a British man-of-war. Found him dazed beneath a Halifax wharf as we were casting off our lines. He was hiding from a redcoat patrol. Smoke jumped down from the pier. The two of us picked him up and pushed and pulled him over the gunwale—none too soon either. As Smoke swung aboard, the patrol had come around the corner of the warehouse. We hid Gaspar beneath a tarp. The marine patrol did not see him, and the *Pegasus*, free of her moorings, drifted away from the pier. The patrol could not board. We saluted the redcoats and sailed for Beverly. Gaspar has been a patriot ever since."

Logan Whitehall, the *Piper*'s second officer, and Midshipman Robert Jones interrupted Bowden's story when they entered the wardroom.

Captain Morris greeted them. "Good day, gentlemen. Charles was telling Jack how he and Horace Smoke rescued Gaspar Arno from the British."

"Likely story." Logan Whitehall chuckled. "To listen to Gaspar's account, he fended off a patrol of redcoats with his sword and pistol. The man likes to exaggerate. I heard Captain Hargrave relate how Frenchy was dragged aboard the *Pegasus* dead drunk." Whitehall slid an empty bench away from the table and sat down. "No matter how that Frenchman got to Beverly, I for one am glad he is on our side. The man has a good eye for aiming a cannon."

"Aye," Captain Morris said. "I am assigning him as master gunner." The captain nodded at Jack. "I have also appointed Midshipman Hollister to supervise our gun crew."

Midshipman Jones stared at Jack and sat next to him. Jack noticed the boy looked puzzled. Midshipman Jones lowered his chin and glanced in the direction of the captain and Mr. Bowden. "Beggin' your pardon, sir. I thought I was to take charge of the gun crew."

"Jack is older, my lad," Morris said as he laid his arms on the table and clasped his hands. "When your father brought you aboard, he mentioned you were a crack shot with a musket. Firing a musket and shooting a cannon are not the same. Jack has experienced the rigors of the sea and has learned to connect and work with a hardened crew. If we are fired upon, I will allow you to assist Midshipman Hollister. In the meantime you will assist Mr. Bowden, Mr. Whitehall, and me. When our voyage is over, you will have the experience to accept higher responsibilities."

The fourteen-year-old banker's son sucked in a breath and tried to stifle the tears wetting his eyes. He lowered his head and stared at the center of the table.

"Our crew is composed of a few experienced seafarers, but most of the men are maladroit wharf rats who know little of the sea," Captain Morris said. "I will need the sailors to keep this vessel afloat and on course. Jack, you and Gaspar can select gun crews from the dross aboard. Some might be rebellious, but I am confident Gaspar can keep them in line. They are, as you might know, patriots because they volunteered for this mission."

Jack agreed and was about to say something when the cook and his assistant entered the wardroom. They carried platters that contained chunks of roasted beef, slices of ham, various boiled greens, carrots, beets, baked apples, and potatoes. They set the platters on the table and departed. The two men returned with chunks of bread and pitchers of spruce beer, birch beer, and malt beer. "If any of you want tea or coffee," the cook said, "the boy will bring it."

Captain Morris reached out and pulled the platter of roast beef toward him. Stabbing a chunk with a three-pronged serving fork, he transferred it to his plate. "Gentlemen, let us eat. We will discuss the course and needs of our voyage later," he said, and he reached for the plate of greens.

The officers attempted to converse and get to know each other. However, they had to almost shout because of the boisterous noise, lusty singing, and impassioned voices coming from the crew's mess.

"Sounds as if the crew members are enjoying their meals," Bowden said. "It is good. Once we are at sea, the meals will be less gratifying, and there will be more demands on the crew's time."

"Aye," Captain Morris said. "In a week they will be more disciplined…and tired." He faced Jack. "After you select your crew, I expect you and Gaspar to run them through some exercises. Train them. Remember, though, we have a limited amount of powder. You will have to use it sparingly. We would not want to get caught short in the heat of battle."

"Aye, sir. I will undertake mock firings until the men become more familiar with the guns."

"Worry not. All British vessels carry a sufficient amount of powder to supply their need," Whitehall said. "Our first capture should supplement what Jack uses to train his crew."

"But what if we encounter a man-o'-war?" Robert whimpered.

"Ha-ha. We'll shoot it in the ass and run like hell," Whitehall said.

Captain Morris and Bowden chuckled.

"Hopefully that will not happen," the captain said. "I do not plan to confront a British man-of-war. We will stay clear, but once we are at sea, I will allow the gun crews to fire a few salvos. The gun crew needs to feel the anger and roar of the cannons."

Jack smiled in satisfaction. "Thank you, Captain. I will inform Gaspar and have him select ten men—enough for two crews. Gunnery training will start this afternoon."

"Perhaps you should wait until morning," Captain Morris said. "After a raucous celebration, I do not believe many will be open to discussion."

Everyone agreed. The cook poked his head through the wardroom door. "Does anyone need anything?" he asked.

"Aye, my good man," the captain answered. "Bring in the rum, wort whiskey, and some glasses. And bring a glass for yourself. I would like to offer a toast to your fine meal and the dawning of our new venture. May we have a lucrative maiden voyage."

Whitehall thumped his fist on the table, and the other officers called out, "Huzzah!"

Squeals and caws of a flock of herring gulls flying overhead caused Jack's concentration on the diminishing shoreline to break. He looked up. The cloud layer had thinned but still covered the sky. Through the diffused morning light, he could see the *Piper*'s foresail and mainsail fill to capacity and tighten. Then the schooner's larboard side began to hike. His body automatically leaned left. While listening to the sound of the water whooshing past the bow intensify, he suddenly heard Whitehall's command to strike the mainsail. This drowned out the sea's music.

Almost immediately the crew members who had just finished cleating the sheets grabbed the lines and unsecured them. The gaff and hoops came rattling and scraping down the mast along with the large mass of canvas. The *Piper* quickly was brought around. This caused Jack to step about lively to maintain his balance. The foresail flapped and slapped as the bow came up into the wind. The schooner slowed and stopped as if mired in a sea of molasses.

Why are we stopping? Jack wondered. He scanned the sea around the vessel and saw a small coastal packet hiked to larboard. It was rapidly approaching from shore. A police ribbon fluttered from its masthead.

"Stand by," Captain Morris commanded. "Make ready to accept Constable William aboard."

The packet passed the *Piper* fifty yards to larboard, struck its sails while rounding behind the schooner, slowed, and approached to starboard. When the little sloop came abreast of the *Piper*'s hull, a crew member in the bow and one in the stern threw lines to men on the schooner. The sea was calm and allowed the packet to approach to within a few feet of the schooner's hull. This permitted others aboard the *Piper* to lower and secure a gangway between the vessels and connect them. The two vessels now drifted as one.

Captain Morris, Bowden, and Jack stood at the head of the gangway as Constable William and another man crossed over the planks to the *Piper*.

"To what do we owe this visit?" Morris said in a welcoming voice.

"Sorry for the intrusion," William said, and he stepped onto the deck. His brow furrowed, and the right side of his mouth opened and twisted downward. He shook his head when he extended his hand to Captain Morris. "A terrible event has happened." While the men clasped hands, William looked at Jack and Bowden and then stared back at the captain. "Excuse me. I'm being improper." William turned to the man who had come aboard with him. "Captain Morris, this is Dr. Herman Voors." William paused for a breath. "Our noted surgeon."

"Yes, yes," Morris said. "Surgeon Voors and I have met previously. It is good to see you again, Herman." The captain placed his hand on the doctor's shoulder. "I believe you have not come aboard for an outing at sea."

The constable spoke. "No." He lowered his head and shook it rapidly for a moment. "Terrible, terrible things are happening. The British—those goddamn lobsterbacks!" The constable sucked in a breath. "They have attacked their people. *Our* people."

"Calm down, Constable," Captain Morris said. "Come. Let us retire to the wardroom."

William nodded. Jack watched the constable clasp and wring his hands, relax, and follow the captain aft toward the hatchway. Jack trailed the group.

William continued. "Last evening, a fisherman who normally works off Portsmouth came to our office. He told the duty officer that two weeks ago three Royal Navy men-of-war released their broadsides on the village of Falmouth and destroyed it. The commander of this dastardly fleet disregarded frightened men, women, and children in the streets running for cover. The British commander did not seem to care. 'He just opened fire on the city,' the fisherman said. The bombardment continued all day."

"Good God! Are those bastards crazy?" Captain Morris ranted as he stomped into the wardroom. "What were they trying to attain? What caused this outrage?"

"When I interviewed the fisherman, he did not know what caused the deadly outburst."

Jack dropped onto a chair and lowered his head into his hands. Bowden looked somber, glared up, and said, "The people of Falmouth are an independent bunch. Most are patriots. I have visited this town many times, and I can think of two possible reasons for the attack. For one, revenge for the battle that occurred at Machias this past summer. I am certain Admiral Graves did not take well to the loss of a naval vessel, the death of its captain, and the capture of twenty of his well-trained men."

"Perhaps," Captain Morris said, "but the people of Falmouth did not deserve to be bombarded for something in which they had no part."

"Agreed," Bowden said.

"What is the second reason?" the captain asked.

"The actions of a radical patriot," Bowden said. "Colonel Samuel Thompson of nearby Brunswick leads a large band of rebels. The last time I put into Falmouth, I heard he had ordered his men to capture and detain a Lieutenant Henry Mowat this past spring. They did so. This action might also have aroused the ire of the British commanders."

"Yes, but they released him some days later," the constable said. "I heard Mowat returned to his vessel and sailed."

"You heard correctly," Bowden continued, "but his release was temporary—a parole so to speak to tend to matters aboard his vessel. Mowat was to return but did not do so. He instead sailed. His escape angered Thompson, but the city elders believed the lieutenant's release was necessary. They felt imprisoning a British officer would bring the force of Britain upon them. The Falmouth leaders did not want such a confrontation."

"Maybe the city leaders were wrong," Captain Morris said.

"Yes. It appears they were," Bowden agreed. "Thompson got angry. He considered Mowat's release an escape and had his men fire on the vessel as it cleared the harbor. The British considered this deed rebellious. Then they added to this infraction the imprisonment of a British officer. Those nervous idiots in Boston might look upon Thompson's actions as major violations against British laws."

Captain Morris tightened his fists. "Nevertheless bombarding a defenseless village that had no part in the fray is incomprehensible. Those men-of-war were never in any danger. A few musket balls fired from shore is no call to answer with cannonballs."

"Aye," Bowden said. "Though a conflict with a few poorly armed insurgents might have been what the fleet commanders wanted. It provided an excuse to create an example they thought would diminish the colonials' desire for freedom. By exerting exaggerated violence as punishment, they probably thought it would frighten us into submission." Bowden tightened his lips and clenched his fists. "Not this time! Their action has only strengthened patriot resolve."

Jack looked up. Everyone could see the anger in his eyes and face. "What does Great Britain think colonist are? Cattle? Vermin? Do they think they can lord over us? Do they believe they can use tyrannous acts to suppress innocent people's desires? I feel King George and his minions have exceeded their bounds. I stand with you and the patriots, Mr. Bowden."

Bowden strengthened and nodded. Captain Morris scanned the *Piper*'s officers. Their utterings and facial expressions signified agreement. He smiled and commented to the constable. "I believe, William, you brought me news of Falmouth's destruction to provoke a supportive response. And this, indeed, you shall have. Though I do not have the armament to face a man-of-war, I can set a course for Falmouth. The *Piper* should be there in three to four days. I am certain the town could use help."

"I was hoping that would be your decision," the constable said. "Falmouth primarily needs medical assistance. Dr. Voors volunteered to accompany you if you feel this proper. Your vessel is the fastest way to get him to Falmouth. I had him bring his medical supplies, and I brought a few provisions. The crew on the packet will transfer this cargo to the schooner as soon as they are summoned."

"Aye," Captain Morris said. "Dr. Voors, you are welcome to come along with us. A medical man will be good to have aboard should we encounter a British vessel. Jack, collect Midshipman Jones. Inform him to help transfer Dr. Voors's luggage and the other supplies to our vessel. You, please arrange for the good doctor to have a berth."

———•◦•———

Transferring Voors's medical supplies, food, and the dry goods Constable William brought took about an hour. Upon completion the constable returned to the packet, and the *Piper*'s crew hauled in the gangway and disengaged the two vessels. Crewmen standing in the bow used boat hooks to push the little craft away from the schooner, and others hoisted its sails. The force caused the packet's hull to rotate to starboard, and this allowed the slight offshore breeze to flow across its beam and fill the sails. The packet continued its turn to starboard and pulled away from the schooner. Constable William stood in the packet's stern. He raised his right arm, called back to the *Piper*, and wished everyone aboard a safe journey.

Dr. Voors and Jack missed the constable's departure. Both were belowdecks. Jack provided a berth for the doctor in an unused compartment forward of the midshipmen's cabin, and together they made up the cot. Both overheard Midshipman Jones tell Captain Morris, who was standing at the opening of the after hatchway, that all the cargo from the packet was stowed. Then they heard Captain Morris shout, "Hoist the sail. Let us get under way."

"Excuse me, Doctor," said Jack. "I believe we are finished here, and I need to go tend to my duties on deck."

"Yes, yes, Midshipman. I can complete what needs to be done. Thank you for your help."

Jack nodded and dashed up the ladder to the deck.

———•◦•———

Captain Morris had the crew set all the sails. This included the topgallants. With the offshore breeze pushing the vessel seaward, the shoreline disappeared below the western horizon within two hours. The wind strengthened and became constant. It blew from the southeast at about ten knots. When the captain commanded the *Piper*'s bow be pointed eastward and the helmsman responded, the schooner hiked slightly to larboard and sliced across the sea surface at nine knots.

While Gaspar explained the workings of a 4-pounder to the group of sailors he collected to serve as gun crews, Jack sat on the breech of another cannon. He felt the little cannon shift under him when the deck skewed from the force of the sails and swells. Jack jumped off the cannon and walked to where the master gunner instructed his crew. "Begging your pardon," Jack said. "Would it not be better if the crew went through the motions of firing this cannon? One learns faster through experience."

"*Oui*, Mr. Hollister. Rehearsal sans powder and shot. *Oui*. 'Tis good. Crew gain experience by doing."

"Yes. Dry firing the guns will not lessen our powder and ammunition. We have many powder bags, but most are empty." Jack turned to a young, detached, inattentive fellow. "Holder, go below and bring two or three empty powder bags."

Henry Holder shook his head and kept his eyes on the deck. He turned and started walking toward the amidships hatchway. Jack tapped a skinny boy of fifteen on the back. The little guy was dressed in clothes too big for him. "Tyler, go with Holder, and bring back a few fragments of wood and a slow match." Jack smiled at Tyler. The unkempt urchin turned and looked up at him. He was pleased at being assigned a task. "Even in practice a cannon needs to have shot."

"Aye, Mr. Hollister," Tyler sang out as he darted after Henry Holder.

"Mr. Gaspar, what other material does the crew need to fire the cannon?"

"A rammer, Mr. Hollister." Gaspar scanned the remaining men surrounding the 4-pounder. "Savage, find the rammer. Make sure sponge is tied on end. Do not forget bucket *avec* rainwater."

A rugged, dark-complexioned, buckskin-clad Iroquois with a clump of shiny black hair tied in a queue glared at Gaspar and grumbled. "I named Nightjar. I not savage. Fight with French. Now fight for Continental army. I learn. No like be called 'savage.'" The young Iroquois Indian leaned against the mainmast.

"*L'homme très raisonnable,*" Gaspar said with a smile. "Good man. Can be trusted. Know him from Montreal. M. Widget and Stokes, push this 4-pounder to a larboard gunport," Gaspar said to the two other men standing nearby, and he pointed to the cannon next to him. "Guns not fired from midship."

"Aye," the two slender, seasoned sailors said together.

They bent over and manhandled the little blackened bronze cannon, which weighed about 150 pounds, to the schooner's left side. The maneuver was not as difficult as they suspected because the gun sat on a four-wheeled wooden carriage.

By the time Stokes and Widget aligned the 4-pounder to a gunport, Holder and Tyler had returned from below deck. Holder carelessly tossed three powder bags to Gaspar. Gaspar gave him an angry look as he set the bags to the side of the cannon. Tyler smiled and put a bucket filled with blocks and splinters of wood beside the bags. In his right hand, he held a hemp cord with smoke curling from one end.

"Keep that cord away from those powder bags," Gaspar grumbled. "Should they contain powder sparks from the match, cause fire."

Gaspar placed a finger into the bucket of water Nightjar had set on the deck next to the mast. Leaning nearby was the rammer the Iroquois had brought. It was a pole with a flared knob on one end and a sponge tied to the other.

"*Bien*, M. Nightjar," the gunnery master said. "Water is sweet. Saltwater is not good inside gun."

Nightjar nodded and rested back against the larboard rail. Looking at the men standing around the cannon, Jack said, "Master Gunner, I will demonstrate loading and firing the cannon while you give the commands. Pay attention, men. Your lives depend on doing this properly." He paused for a moment. "A proper gun crew requires the coordinated effort of five men. Each man has a job to fulfill. The jobs need to be done quickly, completely, and in proper order. At the master gunner's command, I will perform the maneuvers. As I do, I will explain and do the action slowly." Jack took a breath and grabbed the ramrod. "Voice your commands, Master Gunner."

"Aye, sir." Mr. Gaspar issued his command. "Sponge the bore!" His voice sounded as if it had sprung from the recesses of the bilge.

Jack dunked the sponge end of the ramrod into the bucket of water and then shoved it into the cannon's barrel. "Before loading, the bore must be clean and any remaining embers doused. Powder bags can prematurely ignite. This is not good." He rotated the rod a couple times before withdrawing the sponge.

"Load!"

Picking up a powder bag, Jack shoved it through the muzzle. He then lifted the ramrod, spun it like a baton, and used both hands to shove the flared end of the rod down the barrel. He thumped it to compress the bag into the breach. Jack removed the ramrod, picked up a handful of wood splinters and blocks from the bucket Tyler had brought, and thrust them through the muzzle.

Again taking the flared end of the ramrod, he drove the shot into the charged cylinder of the cannon and removed the rod. "Cannon loaded!" Jack yelled.

As Jack was compressing the shot, Gaspar placed his thumb over the cannon's touchhole. "Must keep draft from blowing powder out hole," he explained. From a pouch on his belt, he removed a porcupine quill. He pushed it into the touchhole and immediately removed it. Lifting the pouch from his belt, Gaspar poured a small amount of gunpowder into the hole and nodded at Jack. "Forgive interruption."

Jack continued his instructions. "The vent man always has a thumb covering the touchhole. As Gaspar said, this is to keep any powder from blowing out of the hole when the loader is thumping the charge. The powder dust could ignite if there is any flame about and prematurely fire the cannon. Disastrous to a gun crew."

Jack stepped away from the cannon. He motioned for Gaspar to hand him the powder pouch and quill he had used. "As you saw," Jack continued, "Mr. Gaspar pierced the powder bag in the cannon's breech with this quill." He held up the quill. "Our master gunner told me he received this porcupine quill from his Passamaquoddy friends as an honor to him for saving one of their people." Jack smiled at Gaspar, and Jack put his finger next to the touchhole. "The master gunner acts as the vent man and then fills the hole with a small amount of powder. This readies the cannon to be fired."

"Aye, Midshipman Hollister," Gaspar said and inflated his chest. "As master gunner I now aim cannon. When ready I yell 'Fire.' When I do, man holding slow match put glowing end to hole."

Gaspar did what he said and jumped back. "Fire!"

Jack laid the smoldering end of the piece of hemp cord he had taken from Tyler on the touchhole. There was a fizz, and an instantaneous jet of white smoke flared from the touchhole. Everyone heard a pop. The gun crews erupted in a cacophony of whistles and huzzahs.

Jack clapped his hands over his ears. "Had there been a full bag of powder in the breech, we would all be holding our ears and shaking our heads." Jack laughed. "All right, men. Move the other cannons to their stations and practice loading and firing them. Mr. Gaspar will see that every man has a chance to experience each gunnery post. He will then assign your positions."

For the rest of the day, the schooner *Piper* progressed to the northeast. The men selected as gun crewmen rotated through each position necessary to load and fire a ship's cannon. Jack could see they were tiring and getting bored. One extra step after each rotation had to be performed that had nothing to do with the shooting of a cannon. Jack had ordered Tyler and Holder to remove the empty powder bag and scraps of wood from inside the barrel after each dry shot. Jack suggested the boys use hooks to pull out the rubbish and splinters that would normally be shot. Hooks turned out to be awkward and time-consuming, and they tended to scratch the inside of the barrels. During this interval the other men relaxed and taunted the boys.

After a series of trials, Tyler decided it was easier and quicker to stick his hand in the barrel and pull out the debris. He even created a chantey to sing while he performed this task. As he pushed his hand in the barrel, he sang, "Stick in you' arm an' nose de muzzle. Wiggle you' fingers, grab the crap, an' huzzle you' buzzle."

During the latter stanza, Tyler shoved his arm up the cannon's barrel then danced about and wiggled his butt. Everyone except Holder laughed and gibed at him. Holder glared at the boy, and Tyler yanked out his arm and sang the chorus of his chantey. "Outcome the chit to muddle de deck. Huzzah, huzzah, huzzah."

Then he straightened up, smiled, and faced Holder, who had to sweep the debris into a pile and shovel it over the gunwale. About halfway through the day, Holder tried to trade jobs with Tyler, but Holder got his arm stuck in the barrel. Jack had a couple of men use water and oil to free him. When the arm was finally extracted, Holder's elbow had several bloody gashes. Dr. Voors quickly cleaned and bandaged Holder's injuries and sent him back to his station.

Jack realized it was close to four o'clock in the afternoon. With the waning daylight; the beginning of the dogwatches; supper; and the tension building between Holder, Tyler, and the other crew members, Jack anticipated trouble. *The men need a distraction. They appear sufficiently competent to actually fire the cannons.*

"Holder," Jack called, "go below and bring two full powder bags and some grapeshot. Each crew will fire a cannon with live ammunition before the watch changes. When both guns have been fired, I will conclude today's training session."

As if struck by a bolt of lightning, the crew snapped to alertness. Gaspar divided the crewmen around him between the starboard and larboard amidships cannons and assigned each man a job. Widget and Stokes fell in with Jack's crew on the starboard 4-pounder. Widget was a sponge rammer and Stokes a loader. Tyler held the slow match and remained with the midshipman's crew. Because of his humiliating job during the training session, Jack gave him the honor of firing the cannon.

When Holder returned, Gaspar assigned him and Nightjar to his crew. Taking Midshipman Hollister's lead, the master gunner gave Holder the job of firing the larboard cannon. Within minutes the starboard 4-pounder was prepared and loaded. Its barrel was wheeled through the gunport. Jack angled the barrel for maximum distance, aimed at a passing wave, and yelled, "Fire!"

Tyler laid the burning end of the slow match on the touchhole and jumped back. Almost immediately a flare of white smoke shot upward. Within seconds the schooner's deck shuddered from the explosion, and a streak of fire jetted from the cannon's muzzle. As the noise of the shot reverberated, a thick cloud of acrid smoke drifted aft along the *Piper*'s starboard side. It almost obscured the geyser of seawater that spewed skyward about twenty-five yards away.

Jack nodded as his astonished crew stared at the gun, him, and the sea. "Good job, men. Tyler, run the slow match to the larboard gun crew. The rest of you are dismissed."

Jack strolled to the foremast to watch Gaspar's crew fire its cannon. Tyler faced Gaspar and held the slow match for him to see. "Aye, mate. Hand it to Holder. He is to fire the cannon."

Before Tyler had a chance to acknowledge the master gunner's command, Holder twisted forward and ripped the burning hemp cord from the boy's hand. "That's mine, pamby. I'll take charge of it."

Holder's impudence startled Gaspar and the rest of the larboard gun crew, but they carried on. The master gunner knelt next to the cannon and placed his cheek against the cannon's reinforce ring. He peered along the barrel and at the gunner's quadrant. He tried to set the cannon to the proper angle for the shot. The master gunner's body tensed. He swung his right arm out and to the side. This signaled to abort the shot.

Holder jumped forward and touched the slow match to the touchhole. A split second before the blast occurred, the master gunner rammed his hands against the barrel and shoved himself away. He rolled back onto the deck, flipped himself over, and covered his head with his hands.

Slightly out of alignment with the gunport, the muzzle of the 4-pounder spewed its charge. The shot took a gaping, ovoid hole out of the gunport and shredded several square feet of larboard gunwale.

Jack and two members of the gun crew were knocked to the deck. One man stood stunned with blood staining his left pant leg. Another was a large man who had been resting against the schooner rail about six feet from the gunport. He got thrown seaward with the splintering gunwale, but he managed to catch hold of a torn shroud as he flew out over the water. For several seconds he hung and swung to and fro over and away from the deck as the *Piper* rolled through the swells.

When Jack looked up, he realized the man's grip on the dangling rope was weakening. The fellow was slowly slipping toward the frazzled end of the shroud. Jack jumped to his feet, grabbed the sailor's legs when the schooner rolled to starboard, and swung the man over the deck. The sailor let go of the shroud. Jack's arms were around the sailor's limp, buckskin-covered legs, and he fell to the deck. He released his hold and recognized the Passamaquoddy named Nightjar. The Indian was barely conscious. The side of his face was oozing blood.

Amid muffled moaning, shouting, and chaotic activity, Jack noticed Holder standing dumbfounded amidships. He was cupping his hands over his ears. Jack's own ears were ringing from the blast, and he could barely hear Gaspar berating the young man. Holder had his eyes squeezed closed and lips pursed tight. Rivulets of tears streaked his cheeks.

"Call Dr. Voors!" Jack shouted for anyone who could hear.

Jack watched Holder fixed like a bollard to the deck. It became obvious Holder was not hearing the master gunner railing at him. Another sailor whose leg was injured and bleeding lowered himself to the deck and leaned against the foremast. Within minutes Voors startled Jack by laying his hand on the midshipman's shoulder. The doctor's voice sounded as if it emanated from somewhere deep in a cavern. "I will tend to the Indian," he said and motioned toward the other injured sailor. "Go. Look after him until I get there."

Voors knelt next to Nightjar, and Jack stumbled in the direction of the foremast. On the way he stopped and faced Gaspar. "It was an accident, Master Gunner," Jack said. "Leave the boy be. You can't reprimand a man for his enthusiasm."

Captain Morris and Mr. Bowden appeared next to Gaspar. "Jack is right," Bowden said, took hold of the master gunner's shoulders, and pulled him away from Holder. The captain put his arm around the young sailor and urged him to follow. Before anyone left the area, however, the captain snapped his eyes upward. Jack's ears had cleared sufficiently for him to hear, "Sail ho. Off the larboard bow."

Briskly the captain lifted his head and stared into the rigging. High above him he saw the foremast lookout pointing to the east and shouting again. "Three vessels. Four leagues. Hauling toward us."

Morris released Holder and ran with Bowden toward the bow. Jack looked in the direction of the approaching ships. All he could see were the tops of several sets of sails reflecting the setting sun's reddish-orange beams. Then he heard Morris shout to the helmsman, "Hard to starboard! Head for the coast."

CHAPTER 5

Luckily the brisk, southwesterly breeze caused the *Piper*'s larboard side to hike when the schooner turned to the west and toward shore. With only a slight chop on the ocean's surface, the damaged area remained dry and allowed the ship's carpenter and his helpers to make repairs.

Amid the clamor of pounding hammers and grating saws, Jack carried a plank to the repair area. Jack handed the board to a pair of seamen, straightened, and looked aft. *Morris is at the helm*, he thought. *Sky is darkening. We are approaching shallows. Reefs. Captain knows these waters though.* About a league behind, Jack also saw the taut sails of one of the British frigates hauling down on the *Piper. It is closing fast.*

A puff of white smoke obscured the frigate's bow. Within a few seconds, Jack heard the cannon grumble. He sucked in a breath, and his body reflexively cowered. He sighed when the shot hit the sea surface a hundred yards away.

"Assemble gun crews!" Morris yelled. "Ready starboard cannons!"

Jack sped to the mainmast where the ship's bell hung. Rapidly he shook the clapper's cord side to side and caused the bell to peal a series of staccato rings. This signal called the crew to battle stations.

Within moments Gaspar, Stokes, Widget, and others stumbled out of the amidships hatch and onto the deck. The master gunner signaled with his arms and yelled commands. The gun crews maneuvered all the 4-pounders to the starboard side.

Tyler and Holder bounded onto the deck, and each carried a bucket of shot and a powder bag. The cannon barrels were sponged, and Gaspar shouted, "Load!" As soon as the rammers pounded in the shot and powder, the crews pushed the muzzles of two cannons through the starboard gunports.

"Stand by!" commanded Gaspar.

Jack felt the schooner bounce just as the bow lookout yelled, "Keel's smelling ground."

Morris swung the *Piper* hard ninety degrees to starboard. Jack's hands pushed forward against the cannon in an attempt to keep himself from falling. The vessel complained with creaks and groans and laid into the turn. Deck crews scrambled to trim the slapping sails and rigging. They loosened some lines and tightened others until the sails filled, and the *Piper* took hold of the freshened offshore breeze. The schooner sped forward through the darkness. It slashed the sea surface and occasionally bounced off the sandy bottom. Easing his grip on the cannon, Jack shook his head. *Captain Morris knows these waters. I hope.*

Continuous gurgling and sloshing seemed to ease everyone until the schooner again lurched to the right.

The anxiety and chaos of being pursued by a British man-of-war mollified. A quick ninety-degree starboard turn directed the *Piper*'s bow seaward.

A command was quietly echoed around the vessel. "No talk. No light."

After about a half hour, Morris slowly brought the *Piper*'s direction to the northeast.

"Lookouts to the rails," Jack heard the captain mumble to Mr. Bowden. "Listen. Any sound, yell out."

The command made its way to the crew, and Morris adjusted the schooner's attitude to sail as silently as possible. Only the sliding splash of water against the hull and a dampened tick or thud of a rope hitting against a mast or yardarm evinced the existence of the schooner *Piper*. With his hands on the rail, Jack stood a few feet from an amidships gunport and slowly inhaled and exhaled the humid, salty air. He could not see the black cannon in the dark. If anyone stood nearby, only a sniffle or shuffle would suggest the individual's presence. Though there was a chill in the air, Jack could feel his body warm, and droplets of sweat began to ooze down his chest and underarms. He expected a cannonball to hit the schooner's hull at any moment. He sighed and held an ear to the breeze.

At first this quiet stance felt comfortable and relaxing. After a while, however, Jack's face began to feel cold. The moisture in his shirt caused him to shiver. He shuffled and looked seaward and then at his feet. He could see nothing. The stiff breeze blowing in his face caused tears to moisten his eyes. They prickled his eyelids, prodding him to rub them. Moving one leg to relieve the pain in the other, he tightened his hands on the rail. Again he shuffled. He heard nothing but the movement of water against the schooner's hull.

After what felt like hours, no one had heard any unusual sounds. Captain Morris gave the command to stand down from the battle alert. Mr. Bowden lit an oil lamp, placed a dimming hood over it, and held it low along his leg.

Jack looked aft and saw the captain turn over the helm to the quartermaster and descend through the after hatchway. The midshipman made his way to where Bowden stood.

"Captain Morris assumed the British gave up the chase," Mr. Bowden said. "His strategy to sail onto the shoals kept the frigates from following in the dark. Their captains are not familiar with these waters. They did not want to jeopardize their ships to take only an unknown schooner as prize."

"Aye," Jack said. "Captain Morris's strategy was good. Thank the Lord he knows these waters."

Bowden nodded. "Have your gun crew disarm the cannons and then dismiss them. I see Mr. Holder did his part. Perhaps he will do his duty like everyone else."

"Aye," Jack said. "He's trying."

———•◦•———

A string of clouds lying to the southwest brightened as the sky lightened. Jack was standing next to the starboard rail and clasping a mug of hot coffee. He lowered his eyes as the sun broke the eastern horizon. After the captain dismissed the men from the battle alert, the atmosphere aboard the ship relaxed. Even so, Morris doubled the number of lookouts in the rigging. When the sky began to be illuminated, no sentinel sounded a warning.

Jack scanned the eastern horizon on each side of the growing flame. He saw no sails anywhere—only the straight line separating the sky and sea. A flock of herring gulls glided over the schooner's wake. Some dropped low and settled in the slightly choppy waves off the vessel's beam. The gulls faced the schooner and were no doubt waiting for the cook to throw breakfast scraps over the side. When Jack dumped the remains of his coffee overboard, four gulls nearest the schooner zipped down only to be disappointed. The seagulls took to the air once the *Piper* passed and no scraps were provided. They joined the flock following to the aft.

Bowden came up behind Jack and jolted him from his serene stare. He sidled to the rail, leaned against it, and said, "Morris has given me leave when we arrive in Falmouth. I am hoping there will be a sloop from Machias in the harbor. If so, I plan to return with it to learn of Horace Smoke's condition. If he is well enough, we will return together."

"Is there a possibility I may also go?" Jack pushed himself away from the schooner's rail and faced Charles.

"No. You are needed aboard the *Piper*." Bowden nodded, turned, and moved toward the helm. "Come. Walk with me. Captain Morris has given Mr. Whitehall permission to visit relatives in Brunswick. So he will be away from the vessel for several days. After seeing how positively the gun crews responded to your supervision, and because of your past seamanship experiences, the captain wants you to fulfill the duties of second officer while Mr. Whitehall is ashore. I believe he is correct in his assessment of your abilities."

Jack sighed. A knot of anxiety had formed in his stomach, but then pride took hold of him. He grinned and straightened. "Thank you for your confidence in me, and thank Captain Morris. I will not let either of you down."

————•+•+•————

Though the *Piper* slid and bobbed over the chop of one- and two-foot waves, she occasionally jolted when her bow smashed into a rogue five- or six-footer. This caused the hull to groan and the rigging to rattle and twang. Along the western horizon lay a carpet of puffy clouds bleached of their morning tints. They disrupted an otherwise azure sky and delineated the shoreline the earth's curvature obscured. A mixture of cool and warm seaward breezes pushed the schooner northeast. The slight wind and nearly calm sea made for a comfortable sail on the Gulf of Maine.

On-deck hammers clunked and saws grated as the carpenter and his crew continued to make temporary repairs to the larboard gunwale and rail. Jack, Gaspar, and several gun-crew members worked to repair the 4-pounder. Its barrel needed paint, and the quadrant was torn away.

Gaspar gently finished tapping the quadrant back into shape and reattached it to the cannon. The quartermaster rang the ship's bell and signaled the change from the morning to the forenoon watch. This caused a bit of chaos on deck as crewmen scurried about and changed their stations. Tyler and Holder continued to work on the damaged cannon. Widget and Stokes had to leave and man their watch stations. Behind the 4-pounder, Nightjar convalesced from his injury. A bandage covered his head and left ear. The cold air did not appear to affect him. All he wore were a pair of buckskin pants, moccasins, and a buckskin vest. The vest's front was open and exposed the bandage that encircled his chest and back. When Jack asked him about his condition, Nightjar answered, "Sun warm. Heal body fast." Then he lay back on the deckhouse roof.

Several other gun-crew members dallied about the area and seemed not to have anything to do. Jack ordered them to mount the ten swivel guns the *Piper* carried. These small-bore, portable, antipersonnel cannons mounted on swivels could be attached to any secure protuberances on the schooner. The swivel gave each little weapon a wide arc of movement. "Attach them to the gunwales. Four on each side of the hull, one on the bow, and one on the taffrail," Jack commanded. "The *Piper* is a warship. It needs to look fierce when it enters Falmouth Harbor. It must give hope and confidence to the townspeople."

Holder chuckled. Jack stepped away from the cannon and did not notice the young man's actions, but Tyler did. Tyler heard his painting partner say, "Confidence? We are puny. Does that instill confidence? Last night we ran from a frigate."

Tyler hit his paintbrush against the carriage of the 4-pounder. "We might be puny, but I have confidence in the captain and Midshipman Hollister. They have fought the British."

Holder narrowed his eyes. "Perhaps so." The doubting fellow slapped a brush full of paint across the barrel and spattered Tyler's arm. "We will see."

———•◦•———

Shortly after the ship's bell sounded four times during the afternoon watch, Captain Morris ordered the *Piper* brought to a west-northwest direction. After about two hours, the sharp line dividing the ocean and sky thickened, darkened, and became fuzzy and irregular when the sun touched the horizon. Everyone on deck heard the shout from the rigging. "Land ho!"

As the schooner continued toward the coast, the shoreline grew, became more distinct, and divided into a series of islands.

Captain Morris stood with Bowden, Jack, and Whitehall behind the helm and said, "The sky will darken within the hour. We will lay off Mackworth Island tonight and enter the harbor at daylight."

Morris pointed to what appeared to be a small floating mass of trees and flatland lying a league or so to starboard. The helmsman readjusted the course to a more westerly direction. A moderate breeze came offshore, and the *Piper* came about quickly.

"Strike the foresa'l," Bowden shouted.

The deck crew scurried about the deck and into the rigging. They loosened lines and furled the massive canvas as it dropped onto the boom. Within minutes the foresail was secure, and the schooner slowed.

"Leadsman, to the chains."

Bowden's command caused a sailor from amidships to dash to the bow. Jack watched as the young man removed the sounding line from a rack. The leadsman tossed up the lead weight attached to the end of the line and caught it in his right hand. He dropped the bitter end to the deck, placed his foot on it, leaned over the rail, and let loose the lead. When it fell two yards down the vessel's side, the leadsman gripped the line. He then swung it forward and released it. The lead line flew well beyond the bow and splashed into the sea. It quickly became vertical and taut against the hull.

"Eight fathoms," the leadsman yelled back, "and no bottom!"

The *Piper* continued to move toward Mackworth Island. Bowden's command to strike the mainsail again generated a swarm of activity. With the foremast and mainmast bare, the schooner remained only under the power of the jibs. The *Piper* slowed to the forward speed of a stealthy snake.

"Mark. Five fathoms," the leadsman shouted.

"Anchor. Make ready," Bowden commanded.

Four robust men assembled on the forward deck and situated themselves near the anchor hawsers. The leadsman again tossed the lead line, but this time the line hit the sea bottom just ahead of the bow. As the schooner moved forward, the sailor gathered the access line until it came vertical. "Four fathoms and bottom!" he shouted back.

Bowden called, "Drop anchors."

The *Piper* shuttered as the chains and hawsers the heavy anchors pulled slid down the hull's side. When the giant clawed weights hit the bottom, the anchor lines continued to play out as the *Piper* glided forward. The leadsman took another sounding. "Three fathoms! Keel will be smellin' the bottom, sir!"

"Secure anchors! Strike jibs!"

Within five minutes the schooner crawled to a stop. When the helmsman fastened the ship's wheel to hold the rudder amidships, Bowden turned to Captain Morris and said, "Schooner *Piper* at anchor, sir."

"Thank you, Mr. Bowden."

The first officer then shouted, "Anchor Watch, to stations." He sighed, clapped Jack on the shoulder, and said, "Let us retire below. Cook will have supper awaiting us."

As oil lamps were lit at strategic points about the vessel, the officers and most of the *Piper*'s crew cleared the deck and headed for their mess areas.

———————

When Jack Hollister came on deck at first light, he understood why he had felt chilled during the night. Heavy dark clouds curled above. A stiff breeze blew across the *Piper*'s starboard beam. Seaward he could see the water's surface growing angry. *Wintry weather is making itself known,* the young man thought. *The fifth of November. It is late.* "I am glad we are near shore and in the island's lee," he mumbled to himself.

He tightened the collar of his pea jacket, buttoned its top button, walked toward the bow, and avoided the crew members clambering about the deck. The capstan creaked and groaned as the anchors were raised. The mainsail and a single jib were hoisted and reefed, and they caught the northerly wind. Jack walked forward as the schooner's bow rotated away from Mackworth Island, and he felt a twinge of vertigo as he watched the shoreline move in an apparent arc. Only several leagues lay between the *Piper* and Falmouth Harbor.

Jack used his glass to focus on the shore ahead. A horrible scene impinged on his right eye. It contained broken pilings, twisted and shattered piers and wharves, and scattered piles of burned debris where once sheds and warehouses had stood.

When the schooner came abreast of Back Cove's mouth and Falmouth Neck's head, Jack saw the stone wall that defined the eastern boundary of Falmouth Town. Beyond lay broken buildings and smoldering heaps of rubble. Though some buildings still appeared intact, a misty pallor of solitude hung over the town. As the *Piper* neared the destroyed wharves and sunken vessels, though, people wandered about. Some moved slowly and aimlessly with their heads bowed. Others walked as if they had a destination, either empty-handed or carrying things. Jack observed armed groups in gatherings of threes, fours, and occasionally fives on what remained of the once-developed shoreline or in doorways of partially burned buildings. A disbanded group of six men strode along the street paralleling the broken quay. They seemed to be stalking the *Piper*'s movements. Each carried a musket. Occasionally one would point his weapon toward the vessel.

Captain Morris came amidships and yelled, "Post the colors!"

Midshipman Robert Jones scampered down the after hatchway, and within moments he was back on deck and carrying a folded white cloth. "Aye, Captain," he said and handed Morris the flag.

"Go, boy! Display it!"

Jones took the flag back and ran to the mainmast. He undid the flag line from its cleat and tied the flag to the cord. The folds fell open. Jones stepped back and ran the ship's colors to the top of the mast.

The wind quickly unfurled the white cloth, and everyone who could see it saw a green pine tree was stitched on the flag's center. Written above the pine tree was the motto, "An Appeal to Freedom."

"General Washington presented the *Piper* with this ensign," Captain Morris said as Jack approached him. "Said it would define us as an American man-of-war." He scanned the activity along the shoreline. "That should satisfy those men who seem to question our presence."

Several shoreline stalkers stood for a moment and glared toward the vessel. Jack heard them cheer. They then started shaking their muskets and jumping around. One even fired a shot into the air. They began to run down the street to the most intact pier that jutted into the harbor.

Several men ran to the water's edge, scampered into open boats, and began pulling toward the *Piper*.

"Floating trash ahead and to larboard," yelled the forward lookout.

"Helmsman, make for clear water," shouted Captain Morris, and he pointed his arm toward the remains of a large wharf. "We will lay off Preble's Wharf. Mr. Bowden, have the crew strike the mainsa'l and ready the anchors."

"Aye, Captain," Bowden said and commanded the order.

This caused the deck crew to scurry to activity. While the schooner *Piper* was being brought to anchor, Dr. Voors leaned against the starboard rail aft of the mainmast and observed the liveliness ashore.

As soon as the vessel was secure, Mr. Bowden called, "Mr. Hollister, have a detail lower the longboat and ready a rowing crew. Dr. Voors, Mr. Whitehall, Midshipman Jones and I will be going ashore. While we are gone, have the remainder of the crew ready to unload Dr. Voors's materials and the other cargo. I am certain some townsmen will be happy to lighter the freight ashore."

"Aye, sir," Jack said and went off in search of the boatswain Stokes, and seamen Widget, Holder, and Tyler, as well as several others.

Holder stood in the longboat near its bow and steadied himself by holding one of the haul lines. He continued to grumble as the longboat was lowered down the schooner's side. Being ordered to the rowing crew angered him. His brow furrowed and jaw clenched tightly. He raised a fist and stared up at the schooner's rail.

Tyler's hands gripped the after haul line, and he sneered at Holder. "You thinkin' you should not be here haulin' a line?" the boy said. "You're no better. Just a common seaman like me."

Captain Morris leaned over the starboard rail and yelled, "Tighten your lip, Mr. Holder. Someone might believe we have a morale problem aboard this vessel."

Before the longboat's keel touched the sea surface, several prams were being jostled fore and aft against the hull.

Morris shouted at the enthusiastic townsmen maneuvering these little barges. "Mind your ways down there. I am not looking to have my vessel damaged. Do not interfere with the longboat."

"Aye, master," a burly man grumbled.

"We bein' careful, Cap'in," another grunted.

"Ya young jacks, hol' tight to those lines," Boatswain Stokes shouted. "Keep tha' longboat from wobblin'. Crew comin' down." He straightened and looked at Widget and Nightjar. "O'er the side, you rascals. Officers awaitin'."

The two seamen climbed over the rail and down the rope netting that had been hung down the hull's side earlier. Stokes followed. When he stepped into the longboat, he moved to the stern, set the rudder in place, and called, "Prepare to receive officers."

Bowden and Jones descended down the hull. When they took their positions in the rowboat, Dr. Voors tossed his black satchel to Mr. Jones and lowered himself down.

"God be with you, gentlemen," Captain Morris yelled.

Stokes commanded, "Larboard, shove off."

As the longboat drifted away from the *Piper* and the oarsmen dug in the oars, Morris called out from above, "It will be some days until you return. Have safe journeys. Mr. Jones, you are in charge of the longboat crew. Return immediately with the crew after Messrs. Bowden and Whitehall and Dr. Voors step ashore."

Before Stokes could answer, everyone heard, "Damn! The captain gives us no time...no liberty, an' no moment ta breathe."

Then the voice trailed off. Though his head was tilted toward the longboat's deck, the captain and all aboard knew who had spoken those words. Holder had a distinctive whiny pitch to his voice.

Momentarily taken aback, Stokes shrugged when he acknowledged the captain. Then he shook his head and said, "Pull for shore! Lay your backs into it!"

"Impudent little bastard," Captain Morris muttered. "When he is back aboard, Mr. Hollister, you need to punish his indiscretions."

Jack felt a twinge of nervousness. "Aye, sir."

"You are now second in charge. The position requires a sense of authority."

Jack nodded. "Aye, sir."

"I am going below. Have the crew ready the cargo for unloading," Captain Morris said.

He walked to the after hatchway and descended. Jack watched as the *Piper*'s longboat neared the shore. Within a few minutes, he saw the four crewmen jump into the water and pull the boat's bow onto the shore. The officers stood and stumbled to the bow, and they disembarked onto moist sand and gravel.

When Jack turned, he observed a small coaster passing slowly about a hundred yards behind the *Piper*'s stern. His eyes widened, and his heart skipped a couple beats. He scrambled to the aft rail and wanted to yell out to the vessel, but he did not recognize the helmsman or anyone else on deck. "Benjamin Foster's vessel," he mumbled. "The *Machias Packet*. Wonder if there is anyone aboard from Machias that I know."

Then a moment of sadness enveloped him. *Mr. Bowden will be departing aboard her tomorrow. Wish I were also. I miss my days in Machias. They seem so long ago. One day perhaps.*

"Ah, M. Hollister," Gaspar said as he came up behind Jack. "Is not that the vessel that brings lumber from Machias?"

"Aye. It is."

"Will you be going aboard?"

"No. They will be sailing in the morning. Captain Morris is going ashore this evening, and I cannot. During his absence the *Piper* will be under my command."

"'Tis good. I will remain and assist."

"Thank you, Gaspar."

"Our cutter is returning." Gaspar pointed to the long-boat. It was about a quarter mile to starboard. "Something unusual, sir. They are rowing fast. Mr. Jones and only four men aboard."

"Good God!" Jack pulled the telescope from his belt and sighted on the longboat. "Holder is missing." He quickly focused on the site where the officers were unloaded. Then he scanned the beach and street but recognized no one. "The captain is not going to look well on this."

———•◦•———

Under the broken dock, Seaman Henry Holder grabbed a piling and glanced back toward the longboat. He saw the commotion his sudden departure had caused. It tickled him for a moment to see the crew still floundering about some fifty yards away and trying to retrieve the oar he had tossed over the side. Once they mustered themselves, he reasoned it would not take very long for them to return to the schooner and send a posse.

Henry reached out and took hold of a board projecting from what remained of a once-ordered dock. He pulled himself along until the tips of his moccasins touched the bottom. As soon as he could, he jammed his feet into the mud to aid his escape. In the process he lost both moccasins. Now barefoot, Henry simultaneously upreared his body flat onto the water's surface and performed scissors kicks. This action shot him toward the broken, twisted framework. He seized a post to which supports were still attached, and then he climbed onto the broken dock. He grimaced and stumbled when a splinter punctured the side of his left foot. He threw his hands forward to cushion the fall, but he still landed hard on his knees. This caused him to cry out as pain shot up his arms and legs.

He crawled forward, found a quiet, hidden place among the twisted wreckage, and sat. He began to rub his injured knees and punctured foot, but fatigue, stress, pain and intense agitation caused him to pass out.

———•·•·•———

The larboard oarsmen boated their oars just before the longboat crashed against the *Piper*'s hull. As the little vessel ricocheted away from the *Piper*, Midshipman Robert Jones launched himself from the amidships thwart and scrambled up the rope net.

"Henry Holder's jumped ship," Jones cried. He wiped his nose and covered his right eye. A smear of blood extended across the lower part of his right cheek.

"At ease, Midshipman," Jack said.

"He hit me, sir, after we shoved off the beach. An' 'e jumped overboard and swam like hell."

"Mr. Widget," Jack said, and he gestured for the seaman to step closer.

The oarsman climbed over the rail and came forward. He put his hand on Midshipman Jones's shoulder. Robert rubbed his right eye and lowered his hand. Jack saw the eye the boy covered had blackened, and tears welled forth in both his eyes.

"Please calm Midshipman Jones, Mr. Widget. Aid him as you can." Jack turned to the others in the rowing crew and said, "Can someone tell me what happened?"

Tyler had been sitting next to Holder in the cutter, and Stokes had seen everything from his location at the tiller. They both began rattling off their observations together. From the chaos of their words and phrases, Jack learned that when the longboat had moved some fifty yards away from shore on its return, Holder had thrown his oar into the water. He had then turned, struck Jones across the face, and flung himself over the gunwale.

"Swam like hell, 'e did, toward some broken timbers. Climbed up 'em," Widget said.

"Mr. Gaspar, organize a detail of armed men to go ashore and find him. Seaman Holder has abandoned his duty—a serious offense. I will go below and inform Captain Morris. I believe Seaman Holder to be in much trouble. He faces court-martial."

Jack dashed down the after ladder to the captain's cabin.

CHAPTER 6

Shortly after Jack scampered off to Captain Morris's cabin, the stern-faced, square-jawed master-at-arms, Sergeant Bobby Turner, erupted through the after hatchway. His downturned white-trimmed tricorne shadowed a pair of squinted, serious eyes. Six more men followed behind him. They bolted out wearing basic cocked hats. All were dressed in dark-blue regimental coats with white linings and facings, pewter buttons, and high leather collars. They wore white waistcoats and jumpers, calf-length white breeches, and white socks. The hard leather heels of their black boots crashed loudly on the deck when the men bounded onto it. Each carried a musket and had a sword swinging at his side. Jack and Captain Morris followed this rank and surged up the ladder. These uniformed men fell in line amidships. When Captain Morris stepped in front of them, they snapped to attention.

Jack was standing behind the captain and recognized these men. He had seen them in slovenly dress during the voyage. They had been doing chores delegated to common jacks. *Solitary fellows*, he thought. *Kept to themselves. Didn't mingle with the other seamen.*

Captain Morris edged next to Jack and said, "Have the ship's crew gather around." He then stepped back and repositioned himself in front of the uniformed men.

"Aye, aye, sir," Jack said, and he called everyone to assemble on deck.

It took a few minutes for Jack's command to be echoed throughout the schooner and for the sailors to gather on deck. When all had assembled, Captain Morris said, "The seven men you see standing before me dressed in uniforms are Marbleheaders—representatives of the New England regiments. Colonel John Glover trained them, and they have been selected for their superior military abilities and seamanship. They are the *Piper*'s contingent of shipboard marines."

A cacophony of confused voices murmured about the deck.

"Come to order, men," Morris commanded. "You know these men. Holystoned with them. Ate and drank with them. They are on board this schooner, however, as soldiers who can be called on my orders for special missions." Morris paused for a moment, looked at the marines, and then scanned the crew. "I have held their identities in secret in case there were some on board who would plan to subvert this vessel's goals." The captain looked up. "It seems we have just such an individual. A deserter—Seaman Henry Holder. Sergeant Turner and his patrol will go ashore and find Holder. Though our deserter comes from a fine patriotic family, I believe he is a loyalist. He needs to be captured and returned to face his punishment." The captain turned to Jack. "Mr. Hollister, your men are to transport these marines to shore. I will also go and meet with Colonel Thompson. During my absence you are in charge. Marines, at ease. Collect your gear. Report to the chains. Ship's crew, dismissed."

Jack signaled Stokes, Widget, Nightjar, and the other oarsmen.

Tyler ran forward and said, "Can I go, too, sir?"

"Not on this trip," Jack answered. "I need you and Gaspar aboard."

Tyler was disappointed, and wallowed off with his head lowered. Within half an hour, everything was prepared, and everyone had boarded the longboat. Captain Morris was in dress uniform, and he stood in front of the forward thwart. The smart-looking marines had seated themselves on the amidships benches and sat as if at attention. They were holding their muskets vertically. Nightjar and Widget pulled on the starboard oars, while two other seamen manned the larboard sweeps. Stokes stood in the stern and handled the tiller. The longboat presented itself with all naval formality as it disappeared into the blaze of the setting sun. A long linear flock of herring gulls flew overhead and paralleled the shoreline.

———•·•·•———

A nearby crunching sound snapped Henry into consciousness. He twisted back and saw the longboat filled with marines grind against the sand. The crewmen were jumping into the shallow water. This sight and the thought of being captured caused him to forget the pain coming from his scraped knees and punctured foot. Henry lunged onto his feet, loped over the broken boards, and scampered toward the street like a mountain goat bounding up a crag.

When Henry heard Stokes call his name, he froze. For a moment the grit and cobblestones of the street aggravated the sting of his punctured foot. After a spasmodic tremor like a dog shaking after a bath, Henry dashed down the street and ducked behind a burned-out building. Realizing no one was following him, he continued to run.

He noticed the road crossed a stream a few yards ahead. Stumbling into the creek, he waded to where the creek passed under a bridge. There Henry sat upon a rock. He caught his breath, buried his face in his hands, and started to cry.

The water abated the pain and cooled his feet. He reached down, wetted his hands, and then rubbed them against his face. Breathing shallowly and watching eddies curl around his ankles, he began to think. *I'm a deserter. They hang deserters.* Tears again filled his eyes. He scooted off the rock and crawled up the bank and under the bridge. The bleeding from his foot and knees had stopped, but the pain pulsed and surged through his legs. He lay back on the dirt. Saltwater-soaked garments clung to his body and caused him to shiver. He sat up, pulled his legs to his chest, wrapped his arms around his legs, and tightened his muscles. For a moment his body warmed. Henry lowered his head against his knees. "I'm gonna hang," he groaned. "Hang," he moaned.

The words *hang, if caught, swing, yardarm*…trailed off in his mind. He was frightened and curled in an upright fetal position. He held his breath and didn't move, eventually falling asleep.

The rumble and vibration of horses, men, and a carriage crossing the little bridge awakened him. Debris ejected from above fell on his face and caused him to wipe his eyes. He opened them and could not see through the cracks between the bridge-deck boards. He rubbed his eyes again. They acclimated to the darkness. He rolled to the side and realized twilight had dimmed to night.

Though the burning sensations in his legs tormented him, he knew his pain was not the major problem. His saltwater-soaked clothing irritated him and made him colder. Whenever he moved, the damp cloth pressed against his skin. He shuddered. Henry crawled out from under the bridge and stood. Cold wrapped about him.

Night's not good to search.

He wrapped his arms about him but continued to shiver. A nauseating, sweet aroma muted the surrounding smells of charred wood and vegetation. Other unpleasant, earthy odors emanated from the muddy stream bank. He looked around. In the waning twilight, he saw the decaying, partially burned corpses of two horses on the far bank. Then the buzz of the flies feeding upon them impinged on his ears. Again his body shook. *Darkness, cold, death.* He stomped about and tried to warm himself. "The devil waits for me, but by God I will disappoint him."

Henry stooped and began to collect armfuls of dried grass and leaves from near the stream bank. *Stream musta been flooded when the city burned.* He carried the dried vegetation under the bridge. When he had gathered a pile sufficient to make a bed, he lay down on it and blanketed himself from the cold. The smell of the dried grass dampened the stench of the dead horses but did not eliminate the hungry grumble in his stomach. "My adventure and revenge will begin in the morning," he mumbled then rubbed his legs and curled into the fetal position.

———•••———

Stokes increased the longboat's speed by commanding the four oarsmen to pull hard for several strokes. Then he yelled, "Toss oars!"

In unison the oarsmen reached out and lifted their oars. Pushing the oars' handles downward between their legs caused the ends of the poles to drop and hit the deck. The vessel drifted with the four oars vertical and the flats of the blades facing forward. The boatswain then steered the boat so the bow pointed to shore. When he had the boat properly aligned and stable, he cried, "Oars! Pull hard together!"

The crew dropped the oars back into the water. Together they leaned forward, dug the blades deep, and pulled back. This maneuver caused everyone seated in the longboat to pitch as the vessel shot ahead. After a second rowing cycle, Stokes yelled, "Boat oars!"

The oarsmen again lifted and rotated the oars parallel to the boat's hull and laid them against the gunwale with the oars' blades directed forward. The longboat maintained its headway and caused the bow to crunch onto the gravelly shoreline. Oarsmen jumped over the side, took hold of the gunwale, and pulled the longboat higher onto the shore. The people in the boat could now exit over the bow and not get their shoes wet.

Eight buckskin-garbed men stood on the street and watched the approach and docking of the *Piper*'s longboat. Several shouldered muskets, two leaned against theirs, and one held his weapon in his left hand and gripped the barrel at its midpoint. This fellow wore a tricorne with a sprig of balsam stuck in the hatband. He was older than the others and looked more rugged and confident. As soon as Nightjar assisted Captain Morris off the longboat, the man stepped toward the *Piper*'s crew. The buckskin-clad fellow extended his hand and said, "From your gold and attire, I dare say you are that proud vessel's captain."

"Aye. That is so. Captain Thomas Morris of the Continental navy." The two joined hands. "I take it I am addressing Colonel Samuel Thompson," Morris continued while shaking Thompson's hand. "That makes those fine fellows behind you the Brunswick militia."

"Aye. Indeed. Welcome to Falmouth." Thompson glanced around at the town. "As you can see, we have not had time to rebuild since our encounter with the king's men." He looked at the longboat and saw the armed marines. "You come as if prepared for trouble. Please have your men come ashore."

"Aye. A matter of a deserter." Morris motioned to Bobby Turner. "Sergeant Turner, have your men disembark."

The colonel nodded and asked, "Did you say a deserter?"

"Seaman by the name of Henry Holder," Captain Morris explained. "He was part of the rowing crew of the boat that arrived earlier transporting Dr. Voors and Messrs. Bowden and Whitehall. He jumped from the longboat on its return." Morris turned his head toward the destroyed wharf. "My people say the seaman escaped by swimming to that wharf. My marines have come to search him out."

"Aye, Captain," said Thompson. "Have you had prior trouble with this man?"

"Yes. He has been a problem since we departed Beverly. Comes from a fine family, but I believe young Holder's loyalties lie with King George."

"Fortunately, Captain, my men know the area well. They will aid your marines. We will have this Holder fellow in hand by tomorrow's nightfall." Colonel Thompson paused and gestured for his men to join the group. "I have a wagon and horses on the street above. We will head to my camp. It is about two miles inland. You will not be alone. Dr. Voors has established his surgery and is billeted at the camp. Most townspeople have their camps nearby, and they have planned a welcoming dinner for you. Are you free to stay the night?"

"Aye."

"Very good." Thompson caught one of his men by the arm. "This is Sergeant Daily of the Brunswick militia. He has been on the street most of the day. Sergeant, did you see anything unusual after the *Piper* arrived? Anyone running? An unfamiliar person?"

"Yes, Colonel. Saw a lad scamper off that pile of lumber as your boat made for shore." Daily pointed to the broken wharf. "Then he scuttled down the street as if his feet hurt. Turned down the street. Looked as if he was headin' toward the camps. So I figured he was there."

"Very well. Perhaps someone in camp has seen him." Colonel Thompson put his arm on Captain Morris's shoulder and directed him to the horses and wagon. "I have a horse saddled for you, sir. Your marines can follow behind the wagon. The distance is not far—two miles as I mentioned."

On the street Captain Morris mounted the horse Thompson had provided. Once in the saddle, he said, "Sergeant Turner, have your men follow us. Mr. Stokes, you and your crew return to the *Piper.* Return in the morning by four bells of the forenoon watch."

The sky darkened and the seagulls ended their alongshore migration when horses carrying Captain Morris and Colonel Thompson stepped onto and crossed a little wooden bridge. The troops of the Continental Marines and Brunswick militiamen marched across behind the riders. The two draft horses clomped hard onto the deck of the bridge. When the wheels of the heavy wagon the horses were pulling rolled over the spaces between the planks, they snapped, thumped, and shuddered, and they loosened debris lodged between the deck boards. Bits of dried mud, splinters of wood, and dust bombarded Henry.

— • ◆ • —

As the morning sky brightened, caws, shrills, hisses, and grunts woke Henry Holder from a fitful sleep. He stirred his arms around and broke free of his grassy cocoon. He rose, looked toward the origin of the noise, and saw on the far bank of the creek ravens, black vultures, and a bald eagle fighting over the tasty morsels of putrid horsemeat. He caught a whiff of the fetid odor emanating from the rotting mass. His stomach twisted. The smell made him choke and gag. He wondered how the scavengers could endure such a stink. He brushed the grass off his still-damp clothing, and he started to rise to his feet. Forgetting his bed was under a bridge, the top of his head conked the planking as he attempted to straighten. He dropped to his knees. Pain filled his head. He grabbed the sore spot with both hands and squeezed, and then he carefully duck walked out from under the bridge. The headache lasted only a moment. Cold air surrounding him reigned over his senses. He began to shiver.

To warm himself, Henry rubbed his sides, wrapped his arms around himself, and tightened his muscles. For a few moments, he jumped around in place. His activity frightened the squabbling scavengers. They all took flight, but within moments the ravens dropped to the grass a few hundred feet away, the bald eagle perched atop a nearby leafless, scorched tree, and the vultures remained aloft. They soared in a big circle over the carcasses.

As Henry hitched about, the air around him sweetened to the smell of dried grass. Though his stomach continued to contract and rumble, the urge to vomit left him. Need dry clothes," he stammered, "and food." He squeezed his arms around himself tighter, rubbed the soreness on his head, and relaxed. Though his feet were cold and the left one hurt from the puncture, he stumbled out of the ditch and onto the roadway. Scanning the surrounding, he saw piles of soot-darkened bricks and burned lumber where buildings had once stood. About seventy-five yards to his right, he noticed groups of people, makeshift shacks, and tents. Henry suspected that was the part of town beyond the range of the British cannons.

There is help there, Henry thought, but the idea generated an anxious feeling that momentarily quelled his hunger. *Do not think I should go there.*

The appearance of three men at the far end of the road frightened him. Two were wearing black cocked hats and blue regimental coats, and the third was dressed in buckskin. Each held a musket. He started to hobble across the street to the rear of a complete but partially scorched building.

One of the men shouted, "There's our man!"

The loud voice startled him. Though the pain in his foot intensified, Henry scudded across the street and jumped for cover between the building and a heap of burned debris. Taking several short deep breaths and rubbing his head and left leg, he limped and jumped farther down the alleyway.

"In here!" a gruff voice behind him yelled. "Saw that cuss duck in here."

Henry heard boots begin to thud on the road, shouts, and swords being whacked against various objects. He bent low and lunged under a mass of twisted boards. His dodge caused an outburst of frightened pigeons and crows. They erupted into the air, and their wingbeats thundered over his head. Then a feral cat jumped from a crate into the alleyway. Seconds following this foray, a musket blasted, and its ball ricocheted off the wall where Henry crouched. The cat ran past as Henry dashed straight ahead.

Leaning against the remains of a porch, Henry hyperventilated. In front of him was Fore Street. Beyond and anchored in the harbor floated the schooner *Piper.* Not far away, to the left lay the warped, charred remains of four large wharves. He glanced to the right. About one hundred yards away, the burned area ended. The green glow of weeds and brush beyond beckoned.

Henry groaned. He sighed, gritted his teeth, and softly growled, "Minutes. Those sons of bitches." He winced in pain. "They'll be on me. Got to get away. Bastard Americans."

He wrung his hands together, bent forward, and stayed close to the rubble. Using a thin, splintered board he picked up as a walking stick, he limped toward the vital area.

"There's the knave!" a gruff voice yelled.

"Shoot the blackguard!" another shouted.

"Oh my!" Henry cried and bounded over some trash. The click of a musket cocking urged him into a scamper. He tossed the walking stick behind him. The musket discharged. Henry felt the shot whiz past his ear. *I'm dead,* he thought.

Then from behind he heard, "Alive! Hold fire! Captain wants that blackguard alive."

Henry stumbled and fell to his knees. Suddenly he felt a hand grab his shoulder. It was not a hard grip as he would have expected of a soldier. It was strong but soft. It pulled him to the left into the rubble.

"Crawl! Fast!" a voice said.

———•◦•———

"Where'd that son of a bitch go?" a soldier grumbled.

"Damned blackguard was here," someone else growled.

The sound of clomping boots and swearing men filled the site where Holder was last seen. Two Continental marines hurried farther ahead. A militiaman ran into a space between broken and burned building timbers. Within moments additional marines and militia arrived.

"We seen the bastard here," Sergeant Turner shouted, "not a moment ago. Where the hell'd he go?"

"Most likely into da rubble," answered a militiaman.

Marine Sergeant Turner recognized the man as the slow-witted fellow who had held the horse reins yesterday. "Are there hiding places under that trash?" Turner asked.

"Rightly so, Mr. Marine. There's spaces an' holes under tha' trash. Ye know timbers don't fall in stacks."

Turner raised his eyebrows, wrinkled his nose, and stared down at Terry. The sergeant removed his tricorne and scratched his head. "You jacks get your asses over here and pull this pile apart."

The crunch and clatter of boards being lifted and tossed and then landing to the side and hitting each other surrounded the troops.

"Ow!" someone screamed. "Damn it. Be careful where you're throwin' that shit."

Dust, bricks, and splinters flew. The hubbub continued.

"Wastin' your time," Dailey, a sergeant in Colonel Thompson's militia, said, and he strolled up next to Turner. "Tirin' your men. Only dirtyin' up their uniforms, Sergeant Turner. Nothin' but a wharf rat could get under that mass."

Turner stepped back and shrugged his shoulders. "Relax, men," he shouted. "We *are* wasting time."

From across the way, a loud crunch suddenly sounded, and a flock of cawing crows exploded into the air from behind a nearby still-standing brick wall of a building. Then a feral cat dashed out and streaked between the legs and over the feet of several of the men. This surprise caused them to jump and stumble about. During this turmoil a series of profane shouts, cries, and screams of pain blared forth. Before anyone looked the cat disappeared into the pile of rubble.

"What in the hell?" yelled Turner. He whirled around and saw Terry standing in a doorway up to his waist in a hole. A cloud of dust twirled and dissipated above the distressed militiaman's head. "Pull that fat man out of the hole before he wakes the dead."

Hearing several others laughing, Turner calmed.

Sergeant Dailey's lips pursed and twisted up to the left. He nodded and stepped next to Turner. "That fat clod may 'ave found how your deserter's escaped."

Turner frowned at the militiaman. "And how so?"

"Many of the larger buildings had cellars for storage. Their entranceways were located near doors to the outside. That way merchandise, wine, beer, and firewood could be easily brought in. Your Mr. Holder must have found an opening into one."

"Can we search for them?"

"Doubt he'd be awaitin'. Many cellars connect to each other by tunnels. If he got in an' the floors did not wholly collapse, he probably found a way out a block or two from here. Best we can do is patrol the perimeter of this burned area and stay alert. He cannot get far with his injuries, and he cannot hide down there forever."

———•◦•———

Henry kept his eyes fixed on the ground and crawled fast to his left. Though the hand released his shoulder, he felt it grip his collar and pull. His body stretched forward. His knees ground against gravel as he crawled forward and reopened earlier abrasions. It deepened the cuts and created more. "Ow!" he whined.

"Quiet," the soft voice ahead said. "You will be heard." The knuckles on the hand that held his collar dug into the base of his neck and tugged. "Hurry. Crawl." The hand released the collar.

The two crawled under the fallen sides of a building. As Holder followed, the illumination around him dimmed. He lifted his head and saw a left hip and butt covered in a scorched, stained, rugged gray material. Moccasins covered the feet that shuffled ahead of him. There was no question in his mind the person leading him was young, agile, and female—a girl about his age. His savior turned around a corner and entered a darker vacuity. "Quick. Follow me," she said.

Not only did the commands press Henry on, but the sounds of boards crashing and men shouting somewhere behind prompted him to hustle even faster. He pursued the girl into the dark hole. He was close enough to smell her scent. Her odor suddenly vanished, and there was the sound of a muffled thump as if someone had jumped. His hand lost touch with the ground in front of him, and he fell headfirst into the void. "Arg."

"So sorry. Should have warned you," the soft voice said. "You fall into cellar."

In the pitch-black space, Henry pulled himself to a sitting position and rubbed the shoulder that broke his fall. He soothed his knees. "I cannot see anything."

"Sunlight make you blind. In minute eyes adjust. Then you see and stand. For now we safe."

After soothing his knees and punctured foot, Henry squeezed his left shoulder. In front of him, the edge of a crate resolved itself in the blackness. A pair of ankles appeared like dull pewter. He looked up. The girl's face was shadowed. Above and behind her silhouette was a pair of broken and jagged timbers. They were angled downward. He surmised they were floor beams. A stack of barrels, several chests, and a chair materialized, and then the chasm formed by the downward-sloping floor took shape. When his eyes acclimated, this cleft seemed illuminated by starlight. With his chin against his chest, Henry stood. "It appears you see well in this darkness," he said.

"Yes. Know this place. Work here. It was store before British destroy. I sweep floor and sell things." The black image bent toward him. He felt her grab the front of his shirt, and then the ankles turned away. "Stand. We best go," she said.

Though hunger continued to aggravate him, his body relaxed. He nodded, even though he knew she could not see. Henry felt himself being led along as if on a leash.

"Duck ahead," she said. "Crawl again."

She released his shirt, and he watched as the girl squatted in front of a lightless void and disappeared into it. He knelt and followed. He gritted his teeth and took shallow breaths. The air smelled burned, dusty, and dry. She crept ahead and sounded like a rodent traipsing through its burrow. His shoulder brushed the edge of something. It moved and fell. *A loose board.* Then his side nudged against a more solid object. The girl's crawling sounds grew louder in his left ear. *Need to turn. She is just ahead.* He heard several clinks and soon learned the girl had moved some bricks out of the way. Then the shadowed image of her behind appeared. They were moving into another space, but most of the above flooring in this building had fallen down.

The girl passed through a distorted angular hole and stood. All Henry could see of her now as he crept toward the opening was the lower part of her skirt. From his almost kowtowed position, he again noticed her ankles. In this new light, they glowed a dull white, and her moccasins were scuffed and abraded. *Like my knees.* This thought rekindled the sensations in his wounds. When he emerged and stood, a dizzying, disheveled sight confronted him. Henry stood in the crevice created by the building's collapsed floors. The sides angled upward and away. They connected with twisted walls and piles of bricks and broken boards. There were no sounds of the marines or militia.

The girl in front of him was young, frail, and plain. Long, tangled, mousy hair covered most of her face. She reached up and pushed some of it to the side. This exposed pale freckled skin and a thin nose that turned down at its tip. *She has a little beak,* he mused. She had a small mouth, lined by colorless, reedy lips, and violet eyes. Her blouse and skirt hung on her as if they had been thrown over a pole. They went straight down on all sides. "Follow me," she said. "Patriots behind."

"Wait! Who are you? My name is Henry Holder."

"Know your name. Men in patriot camp say much about you. Say you are traitor." She turned and gave him a thin smile. "They call me Luce. Name really Lucinda."

"Never known a Lucinder."

"Lucinda! My name not end in 'er.' Call me Luce, like everybody do."

"As you wish."

"Now follow. We must leave. Soldiers find us if we not go." Luce scampered through the crevice of disarray and emerged onto the street. She snuck along to the edge of the devastated building and peered around the corner. "Soldiers still looking," she whispered, and she turned and began running across the street. "They not know what they do."

She gestured for Henry to follow. Hidden by the rubble behind them, the two ran down an alleyway. It ended at a ditch. They slid down the bank and into the creek below. It was about one hundred yards upstream of the bridge under which Henry had spent the night. They continued wading upstream to where the runnel entered a small sedge and cattail marsh. The height of the cattails rose to six feet as they slogged upstream. Then the brook opened into a concealed pond. Luce led Henry through the shallows and along the edge of the vegetation to a hummock where alder bushes grew. They waded to shore. The elevation on the alder knoll was a few inches above the pond's surface. Luce let go of Henry's shirt and walked up the bank. Small, open, weedy plots between the alders provided them dry spaces to lie back and relax.

Holder did just that. As soon as his head hit a grassy pillow, he exhaled a deep sigh, groaned, and stretched out on the grassy bed. The sunlight warmed his body. His knees and the puncture in his foot burned. Momentary twinges shot through his legs, but his muscles felt as if they were melting. He closed his eyes. Feeling additional warmth and a small increase in the weight on his body, he parted his eyelids. A blurred image of a drab, light-colored petticoat stood over him. "Luce, what are you doing?"

"My skirt keep you warm. You sleep. I return."

"Um...yes."

Henry yawned, and his eyes closed. He did not hear Lucinda wade into the pond and disappear through an opening in the cattail barrier.

———•◦•———

An indistinct squish and crunch caused Henry to stir. Pushing his leg from under the skirt made him shiver. He stretched and noticed the sun had moved westward. It cast its light lower. The alder bushes blocked the warmth. Lying on the ground and in damp clothing, he felt a layer of goose bumps rise across his shoulders. His muscles tightened. *Damn saltwater. Never dries.*

He rolled the woolen skirt tight around himself and curled into the fetal position. Then he heard it—a metallic click nearby.

"Where's that trollop?" a voice growled. "Is she coming? Said she left the deserter around here."

"Hush up," another deep voice scolded. "You'll scare the blackguard."

Squishes, crunches, and splashes came closer. Henry scrambled to untangle himself from Luce's wool skirt but was not fast enough. He felt the coldness of a musket's muzzle against his neck. He opened his eyes and saw another set of eyes staring him in the face. Only swinging a sledgehammer could have created the muscles of the man standing in front of him. He put the muzzle under Henry's chin and lifted.

"On your feet, boy!"

Henry's body trembled as he struggled to stand. Luce broke from the cattails. "He's got no weapons, and 'e's injured," she said. "Mind yourselves."

She walked up to the men and carried a bundle in her arms. The muscular man laughed and lowered his weapon. Luce turned to the thinner fellow. She dropped the bundle onto a dried clump of grass and grabbed his arm. "Reverend," she said.

"Careful, girlie," he warned. "Surprising me as you did could 'ave made me pull the trigger. Then we would 'ave 'ad a bloody mess."

The tall, rangy man of God pulled his musket away and set the butt of its stock on the ground beside him. Luce turned to Henry. "Strip off those duds," she commanded. "Wash off in pond. You smell like rottin' fish and dung. When you finish, here is clothing. Clean an' dry."

She pointed to the bundle lying in the grass, and Henry backed toward the water's edge. He stared at Luce. His eyes widened and mouth opened. "I ain't never divested in front of a girl."

"It will be all right, lad. Little Luce has seen more than you are going to show her. Now get along. The day is getting late."

Luce giggled and said, "I look away." She continued to chuckle as she rotated, but she snapped her head around as she stepped into the grass.

The muscular man laughed as Henry removed his clothes. When the boy took an article off and threw it onto the ground, the big guy pushed it into the weeds with the barrel of his musket. "Burn later," he said. When Henry stood naked and shivering, the muscular man waved the barrel of his musket toward the water and motioned the boy to enter the pond. "Wash you'self!"

Henry made some muffled sounds, waded into waist-deep water, and did as he was told. Luce snickered and put her hand over her mouth. She looked away and wrapped a towel around Henry's shoulders when he walked out of the water. She handed him another and then proceeded to wipe the water off his back. While Henry worked on his chest, the young woman lowered the towel, stepped to the boy's side, and began to rub Henry's right buttock. She progressed to the outer portion of his thigh, knelt, reached around to the front of his upper leg, and continued wiping.

Henry staggered, snapped his towel down to his crotch, and pushed her hands off him in the process. His action was not fast enough, however, to hide his arousal.

"Ho, ho, ho," the muscular man said and nodded his head toward Henry.

"Control yourself, boy," Reverend said.

Luce was on her knees about a foot from the boy's side. She squeezed the ends of the towel in her hands, placed them against her cheeks, and giggled. "He pretty man," Luce said. "I like."

Henry stared down at himself and pulled his towel tight about his hips. He then grabbed his crotch and allowed the sides of the cloth to drop off his hips. He stood buck naked for a moment with the towel hanging between his legs and covering his privates. He stumbled backward into the cover of the vegetation. "Oh! I'm sorry," he cried as he tried to conceal himself.

The reverend sidestepped and cuffed the top of Luce's head. "You vixen," he groaned. "You knew that would happen. Planned it, did you not?"

"Ow," cried Luce, but she continued to giggle and stare at Henry.

The reverend picked up Luce's skirt and threw it to Henry. "Cover yourself, boy. Get dressed. You will learn that trollop has a foul streak."

"Nah!" Luce interrupted. "Only havin' fun. I'm a good girl. You will see."

She sheepishly picked up the bundle of dry clothes, carried them to Henry, dropped them at his feet, turned, and walked into the cattails.

"Hurry, boy. Dress and sit," Reverend said, and he pulled a bottle of rum from a pouch he carried. Before Henry pulled on pants, the reverend pushed him into a sitting position. "Straighten your legs."

Yanking the cork from the bottle, he poured some rum on the boy's knees and the rest on his punctured foot. Henry squealed from the momentary sting.

"Now put on the pants and moccasins. We need to return to camp. There are many questions you need to answer."

------◆------

The reverend's camp was located about three miles inland from the pond in a forested clearing. It was a collection of loosely constructed tents and lean-tos dispersed between several hillocks denuded of most ground vegetation. Several campfires burned in a depression. A group of women collected around one and appeared to be cooking.

Men stood, sat, or reclined near the other fires. Some conversed, several were cleaning muskets, and a few seemed
to be asleep. When the reverend, Henry, Luce, and the
muscular man walked into the depression, the subdued
hubbub of the camp silenced. Not even a bird's chirp was
heard. All eyes focused on Henry.

The reverend waved his musket. Everyone returned to
the business at hand, but for the moment they remained
distracted. Though voices and other camp noises could
be heard, heads turned to follow the small party past the
campfires and up a rise to where the group stopped in
front of a large tent. They watched the muscular man
shove Henry and Luce through the tent's opening, and
then most saw the reverend enter.

The muscular man signaled toward the group of
women. Two broke from their tasks and quickly moved
off in opposite directions. Within a few moments, they
returned. They were carrying pieces of cloth and a couple
sacks and bottles. They ran up the rise and entered the
large tent. Shortly thereafter, the women exited. The reverend followed. Then he and the muscular man headed
off to another tent. The women returned to the campfires.
After about an hour, the disruption Henry's appearance
had caused in the camp dissipated. When he next left the
tent, few took notice.

Henry was wearing dry clothing. His wounds were
treated, he had eaten, and a bunch of curious folks were
not staring at him. Henry placed a dried-grass-stuffed
feed bag on the ground next to a tree and sat down. He
leaned back against the tree trunk, yawned, and accepted

a cup of tea Luce had brought. His eyes were heavy, and he closed them.

"Do not fall asleep," the girl said. "The reverend wants to ask you questions. He be here in a moment."

"I will be"—Henry yawned—"ready to answer when he comes."

The sky that was visible through the trees had colored into streaks of deep red, brown, and black. The unusual warmth of the November day had cooled. His head rolled to the side and came to rest on his shoulder. Henry tightened the coat around him, sighed, and closed his eyes. The boy did not hear the girl's warning, but he felt the boot that sent him scooting a few feet away from the tree.

"Hey! What did ya do that for?" Henry cried. He pushed off the ground and jumped to a standing position. He stumbled about before catching his balance. "No call for doin' that. Could 'ave just shouted. I'd 'ave woken."

Reverend held his arms akimbo and stared at Henry. The preacher's face crinkled into a grin. "We do not tolerate siestas around here," he said. "My people sleep when they are told."

"I was just takin' a nap." Henry's shoulders slumped. He felt shaken and frightened. "Doin' nothing wrong. What's a siesta?"

The reverend glanced toward the muscular man. He stood at the reverend's side and winked. "Siesta is nappin' when you are expected to be open-eyed."

Henry scrunched his eyes and shook his head. "My day's been hard. Didn't know it be a sin to be sleepin'."

The reverend's face reddened. "In my camp no one sleeps until I say so." He nodded toward the muscular man. "Bork, take that rope you are twistin' about, and tie this rascal's hands behind him." The reverend stared into Henry's eyes. "You are now a prisoner. In the morning Bork and I are going to turn you over to Colonel Thompson's militia. Then they'll have their deserter, and I will be credited with the capture. That will put me and Bork in good stead with that bunch of patriots."

Henry Holder's jaw dropped. He stared speechless and confused at the two men. Before Henry's thoughts of escape could connect with his legs, Bork grabbed and twisted the boy's arms around to his back and secured his hands with the rope. As the boy struggled, he saw Luce near a campfire. Her back was to him.

CHAPTER 7

Captain Morris and Colonel Thompson exited Greele Tavern where they and Sergeants Turner and Dailey had breakfasted. This was the only building in the burned-out area of Falmouth that remained standing. The owners and a volunteer crew took a week to clean the place and make the necessary repairs so the tavern could be opened for business. Unfortunately Greele's was the only establishment of its kind within many miles. Not only did it attract the townspeople but also the scum of the earth.

When Thompson told Morris that Greele's bolstered the town's morale, Morris asked, "Do many of those miscreants live about? Some appear to be runagates."

"Aye. The tavern does entice the muckers."

The six marines and a collection of motley militiamen milled about the street in front of the tavern. They had all been up since daybreak trying to find Henry Holder. A group of the militiamen had stayed in the area where the deserter had last been seen to search and patrol.

"The *Piper* has considerable amounts of food aboard," Morris said. "More than is needed and enough to supply the crew for a month or more. I would like to send the extra to the villagers to help them through this difficult time."

"Your desire to send what food you can spare is most welcome, Captain Morris. It will invigorate the townspeople. Perhaps it will dispel the reverend's jeremiads."

"Who is this reverend fellow?" Morris asked.

"A questionable man of the cloth," Thompson said. "You'll meet him this evening."

"Aye. I'll be aware. Now let us get back to the food I will provide." Morris paused. "When the craft is loaded and ready to make for shore, I will have the bosun haul up a signal flag. It should be visible from Greele's."

"That will be good. We will be ready," Colonel Thompson said.

He stepped back to allow Captain Morris to go before him. Captain Morris heard three clangs of the ship's bell float across the water. "My boat crew will be here in a half hour," he announced. "It angers me we were not able to catch that blackguard who deserted my vessel. I hate to sail and have him free to roam."

"Not to fret," said Colonel Thompson while trying to dislodge a crumb from between his front teeth with a knife. "My men will catch the bastard and hold him hostage till you return." After success with the crumb, he wiped the dagger's tip against his leg and sheathed the knife. "He will not have gotten far."

The two men strolled along the street to the beach where the longboat was to land. Above them the herring gulls squealed and cawed, and the harbor's smell filled the air with musty, salty, fishy aromas. A placid, humid atmosphere engulfed Falmouth.

Sergeant Turner led the Continental Marines, and they marched in rank about thirty feet behind the officers. With Sergeant Dailey in the lead, scattered groups and pairs of militiamen dawdled along the street to the broken wharf.

When the assembly came abreast of this wharf, those listening heard the *Piper*'s bell ring four times. Morris glanced ahead and toward the shoreline. He saw Gaspar and Widget knee-deep in the water. They were pulling the longboat's bow onto the shore. The captain also noticed the chain and handcuffs wrapped around the Frenchman's waist. *Sorry, my friend. There will be no use for them on this trip.*

Stokes was tying down the tiller. Tyler sat to starboard and looked proud. Morris reasoned Midshipman Hollister had assigned him to the boat crew to replace Henry Holder. Seaman Robert Marvel, another young, patriotic fisherman from Beverly, sat to larboard and rounded out the rowing crew.

"You have a punctual crew, John," said Thompson.

Morris nodded. A grin softened his wrathful face. "Aye. Colonel Glover and I expect discipline and promptness from our men."

"John Glover picked your crew?"

"Aye. He is a good judge of men and trains them well. Those he mentors would follow him into the fires of hell."

"As you say, Captain, but the colonel does make mistakes."

Morris moved toward a path between two boulders that led to the beach. "Do you mean selecting Seaman Henry Holder? The deserter was not Glover's selection. Two days before the *Piper* sailed, Henry Holder's father—a diligent and patriotic Marbleheader—brought him aboard. Asked I take him on, teach him discipline, and make a man of him. His father is a friend. I accepted the boy." Morris shook his head. He placed his hands on the boulders and proceeded down the path. "The blackguard is a disappointment to his father. Sad day when I have to apprise Henry Senior of his son's treachery."

"Aye. Be easier to tell the man his son was lost at sea," Colonel Thompson said, and he followed Captain Morris to the beach and toward the longboat.

Gaspar stepped forward. "Longboat ready to transport the captain to his vessel, *mon ami.*"

Captain Morris took a long look at Gaspar. "Thank you, gunnery master." The captain placed his hands on the boat rail and turned to Thompson. "Thank you for your hospitality," he said. "Mr. Whitehall will be returning on the morrow. Today is already the twenty-third of November. The *Piper* needs to be at sea to accomplish her tasks. I plan to sail on the tide in two days—the twenty-fifth. I will expect Lieutenant Whitehall and Dr. Voors to be aboard."

"Will Charles Bowden also be returning?"

"No. Perhaps sometime later he will find his way here or to Beverly. He is with O'Brien's Machias militia. I expect they will harass British shipping in waters to the east. The *Piper* will patrol off Boston."

"Perhaps your marines could stay and assist in the search for the deserter. They can return to the schooner on the morrow with the others."

Morris nodded as he turned and stared toward the path beyond the boulders. The tide had ebbed and exposed the slippery expanse of rocky beach. He saw Sergeant Turner stepping gingerly onto the algae-covered stones. "Hold up, Sergeant. You and your men remain on shore. Assist the militia in the hunt for Holder. Return tomorrow with the good doctor and Mr. Whitehall."

"Aye, sir," the sergeant said, and he looked relieved as he stumbled back onto more solid footing.

Thompson moved next to a militiaman who stood nearby and held two muskets. The colonel took one and hung it on his shoulder. "We will watch for your signal flag, Captain, and accept the supplies you provide with appreciation."

Captain Morris gripped the longboat's rail for balance and climbed aboard. Gaspar and Widget shoved the boat off the shore and swung themselves aboard. Before the captain sat, he called to Thompson. "My midshipman, whom I left in charge of the *Piper* in my absence, expressed a desire to come ashore. As soon as I relieve Mr. Hollister of his duties aboard, I will allow him and Mr. Gaspar to return. They can have a bit of liberty and if necessary assist Dr. Voors and Sergeant Turner."

"Very good," Thompson said, and he raised his arm in farewell. "Pleasure to have met you, sir. Do not fret. We will capture your deserter."

———•◦•———

Though those on shore enjoyed an unusual day of late-autumn warmth, out in the harbor, the quiet breeze added a chilling bite to the air. Jack stood at attention until the boatswain's mate hailed Captain Morris aboard.

"Mr. Hollister, at ease. Walk with me while I inspect the repairs to the gunwale."

"Aye, sir. Welcome back. I hope your trip ashore was enlightening."

The two men strolled to the larboard side of the schooner.

"Everything aboard proper?" Captain Morris asked.

"Yes, sir. The *Piper* had a quiet night."

As the captain approached the portion of the hull the accidental cannon firing had razed, he clutched his chin and nodded. The gunwale, deck, and gunport looked pristine. It appeared as if nothing had ever happened.

"The carpenter has done a fine piece of work," the captain said. "The man can do wonders with wood." Morris placed his hand on the rail and then slid it along the newly painted boards. Even on close inspection, it was difficult to see any evidence of the once-gaping hole and splintered wood. "Fine work indeed." He straightened, sighed, and turned toward the after hatchway. "I will meet you in my quarters. Bring Gaspar. Stop by the galley. I am sure the cook has hot coffee waiting."

Jack entered the captain's cabin holding two mugs of steaming coffee, and he placed one on the table in front of where Morris stood. Gaspar followed. He was holding his own mug of coffee.

The captain motioned for the two to sit. He shuffled several sheets of paper about his desk and lifted one. "In two days the tide will be proper during the forenoon watch to make for open water. We will sail for Beverly. A short trip. We can be there in two days with good weather." He raised the sheet of paper and held it in front of him. "This is the consignment of food for this voyage. Have the cook bring it to date and determine the least amount we will need to get us back to Beverly. Have the crew load what we will not need in the longboat for transfer to the people of Falmouth. The bombardment of their village has made them weary, anxious, and skeptical. The food will be a boost to morale. Otherwise I fear we will lose them to the British." Morris handed the consignment list to Jack. "If Fortune is with us, she might place a British transport across our course."

"Aye, sir. The crew would enjoy a good fight," Gaspar said, and he and Jack took their leave.

By noon two longboats were loaded with casks of flour, oats, hardtack, carrots, potatoes, salt pork, and salted cod; a barrel of lard, one of rum, and another of cooking oil; bags of salt and other spices; the captain's chest of fine tea; and three loaves of bread the cook had baked the day before for the crew. On deck were three cages of live chickens and a box of eggs protected in flour. The load to Falmouth contained enough food to supply *Piper*'s crew for a month. The cook kept enough victuals for the few days needed to return.

As Jack stood checking the list, Captain Morris came up behind him. "Make sure this food gets to the camp Colonel Thompson and the townspeople have set up on the edge of town," he said. "Thompson is in charge of the militia. You will recognize him. He is a rugged curmudgeon but a fair man. A red beard covers his face. He will ask you many questions, but he will tell you how things should be. You can trust him and his men." Morris placed his hand on Jack's shoulder. "Many of the townspeople are wavering toward the pronouncements of a man they call Reverend—a supposed clergyman of dubious persuasion. He arrived late to the gathering last evening with a strange waif. His concubine no doubt. When Thompson asked the reverend for an explanation of his delay, he answered quite vaguely. The reverend and his woman departed before dinner was completed. I do not trust them."

"Aye, sir. I will be on my guard."

"Gaspar will be your sentinel. Remember, though, you are his guard also."

The two men walked to the chains. Jack look toward the longboat tethered below. He saw the brawny Frenchman assisting a seaman who was lashing down some barrels.

"A bit of advice," the captain continued. "The food in Greele Tavern is edible. So eat before you go to where all are encamped. The women have little to work with, and Thompson's cooks need a few lessons."

"Everyone should do better with the food you are providing," Jack said, and he took hold of the rail and stepped onto the top rung of the boarding ladder.

"Aye. Perhaps so," Morris said, and he stationed himself against the gunwale. "Lieutenant Whitehall is to return on the morrow. I will send a boat for all of you in the afternoon. I hope by then you will have Mr. Holder in chains. Take care." The captain stood for a moment facing the shore. Then he turned and shouted, "Bosun, hoist a signal pennant."

"By your leave, sir," Jack said, and he climbed down the ladder and boarded the longboat.

———————

Heavy gray clouds created a specious mountain range across the western horizon. A featureless white sky glowed above that paled the blue displayed earlier in the day. From the northwest a blustery cold wind riled the harbor waters into choppy waves. Jack tightened his coat's collar as the longboat ground ashore. The afterglow of a late warm autumnal clime was ending.

Boatswain Stokes threw his arms up as he approached Jack. "The boat has been unloaded, Mr. Hollister," he said. "Supplies on the street. No thanks to those patriots. None of 'em showed to help, even though Captain Morris's signal flag can clearly be seen tearin' at her ties. Got Marvel, Tyler, and Widget guardin' the cargo."

As he finished speaking, two horse-drawn wagons rolled in next to the pile of provisions. A scrawny man was driving each wagon. When they pulled abreast of the longboat's crew, they brought the horses to a halt.

"Colonel Thompson sent us to collect the victuals you boys brought ashore," one of the men said. "The colonel and his men will be along shortly."

Stokes sidled next to one of the wagons. "You expectin' us to load that stuff on those wagons?" He chuckled. "You don't look strong enough to lift that horse's tail off his ass."

Tyler, Widget, and several other longboat crew members started laughing. The scrawny man thumped the horsewhip's handle on the wagon's floor. "Don't want to put you boys out any," he said. "We watched you bustin' your backs haulin' those barrels and casks through the mud. Soon as the colonel comes, his men will do the loadin'. We've got some hot grog awaitin' o'er at the camp to freshen your gullets."

"Now that is very considerate of you, sir," Stokes said.

He put his hands on his hips, flicked his head, and motioned for his men to take their ease. Jack grinned when he looked at the boatswain. "Mr. Gaspar and I will wait until the colonel comes. He can oversee the loading while you men rest. Captain Morris wants you back aboard the *Piper* before sunset. In the meantime enjoy the patriots' hospitality."

"Remember, the captain doesn't take kindly to rum-dum people," Gaspar warned. "So temper yourselves."

"Aye. We'll be mindful of what you say," Stokes said.

The boatswain waved his arm, and the rest of the longboat's crew perched on the boulders along the street. Jack grinned as he looked up the street. A weathered man wearing a buckskin jacket, heavy pants, and mud-covered boots headed toward him. A black cocked hat with a sprig of spruce stuck in its band topped off his outfit. Jack took notice of the man's red beard.

"I expect you are Colonel Thompson," Jack said.

"Aye. And you are Midshipman Hollister." The colonel motioned to several motley men following him. "Rest your muskets, and load those wagons. The cooks are waiting for these supplies. You boys from the longboat are welcome to share in our fortune."

"Appreciate your kindness, sir," Stokes said.

In about fifteen minutes the militiamen had loaded the wagons.

"Your marines are camped near Greele Tavern," Thompson said to Jack. "I expect you have orders for them." Jack nodded, and the colonel pointed down the street. "When you have completed your visit, I will welcome you and the marines at our camp. It is only a short walk. Sergeant Turner knows the way."

The colonel grabbed the reins and mounted his horse. He motioned to the wagon drivers to commence the journey to the patriot camp. The longboat's crew fell in with the militiamen, and all headed off together behind the wagons. Jack tipped his head in the direction of Greele Tavern, and he and Gaspar walked toward it.

<hr />

The marines had set up a temporary camp in a grassy field on the street a block away from Greele Tavern. Sergeant Turner and his six men were relaxing when Jack and Gaspar came up. Smoke from a smoldering campfire enveloped the area and wafted through the two mud-colored tents the marines had pitched nearby.

Sergeant Turner jumped to attention. "Midshipman Hollister, welcome," he stuttered as Jack and Gaspar walked into the group. "I...uh...the men have been searching all day. They needed a—"

"At ease, Sergeant," Jack said. "I am not here to inspect. Only wanted to inform you Mr. Gaspar and I are here.

We will sup at the tavern before continuing to the patriot camp. Have you any leads on Holder's location?"

"Nay, sir. Several militiamen suggested he is hiding in the swamp." Turner pointed toward a rangy stand of larch trees about a mile away. "We plan to search there tomorrow."

"Aye. It will have to be in the morning. The captain wants everyone aboard in the afternoon."

"Yes, sir. Captain Morris has informed us. We will be ready."

"Hopefully with Holder in chains."

"Aye, sir."

Jack cuffed Gaspar's arm and flicked his head toward Greele Tavern. "We will take our leave now, Sergeant. I would like to finish supper and join Colonel Thompson and his militiamen before the evening gets too dark. Please inform him when you return to the patriot camp this evening."

"Perhaps we should join you, Mr. Hollister. The tavern is a nest of roughs, rogues, and renegades."

Jack placed his hand on his sword's hilt. "Mr. Gaspar and I are well armed. We should have no trouble. We will only be eating. Thank you for your concern, Sergeant."

"As you wish, sir, but pay close attention to your surroundings."

"So we shall," Gaspar said. He inhaled, expanded his chest, removed a pistol from his waistband, and wiped the barrel down his pant leg. "I will use this if need be."

Sergeant Turner nodded. "You are a big fellow, but I meant for you two to listen. You might hear word of Henry Holder's whereabouts."

"Very true, Sergeant," Jack said. "We will take your advice."

———•◦•———

Midshipman Hollister and Mr. Gaspar entered Greele Tavern. Almost immediately Jack rubbed his eyes to comfort them. Acrid tobacco smoke, candle wax vapors, oil-flame exhaust, smells of food and stale beer, and smoke from burning wood in the hearth filled the interior and irritated his eyes. Gaspar coughed several times before he adjusted to the pungent air. Gazing about the dimly lit room, the men saw several people working behind a rough-hewed counter. They were silhouetted against the flaming orange cooking fire. Jack led the way along the left wall to an empty table upon which a candle flickered.

Both men noticed the din inside the tavern immediately quieted when the flash of daylight blazed into the room as they entered. When Gaspar closed the door, the inside babble returned. Besides the candle flames and hanging oil lamps, the only light penetrating the room came from a single, grubby, smoke-fouled window located on the right side wall. Jack estimated the tavern contained about thirty patrons of unknown disposition. *Quite an assortment for this early in the evening*, he thought.

As Gaspar pulled a chair away from the table, he noticed two men seated nearby. They were glaring at him and Jack, but a waitress distracted him.

"How you fellows doin'?" she said. "Bring you a pint, or would you want something else?"

Jack looked up. "My God," he said, "Kara? Kara Balch? It is you."

"Jack!"

"Ian told me the redcoats took you, along with him. He said some officer held you prisoner onboard the vessel. That he saw little of you during his impressment. Did you escape?"

"No." Kara clasped her hands together and lowered her head. "That bastard officer left me stranded on the streets of Boston. 'You can go home now, wench,' he said. Pushed me into an alley an' walked away. A real son of a bitch, he was."

"I am so sorry. Your sister, Maire, was livid. Said she would kill the redcoats who took you if she ever found them."

"I believe she would. Maire hates the British. Have you seen her or Dunkin? Is Ian well? I know he was released in Boston. Never heard what happened to him though."

"Maire and Dunkin are well. They transported Mr. Bowden, Mr. Smoke, Sara Hargrave, and me to Machias the afternoon we returned from hunting. They both returned to rebuild their camp. Damn British really destroyed it." Jack paused and pursed his lips. "Bowden, Smoke, Sara Hargrave, and I remained in Machias through the winter. Sara, bless her soul, died after Christmas. Pneumonia. We buried her in spring."

"So sorry to hear that. A pleasant woman she was."

"The three of us men joined the Machias militia. Helped capture the Royal Navy's sloop of war HMS *Margaretta*. Exciting battle, but Mr. Smoke was wounded.

About a week after the battle, Maire and Dunkin returned and transported Bowden and me to Beverly. I went to Boston and found my brother living with family members. Ian was in good health. He and the other Hollisters left Boston and sailed back to England."

Gaspar groaned and nudged Jack.

"Excuse my manners," Jack said. "Let me introduce my gunnery master, Mr. Gaspar. He and I are sailing aboard the *Piper.* She is the vessel floating in the harbor."

Kara nodded at the burly Frenchman. "Pleasure to meet you, Mr. Gaspar. Your captain and our Colonel Thompson were in here this morning." She touched the collar of Jack's coat. "Looks as if the Americans made you an officer."

"Aye. A midshipman. I want to tell you, though," Jack continued, "Mr. Bowden also arrived with me on the schooner *Piper.* He sailed two days ago for Machias to check on Mr. Smoke. While there I believe he plans to visit Maire and Dunkin."

"Everyone in Falmouth has heard of the battle that took place in Machias," Kara said. "Many believe it is why the British bombarded our village. I am glad you took part and were not injured, but the battle created anger among many in Falmouth." She shrugged and rolled her eyes. "Shall I bring you something to drink or eat?"

"Aye," Gaspar said, and he patted his belly. "A pint for me and one for Midshipman Hollister. We would also like bowls of that fine-smellin' stew and a tray of bread."

"Aye. Venison stew it is." Kara straightened and rubbed her hands down her apron. "Perhaps we can talk later."

"Yes. I would like that, but we have not much time. Need to be back aboard the *Piper* tomorrow afternoon. The captain wants to set sail in two days for Beverly, but first a deserter must be captured."

"Aye. There is talk of that youngster also," Kara said, and she turned and moved toward the counter.

While watching Kara, Jack noticed the two men at a nearby table. They were sitting with two others and glaring at him and Gaspar. In the dim light, he could only make out that they were heavily garbed. This made them look robust. When the one sitting in profile leaned toward the candlelit center of the table and turned his head, Jack saw the candle's flame flicker in the man's dark eyes. A thick growth of snarled beard covered the face, but a flattened nose projected beyond a dense mustache. Its tip twisted to the left. The face appeared to gawk in Jack's direction as this man babbled heatedly to the other three.

The fellow with his back to Jack leaned forward and shadowed the others. His oversize head and unruly mass of hair silhouetted by the candle's aura created an image of wild spikes and curls. When he straightened, Jack could see clumps and strands of greasy hair twist down the man's neck and fall toward his shoulders. The movement of this slovenly coiffed rascal revealed the face of the rogue sitting opposite him.

This individual wore a frayed and faded red coat. Eroded trimming suggested the uniform of a British soldier. This fellow had intense eyes, a scarred, unshaven face, and light-colored hair that laid flat on his head. He moved his hands about the table as he spoke. Jack glanced and saw this blond fellow subtly point at him and Gaspar. "I feel there are some here who are interested in us, Mr. Gaspar," he said.

"Aye, sir. When we sat at this table, I espied that group take particular note of our presence."

A chair scraped against the floor. Jack gripped his sword's hilt, and he saw the man with the twisted nose stand and swing a cutlass from his waist. The rogue's dark, squinted eyes glared at him. Jack removed his pistol from his belt and passed it beneath the table to Gaspar. He then slid back the bench on which he sat, rose, and unsheathed his sword. Directing the tip of the cutlass at Jack, the rogue moved toward the midshipman. In a clatter of scrapes and clunks, the other three at the table stood and trod behind him.

Gaspar leaped up. The action caused his chair to twirl onto its back and clack against the wall. He pointed both pistols at the approaching miscreants.

Words rolled from the beard-hidden mouth. "Remembers you from Halifax. A milk-faced lad you were back then," the knave said and raised his left arm.

Jack saw the fore-end of his opponent's arm was twisted as if it had once been broken and never properly healed.

"My arm spoke to me when I looked upon your sweet face," the man grumbled. "I remembers you...an' the old white-haired sea dog ye was protectin'. Heard he'd joined Neptune's navy."

"Aye." Jack pursed his lips and tightened his grip on the sword. The thought of Captain Hargrave's demise caused his stomach to contract. "The beard masks your identity, but you have not changed the slovenly uniform you were wearing back then."

The man raised his shoulders and inflated his chest. He lifted his left hand and tried to make a fist, but the fingers would not close. "That belayin' pin ruined my arm. Vowed to avenge it if ever the chance came. The gods have answered my prayer. They've brought us together again."

The renegade pushed Jack's table aside, raised the cutlass above his head, and sliced it down at Jack. Jack jumped back and twisted to the left. He snapped his blade diagonally across his chest and aimed the tip at the opponent's neck. With his body bending low, the bearded man raised the cutlass and thrust it forward. Jack sidestepped right, snapped himself up onto the balls of his feet, jutted his rear, and swung the blade of his sword down and across his body. A clack rang out when the tip of Jack's blade connected with the cutlass. The sound became a screech as the sword slid past the cutlass's hilt. The blade opened the renegade's coat sleeve and sliced a chunk from the bearded man's right arm. The rogue dropped the cutlass, grabbed his bleeding arm, and fell on his knees. Two of his closest henchmen yanked their daggers out and were about to dive forward, but Gaspar fired a pistol. The shot tore through the blond rascal's shoulder. The master gunner dropped the gun and then snatched a dagger from his belt. "I move faster than you, *mes amis*," he growled and aimed the other pistol at the remaining blackguards.

No doubt thinking of their well-being, the two uninjured renegades backed off and went to the aid of their friends. They helped them to their feet and staggered out the door of Greele Tavern. "We will have our revenge," the one with a big head and disheveled hair grumbled, and he stumbled out while supporting his wounded friend.

Jack took a deep breath and sheathed his sword. "Never thought I would see them again."

Gaspar handed the unfired gun to Jack, holstered his dagger, and picked up the discarded pistol. Together the two men righted the table, returned the fallen chairs to their places, and sat down. The master gunner reloaded the fired gun and stuck it into his belt. "You good with sword."

"Father hired an exemplary swordsman to train my brother and me. My opponent had little instruction. From the infantry no doubt. Knew only to whack and stab," Jack said, and he wiped some perspiration from his brow and adjusted his coat.

The two sat for some moments to allow themselves to cool from the intoxication of the encounter. Within a short time, disorder among the tavern patrons calmed. Several approached. "Those were some dangerous fellows you tangled with," one said.

"Murderers," said another.

"Cutthroats, thieves, and kidnappers from Canada they are," the first man added. "Scattered about the backcountry they are. Come in small gangs. Prey on patriots...and loyalists. Heard they answer to a woodsman named Jacob Wrack. No one about here has ever seen this man Wrack. A phantom he is."

Kara elbowed her way through the group and placed two bowls of steaming venison stew on the table. "Hope your bellies have quieted sufficiently to enjoy your supper," she said. Then she straightened and calmly announced, "I've seen this phantom you speak of. The man Jacob Wrack."

Astonished looks fell across the faces of Gaspar and the men standing around. Jack scratched his head. "I know of this man also, but have never met him. My brother Ian mentioned his encounter with this Mr. Wrack—an undeniable cutthroat, he called him."

"Aye," said Kara. "He served aboard the HMS *Buzzard* until he murdered one of the sailors while the frigate wintered in Halifax. Escaped into the forest when the *Buzzard*'s marines pursued him. He was never captured."

Jack nodded. "Aye. Kara is correct. The redcoats aboard this vessel kidnapped my brother, her, and others. Ian spent a year in servitude aboard the *Buzzard*."

Kara turned from the men and walked to the counter. She quickly returned with two pints of ale. "It is time to eat. You will need your strength should you meet those renegades again. They have been here before." She turned and shooed away those standing about. "Allow these men to eat."

"Thank you for your concern, Kara, but Mr. Gaspar and I will return to the *Piper* tomorrow. We sail for Beverly on the twenty-fifth. I doubt if we will meet those fellows again"

"Aye. You plan to lodge here? I can inform Mistress Greele to prepare a room for you."

"No. Colonel Thompson has quarters at his camp. He is expecting us."

"That's a two-mile hike, and the sun is waning." Kara wiped her hands on her apron. A look of concern covered her face. "Perhaps you'll stop by before you leave tomorrow."

"*Merci, ma chère*. A coffee to warm our innards would be nice before we return to the *Piper*," Gaspar said.

"Hot coffee will be waiting." Kara waved as she walked back to the counter.

Jack and Gaspar ate quietly. As they finished, the gunnery master said, "I fear we have not seen the last of those scoundrels."

CHAPTER 8

Except for a flickering circle of light from the campfire outside the reverend's shack, darkness covered the rest of the camp. The reverend and Bork sat, drank, and warmed themselves next to the fire. At the sound of snapping twigs, the two men dropped their mugs and rolled backward into the shadows. Each jumped to his feet, grabbed a musket, and aimed in the direction of the sounds.

"Who goes there?" the reverend yelled. "Identify yourselves."

"Need help. It's me. Elvy," a robust man with an enlarged head and long, spiky hair growled, and he entered the circle of light.

Partially tossed over his right shoulder was another man. His head hung down, and his bleeding right arm dangled at his side. The injured fellow's boots dragged along the ground until his bearer came abreast of the campfire. He then straightened, twisted, and let the mangled body fall onto the dirt. "He 'ad a disagreement."

Their muskets were trained on the grubbily dressed man, and the reverend and Bork stepped out of the shadows. Before either could utter a word, two other roguish men came out of the darkness. One strolled in, and the other stumbled forward and clutched his shoulder. Spatters of blood decorated the tottering fellow's blond hair and right ear. The seam connecting this man's coat sleeve to the shoulder was torn apart. The remaining shreds of cloth bore rose-colored stains.

"Appears more than a disagreement," the reverend said. "Someone at Greele's get the better of you, Elvy?"

"Jay," Elvy said and pointed to the unconscious fellow lying on the ground, "'e recognized an Englishman said confronted him last year in Halifax. Said he's the one who caused a couple American jacks to mangle his hand. Wanted revenge, but the lad was quicker with his sword."

"What of your other partner?"

"We were gonna shoot the whipster, but his henchman shot first."

"Aye. Bad evening for all you." The reverend lowered his musket's barrel. "Bork, fetch a couple women. Have them bring what they can to repair these men." He glanced down at Jay. "I fear your friend is steppin' on the ladder to his maker. All he'll be needin' is a prayer to speed him along."

Bork jumped up and disappeared into the darkness. Seeing the renegades carried no firearms, the reverend leaned his musket in the shack's doorway and strolled back to the campfire. He lowered himself onto a bench. From under it he brought up a jug and took a swig. "Seat yourselves. The fire will warm your faces and the rum your innards," he said and passed the jug as soon as the renegades found a perch near the campfire.

"I believe your friend Jay challenged a marine or sailor from the schooner *Piper*," the reverend said.

"Aye," Elvy said. "The lad was a young, sandy-haired fellow wearin' a uniform I did not recognize. He was no marine. His partner wore a sailor's garb."

The reverend nodded his head. "Your friend matched swords with Captain Morris's spirited midshipman. Haven't met him, but the captain said he's an Englishman well connected with the British aristocracy. Jack's his name. Jack Hollister. Decided to remain in the colonies and become a patriot rather than return to England."

Elvy scratched his head and smoothed his unruly hair. "Heard Jacob Wrack mention the Hollister name. Says a Hollister was aboard the HMS *Buzzard*." He squinted his eyes. As the rum jug passed, he took another swig. "Mr. Wrack might find this midshipman to his interests. A golden cow so to speak."

"Aye. A dead golden cow," the rascal nursing the injured shoulder said. "And that son of a bitch who shot me. Like to put an end to both of them."

"Mind your shoulder," Elvy said. "We've no means to capture this fellow."

Three women carrying buckets and baskets followed Bork as he returned. The reverend was deep in thought and looked out toward the dark forest. He slapped the lead woman on the back and caused her to lurch forward. "Tend to these injured men. One is beyond help. Bury him." He snapped his attention to Elvy. "How long have you been gone from Greele Tavern?"

"An hour maybe."

"If we hurry, we can catch them as they walk to the patriot camp. Bork, go fetch Luce. She can bewilder the lad while you and your man disarm the midshipman's henchman."

The reverend jumped to his feet and grabbed the musket and a powder horn. Elvy readjusted a short club tied to his belt and motioned to the uninjured renegade. Bork ran to the lean-to where Luce normally slept.

"I know a shortcut to the main road," the reverend said. "No doubt they will be cautious after the encounter. There's much cover along the route though. We can apprehend the lad and his man once they cross the bridge. The boy's the prize. He'll fetch a good ransom."

Bork returned. "I not find Luce. She not where she should be."

"Damn that woman! With that deserter no doubt."

———•◦•———

With sufficient light in the forest, Luce found the depression where the reverend and Bork had tied Henry to a tree. She observed him from her hiding place—a clump of bushes about one hundred feet up the rise. She saw people still milling about, and she touched her finger to the tip of her dagger and slowly squatted. *Those rascals are going to hurt that boy.* She turned and crawled through the brush to a boulder atop the hill.

Traversing a wide arc around the campsite, Luce secreted herself in a clump of low balsam trees near the reverend's shack. She sat on the ground and waited. Low-hanging branches hid her. When the two men emerged from the shack and comforted themselves next to the fire, she listened. They talked in low voices, and she was unable to hear what they were saying. Cloaked in darkness, she crawled on her knees to the side of the dwelling and closed the distance behind the men to about fifteen feet. Their words were now clear. Henry's name came up several times, but Luce's stomach tightened when she heard what the reverend had planned for the boy.

Luce's hand snapped to her mouth. She sighed and gasped. She pushed herself flat against the building, yanked the knife from her belt, and raised it to shoulder height. She shuddered. Her skin was hot, but she stood. A splinter pierced her shoulder as she scraped against the rough wood siding. She shook off the pain, gripped the dagger tighter, and held it above her head. She gritted her teeth and was about to jump out when some twigs snapped a short distance from the campfire.

She peered around the corner of the shack, and Luce saw a raggedly dressed man emerge. He was dragging another from the darkness. She rolled back against the shack and took a deep breath. Subconsciously she lowered the knife to her side.

Luce remained long enough to see two more men enter the circle of firelight. After hearing their story and the reverend's new plan, she crawled away from the shack and ran to the depression where Henry Holder was tied to a tree. With a couple swift swipes, Luce severed the ropes that bound him. She grabbed his shoulder, pulled him around to face her, and said in a harsh whisper, "We must go."

Henry felt her warm breath across his cheek. He nodded. He was aware of her concern and jumped to a standing position. "We need a weapon," he said as he stretched.

Bork pulled a flaming branch from the fire to use as a torch, and he hurried to the tree where he had tied Henry.

Luce heard heavy footsteps approaching, yanked Henry's arm, and urged him away from the tree. They lurched forward and dropped to their knees. On all fours they crawled over the mossy ground and lichen-covered sticks and stones. The latter irritated Henry's scraped knees, but the coolness of the squishy sphagnum eased the pain. About twenty feet from the tree, they rolled around and sat still. They breathed quickly and watched as Bork waved his torch around the area near the tree. They heard him yell and saw him turn and run back to the campfire.

———•◦•———

"Argh!" Bork shouted from the darkness. "Gone." The torch flame blustered as he ran back into the circle the campfire lit. "He's been cut free."

"Goddamn!" the reverend shouted. "That bitch cut him loose." He buried the cutting edge of a tomahawk into the tree next to him and broke the handle in the process. "Leave 'em be. The midshipman is a better prize. Let's get to it."

Bork grabbed up two muskets and tossed them to the two uninjured renegades. He picked up the two weapons leaning against the shack and handed one to the reverend. The four men ran off into the darkness as several women tended to Jay's corpse and the blond fellow's shoulder.

"We has to hurry," Bork said while trotting behind the reverend.

"Aye."

The reverend puffed as he sidestepped several boulders and jumped over a fallen birch trunk.

"Ow!"

The two men heard a crack of steel. One of the renegades had stepped in a hole, tripped, and clanked his musket on a rock.

"Keep it quiet." The reverend barked the command to the rear. "A disturbance will alert the patriots."

"My ankle!" one of the renegades whined.

The reverend came to a stop and snapped around. After a quick leap to the rear, he stood over a trembling black mass. The renegade lifted his head. "Cannot stand," he cried.

In a well-directed swing, the reverend arced his dagger past a mat of hair.

"Argh," the voice gurgled, and the dark bulk rolled forward and was quiet.

"What in the *hell* did you do?"

Though he could not see him, the reverend recognized Elvy's voice. "What needed to be done!" he said. "Injuries do us no good. Hurry along, or we'll lose our prize."

He swiped the blade of his dagger against his pants, and he dashed off toward the road to the patriots' camp.

Luce caught her breath and sighed. She jabbed Henry's side as she rose to her feet. He stood, took her hand, and tiptoed forward and away from the campfire. Within less than ten feet, he caught his foot beneath a tree root and fell forward. His knees plashed into a spongy bed of sphagnum. He was still holding Luce's hand, and he felt her grip tighten when she stepped around to the front of him. He knew she had a knack for seeing in the dark, so he stood and let her take the lead.

After moving about one hundred feet, they came to the western edge of the reverend's camp. Dim moonlight filtered through the trees, and they saw a tent not far ahead. They approached, and they heard heavy snoring and noticed three muskets against a nearby tree trunk. Several powder horns and shot bags hung from the tree's branches.

Luce released Henry's hand, touched his chest, and glared at him. He saw her eyes widen and her finger press against her lips. He stopped. With the silence of a cat approaching its prey, she stepped toward the tree. She took a musket, reached up, and noiselessly removed a powder horn and a bag of shot. She saw a ragged mound outside of the tent, and she went to it. She stooped over, took hold of the furry mass, and lifted it. As she raised her arm, the mass unfurled into a bearskin. She shook it toward Henry and motioned for him to follow. She flipped the bearskin over her shoulder and quietly headed back into the forest.

They shortly came to a well-worn path, and they increased their pace. Sprinkles of moonlight lit the way, and they hurried from the campsite. When they reached a barren plateau atop a hill, they stopped.

Luce looked skyward. She then glanced down the path and noticed its direction lay to the right of the moon. "Must follow path," she said. "Take us to river but rest first. Wait for morning twilight."

She grabbed and pulled him along as she moved down the far side of the hill and back into the forest's cover.

———•◦•———

Elvy followed the sound of the reverend's footsteps and almost ran into him when the man of God slowed. "Cutthroat," he mumbled loudly enough for the reverend to hear. "Murdering my man will not sit well with Mr. Wrack."

"So be it. Wrack's ire will be pacified when we present him with his prize."

In the next moment, the reverend threw his arms out to the side and caused Elvy to run into one. Both men stilled and waited. The sound of voices a short distance away filtered through the trees.

"Bork, stop," the reverend vented softly. "We're here. Conceal yourselves."

———•◦•———

When Luce and Henry reached the bottom of the hill, she led him into the trees. About twenty feet off the path, she came to a mound and stopped. She kicked off her moccasins and stepped around. "Grass dry. We rest here." She spread the bearskin and lay down on it. "Come. Roll in skin. Cuddle. Keep warm."

Though she raised her arm, Henry could not see it in the darkness. She turned and pulled the bearskin over her. Henry removed his jacket, kicked off his shoes, and stretched out near Luce. His left elbow touched her back. He rolled to the right, grabbed the edge of the bearskin, and rolled back. The maneuver partially covered both. The interior of this cocoon quickly warmed. Luce pushed her body closer to Henry's. She twisted herself against him and pushed her buttocks against his groin.

Henry's entire trunk tensed and became hot and moist. He had never bedded with a woman. Her hair buried his nose, and he smelled her musky odor. He held his breath, and when he did exhale and breathe, his gasps were quick and shallow. Every time he twisted, moved, or sighed, Luce pushed closer.

She slid her right arm back and let her fingers slide along his arm. When the fingers reached his wrist, she tightened them. She then dragged his arm over and around her and pushed his hand against her. Henry balled his hand into a fist. Luce caressed and squeezed it. With the pressure of a feather, her fingers touched and slid over his wrist and hand.

Slowly Henry's hand opened and flattened below her breasts. She felt his arm relax, but he kept it firm around her. She flattened her hand over his, applied a little pressure, and moved it to her left breast. His hand and fingers tensed. She held him fast and pressed his hand gently into her softness. She eventually felt Henry relax, and he began to fondle her. After a few moments, her fingers tightened around his hand. She held tight and moved the hand away and down to the edge of her blouse. She then pushed it under her blouse and up to her naked breasts. Henry's fingers touched her hot, moist skin. When he reached her nipple, his hand splayed.

Luce made a quiet squeal when Henry's moving fingers touched and then squeezed a nipple. She took her hand away and allowed him to fondle first one and then the other breast. She slightly shifted her rear and slid her right arm over and behind her. Luce spread her fingers and pressed them against Henry's groin. "You have now warmed," she said and giggled softly.

She squirmed. Her fingers tightened around Henry's member. While she caressed it, she softened and allowed him to enjoy her.

———•◦•———

The reverend bent forward in an attempt to peer through the brush. He could hear two men talking as they approached but could not see them. Flashes of light indicated each carried a lantern, but beyond the glow the intended victims were lost in the darkness. He straightened and pushed apart the dried vegetation. A thin limb snapped and caused him to drop to his knees and hold quiet. After a moment he realized the snap had not alarmed the approaching men. He then heard a crunch to his side.

"Elvy and me ready," Bork whispered.

The reverend reached over and patted his assistant's back. "We'll ambush them when they get forward of us," he said.

The rogues readied themselves. As their quarry approached, the lantern light that swung at their sides glowed and gleamed high and low and illuminated the path ahead. Silhouettes materialized as they passed the ambushers. There was a robust man wearing a knit cap, and next to him on his far side was a thinner fellow topped with a tricorne.

Elvy jumped clear of the brush and swung his club. His arm jarred as the club's knob connected with the solidness the knit cap covered.

Gaspar swung his lantern around as he twirled. It flew out of his hand as the butt of Bork's musket jabbed the hefty fellow's gut, and Elvy slashed at his side. The lantern tumbled down the path and extinguished itself. The master gunner doubled over and fell into the brush.

"Gaspar!" Jack yelled as he turned, brandished his pistol, and raised the lantern he held over his head.

A sudden shot of pain erupted from his upper right arm and sent his weapon flying. He howled as he felt his injured arm yanked behind him. Jack dropped the lantern and attempted to pull his dagger, but someone else's arm locked tight around his head and knocked the tricorne into the weeds.

"Jack Hollister, I presume," the reverend said.

———•◦•———

When Henry felt a delicate nudge against his side, he opened his eyes. Fragments of dark-gray light silhouetted the fir boughs above him. Aware of the dissipating somnolence, Henry rotated his head to the side and saw Luce's toes. He glanced up. "It's no wonder I'm cold. You have left me," he said and pulled the bearskin tighter about him.

"Time to rise. We must go," Luce said.

She reached down, grabbed the edge of the bearskin, and yanked. This flipped Henry onto a cold, wet, spongy carpet of reindeer moss. Henry jumped to his feet. His pants slid down his legs. He bent down, gripped them, and pulled them up. After securing his belt, he wrapped his arms around himself and began slapping his upper arms. "Luce, where's my coat?" He hopped about the mossy bed. "And where are my shoes?"

"Such a boy! How you survived so long I do not know." She reached down, found his shoes next to a boulder, and tossed them to him. "Your coat is on the branch. Hurry. We must get to the river."

She took up the bearskin, threw it over her shoulder, and wrapped it around herself. Luce led the way to the path, and the two hastened down it. Their backs were to the overcast but lightening sky. They reached the shoreline, and she put her finger to her lips. Looking up and down the shore, she motioned for Henry to follow quietly.

After walking a few minutes, Luce stopped. "Ahead," she whispered and pointed. "Canoes." Henry nodded. "Indian camp near."

Luce sneaked forward and used the alder bushes and other brush for cover. The first canoe sat upright on the bank about ten feet from the water's edge. When she got opposite it, she stopped, squatted down into the tall weeds, and waited. With similar stealth Henry followed. He watched as Luce raised her nose into the air and sniffed.

"Red men not cooking," she whispered. "They in forest hunting. We take canoe. Must be quick...an' quiet."

Henry's body tensed. He watched Luce rise and lightly tread to the boat. Her back was to him, but he saw her gesture to follow. He breathed deeply and duck walked through the grass, into the mud, and to the head of the canoe.

"Go to side," she commanded. "Paddles in bottom." He did as he was told. "Quick. Lift. Run into water."

With only a slight swish, the canoe floated between them.

"Get in," she commanded.

As he crawled over the gunwale, Henry struggled for balance. Luce pushed the canoe forward as she slid into the rear. They both grabbed the paddles and dug in. In minutes they were gliding parallel to the reed beds growing along the far shore.

Luce steered the canoe into a creek. "Long Creek," she said. "Know this place."

They paddled up Long Creek for about two miles to where it narrowed to a shallow, rippling stream. They disembarked, pulled the canoe up the stream for about one hundred yards, and hid it in the forest.

"We walk now. My people, they are not far. Live near Gorham Village."

CHAPTER 9

A cold, overcast morning greeted Sergeant Turner when he exited his tent at Thompson's patriot camp. Above, the steel-gray clouds curled and billowed. The threat of snow filled the air. A second marine pushed back the tent flap, crawled out, stood, stretched, and yawned.

"Turned in early last evening," Turner said. "Did you see Midshipman Hollister and Mr. Gaspar come into camp?"

"Did not take notice," the marine said. "It was dark. Cold. Could not see 'cause several of us sat bundled around the campfire enjoyin' the colonel's offer of rum. The ol' man said it would keep us warm and make us sleep. Did indeed do so."

"Aye. Where was the midshipman to be tented?"

"Bein' an officer, he would be stayin' in the colonel's quarters." The marine pointed to a house–barn complex occupying a forested opening some five hundred feet away and up a slight rise. A column of dark smoke twisted upward from one of the chimneys on the far side. "They are stokin' the breakfast fire."

"Could do with a cup of coffee," Turner said. "I will amble over and wake the lad."

The sergeant pulled his coat about him and thrust his hands into the pockets as he strolled off toward the colonel's house. The house's back door opened into the scullery. Turner had to shed his coat because of the heat coming from the kitchen. He strolled into the cooking area and found two of Thompson's men—cooks, he assumed—frying up a batch of johnnycakes and chunks of smoked, greasy meat. To him it smelled like bacon, but he remembered little bacon had been aboard the *Piper*, so none had been brought ashore to supply the village.

"Any coffee?" he asked of the man closest to him.

"In the pot hangin' by the hearth. Help yourself," the man said. "Take with it a cloth. The handle is hot."

Turner pulled a mug off a shelf, grabbed a towel to insulate his hand, and poured himself a cup. "Much obliged." The sergeant took a swig, shook his head, and swallowed. "That will guarantee to curl your hair."

"Colonel likes it strong," the cook said. "Keeps him alert."

"Aye. Do either of you know where Midshipman Hollister and his man are berthed? They should have arrived last evening."

"Nay. The colonel asked the same question before he turned in. Do not believe anyone came in last night. Colonel thinks the midshipman and his man stayed overnight at Greele Tavern."

"Aye. Perhaps, but that was not Mr. Hollister's plan."

Turner drank the rest of his coffee, shrugged, and scratched his chin.

"Do not believe anyone took note of the midshipman's arrival," the cook said and continued to push and flip greasy strips around the skillet.

"Thank you again for the coffee," the sergeant said, and he grabbed his coat and headed for the back door.

"Sergeant!" the cook yelled. "Take this bundle o' crisps and cakes with you. Your boys will be likin' to fill their bellies 'fore they go off."

The cook held a cloth bundle tied together by its four corners and handed it to Turner. Splays of grease stained and deepened the towel's color.

"Aye. They would appreciate a hearty breakfast. It is cold out this morning."

As the marine sergeant approached his six men, he found them congregated around a small campfire. They stood and drank coffee they had brewed. He held out the parcel. "Thompson's cook sent these freshly cooked victuals. Enough for all of us."

The marine nearest Turner accepted the bundle, set it on a stump, and untied it. The corners fell away and exposed a pile of johnnycakes and strips of fried meat.

Sergeant Turner filled a mug with coffee. Though he joined his men as they partook of the unexpected breakfast, he appeared disconnected. He did not join in their chitchat but instead stared off into the distance.

"You look concerned, sir," one of his marines said.

"Aye. There is concern to be had."

"Is it something the midshipman said when you met with him at the house?" another asked.

"To the contrary. Midshipman Hollister and Master Gunner Gaspar did not arrive at the camp last night. The colonel suggested they might have lodged at the tavern." Turner looked at the marine who had addressed him. "Mr. Hollister did not tell me he was staying in the town."

Turner wrapped his hands around the mug and looked into it. He then lifted it to his mouth and gulped down the coffee. "Finish up! Ready your muskets, and grab your packs. We are going into town to look into this."

In less than fifteen minutes, the Continental Marines were hoofing it toward the Falmouth waterfront and Greele Tavern. About a half mile from the patriot camp, the marine moving along the edge of the road and ahead of the troop cried out, "Over here!"

Sergeant Turner lowered the arm holding his musket and ran forward.

"Sir, the brush has been crushed." The marine stepped to the edge of the road and picked up several leaves. "Blood, sir."

"Aye. And the gravel on the road has been disturbed," Turner said as he quickly sidestepped the disarranged roadbed.

The six other marines joined in.

"Search the area," Turner commanded.

"Boot tracks over here. Several different ones," a marine said.

"No direction. Looks as if a scuffle took place here," another announced.

"Moccasin prints. Indians?"

"Been told no hostile savages about," Turner said, and he glanced down on several obvious moccasin foot-prints. "Some loyalists wear moccasins. The boot prints are British. Here." He pointed to some smaller indenta-tions. "Shoe prints."

"A tricorne, sir," the marine who had been searching the scrub several feet off the road yelled. "Looks to be that of a midshipman." He held it up for the others to see, lowered it to eye level, and rotated it. "There's a broken spruce sprig caught in the band and a patch of blood on the inside."

"Midshipman Hollister," Turner barked. "He has been here. That is his hat."

The marine holding the tricorne came crashing out of the brush. He handed it to Turner.

"Search the area!" the sergeant commanded.

A flock of crows and ravens flew up from the far side of a rise about fifty feet from the road when the marines clamored into the scrub and pushed down clumps of high grass, tangled briars, and stiff bushes.

"Over there," Turner yelled, and he pointed to where the birds had taken flight. "What are those scavengers eat-ing? Go look."

Two marines made their way to the site. "Argh!" one exclaimed. "Not a pretty sight, sir. A man with his throat cut. Blood all over."

"Goddamn!" Turner cried out.

The sergeant stumbled as he pushed through the brush. He caught his balance and remained upright but tripped forward. The musket he carried flew ahead of him. He bumbled for a few feet, retrieved the musket, and arrived at the carnage. "Terrible!" he called out. "But not Hollister I see."

The sergeant drew his sword. He used its tip as a probe, bent over, and pushed away bits of debris. "British. Wearin' a red coat. Torn. Trim dirty. Buttons missing. Renegade. British no doubt."

"Boot track over here," one of the men called out. "Directed to the road."

"Leave 'im," the sergeant said, and he motioned for the men to follow the footprints.

A yell caught Turner's attention. "Man down!"

He looked up and spotted the two marines searching the forest edge and brush on the opposite side of the road. Both were waving everyone over. When Turner got to the site, he found another body lying face down. Blood covered the back of the man's head. It was mostly dried and blackened. The robust person wore a dark, heavy coat. One of his shoes was missing. The sergeant stooped down and turned the body over. "Mr. Gaspar!" The sergeant released his musket, and it dropped to the ground. He stiffened the fingers of his right hand and gently touched the gunnery master's neck just below his ear. His eyes widened. "This man is alive! Get some poles. Make a stretcher. He needs to be taken to camp where Mr. Voors can tend to him."

"He was dragged here, sir." A marine handed Turner a shoe. "Found it just off the road."

In a very short time, the marines had cut down two small fir trees, stripped the trunks of branches, and threaded the poles through a couple coats to create a makeshift stretcher. They rolled Gaspar onto the stretcher and lifted it slightly. The gunnery master's weight held the coats in place. Sergeant Turner ordered two marines to transport Mr. Gaspar back to the patriot camp.

"We will continue to search the area for Mr. Hollister." He removed his hat and scratched his head. "Though, I believe if he were here, we would have found him." He looked at the men preparing to carry Mr. Gaspar back to camp. "Inform Colonel Thompson of what we found. Tell him the five of us are going to Greele Tavern to question everyone we find there. Have him send his militia. Also tell him I would appreciate if he would send someone to inform Captain Morris of the possibility Midshipman Hollister has been taken hostage." He shook his head. "For reasons I do not know. Mention also that Mr. Holder is still at large."

------ • ------

Inside Greele Tavern Kara was sweeping sawdust into a pile when Sergeant Turner and his two marines entered. Rather than looking dark and gray as it usually did after being trodden upon for several days, some of the sawdust had a fresh beige coloration. Much of it was clumped in reddish-brown chunks.

"Cleaning up after last evening's brawl," Kara said. She pointed to a less tainted area. "This area is clean. You can sit here." She set the broom aside, grabbed her apron, and wiped her hands. "Get you coffee or beer? Breakfast maybe?"

"Nay, ma'am, or should I say Kara? We met yesterday when we lunched here," Turner said. "We are searching for spoors a young midshipman and his rugged partner might have left. They were to sup here last evening and join our camp after. The older fellow we found this morning along the road. He had been maimed." The sergeant turned to the marine who stood behind him. The marine handed him Jack's tricorne. "We also found this. The midshipman's hat." He glared at Kara. "Were they here?"

Kara raised a hand and covered her mouth. A look of concern cloaked her face. "Aye. Indeed. They did eat here." Then her eyes widened. She placed her hands against her cheeks. "Aye. Jack...Jack Hollister. Oh my God!" she gasped. "Those awful men. Overheard one say 'Halifax,' and then Jack and he wrangled. The boy chopped his arm. He's good with a sword, he is. There." Kara pointed to the stained pile of sawdust. "Jack cut the renegade's arm."

"Was Mr. Hollister hurt?"

"No. Jack's man shot another. Then the fighting stopped. The bad men went." Kara choked, and tears wetted her eyes. "Wicked men. They said they would return to get even."

One of the marines muttered, "Those bastards ambushed Mr. Hollister and Gaspar."

"Not on their own," Turner interrupted. "They were wounded. Badly perhaps. How many others were there?"

"Four."

"Two uninjured?"

"Aye." Kara wiped her eyes with the edge of the apron. "They helped their friends leave."

"Still. Two against Gaspar and Mr. Hollister? No. They are well-trained fighters. Those renegades would have needed help to take down the gunnery master. And Jack, he is a highly trained swordsman." Sergeant Turner nodded, strolled to the table Kara pointed to, and sat down. Kara and the marines followed. He looked up at the woman. "How do you know the midshipman?"

Kara took a deep breath, pulled back a chair, sat, and told of how she came to know Jack and his brother, Ian. She recounted their activities with her sister, pirate leader Maire Balch, Maire's assistant, Dunkin, Bowden, and the other company at the pirates' camp. She then told Turner about the raid of the Royal Marines and how the brothers had become separated. Sniffling, sighing, and wringing her hands, she divulged her experience aboard the royal naval frigate and how she was discarded in Boston. She sat and buried her face in her hands. "Jack is in trouble," she mumbled.

Turner placed his hand on her back and softly patted it. "Do you know of anyone who would aid those renegades?"

Kara looked up, rubbed her nose, and nodded. She looked around the tavern and saw that, except for her and the Continental Marines, the place was empty. "Aye. There is someone, but you must tell no one…it was I… who told you. There is a man. They call him Reverend. He shepherds a group of religious Tories who are camped a few miles to the west. I saw him with the renegade named Jay—the one who fought with Jack—and another man. His henchman, no doubt…terrible men. Deserters from the Royal Navy. Met them at the tavern before the British poured broadsides into Falmouth." Kara rubbed her eyes. Again she glanced about the tavern. "Reverend speaks as if he is the patriots' friend. Says he himself is one." She clenched her fists, widened her eyes, and whispered, "He is not to be trusted. Not a friend."

Turner looked into her eyes. "Thank you, Mistress Kara. I must talk with the colonel. Tell him of this. You have my word—we will do what it takes to find Mr. Hollister."

He stood and motioned for departure, and the five men left before Kara could pull herself together.

———•◦•———

After Voors completed stitching up Gaspar's head wounds and a knife stab to the left shoulder, several camp women bandaged him. He bent over and touched the master gunner's neck. "Heart's beating slowly," the women heard the doctor mumble. "Temperature is cool."

Voors straightened.

"He gonna live?" one of the women asked.

"Aye. I will know more when he awakes. He has been unconscious since the marines brought him in."

The woman who had spoken nodded. "Need to return to the kitchen."

She left the room. The other two spent a few minutes fussing around Gaspar. They unfolded several blankets and covered him as Voors collected, cleaned, and returned his instruments to his medical bag. When finished, the three stood looking down at the comatose man.

"Looks as if God might call him," one of the women murmured.

Dr. Voors turned away. "We will leave him be. Call me should he awake." He walked from the room.

Downhill from Colonel Thompson's house, life in the patriot camp progressed normally. Voors found the colonel leaning against a rail fence and surrounded by a motley group of militiamen.

"How is Captain Morris's master gunner?" Thompson asked.

"The man took some hard knocks," Voors said. "Has not regained consciousness. It's a wonder he is still alive."

"I have sent a messenger to notify Captain Morris," the colonel said. "He wants to sail in the morning, but two of his men—three if you count the deserter—are disabled or missing. I suspect he will be visiting us before the sun sets." Thompson pushed himself away from the fence. "As soon as Sergeant Turner returns, my men are ready to search for those renegades."

"Aye," Dr. Voors said. "We need information. The women will notify me when Mr. Gaspar awakens."

Surgeon Voors nodded and strolled off to his tent.

———•◦•———

By late morning the thick steel-gray clouds that had been harbingers of snow thinned and began to break up. Beams of sunlight illuminated the patriot camp. For a day in late November, an unexpectedly warm breeze rustled the branches of pine needles as it wafted through the massive fir forest. The burring made by red squirrels seemed to have notified chipmunks, which were scurrying about the camp, to fill their larders with seeds and cones before ice and snow covered the ground.

As Sergeant Turner and two of his marines trudged rapidly into camp, the chipmunks whirred about and looked for cover. Colonel Thompson spotted their approach, left his troops, and met the marines by the water barrel. Before Turner took his turn to drink, he asked about Gaspar's condition.

"Surgeon Voors tended to his wounds," Thompson said. "But he said the man had not regained consciousness. That was two hours ago. We should see how he is doing. He is in my house."

"I believe Midshipman Hollister has been taken hostage," the sergeant said.

"Aye. That is what the two who brought Gaspar to the camp said."

"If he were awake, the gunner might give us some information. Perhaps Dr. Voors can wake him."

"Aye." Thompson started off toward his house.

Turner took a quick drink of water and followed the colonel up the hill. One of the marines headed off to notify Dr. Voors.

As the men slammed open the door and bounded into the kitchen, the two women inside jumped up and dashed to the opposite side of the long table. In the process one hit a cup full of flour and dumped it across the table. The other grabbed a broom and was ready to swing at the intruders.

"Sorry, ladies. Did not mean to startle you," the colonel apologized as he hurried headlong past the table and toward the room where Gaspar lay. "Has he wakened?"

"No, sir," one of the women uttered. She raised her hand to her mouth.

Thompson and Turner stomped over to the cot where the master gunner lay.

"Mr. Gaspar, can you hear me?" the sergeant commanded. "Wake up, man. Jack has been taken."

The gunner's arm moved, but the rest of his body lay still.

"At least he is alive," Turner said as Dr. Voors walked up behind him.

"Easy, Sergeant," Voors said, and he put his hand on Turner's shoulder. "Aggravating him will not bring him around. Let me try something."

He reached into his satchel and extracted a small vial. He unscrewed its cap and passed the vial under Gaspar's nose several times. He allowed the irritating scent of hartshorn to waft into his nostrils. The master gunner's body convulsed. He tossed his head to the side. Voors fluttered the smelling salts near Gaspar's face several more times. A singular spasm caused the man's chest to tighten, and he snapped his body upright.

"All is well, my man," Dr. Voors said, and he gripped the gunner's shoulders.

A strong, roaring sneeze threw Gaspar backward. His eyes opened, blinked, and glared. He sneezed a couple more times. He propped himself forward and then shot his fists forward and looked around. "Where am I?" he moaned, and then he fell back.

"You are safe," Voors said. "You are in Colonel Thompson's house. He is on your right. Sergeant Turner, whom you know, is standing at your feet."

Gaspar focused his eyes forward. "*Oui.*" He shook his head. "*Je recognize.*" His body relaxed. He lay back. Then he popped up again. "M. Hollister, *est-il en vie?*"

"What did he say?" Turner said.

"Asked if the midshipman is alive," Thompson replied.

"He has not been found," Turner said. "He has been kidnapped no doubt."

"Ambushed we were." Gaspar struggled to raise his hands to his head. He felt the bandages and lightly rubbed them. Then he moaned and dropped his left arm. "Two... maybe three. Do not know. Dark. Not see. No remember."

He slid his hand over his head, lowered it, and began to rub his shoulder. His eyes closed, and he lay down onto the pillow.

"Let us leave him be," Thompson said. "The militia is ready to search. We will find those sons of bitches."

Dr. Voors yelled out to the women in the kitchen to bring some water and fresh bandages. He remained in the room to tend to Gaspar, and Thompson and Turner left. When Turner came next to the long table where the women worked, he turned to the colonel. "Sir, please sit. I met with the Greele barmaid, Kara. She told me what happened at the tavern."

Thompson pulled away the chair at the head of the table and sat. The sergeant seated himself to the side.

"Aye," the colonel said. "I know of her. A rugged one she is. She has little love for redcoats."

Turner informed Thompson of what Kara had told him about the confrontation Jack and Gaspar had with the renegades while at Greele Tavern the previous evening. He also told him of the suspicions Kara had about the reverend and his activities and his apparent connection with the renegades.

Thompson rubbed his chin. "I, too, have my suspicions about the reverend. It is possible he and his followers are involved. You, I, your marines, and some of my militia will go to his camp. They will consider it an attack, but so be it."

The colonel pushed back the chair, stood, and headed out the back door. As Turner exited the kitchen behind Thompson, a man on a horse rode up.

"Lieutenant Whitehall!" Turner shouted. "Thank God you are here safely. Midshipman Hollister has been kidnapped. Gaspar is wounded, an' that damn deserter has not been captured."

The second officer of the schooner *Piper* swung himself out of the saddle. "Is that deserter involved?" he barked. "Has the captain been informed?"

"Thompson sent a messenger to the *Piper*. I do not know if Henry Holder was part of last night's attack. Colonel Thompson has the militia ready to find the culprits."

"Today is the twenty-fourth," Whitehall said. "Captain Morris wants to set sail in the morning. Ordered us back aboard this afternoon. That is why I returned."

"Aye, sir." Sergeant Turner's face became serious. "Mr. Hollister needs to be found. My men and I would like the help."

"Aye," Whitehall said.

He was about to continue, but the noise of bouncing wagon wheels and horse hooves startled both men. The following cloud of dust enveloped the wagon as it came to a stop in a clearing, but inertia and wind quickly dissipated it. Turner and Whitehall watched Colonel Thompson trot to the wagon. They saw the driver jump from the wagon's bench and help Captain Morris off. A contingent of sailors poured over the sides and transom and fell into rank. They were all carrying muskets.

"I suspect you will have your answer soon," Whitehall said.

Whitehall tugged his horse's reins and urged the animal to follow him as he and Turner moved to where the others stood. When they approached the wagon, they heard anger in Captain Morris's voice.

"We need to find my midshipman," the captain barked. He raised and pumped his fisted right arm. His left hand was on his saber's hilt. "And the culprits who attacked and kidnapped him. This needs to be done immediately because the *Piper* must get under way. We have some British shipping to disrupt." He turned to the rank of sailors. "I brought these sailors to aid in the search. Lieutenant Whitehall, you will be in charge. I will return to the *Piper* and make ready for immediate departure upon your return."

"Aye, sir," Whitehall said, and he strolled to the group of sailors.

"As you wish, Captain," Colonel Thompson said. "Sergeant Dailey, you and the militia return to the scene of the ambush. Determine the direction those villains took, and then scour the forest and barrens until you find them. Dailey, have those Abenaki friends of yours help out. They are good trackers. Lieutenant Whitehall, you and I will lead the marines and navy to that religious camp. Hopefully we can avoid a shooting battle." The colonel turned his attention to Morris, who had already climbed onto the wagon bench and seated himself next to the elderly driver. "By your leave, Captain," he said. "Do not concern yourself with the miscreants. They will be hung as soon as they are captured."

When the dust from the wagon hauling Captain Morris to the waterfront settled, Colonel Thompson hailed Lieutenant Whitehall. "Are your men ready to move out? We need to get to the reverend's camp. Perhaps he might have some answers."

"Aye!" Whitehall turned and yelled, "Sergeant Turner, ready the crew to march."

Almost immediately the *Piper*'s marines and seamen fell in behind Colonel Thompson and Lieutenant Whitehall. The column headed out of the patriot camp and turned west on a partially worn path that led up a hill and into the fir forest.

"The reverend's camp is just beyond the rise ahead. About a half mile," Thompson said.

The sailors and marines had their weapons readied. They poured from the forest and scattered through the nooks and crannies of the camp. They surprised residents working in the open, and those residents ran haphazardly about looking for cover. A plump, older woman who seemed to be doing laundry quickly turned and grabbed a musket lying against a stump. She lifted it and pointed it at the approaching troops.

"Alma!" Colonel Thompson shouted, and he raised his arm to halt his troops. "I see you are still the reverend's camp cook. We are here only to ask the reverend a few questions."

"Abrupt entrance you make, sir," Alma said, and she glared at him. "Better you come announced." She lowered the gun.

"Appreciate it if you would inform the reverend of our presence."

"Ain't about, sir. Don't know where he's gone. Bork, 'e, an' two renegades went off after dark last night. Ain't been back since."

"Renegades you say?"

"Aye. Four of 'em come last night. Two injured and two not. One died. We buried him. Other shot in the shoulder." Alma turned and pointed to a shack about a hundred feet away. "He's sleeping in there." Colonel Thompson signaled for several sailors to go to the shack and take charge of the injured renegade. "Thank you, Alma," he said. "We have a problem. One of the *Piper*'s midshipmen was kidnapped last night. This morning we found his companion, the master gunner, lying in the brush near the road from Greele Tavern. Left for dead he was, but he regained consciousness after being brought back to camp. The men also found a dead fellow in a dirty, tattered uniform near the road. His throat was cut."

"Don't know anything 'bout that, sir," Alma said.

Thompson nodded and turned to watch his men extract a struggling, light-haired man from the shack. The colonel nodded again. "Thank you, Alma."

He gestured to Lieutenant Whitehall. The two men started off to where the sailors were restraining the complaining renegade.

"Relax, my man," Colonel Thompson said when he came face-to-face with the renegade. "Who might you be, sir?"

The injured man continued to bend, twist, and stomp between the capturers who held him. Suddenly he slouched. "Call your men off. My shoulder is injured."

Thompson shook his head. "I asked who you might be. Answer, and we will talk."

The man stiffened, stood tall, and brushed strands of his blondish hair from his face. "An officer in His Majesty's army. Rob McLeod of the Halifax Fusiliers."

"Aye, Mr. McLeod."

"There will be hell to pay when my unit learns a bunch of rebels is holding me prisoner." McLeod again tried to wrench himself free. "Unhand me, rebel. I will not bend to such treatment."

A smirk crossed Thompson's face, and he slowly shook his head. "Silence! You, sir, are a deserter from His Majesty's army and now a prisoner of Brunswick militia. I believe you know what the British do with deserters." The colonel paused for a moment and glared into McLeod's eyes. "We treat deserters in the same manner."

"I'm a fusilier in His Majesty's service...and an officer. You have no authority over my actions. I'm not a deserter!" The fusilier raised his head and stood tall.

"What do you know of the reverend's business?"

"I am Rob McLeod of the Halifax Fusiliers."

"Aye, Mr. McLeod. You seem to have an aversion to answering questions." Thompson dilatorily surveyed the area around him. His gaze came to rest a bit to the right, and his eyes focused on an old, weathered balsam fir. Its lower branches projected horizontally a short distance from the trunk. "I do believe one of those branches over there has the strength of a proper yardarm. Do you not think so, Mr. Whitehall?" He glanced at the lieutenant. His eyes narrowed and created a sneer. He then returned his attention to Rob. "A proper gallows it will make."

"Aye, Colonel," the lieutenant said and nodded at Rob. "Perhaps we should invite Captain Morris. He missed his chance for a hanging when our deserter escaped."

Whitehall laughed.

"No time," Thompson said. "We need to find the midshipman." He faced the men holding Rob McLeod. "March that rogue to the hanging tree. This fellow is of no use to us. Let us hang him and get on with the search."

Rob twisted and kicked as the militiamen started to drag him to the fir. "Stop! Wait! The reverend...the reverend went to capture the midshipman when your deserter escaped this camp. Said this fellow—he called him

Jack—would be of more value. The reverend said he could ransom him to the colonials or sell him to someone named Wrack. So he and his ugly hunchback went off to capture this Jack fellow."

"Hold up, gentlemen," the colonel said. "I believe the thought of a rope tightening around the neck has tickled His Majesty's fusilier into divulging the information we need. Continue, Mr. McLeod. How are you involved with the reverend?"

"Four of us were in Greele Tavern last night when this Jack fellow and his man attacked us. A keen swordsman he is. With three swings of his sword, this Jack fellow chopped the arm of my partner, Jay. Bad. Then his mate shot me when I went to Jay's aid. We wanted revenge, but our mates, Elvy and Cotton, by themselves were no match. I was shot in the shoulder, and Jay was spurtin' blood like a fountain. Could not help them. We…we needed help ourselves. Elvy and Cotton knew of the reverend's camp. Said it was nearby. Said the reverend had helped them before. So we made our way here."

"Where are your partners?"

"Jay's dead. Women buried him. Cotton and Elvy went with the reverend."

"For now I will stay your execution, Mr. McLeod." Colonel Thompson called four sailors to come to him. "Secure this wharf rat, and take him to my camp. Fusilier Rob McLeod, you are now a prisoner of the Brunswick militia."

Within a few minutes, the sailors had tied Rob's hands behind him and marched him out of the reverend's camp.

"Our task is to find the reverend and his crew, Lieutenant Whitehall. We know one of them had his throat cut, so we are looking for three. Let us head to the undestroyed part of Falmouth. If the reverend plans to sell Mr. Hollister to this Wrack fellow, he will need a schooner. I have heard of this killer. He has been seen in Nova Scotia. We need to catch those three before they find a vessel. Let us be on our way."

———•◦•———

Four Abenaki Indians strained and grunted as they dragged the carcass of a large buck from the forest onto a grassy peninsula that jutted into the Fore River. They pulled their prize to the shoreline. They relaxed somewhat and moved easier because the deer's body now skidded along on the wet mud and grasses. Their canoes lay some yards ahead.

As they approached the landing, the two lead Indians became agitated. They dropped their towlines and dashed ahead. One swung his tomahawk. The other two saw the problem. Only one canoe lay in the grass. A single canoe would not transport four men and a deer carcass two miles up the wide estuary to their village. With the sun lowering in the west, there was not much daylight remaining. They were also concerned about the smell of a dead animal. It would attract the scavengers that prowled in the dark.

Their yammering, scrambling, and stomping caused frightened crows and ravens to explode into the air. They cawed raucously as they flew in random circles and added to the ruckus. All this noise also attracted Sergeant Dailey and his patrol. They were searching the forest for signs of the kidnappers. He signaled his men to move in and surround the Indians.

The sounds of breaking sticks, rustling grass, and squishing mud startled the Indians as the militiamen, with muskets raised, emerged from the forest and onto the river's edge. A tall, stalwart one named Abooksigun brandished a tomahawk and yelled, "What this?"

Almost immediately two other Indians dropped onto their knees. In a split second, they had bows drawn and arrows aimed. The third launched a spear, which impaled itself in the mud short of the militiamen.

"Wildcat, relax! Before someone gets injured," Sergeant Dailey shouted, and he lowered his musket and stepped forward.

"Dailey?" Abooksigun said, and he lowered the tomahawk to his side. He motioned for the others to ease off. "Why you attack? We hunt."

"Heard the clamor." Dailey raised and lowered his arm to signal his men to put down their firearms. "Sounded like a scalping party."

"Someone take Chogan's canoe. Now night come. Cannot go to village."

Dailey removed his cap and scratched his head. "Sorry about your canoe, Blackbird. We are searching for some kidnappers. They took a young midshipman from the vessel in the harbor. Did you see any signs of others moving around?"

"No. We not see any man while we hunt." Wildcat walked to where the missing canoe once lay. Dailey joined him. "Maybe kidnappers take canoe. We look."

Abooksigun, Chogan, and Dailey examined the area. The two Abenaki then followed a set of footprints to the river's edge.

"Only two persons carry canoe to river. None return," said the Abenaki, whom Dailey called Wildcat. "One wear shoes. Other moccasins."

Dailey examined the footprints. He shook his head. "The footprints where the attack took place do not match. The kidnappers did not take your canoe."

The three returned to where the other Indians and militiamen were waiting.

"My men will help you build a raft," Sergeant Dailey said. "If everyone hurries, you can get your deer back to the village before dark."

Wildcat's deep brown eyes sparkled. He smiled and nodded. "We will have party as you say when you come to visit," he said.

CHAPTER 10

Spared from Royal Navy bombardment, the western edge of Falmouth contained structures that were still intact and habitable. Scattered about were residences, storage buildings, and a few commercial buildings. Nan and Edward Peevy were both in their late sixties. They had lived in one of the cottages for the past twenty-some years growing vegetables for the town on a plot of land behind the house.

When word of the redcoats' attacks on Concord and Lexington had reached Falmouth, Edward had taken up his musket, hobbled through the kitchen door, and told Nan he was going to join the patriots.

She had called him an old fool who needed a crutch rather than a musket. "Those redcoats will hang you when they catch you," she had warned.

"They would not. They would not bother with an old man." Edward had shuffled back through the door.

About a month later, when news of the Battle of Machias got to Falmouth, Edward had again grabbed his musket and headed out. He had limped as far as the bench on the porch and seated himself. "Nan! I am ready. Tell Colonel Thompson where to find me."

Nan had brought him some water and said, "Colonel Thompson likes younger men in his militia."

Edward had shaken his head, taken a deep breath, and drunk the water. He had laid the musket on the floor, scratched his head, and gazed down the road.

On October 17, 1775, the British began lobbing cannonballs into Falmouth Village. The Peevys took shelter in the root cellar Edward had built under the house. They stayed there during the two-day bombardment. They sat and slept next to piles of potatoes. Luckily their house was out of range of the ships' cannons and outside the main part of the village. Both decided the British had superior firepower and the patriots had no chance of winning.

"Nan, if we survive this," Edward said, "and we remain in the colonies, I do believe it best if we follow King George's laws."

"As you say, Mr. Peevy." She tore a chunk of bread in half and placed it next to her husband. Then she poured him a mug of water. "Now eat. Keep yourself fortified."

"Aye." Edward took a bite of bread and started chewing, but he continued to talk. "Soon as those boys quit their shootin', they will sail away and return with fresh seeds for plantin' in the spring."

The low thud of a bursting cannonball startled the old man, and he spilled the water.

"I am sure they will, Mr. Peevy." Nan refilled the mug and patted his shoulder and back. "All will be fine, but for now you must remain calm. When the shootin' stops, you can go prepare the garden."

When the bombardment ended on the afternoon of the eighteenth, the Royal Navy vessels sailed away. Since their departure, on days of good weather, Edward Peevy only ventured as far as the porch where he spent the days gazing down the road. On inclement days he remained in the cabin. During all this time, Nan tended to his needs.

In the early morning hours of the twenty-fourth of November, a disturbance woke Nan. She slid from the bed and tiptoed to a window. She gazed toward the street but saw very little because her breath fogged the windowpane. She used the edge of her gown to clear a spot to see what might have made the noise. The almost-total darkness hid whatever was going on outside. Then for several moments the light from a nearly full moon shone through a crack in the overcast and illuminated the street. Some way past the house, she saw three men, two dragging a fourth man. She gasped. Subconsciously her hand snapped up and covered her mouth. Then the heavy clouds again covered the moon, and she could see nothing.

"What is goin' on?" Edward grumbled, and he began shuffling about in the bed.

"Hush!" Nan moved to the side of the window. "Two men draggin' another," she whispered. "They are followin' a tall, lanky man wearin' a long coat."

The bed creaked. A pillow puffed when it fell to the floor. Sounds of flopping and ruffling filled the room as a heavy quilt was pushed to the side. Then the thud of feet hitting a small bedside rug excited the air.

"Stay in bed, you ol' fool. Do not light any candles."

She again wiped the window and looked out. Nan heard distant sounds of boards falling or being shoved aside. Shortly thereafter, rusty hinges discharged several long, sharp screeches. She looked in the direction of the shrill sounds as moonlight again broke through the clouds, and she spotted the men near a building about a block away. She watched as the tall, lanky one in the long coat held a door open while the other two dragged the third inside.

"Mr. Peevy!" Nan hissed. "It is that deposed minister. He's up to no good again."

"You sure?" Edward stumbled to the window. "I want to see."

"Get yourself back to bed 'fore you catch your death of cold."

Nan felt Edward's shoulder brush against her as he turned and waddled back to bed. The heavy overcast clouds again masked the moonlight. She heard the squeal of the door being closed. "That is the reverend all right. He is the only one in town whose coat hangs to the soles of his boots."

"Methinks," Edward wheezed as he crawled beneath the bedcovers, "we should tell Colonel Thompson what you saw."

"Do not know if I should. Could anger the reverend if he learned we told on him—to the militia head no less. That charlatan believes we are loyalists and part of his fold. His group could turn on us and be nasty."

"Aye," Edward mumbled. "Do what you want, ma'am. The colonel will..." The old fellow's voice drifted off as he fell into sleep.

Nan continued to look out. The moonlight again lit up the street, but all looked normal and empty.

———•◦•———

Jack's eyes were closed. He moved his head and felt his right cheek scrape against a gritty floor. He shifted his weight against his shoulder and winced. He pulled his knees up toward his body and attempted to stand. He could not bring his arms and hands around to his sides or front to gain the support he needed. *Damn. My hands are tied behind me*, Jack realized. He tensed, twisted, and struggled to spread his legs and lift his body upright, but he could not. *Legs are bound, too.* His cheek scraped farther along the dirt.

Jack's head throbbed. He opened his eyes, and he saw blurry shafts of light divide the darkness. He shook his head and squinted. The eyes cleared. Daylight penetrated through some chinks at the top of the wall in front of him and provided enough illumination to discern his prison. He rolled his head and looked above and around. *Rafters above. Stone wall. I am in a cellar.*

His headache intensified. He took a deep breath, laid his head back, and closed his eyes. He choked and spat and then coughed and spat again. He struggled to rid his mouth of silt and the taste of mud. He turned onto his back and pulled his knees up. A burning pain at his wrists caused him to flinch when he twisted his arms. He rolled again onto his side.

He contorted and shuffled like a tethered snake, and Jack strove to wiggle to the wall. There he knew he could force himself up the side of the wall to a sitting position. After a few moments of painful exertion, he maneuvered the few feet to the edge of the floor. He turned onto his back and shoved his body against the wall and to an upright position. He then shifted to a comfortable position against the cold, damp stones and relaxed. He let his shoulders droop. He lowered his head and gazed at the floor. *I am alone. Gaspar. Where is Gaspar?*

Jack heard the sound of voices and tensed. They were muffled and coming from outside the cellar. From the tones of speech, Jack determined there were three different men, and they were arguing. After a few moments, though, he realized one of the individual's curt utterances were gruff commands.

With a sudden wham as if the heavens had abruptly opened, a blare of light blinded Jack. He closed his eyes, squeezed the eyelids, and shook his head. Slowly he opened his eyes and squinted. It appeared as if something had swung open the wall in front of him. He looked into the dazzle. A shimmering silhouette of someone in a long coat appeared above him and blackened the center of the blaze. The image seemed to descend through the glare. Two shadowy figures, one on each side of the long coat, further impeded the radiance. Jack's eyes acclimated to the light, and they began to focus. The three images appeared to float downward toward him through a wide opening in the ceiling.

Turning his eyes slightly to the left, he recognized the large head of unruly spikes and curls to the left of the tall, lanky man in the center. That head belonged to one of the four renegades from Greele Tavern. Jack took a deep breath and tensed his muscles. *Damn sons of bitches. They're the ones who ambushed Gaspar and me last night.*

He felt his body heat rise. He squirmed backward on his rump and pushed himself harder against the wall. As he pulled his knees up to his chest, he noticed the rope binding his legs was only wrapped several times around and not tied. He shuffled his legs, and the binding loosened.

The three images clarified. Above the collar of the long coat appeared a narrow face with a pointed nose and a thin, dark mustache. A hefty pair of black eyebrows amplified the deeply set, squinting eyes that were locked on Jack. The rogue's straight peppered hair fell below his small ears. On his right came a slovenly dressed, partially bent robust man with a round, nodule-covered head and face. Jack noticed this gnomish figure was carrying a wooden bucket in one hand and a mug in the other. The renegade from Greele Tavern with an enlarged head, unkempt mane, and dirty, tattered uniform completed the trio.

"Bork," the reverend said, "give the boy the gruel and that swill you call coffee." He continued across the floor, came to a stop in front of Jack, and looked down. "I see you are awake and not too damaged. Figured you would be hungry from all your activity. Sorry I cannot offer you a venison steak and fine ale. Bork's porridge will fill your belly, though, and keep your strength up."

Jack blinked his eyes. "I need use of my hands."

"Aye. Elvy, cut him free."

The renegade pulled a dagger, stepped toward Jack, and straddled his legs. He bent down, and Jack leaned forward. Jack felt the cold steel slide between his wrists. When he heard the cord snap, he quickly worked his feet back and forth and catapulted his toes hard into Elvy's groin. The renegade screamed and folded. Jack jumped to his feet, grabbed the bucket from Bork, threw its contents in his face, and flung the empty bucket at the reverend.

The reverend ducked and swung the blackjack he was holding. It connected with Jack's shoulder and knocked him against the wall and off-balance. Bork spat gruel, wiped his face, grabbed the midshipman, spun him around, and locked his heavy arms over his chest in a bear hug. Smacking the business end of the blackjack against his hand, the reverend smirked at Elvy. He was holding his crotch, moaning, and writhing on the floor.

"Nice try, Mr. Hollister," the reverend said.

"How do you know my name?"

"Your Captain Morris spoke of you at Thompson's gathering several evenings ago. The Hollister name is not unfamiliar to us in the sea trade. I do believe the Hollisters are owners of one of Great Britain's prominent exchange and transport companies. You are one of the family, and that makes you an aristocrat of sorts. A person of much importance. A precious commodity that men in my trade can sell or ransom. Aristocrats bring a good price."

"A kidnapper and scoundrel you are then, sir!" Jack choked, squirmed, and tried to take a breath.

The reverend laughed. "Not so different from what your people do. My brother and I, we also exchange commodities."

"Is this oaf holding me your brother?"

Bork snapped his elbow against Jack's ribs. "I no oaf! An' not his brother!"

The reverend grinned and shook his head. "No. That empty-headed fellow embracing you would never be a brother of mine. Mr. Bork can only take orders. Not give them. My brother gives them and ensures they are carried out."

Bork's arms tightened around Jack and suffocated him. Bork stomped back and forth and tried to speak.

"Know your place, dullard," the reverend barked. "Do not open that stupid mouth, or I will ventilate what remains of that skull of yours. Relax. You are choking our prize. We need him alive."

Bork loosened his grip.

Jack sucked in a deep breath and asked, "Who is this brother of yours?"

"Jacob Wrack." Jack stiffened and stared at the reverend. "Except for Mr. Bork, who has never met him, no one in this area knows we are brothers. Now, you know. It will not matter though. You will be meeting him soon."

"The murderer and renegade," Jack growled. "He is known in the area. During my brother's imprisonment aboard the HMS *Buzzard,* he met your recreant brother when that frigate overwintered in Halifax."

"Aye." The reverend nodded and smirked. "Jacob had his problems aboard that vessel. Escaped. We will be meeting him in Halifax." He shoved the blackjack into his belt and looked at Bork. "Secure him. This time properly. We need to locate a seaworthy vessel and be off before those patriotic interlopers find us."

"Aye," Bork said. "Is *Rosebud* not good?"

"That tub's ready to sink," the reverend growled. "Need a vessel that will float." He stepped back and turned toward Elvy, who was sitting on the floor and rubbing his crotch. "Get your ass up, and get to Greele Tavern. Go. Watch what goes on with the *Piper.* Be inconspicuous. We will need to get past that rebel schooner. Son of a bitch is armed to the teeth."

The renegade twisted onto his knees. Like a broken man, he contorted his body to a standing position and stumbled up the stairs and into the daylight.

Cracks appeared in the cloud blanket after lunch, and patches of blue began to show as Henry and Luce hiked up the side of a nearby knoll. Though it was the twenty-fourth of November, it turned out to be a beautiful autumn day. Below and across the meadow stood a log cabin where the two had spent the night with Luce's friends, Martha and Birdie. The air temperature warmed as they walked through the grass. Stopping just below the hill's summit, Henry scanned down the hill, walked beyond a tree, looked toward the top, and returned. He turned, glanced over his shoulder, and then faced Luce. Her attention seemed fixed on a few flowers that remained in bloom.

"We are not safe here," he said. "The reverend and his people will find us. We need to move on."

"We safe. Reverend not know this place." Luce picked a wild carrot flower and brushed it against her cheek. "Martha and Birdie sneak away from Reverend's camp last spring. Come here. When try to capture them, Reverend never search across river. So he not find them." She flicked the lacy white flower at Henry and dropped down next to him. "He not care we go. I heard bad men who come to camp. Talk of sailor they fight with in tavern. When Reverend hear this, he get excited. Say sailor is English a-a'isthocras. Expert swordsman, he say. Name Jack Holl'st'. Reverend want to capture this Jack Holl'st'. Say he important. Golden cow he called him. Get ransom from patriots." She smiled and scratched her head. "If not, he say he take boy to Halifax and sell to brother. Brother like boys." Luce picked a long blade of grass and glanced over at Henry. "We safe. Reverend not look for us."

She smiled. Henry fisted his right hand, smacked it into his left, and shook his downturned head. He flipped onto his butt, jumped to his feet, and stomped to a nearby tree. He pushed his head against the trunk and held it there for a moment. He then quickly straightened, snapped around, and faced Luce. "Damn it, Luce. This is not good."

She saw his eyes narrow and his jaw tighten. He still clenched his fists. He returned to where Luce sat on the ground and dropped to his knees. "Who the hell is this reverend? And how do you know him?"

Luce jerked away. A startled look was on her face. "Why you howl at me?" she cried. "I not do anything."

She scrambled to her feet and backed away from Henry.

"I am sorry, Luce," Henry said as he stood. "Midshipman Hollister was the only person aboard the *Piper* who was civil to me." He raised his hands, turned the palms out, and moved slowly toward the girl. "Mr. Hollister is my friend. I need to help him." Henry moved away from Luce and began nodding and pacing about. "But I do not know what to do." He stopped for a moment and looked up. His eyes softened. "Who is this evil reverend? How did you come to know him?"

Luce wrung her hands together. Tears filled her eyes. She lowered her head and took a deep breath. "My father Dutch trapper. He no wants my mother. Send her back to tribe. Tribe take my mother in but not want me. Two men in tribe take me to Portsmouth Town. Trade me to old woman for musket. She have house, and other girls live there, too. Woman make us work for her in daytime. At night men come. Woman force girls to go with them."

"How old were you?"

"Fourteen years."

Henry ran his hand through his hair. "Please continue."

"Reverend come one night. He smelly. Bad drunk. Want me. Ol' woman say I go with him, but I not want to. He pull me upstairs. Hurt arm. I cry, but he not care. Push me in room and rip away dress. Tie me to bed, do things, and fall asleep. I scream, but no one come." Luce wiped her eyes. "Reverend wake. Throw blanket over me and drag me downstairs. He gives ol' woman money and takes me with him. He say because I know his real name, and he want others to know him as 'Reverend.' Said he kill me if I call him by his real name."

"I am so sorry." Henry put his arm around Luce and pulled her to him. "That son of a bitch hurt you. Made you his slave. I want to kill that bastard, but first I need to help Mr. Hollister."

Henry took Luce's hand and started to pull her to the house. "I need to get going. Get back to the other side of the river. We must hurry."

"Cannot go back. Get caught, and they hang you."

"Perhaps, but Mr. Hollister needs help. And he would help me if I needed him."

"Then I go, too. Guide you. Keep you safe."

"There is danger," Henry said. "I would rather you not go."

"I go!" Luce grabbed his shirt sleeve. "You need my help. I be careful."

"Very well. But I sure would not want for you to get hurt." Henry shook his head. "By the way, what is the reverend's real name?"

"Enoch Wrack," Luce said.

The name stopped Henry in his tracks. "Mr. Hollister spoke of a man named Jacob Wrack. Not a good man. A killer whom the redcoats and patriots are hunting."

"Aye. Reverend's brother."

By the time Henry and Luce reached Martha and Birdie's log cabin, the sun lay on the horizon.

"We must hurry," Henry said.

"It be dark before we can find canoe," Luce said. "Martha cook fish and lobster. We eat good. Sleep. Leave tomorrow before sunrise."

"Midshipman Hollister needs my help," Henry said, and he ran into the cabin and started gathering his gear.

Luce laid her hand on his back. "Not good if you injured or lost. Go in morning. All will be good."

Birdie came through the door. "What are you two in such a hurry for?" she asked. "Martha will have victuals ready in a little time. We can eat soon."

"Henry's friend in trouble," Luce said. "We need to go back. Help friend."

"It is miles back to the river. You will be lost."

"Aye," said Luce. "I tell Henry. We wait to morning." She looked at Henry.

"Aye. You're correct." Henry set his pack down and returned the powder and shot bags to the hook. "I would be no good to Midshipman Hollister lost in the woods."

———•◦•———

The pair of big, flat doors slammed when Bork lifted each and flipped it shut upon exiting the cellar. This threw Jack back into darkness. The stout limb scraped as he shoved it between the handles to secure the doors. Bork straightened, wiped his hands against his pant legs, and followed off behind the reverend and Elvy.

Jack took a deep breath and attempted to clear his head. He stared forward. He shifted, forced his shoulder against the wall, and tried to decrease the pain the whack of the blackjack had provoked. Maintaining pressure on it seemed to work. He relaxed as the soreness subsided. *Nothing broken.*

Jack's eyes slowly adjusted to the darkness. Patterns created by slivers of light on the floor and the wall to his side resolved and brightened. He breathed deeply as he slouched and looked around the cellar. Spatters of porridge covered the ground where the bucket he had swung struck Bork. As Jack looked at them, his stomach grumbled.

"I have not eaten since Greele Tavern," he mumbled. "That was last evening." He gasped as he straightened, but his stomach muttered. "Guess I could have swallowed a few spoonfuls of the swill that deformed wart offered." Jack chuckled and moaned. "Those bastards will be back. I need to escape or somehow get the upper hand."

He worked his arms, but they were securely tied behind him. He looked down. The rope that originated at his wrists came under his buttocks and to the front between his legs. This caught his attention. It wound around the legs. Though it encircled them several times from his knees to his ankles, the bitter end was tied in a simple overhand knot. *That fat dwarf was not a sailor,* Jack thought. He raised his knees to his chest and shuffled his feet. The binding loosened. He bent forward and bit down on the cord. He straightened and yanked at the slack. The rope grew taut and tightened against his legs, but it slipped a short distance upward. As it did the knot migrated slightly toward the rope's end. He shuffled his feet for about ten minutes while holding the rope in his mouth. Beads of sweat formed on his brow and formed dark patches on his shirt. He relaxed and spat away the rope. After a while he again began working his legs back and forth. The coils about them loosened. When he tried to move his legs apart, they separated slightly. He slowly slid his feet back and forth and applied pressure on the knot at his ankles with each move. As he did the knot relaxed. Jack stretched his legs out and jiggled them. It untied, and the end of the rope fell to the ground. He leaned back against the wall, took a couple deep breaths, and rested for a few minutes. When he stood, the rope around his legs uncoiled, but it was still attached to his wrists. It secured his hands behind him.

Jack was distracted from hunger, but he worked his hands and tried to free them. His wrists burned where the rope bound them. The knot at his wrists remained secure. *Getting free will not be easy. Got to find something sharp.*

He trailed the free end of the rope and paced along the cellar's wall. Where there was sufficient light to see into the rafters, he examined everything closely for exposed nails, splinters, or other hidden sharp objects. In a darkened corner, he stumbled into a staircase. When he caught his balance, he stood for a moment and allowed his eyes to acclimate to the near blackness. He gently moved his uninjured shoulder against the stairs and rotated his head until it touched the framework of the under casing. He then carefully bent forward and gazed into the darkness under the stairs. He used the toe of his right boot to probe about, and he disrupted several items propped in a corner.

A pole fell forward and struck his chest. Another fell to the floor. He stepped back and kicked both things toward the center of the floor. He looked where the objects came to rest, and his dark-adapted eyes quickly discerned a shovel and hoe.

A feeling of relief came over him. *Tools!* Jack stepped over the implements and dropped on his knees. With his back to the shovel, he took hold of it and manipulated it to a vertical position. He separated his hands, placed the rope that bound them together onto the edge of the blade, and began to saw.

"Damn! Dull edge," he said.

He sawed faster and applied more pressure. The beams of light that had shown through the cracks in the cellar door were gone. Only a couple radiant slivers projected from openings between the building's rafters and its foundation on the wall opposite the doorway. Jack surmised the day was nearly gone. *Perhaps my captors will not return until morning.*

He felt the rope tattering as he continued to saw.

CHAPTER 11

The patriots' camp was abuzz at sunup. Today Captain Morris had planned to sail. Instead the militia and the *Piper*'s marines and sailors had a hurried breakfast and then prepared the gear and weapons they would need to scour the Falmouth peninsula in search of Jack Hollister and the culprits who had kidnapped him. Though a heavily overcast sky blocked the rising sun's warmth, slashes of blue were appearing along the western horizon. It was the morning of the twenty-fifth of November. The nighttime chill remained, but the gusty, salty breezes had calmed. All expected the sky to clear by midmorning.

Several jets of steam shot up when Sergeant Turner tossed the remaining coffee in his mug onto the peripheral embers of the campfire. "Those footprints your men found yesterday, Mr. Dailey, of whoever stole that Abenaki canoe," he said, and he stood. "They must belong to the deserter Holder and his companion."

"Aye," Sergeant Dailey agreed and gulped what was left in his mug. He jumped to his feet. "You will follow them, will you not, across the river? Meanwhile we will search for the midshipman on this side. Capture everyone by nightfall. Your Mr. Holder cannot have gone far. He does not know the area."

Turner's eyes narrowed, and he glared at the militia sergeant. "Nay. Not on your life, sir. Finding the midshipman is more important." He tightened his lips and nodded to intensify his statement. "Even than that damned deserter. From our visit to the reverend's camp, we know who the kidnappers are. The colonel said the reverend and his crew of cutthroats will need a schooner, so they still have to be in the Falmouth area. My marines and sailors will turn this ravaged peninsula inside out to find our boy." He fisted his hands. "We'll get those bastards who abducted him. That will satisfy Captain Morris's desire. He will have his hangin'. Someone in this damn village must have seen them."

"You do not know Falmouth."

"That is where I was hoping you would help out."

"Aye. Then we should combine forces and delegate men as needed," Sergeant Dailey said, and he took hold of his musket's barrel and used it as a staff to stand.

Sergeant Turner caught the boatswain's attention and pointed toward a clump of trees. "Mr. Stokes, have our men muster by those trees in the next five minutes. We need to get the search under way."

"Aye," Stokes said.

He whirled around and headed off to where groups of sailors were mingling. As he walked, he shouted to them to cut their chatter, grab their gear and weapons, and immediately fall in. Believing his command was heard, he changed direction and pointed to the trees, but he continued to shout as he marched toward his troops.

Mingled among the double-timing sailors were Midshipman Hollister's gun crew—Widget, Nightjar, Marvel, and Tyler. The four men mustered next to each other and came to attention in the front rank. Stokes took his stance next to his crewmen. *Piper's* other sailors fell in around them, while the marines took a position to the side of the sailors.

"We is here to help find Master Jack," Tyler said as he stood and fidgeted next to the lanky, ruddy-skinned Nightjar. "We gonna get those rascals who hurt Mr. Gaspar an' kidnapped Master Jack."

Nightjar thumped the stock of his musket onto the ground, grunted, and jumbled the young seaman's hair. Widget and Marvel smiled and nodded. Lieutenant Whitehall and Sergeant Turner stood in front of the sailors. Whitehall addressed them. He told them the evidence suggested Midshipman Hollister was being held prisoner nearby. He explained they and the militia would conduct the search together. They would comb the entire Falmouth peninsula until the midshipman was found and the kidnappers captured.

"Let us be under way," someone yelled.

The other sailors shook their fists and muskets and shouted, "Huzzah!"

"We will get the bastards," Stokes mumbled.

"Sergeant Turner," the lieutenant said, "the searchers are anxious. Let them get under way."

"Hold up a moment, gentlemen," Colonel Thompson shouted as he walked into the rank of troops. He led a large white horse behind him. "Sergeants Turner and Dailey, select a contingent of four men from each of your units. I want them to head off to the reverend's camp under your command, Lieutenant Whitehall, and stand guard on it in case those scoundrels return."

"Aye, aye, sir," Dailey said.

Turner nodded and pointed out Widget, Marvel, and two other sailors. "If the colonel and Lieutenant Whitehall will allow, I would like also to choose one of my marines to lead this patrol."

Both Thompson and Whitehall agreed. Colonel Thompson adjusted the saber around his waist and his tricorne and shouted, "Gentlemen, let us get on with this search."

He turned and mounted his horse.

———•·◆·•———

Henry and Luce had breakfasted and were on their way by the time the overhead blackness began to lighten to gray. Henry clutched the musket Luce had taken from the reverend's camp, and he led the way down the gradient toward the surrounding forest. Except for a few waking birdcalls, the forest still slept. Luce tried to keep up and scurried behind him.

"Be careful," she called out. "Forest dark. Roots cross trail. Trip you. Watch out."

Henry swung his arm up and dismissed her caution. He scampered into the dense cover of the forest. He found the path that led to Long Creek, the stream that flowed to the Fore River, and swirled onto it. Hearing another warning Luce shouted, he slowed, stopped, took a deep breath, and waited for her to catch up.

"Not good to Mr. Holl'st' if you break leg," she said and stepped next to him.

"His name is Mr. Hollister. Can you say that?" Henry sighed deeply as he curled his right leg back and then stretched it forward. "Oh, never mind. Call him Jack. Come along. We need to get to the river and cross it."

He started off down the path at a more reasonable pace. He watched out for the rocks and roots that seemed to pop up in front of him. The downhill trek finally leveled, and Henry began to feel a cool, humid breeze waft past his face. *Not much farther*, he thought.

Ahead, the forest became less dense and exposed more sky. Its floor changed from small lichen-covered boulders, exposed roots, and soggy carpets of sphagnum moss with protruding stones to boulders and rocky overhangs. The path seemed to terminate at a fissure between two craggy outcroppings. He gingerly worked his way through the crack and emerged on a promontory that jutted about ten feet above a marsh. Through this and a short distance away meandered Long Creek.

He heard Luce call out to him. She was about thirty feet to his right and standing between a pair of twisted, aged fir trees growing at an angle from a lower bank. Below her the path wound its way on a low ridge through the sedges and cattails. "We go here," she yelled and pointed farther to the right. "We hide canoe that way. In cattails. Should still be there."

Henry climbed hand over hand up the crevasse and joined her. They followed the ridge, jumped a couple small breaches, and sloshed through low areas to and along the creek for about a mile. Using her tracking skills, Luce led the way. When she saw several subtly bent and broken cattails that progressed in a nearly linear line into the marsh, she waded into the water and examined the area. She probed her way into the reeds. "Canoe here! No one find."

Because Luce was hidden among the cattails, Henry heard her but could not see her until she came backing out of the marsh. She crunched weeds and sloshed water and mud. With a firm grip on the canoe's bow, she pulled the vessel into the stream.

"You hid it very well," Henry said as he watched, "but it has only been hidden for two days."

She glared at him for a moment. "All good. Paddles here, too. We can go now."

After Luce crawled into the canoe and knelt in the bow, Henry laid the musket in the center of the canoe and, holding on to both sides of the canoe, pushed it off, got in, and seated himself in the stern. Raising his knees for comfort, he paddled and scanned the stream ahead. It was midmorning under an overcast sky. There was no apparent breeze, but the air continued to be cold and humid. They did not speak as they paddled. Except for an occasional squawk of a herring gull or strident squall of a belted kingfisher, the only sound that could be heard was the gurgling and swishing of the water against the hull. After about two hours, the air became misty. Henry noticed exposed patches and hillocks of mud and detritus.

"It is near midtide," he whispered.

As the stream widened, Henry and Luce stayed near the starboard shore. The mist thickened, and the left bank disappeared. After some minutes the right bank disappeared. As they kept on into the fog, the canoe's bow began to swing to the right.

"Strong tidal current," he said. "We are on the Fore River. Tide is ebbing." He used the paddle as a rudder, dug deep, and pushed to the left against the water. This forced the bow slightly upstream. "Stroke deep, Luce. I will hold a straight course. We have to cross over before we are pushed out to sea."

After a few minutes of straining against the flow, Henry's muscles tightened and became sore. Sweat began forming on his forehead, chest, and back. With the air around him a thick, white soup, he continued to fight to keep the bow abeam of the current. He could barely see Luce. Only flow streaks etched the water's surface. Occasional clumps of flotsam broke these.

"Watch out for logs," he shouted, and he continued to force the canoe in the direction he wanted it to go. "Current is hell." He pushed hard against the paddle blade. "But the fog is good. No one onshore can see us crossing."

The slug of colder air must have been following the tidal flow along the west side of the Fore River estuary because as Henry and Luce neared the eastern shore, the force of the current and the thickness of the fog began to diminish. "Where are we?" Henry asked.

"South tip of Falmouth Neck," Luce said. "If we go around rocks o'er there"—she pointed toward a bunch of algae-covered boulders about a hundred yards away—"we be in harbor."

Henry continued to slowly paddle and allowed the tidal current to carry the canoe to slightly beyond the point of land. He stretched his body upward and could see over the boulders. About a mile away, the furled topsails, yard-arms, and masts of the schooner *Piper* penetrated the fog bank shrouding the harbor. The *Piper* was lying at anchor. Almost automatically he dug the paddle deep, gave it a pull and twist, and rotated the canoe's bow upstream. He paddled for a few moments and brought the canoe back behind the cover of the point of land.

"We go around bend ahead," Luce said. "Good place to go ashore."

The fog continued to thin, and sunlight broke through patches between the clouds. This cast a silvery sheen across the water's surface. The two rowed hard until Luce boated her paddle and waved her arm toward shore. Henry steered the canoe's bow to a sandy, reedy beach. "This is near where we borrowed this boat," he said as the bow ground into the silty grit.

"Aye," Luce said. "That it is."

She jumped out and pushed the paddle down into the canoe. She grabbed the vessel's bow and pulled it higher up the beach. Henry clambered out. His paddle thudded onto the bottom of the canoe.

"Shush," Luce hissed. "Someone hear us. Must be quiet."

Henry nodded. The two carried the canoe up the shore and set it down beyond the flotsam defining the high-tide line. Henry reached down into the canoe and retrieved the musket they had brought. They climbed up a low bank and hurried across a narrow open strip of low weeds into the cover of a clump of alder bushes. Henry sat down on an old piece of driftwood, took a breath, and sighed. Luce pushed her way through to the edge of the bushes. After a few moments, Henry joined her.

"I see some buildings," he said, "but they are not burned or destroyed."

"Aye." She pointed to the right in the direction of the harbor. "We west of Falmouth Town. British guns not reach this part of village."

"Not much cover," Henry said. "We will be seen if we try to cross to those buildings."

"Need to go back to riverbank and sneak upriver to where forest start." Luce turned and began to make her way back to the river's edge and the cover of brushwood composed mostly of alder. "Must hurry. Know some people can trust. Not far."

They kept low and dashed across the exposed area to the riverbank. They jumped down it. To maintain cover they stayed bent over as they hurried upriver. Henry stumbled through a dip in the riverbank, and he spotted a disheveled rank of men off in a distance. They were carrying muskets. He gripped his musket tightly and dropped to his knees, and Luce scurried into a nearby stand of birch trees. He watched the troop as it proceeded behind some buildings. Immediately he scrambled to his feet and ran into the forest.

"The militia. Over there. Must be looking for Jack," Henry said when he came next to Luce.

She nodded, put a finger to her lips, and moved a little deeper among the trees. With Luce in the lead, they advanced stealthily among the trees. Within a few minutes, they came to the road the militiamen had just passed. Carefully they dashed across. After about twenty minutes, Luce stopped and moved closer to the forest edge. From behind a large oak, she peered across a field toward a farmhouse.

"My friend Nan live in house," she said, "with husband. She good friend. We go."

"We will be seen," Henry cautioned. "That militia, they might even be searching the house or somewhere nearby."

"Nan good cook. I hungry. Feel thirst. We go...with care."

"Yes. Stay low."

"You follow," Luce said, and she stepped back in among the trees and scrambled forward. "Find ditch. Go to Nan's garden."

Within a hundred feet, Luce found the depression. It was dry, and the vegetation stood tall along its banks. The ditch sheltered them almost to the back of the farmhouse.

After leaving Jack on the afternoon of November 24, the reverend, Bork, and Elvy hiked upstream along the east shore of the Fore River estuary. They went for about two miles north to where the estuary narrowed and the river actually entered. They continued upriver for another quarter mile, turned inland, and arrived at the reverend's hideaway well after dark. Alma and a dozen of the reverend's well-armed partisans met the three men. Before they reached the campfire and bivouac area, Alma related her meeting with Colonel Thompson earlier that day. She told the reverend militiamen, marines, and sailors were guarding the loyalist camp. "Those patriotic rebels surround our camp, sir."

"I knew it would not take long for that bunch of traitors to find fault with us," the reverend grumbled. "Since we do not cotton to their ideas of independence, they will find any excuse to incriminate us for anything that goes amiss." He walked to the campfire, sat on a bench next to it, shook his head, and shrugged. "Alma! Get me some victuals and a jug of rum. Need to think. Rest of you, shut up, and get the hell out of here."

———•◦•———

The clang of an iron skillet Alma had dropped startled the reverend awake. He had been sleeping in a nearby tent. He grunted, ran his hands through his hair, and sat up. He kicked away several blankets that tangled around him, and he crawled out of the tent. The morning twilight illuminated the camp. "Alma, fetch me some water," he said, and he blundered about while trying to stand.

"Sorry to wake you, sir," she said, and she handed him a wooden dipper pulled from a bucket containing drinking water.

He slurped and spilled part of the fluid down his chin. "Any of them damn fools awake?"

"Aye. Bork is yonder."

"Fetch him. And some food. We need to get on with our mission."

But as Alma turned to get Bork, the twisted gnome came up behind her. She jerked back as he said, "I here."

"Anyone else awake?" the reverend asked.

"Nay, sir," Bork said, and he looked toward a group of tents about twenty feet away.

As Alma walked back to the fire, the reverend and Bork crunched through dried leaves and twigs. On the way the reverend picked up a fallen branch. As he walked, he flung it about like a club.

"Elvy sleep, there," Bork said, and he pointed to a bundle of blankets lying in the open on a pile of leaves. "Spent most of the night watching that Continental schooner."

"Goddamn it!" came a shout from under the heavy, coarse cloth when the reverend whacked the clump. "What the hell is going on? I will kill the son of a bitch who hit me," the renegade shouted.

Cloth tore and leaves flew as he tried to free himself of the ensnarling mass.

"Get on your feet, and get the rest of those bastards up," the reverend commanded, and he leaned against his club as if it were a walking stick. "Those patriot rebels will be out searching. We have business at hand and must not be found."

"Aye." Elvy scrambled to his feet and brushed himself off. "Could have been gentler," he whimpered.

"Alma," the reverend shouted at the woman as she busied herself next to the fire. "My men need breakfast. Get something to fill their bellies fast."

Within fifteen minutes twenty slovenly dressed men gathered around the campfire. Some were spitting. Others were coughing or dragging blankets or muskets as they stumbled next to a table stacked with wooden plates and mugs. As they stood waiting their turns to collect some food, several twisted about and tried to square the clothes they had slept in to gain more comfort. Some spit in their hands and smoothed their hair. Others put on caps or hats. "What in the hell is this all about?" someone said.

"It is about getting me to Halifax," the reverend said, "with my prisoner. There are patriot patrols searching for us and trying to disrupt my mission."

"An' who might your prisoner be?" a lanky new recruit named Dirk asked.

"The midshipman from the schooner *Piper*."

"What has that got to do with us?" Dirk asked. "Those patriots are after you and those renegade redcoats who have been following you for the past few days." The lanky fellow faced the others. "Our devious reverend got himself into some trouble. Now he wants us to get him out of it. This is not our fight. I don't want to feel a patriot bullet.

My loyalty is to King George and Great Britain. Not this charlatan. Are any of you with me?"

Several men stepped around or turned to look at the recruit. Several moved uneasily. No one stepped forward. All stood around nervous and mumbling. The reverend narrowed his eyes and tightened his jaw. When the fellow glanced about and saw none would follow him, he dropped his arms, shrugged his shoulders, turned around, and strode away from the rest of his supposed comrades. He headed to the path that led to the loyalist camp.

"Get it together, you scalawags," the reverend growled as Dirk walked the short distance to the forest and disappeared among the trees. "That turncoat will wish he had come with us."

The reverend fisted his hand, and the others returned their attention. He then discreetly winked at Bork and then put his right hand against the handle of the dagger stuffed in his belt.

Bork recognized the modest left twist the reverend made with his head as the signal to go, follow, and dispatch the lanky fellow. He nodded and staggered away from the front of the group. He did not hide his intention for leaving.

Several of the reverend's loyalists stared at their leader. Others shook their heads. Audible gasps and wheezes could be heard. Someone said, "Poor bastard."

Elvy raised his musket and pointed it toward the group.

"Goddamn traitor he is," the reverend snarled. "Any you other rascals thinking of joining that bastard on his trip to the afterlife?" He glared at his crew. "I think not.

That is wise. As you now realize, I have a mission, you scurvy rats. A mission I will not be deterred from."

Several men closest to the reverend nodded but moved a few steps back from him. Elvy lowered his musket.

"I want four of you." The reverend pointed to four men on his left. "Want you to return upriver to the *Rosebud* and ready her for the trip to Halifax. Make sure you are not seen. Those damn patriots do not know I have a vessel." He waved his arm. "Now be on your way."

The men ran off down the path to the Fore River. They swung their muskets at their sides.

"The rest of you, follow me and Elvy to the warehouse to collect my prisoner. Make sure you have a complement of shot and powder. Those patriots, militia, and sailors are looking for us and the prisoner. We will probably encounter them, so be on the ready."

Luce crawled up out of the shallow gully to its lip, parted the tall, dry grass and weeds growing along the edge, and looked toward the farmhouse. She crouched while she continued to peruse the meadow and up and down the road, and she waved her right arm behind her back. "You stay," she said. "Hide. Watch house. I not see militia. I go. Signal when all is right."

Henry crawled next to her. "Aye," he whispered and patted her on the back. "Be cautious."

She crept to the edge of the brush, stood, and then took long careful steps as she strolled to the back of the farmhouse. He heard her knocks on the door. After a few moments, the door opened, and a pudgy little woman seemed to pop onto a small porch. The breeze carried the sound of a happy cry as Henry watched the woman embrace Luce and pull her into the house. He relaxed but continued to keep his eyes on the cottage and its surroundings.

———•◆•———

"Lucinda! Lucinda!" Nan Peevy blubbered and squeezed Luce tightly. "My little lassie, you have returned. I became so worried when you disappeared."

Luce coughed and choked. Nan released her.

"The reverend," Luce gasped, "he not good. Want to kill my man." She stepped away from Nan and moved to the door. "He been here? Or soldiers?"

"Aye. Colonel Thompson and some of his men stopped by this morning. Said he was looking for the reverend and some midshipman. I told him the reverend had not been by for some weeks. I do not know of any midshipman. Colonel Thompson said thank you, an' he and his men left. No one else has come by."

"Colonel ask about deserter?"

Before Nan could answer, some noise that came from another room startled both women. Edward Peevy came stumbling into the kitchen. He was wearing a linen nightgown and white stocking cap. "What is going on?" He asked. "Who you talkin' to?"

Nan turned toward the old man and took hold of his shoulder. "I am talking to my friend Lucinda from the reverend's camp."

"Is that scoundrel come by?" Mr. Peevy asked. "He and his people are not my friends. Where is my gun?"

"Easy, Mr. Peevy. The reverend is not here."

"Get my musket. Go for Colonel Thompson." Edward broke free of Nan's hold and staggered toward Luce. His eyes focused on her. "Ah, Luce. Where have you been? Did not know you were here."

Nan caught him by the shoulder. "Now you return to your bed, my dear," she said. "All is well. The reverend has not stopped by."

She tried to guide him back into the bedroom.

"What is that I am smellin'?" Edward asked as he towed Nan around the kitchen.

"Smoked venison, my dear. Now let us go back to bed, and I will bring you some and a mug of tea."

Edward relaxed and allowed Nan to lead him into the bedroom.

She returned quickly. "Mr. Peevy is getting old but still thinks he is the roughneck he once was." She wiped her hands on her apron and focused on Luce. "Your man friend? Where is he, Lucinda?"

Luce returned to the house's back door. "Hidin' in the field."

"Call him in. You two must be hungry and thirsty. I have bread and, of course, venison and tea."

Luce opened the door and waved her scarf to signal Henry to come to the house. Henry peered over the grass blades and spotted Luce's arm and scarf projecting through the doorway. He rose to his feet but remained low. Holding the musket at its midpoint, he scanned his surroundings and dashed to the back porch. Luce grabbed his outstretched hand and yanked him inside the house. The rapid entry made him stumble. Luce caught him as he straightened. She wrapped her arm around his waist. "My Henry!" she said.

"Good day, Henry," Nan said. She was holding a mug of tea in his direction. "A pleasure to meet you."

Henry nodded and mumbled something incoherent while trying to catch his breath.

"You must be thirsty. Have a mug of tea." She moved toward him. Still holding the mug, she gave him a one-armed hug. "A friend of Lucinda's is welcome in the Peevy house."

"Thank you, ma'am," he said, and she released him. "But—"

"And I am sure you two are hungry," Nan interrupted. "There is bread and smoked venison." She gestured toward the table. "Please."

"Mrs. Peevy!"

Henry snapped the musket butt to his shoulder and aimed its barrel in the direction of a guttural voice.

"Is ye ever gonna bring me some vittles?"

Luce placed her hand on the musket barrel and slowly pushed it down. "Only Edward. Mr. Peevy," she whispered and touched her hand to her head. "Old."

"Soon, Mr. Peevy," Nan shouted through the doorway. "I have not forgotten, but we have guests." She moved to the table, tore a chunk of bread, and cut a slice of venison. "Please help yourselves while I take these to Mr. Peevy."

Henry set the musket against the table, tore off a hunk of bread, and stuffed it in his mouth. He chewed rapidly and sliced off a piece of venison. "We need to hurry," he said, and he filled his chops with bread and meat and masticated. "Does Nan know anything?"

"I not ask," Luce said. She was being daintier in her eating. "I tell her what we look for, but Nan say she not know Mr. Jack."

"We need to ask her if she might have seen persons doing anything unusual in the last few days."

After a few minutes, Nan returned to the kitchen. "Mr. Peevy sends his blessings. He would like to meet you, Henry."

"Nan, we eat an' now must go," Luce said.

"Aye," said Henry. "We must find my friend. He has been prisoner of this man they call the reverend."

"So Luce has said," Nan responded. "Colonel Thompson, when he stopped by, also asked about him."

"Have you seen anything unusual?" Henry asked.

Nan paced around the kitchen and then threw her hands to her mouth. "Oh my Lord! Aye. Yes. Two nights ago I saw three men dragging a fourth. Could not see who they were, but a tall, skinny fellow wore clothes I have seen the reverend wear. Went to the warehouse up the road." She again covered her mouth but this time only with her right hand. She lowered it, and her eyes were large and staring at Henry. "I was scared to tell the colonel this." She hurried back into the bedroom. "Come in here. Quickly."

When Henry and Lucy followed her, Nan was standing by the window and clutching the sides of her apron.

"The abandoned warehouse. Over there. The one standing by itself two blocks up the street with broken windows. They went into the basement. The doorway opens into the street. Only three came out."

She moved away from the window to allow Henry to look out. The bed behind them creaked and squealed.

"What chu doin' in my room?" Edward barked. "Wha'chu lookin' for?"

"Those men we saw two nights ago," Nan answered.

"They back?" Edward had rolled from under the blanket, and his naked legs were dangling over the bed. "Gimme my musket."

"Be still, Mr. Peevy."

"The man they been dragging had to be Midshipman Hollister," Henry said. "Come on, Luce. We need to get to that building. That is where they are hiding him." He took hold of Luce's arm and began pulling her into the kitchen and toward the cottage's back door. He paused a moment and grabbed his musket. "It has been two nights. Mr. Hollister needs help."

Luce pulled back and stopped Henry. She turned and thanked Nan.

"The man has been held prisoner for two or more days?" Nan said. "He will be starvin' and thirsty—perhaps injured." From a hook board next to the cupboard, she removed a leather bag and a canteen, and she swung around to the table in the center of the kitchen. She grabbed some leftovers, wrapped them in several cloths, and packed the bundle into the bag. She then dipped water from a jug and filled the canteen. "Here. You take these with you. Your midshipman will be thankful."

Luce smiled, took the satchel, and looped it over her shoulder. "Thank you, Nan. We must go now."

"Yes, yes." Nan took hold of Luce's hand, closed her eyes, and nodded.

Henry took hold of the strap holding the canteen and stepped out onto the porch. "Come on, Luce."

"You two be careful," Nan said with a troubled look on her face. Luce slowly tried to extract her hand from Nan's grip. Nan sighed and nodded. "I will inform Colonel Thompson's people of the location, when they return." She released the girl, reached behind the door, and brought out a musket. She handed it to Luce. "Take this," she said. "Edward's musket. Better you should have it than he. Be careful."

She rubbed her hands against her hips after Luce took the weapon. She stood in the doorway until the two went out of sight around the cottage.

CHAPTER 12

Lying on the cellar floor against a wall, Jack shivered when he awoke. He wiggled himself to a sitting position. Slivers of light penetrated through cracks between the building's foundation and framing, and the split dividing the doors shone on the floor and dimly illuminated Jack's prison. They also informed him of the direction the entrance faced—east. He coughed a dry cough. His throat was parched. He needed water and food, too. Last night's exertion to cut himself free had left him dehydrated and sapped of his strength.

I need water. He shook his head. His wrists ached. They'd become chafed while freeing himself. Slipping his hands and wrists under his armpits and squeezing them momentarily stifled the pain. He gazed around the room. A few feet away lay the shovel. Nearby were the hoe and a confusing pile of rope that had bound him. It was now in two pieces—one long and one short. On the far wall, he saw a dark discoloration. *That surface felt cold and wet when I was searching for a weapon.*

He rolled onto his right knee, placed his left foot on the ground, and raised himself to a standing position. To maintain his balance, he kept his hand on the wall and staggered to the wet area. *A spring I guess.*

For a moment after he placed his tongue on the wetness, he felt a cool, satisfying sensation, but it changed to a bitter, earthy taste. "Ugh."

He spat several times, and the musty taste quickly dissipated.

"It is water," he mumbled. "I need it."

Testing the seepage with his fingers, he found the crevice where the ooze was the greatest. The fresher outflow tasted sweeter and less moldy. Using his tongue, Jack was able to collect enough to relieve his parched mouth and throat. He was satisfied for the moment, and he sighed, returned to the dryer portion of the wall, and sat back against it. He laid his head back and closed his eyes.

After some minutes painful hunger contractions irritated his stomach. *Food. Need food.* He opened his eyes, shifted around, and looked about. *Those damn renegades will be returning soon. Need to defend myself.* The shovel and hoe lay exposed on the floor with the rope that had bound him tangled over and under these farm tools.

"Rope. Yes," Jack mumbled to himself and nodded. "I can fashion a trip line across the entrance. That will slow them."

He stood, walked to the rope, and picked up the longest piece. He held one of the ends in his left hand, and he spread his arms to their full width. He let the rope slide through his right hand for almost its entire length. There was about three feet of additional cord that hung down beyond his right hand and lay against his leg and on the floor. *Good.* He looked at the base of the stairs that led up to the entrance. *About four feet across. Sufficient surplus to make a proper trip.*

Jack walked to the stairs. A floor-to-ceiling post on each side held the steps in place. He tied one end of the trip line to the left post about three inches above the edge of the first step. He stretched the line across the stair, pulled it taut, and tied it to the right post. *Light outside will blind them. Will not see the trip line,* he thought.

He chewed on the inside of his lip and grinned. He returned to the middle of the cellar floor, picked up the hoe, and carried it to the stairs. Estimating the distance a man would fall when tripped, he positioned the hoe so it would lie perpendicular to the stairs with its blade up. Falling forward onto the hoe would inflict considerable damage to the victim. "Might even kill him," Jack grumbled and sneered.

He picked up the shovel, used it to balance himself, and turned. *That will stop one. Maybe two.* He looked at and admired the trap he had just set. He gripped the shovel's handle with both hands and swung it back and forth. *An ungainly sword. It will have to do.*

He held his weapon and slouched against the wall behind the stairs. *Now to wait.* His stomach grumbled and irritated him.

A scraping sound on the door above Jack startled him awake. What seemed like moments turned out to be a longer lapse of time. He noticed the light in his prison had dimmed. The sun had shifted. Its light was now shining through smaller cracks on his right. He had fallen asleep while standing up.

He tensed his muscles and readied the shovel to an attack position. Again he heard something scraping against the door. This time the sound lasted longer than the one that had earlier awakened him. It was as if someone was attempting to pull off the log that latched the door panels. Then he heard a dull thud.

Then one of the door panels was lifted, and daylight poured into the cellar.

He glanced up and to the side but saw no one. The doorway seemed clear. His chest and back tensed, and his leg muscles tautened. He gripped the shovel handle with his arms cocked. Slowly he lifted his head, looked up, and saw only sky. Then a musket barrel appeared to slide in from the side. A soft, nervous male whimper followed. "Mr. Hollister, are you down there?"

A second musket barrel moved into Jack's view from the front of the doorway, and a female voice said, "No hear sound."

"This is the building where your friend Nan said she saw the reverend and his men take someone," the male voice said. "Perhaps he is injured. Or dead."

Jack watched as the musket barrel on the side moved around to the front of the doorway. It was being pointed down the stairs. It moved forward, and Jack could see the image of a person's head appear. His eyes were having difficulty adjusting, but the object continued to rise as it approached the doorway. Then it stopped. He could now see a man's body from his belt to his head. The person wore a cocked hat and aimed the musket down the stairs.

"Mr. Hollister, are you down there? It is Seaman Holder. I have come to rescue you."

Jack relaxed but held the shovel in a position to swing it out if necessary. He watched the backlit image of who he hoped was Henry Holder shrink back from the doorway. Then he heard the top step creak as Henry stepped down on it.

"I am coming down." Henry's voice wavered.

Jack remained behind the stairs and ready to whack the person if not Henry, but his body felt weak and slightly dizzy. He pushed his forehead against a cross board, and he saw boots and legs come into view in the spaces between the steps. *The pants the man is wearing—are those typically worn by a seaman?* "Henry, stop right there," Jack said. "Come down carefully. At the second step from the bottom, jump to the floor. A trip line is set on the first step."

Continuing to hold the shovel tightly and to his side, Jack stepped out from under the stairs and moved around to the post at the base of the steps. He stood in the shadows and leaned against the support as Henry gingerly came down.

Henry raised his musket's barrel across his chest, gripped its midpoint with his left hand, and jumped to the cellar floor. A thud and flurry of ejected dust exploded around his boots when they made contact with the ground. Coming in from the outside brightness into a dark cellar, Henry was momentarily blinded. Setting the butt of the musket on the ground, he used the weapon to stabilize himself.

"You know you are at the risk of being hung," Jack said, and he stepped out of the shadows. "You are a deserter, and Captain Morris has a noose swinging from a yardarm that he would like to loop over your head."

"Aye, Mr. Hollister." After an uneasy glance, Henry lowered his head. "I…I realized a seaman's life is not for me. Hate the sea."

"Is he down there?" a soft voice called down from beyond the doorway.

"Who is with you?" Jack grumbled, and he glanced up to see a musket barrel wavering through the doorway.

"Luce. She has been helping me. Without her I would not have been able to find you. She also helped me avoid others looking for you—militia, sailors, renegades, and that damn reverend."

"Call your friend down, but warn her to be careful." Jack pointed to the trip line and the strategically placed hoe. "She needs to avoid the traps."

"Yes. Mr. Hollister is down here. But he has also rigged a snag to stop the reverend. So you need to come down carefully. Jump to the floor from the second step from the bottom."

"So you know of the reverend?" Jack asked. "That son of a bitch attacked me and Gaspar a couple nights ago. Do not know if Gaspar is alive or dead."

"Aye. The reverend kept me prisoner," Henry said, and he watched Luce step down on the top step. "Was plannin' to kill me, but Luce saved me. She is a good partner."

Luce lowered the barrel of her weapon and was about the place her foot on the next step when a musket ball splintered the doorframe in front of her. She jumped back, lost her balance, and stumbled. She flailed, dropped the weapon, and came tumbling down the steps. The leather bag containing food flew off her shoulder and sailed over her head. It landed in the cellar a few feet from where Jack stood. The trip line slowed her progress, but she flipped over it and hit the floor on her side. The musket fell across her back just as Jack and Henry, who were trying to catch her or deflect her body from the hoe's blade, caught her. Both had their hands on her the moment she hit the floor. They lifted Luce to her feet and held her up.

"You all right?" Henry shouted.

"Shoulder. Hurts."

"Who in the hell is out there?" Jack's hand felt warm and wet. He spread it open in front of him. "Blood. You are bleeding but not from a bullet. Too little blood. You abraded your shoulder when you fell."

He motioned for Henry to take Luce deeper into the cellar, picked up the musket, and checked the tautness of the trip line. Assured his trap was still secure, he nodded and stepped back into the darkness. A couple more musket balls hit the building and doorframe.

"We are under attack," Jack groaned.

"Reverend and his men," Henry whispered. "He is the one who knows you are here."

With Luce secure in a far, dark corner, the two men took cover behind some barrels stacked against a side wall.

"Hope you brought powder and shot," Jack said.

"Aye." Henry felt for the satchel slung over his shoulder and lifted it. "Damn! The bag with food and the canteen Luce carried is lying on the floor near the door."

———•·•·•———

Bork pointed his walking stick up the street and yelled, "Look there! Luce is standin' o'er there. Cellar door opened. Her musket aimed down the stairs."

The reverend and Elvy ran to his side. Several of the reverend's other men gathered around.

"Damn bitch has returned," the reverend grumbled, and he gnashed his teeth. "Found our prisoner. Shoot her!"

Elvy raised his musket, took aim, and fired.

"No wonder those redcoats kicked your ass out. You cannot shoot worth a damn," the reverend yelled.

The reverend grabbed the musket of another man standing nearby and fired it at the same time one of his other loyalists took a shot.

"Nay! I hit her. In the back," Elvy grunted, and he angrily thumped another load down his musket's barrel. "Saw her gun toss. She fall back an' into the cellar."

"What I saw," the reverend growled, and he uttered his words slowly, "is your shot hit the building. Saw wood explode and splinter two feet in front of her. Startled her, you dumb shit, and she stumbled down the steps." He butted his musket on the ground, pulled off the thumping rod, and reloaded. "Get over there, and clean up the mess.

That damn midshipman is probably near dead anyway. Bork did not leave him any water."

"Sergeant Dailey, someone is shooting," a soldier shouted from the scattered militia trampling across the brushy meadow toward the Peevy cottage.

Many stopped and stood. Their eyes moved to the sergeant or where the sound of the shots came from.

"Aye," Dailey yelled. He raised his arm and gestured for formation. He then moved his arm and pointed in the direction of the gunfire. "Let us get over there. Posthaste."

The troops grouped with muskets readied into a disorganized horizontal line. Dailey was in the lead, and they advanced to the street that led to the old warehouses. As they neared, the sergeant signaled for the troops to spread out and move stealthily. When the patrol reached the head of the street that several cottages and old buildings faced, Dailey motioned for all to halt. The group took cover next to buildings, in doorways, and behind anything stacked on the street.

"Over there," a militiaman said, and he pointed toward some commotion about a block and a half down the street. "Sergeant, over there. Men with muskets and pitchforks. Across from that solitary building."

The sergeant called to two of his soldiers and three Abenaki Indians. "I want one of you to go with each patrol that flanks the warehouse. When all are in position, you

Abenaki signal. Whistle, do a birdcall, or grunt. The signal doesn't matter as long as the three of you agree." He turned to the other two men. "Each of you select a dozen men. Sneak up there, and establish a line on each side of that warehouse. I will lead a patrol up the street from this end. We need to surround that building and those damned loyalists. Now get going."

As soon as the flanking patrol headed off behind the buildings, Dailey called to a wiry boy. "Terry, go to Greele Tavern. Find Colonel Thompson. Tell him we have found the reverend and his men. Make sure you are not seen. Be careful."

Terry nodded and ran off. Dailey scattered his men and had them sneak forward along the abandoned houses, sheds, and buildings. He and two others took cover in a doorway. A few yards ahead, a large-headed man accompanied a lanky man in a long black coat. They both bent over, carried muskets, and scrambled across the street. Limping behind them, the hunchback followed. The sergeant also noted the reverend's other men ahead. They were hiding behind stacks of lumber and in doorways. A group of them also squatted against a building across from an open cellar. He looked around at his men. They were all hidden. He felt comfortable. They had not been seen. Dailey crouched and readied his weapon.

A distinctive call of a northern flicker came from the far end of the block near the warehouse. Within a moment there was another, but this one was closer. Dailey looked over at his Abenaki scout. He was lying next to a walkway. The man nodded and cupped his hands around his mouth. The next sound Dailey heard was a rapid string of "wicki-wicki-wicki-wicki" ending in a loud "kleee."

———•◦•———

The doors covering the cellar remained open. No one inside could see what was going on outside, but an occasional indistinct voice could be heard. Both Jack and Henry had their muskets trained on the entrance.

Henry rested his weapon on the barrel he was hiding behind, and then he scrambled to the middle of the cellar to retrieve the satchel lying on the floor. He hurried back to the cover of the barrel. "There is some smoked venison and bread in this bag. Brought it for you." He handed it to Jack along with the canteen. "A Mistress Peevy sent it. She is Luce's friend. Lives in a cottage nearby."

Jack took the food and nodded. "We must thank her," he said, and he chewed off a piece of venison. He tore apart the chunk of bread and was about to shove it into his mouth when he heard a bunch of whoops and hollers and several musket blasts. "Someone is shooting outside but not at us."

Jack took a gulp of water from the canteen. He swallowed and readied himself for an attack. Henry did the same.

"Get in that cellar an' drag that navy kid out. Want him alive. He's worth a fine ransom. Kill whoever else is down there," a gruff voice outside commanded. "Those damn militiamen have found us. They have us..."

Several musket blasts drowned the voice. Two shots splintered the side of the building above the doorway, and a man jumped down. He held his musket high, landed on a middle step, and brought his weapon forward.

"Hold your fire," Jack whispered. "He is blinded by sunlight. Cannot see us."

The intruder lowered his head and cautiously stepped down the stairs. When he reached the second step from the bottom, his eyes must have adjusted to the darkness because he aimed his musket toward the casks and barrels where Jack and Henry hid. He sidestepped with his right foot to the lowest step, twisted, and caught his toe under the trip rope. He attempted to yank it free, and he stumbled and reeled. He flung the barrel of the musket toward the ceiling and pulled the trigger. The blast sent splinters of wood and dirt onto Jack and Henry as the man fell onto his knees, but inertia pushed him forward toward the hoe's blade. Its handle bounced up and down as his body fell onto it. He uttered a gurgling scream when the blade cut through his neck.

Before the dust ejected by the fall could settle, Luce was next to the man with the shovel blade poised above the back of the man's neck. She held her position. "Trap work," she said.

Outside the shooting and hoopla continued.

"They will be sending another," Jack said, "before the militia can rescue us. We must be ready."

Jack took another couple bites of venison and bread. Though his musket rested on the cask, its barrel was aimed at the doorway. Henry wiped his brow and crouched against the wall. The body of the reverend's loyalist lay between him and the entrance. He scanned the cellar, and then he heard a scrape and clunk somewhere in front of him. "Luce, where are you?"

"I here. Behind steps. There passage here. It hidden." She grunted as another scrape sounded. "Blocked by stones and wood." Jack and Henry could hear her chopping, scratching, and digging and her mousy chattering. "I know these places. I hide in them many times." Then she increased the volume of her voice. "Remember, Henry? We sneak through broken cellars when I save you."

Then they heard Luce groan, a longer scrape, and a couple thuds as if several boards were tossed to the ground. A musty, fishy odor released from the sealed compartment wafted through the cellar.

Henry turned to Jack and said, "Yes. Luce was the one who helped me elude the crew from the *Piper*. She guided my escape through those burned-out buildings. That is how I met her."

"Room at end of passage." Luce's voice sounded muffled as if in a tunnel.

The gunfire on the street seemed to escalate. Henry and Jack saw partial images of men dressed like farmers or tattered British soldiers. Others wore worn-out buckskin jackets. Thy all scampered back and forth near the entrance. Then a gruff voice shouted, "Elvy, get your ass in there and kill those bastards. Goddam patriots have us flanked. We are surrounded. Hold your ground."

Before the reverend's command ended, a torso with a large head covered in a mass of unruly black hair appeared at the top of the stairs. He was wearing a soiled, shabby red military coat. He carried a musket in his right hand and a pistol in his left.

Without a second thought, Jack fired his musket. A splatter of red exploded from the center of Elvy's chest. He flipped backward and slid down the stairs. Both his weapons bounced down with him. He lay in a bleeding heap a few feet from the other intruder.

"Bastard from Greele Tavern," Jack said.

"Oh my," Luce said, and she came around from behind the stairs. "Mr. Jack shoot bad man. Henry, he one of four who came to Reverend's camp night we escape."

"Aye," Henry answered. "So you found another room in this basement?"

Luce nodded, and Jack said, "Good! That space will work in our favor. The militia and sailors do not know you are here, and I am not going to tell them. They are looking for me.

"I want you two to hide in that secret space. Make sure to take the leather bags you brought with you and that musket Luce carried. Cover the entrance well. It is in a dark corner behind the stairs. They will not search. I can explain the deaths of these renegades with ease. Stay hidden until after dark. Then go. I wish you and your lady good lives."

Henry was astonished, but he grabbed Jack's hand and started shaking it. "Mr. Hollister, I knew you were a good man. I will never forget you." He threw his arms around Jack and gave him a tight hug. The two men exchanged slaps on the back and then stepped away from each other.

Henry continued to hold Jack's shoulders. "Never forget you, sir. Perhaps we will meet again someday. God be with you."

"Aye," Jack said. "Perhaps. When you leave here, though, do not go home. The navy will be looking for you. You are still a deserter. I suggest you make your way west when you leave this place."

Luce ran to Jack and hugged him. "You good man."

She released Jack and collected everything that would suggest anyone but Jack had been in the cellar. Then she and Henry secreted themselves in the passageway behind the stairs. Jack heard them shoving the stones and boards back into the entrance to the room behind the stairs. He continued to hear screams and yells outside, but the shooting ended. After a few moments, Sergeant Dailey, Colonel Thompson, and Sergeant Turner blocked the sunlight entering the cellar.

"Midshipman Hollister, are you down there?" one of them yelled.

"Aye. Along with two dead renegades."

Sergeant Turner stopped in his tracks when he heard a muffled cough. "Where did that come from?" he asked. "I believe someone is hiding down here."

Jack snapped his hand up to his mouth and made a couple deep-throated grunts. "Sorry, Sergeant. That was me. Have not had much to eat or drink in the last couple days. And the air is not pleasant down here."

"Aye, sir," Turner said, and he called up the stairs to send two people down to help Midshipman Hollister out of the cellar.

"Send four people down," yelled Colonel Thompson, "and have them bring a litter. The man has had a devil of a time. He needs attention. Is Dr. Voors out there?"

"Nay, sir! He's en route," someone shouted down.

Seamen Nightjar, Stokes, and Tyler came stomping down the steps. Another sailor dragging a litter followed.

"Mr. Tyler," one of the sailors said when the group reached the bottom, "methinks a small fellow as yourself might be hurtin' if he carries the midshipman from this place. We come to help." He then focused on the others. "The boy can hold Mr. Hollister's hand. Kinda comfort him as we carries him up."

Tyler curled his lips, narrowed his eyes, and glared at the man. "I am capable!"

"Aye," Nightjar said, and he put his large, weathered hand on the young sailor's shoulder. "That you are, but Seaman Richter is only lookin' out for your welfare, my friend. He means no ill. Carryin' a litter with a man's body shiftin' about on it up some stairs takes some heavy handlin'. Mr. Hollister will need some comfortin' on his journey."

"Do not need any help," Jack said as he moved away from the wall he leaned against. "Just a bit sore and hungry, but I can walk out of here on my own."

Seaman Richter shrugged and rolled up the litter. As he started toward the cellar's entrance, he said, "Tyler, you can let Mr. Hollister lean on your shoulder while he walks up the stairs. That'll make you useful.

Tyler relaxed, nodded, and stepped back. Nightjar removed his jacket and handed it to Jack.

"Come, Mr. Tyler," Jack said as put on the jacket. He chuckled, bent down, and put his hand on the seaman's shoulder. "Be my crutch." The two started up the steps. "For a little fellow, you are a sturdy one."

"Aye, sir. That I am."

Tyler handed him his canteen, when he and Jack stepped onto the street. The boy reached into the leather bag that hung from his shoulder and pulled out a couple mangled biscuits. He handed them to the midshipman as the two walked to a nearby porch.

"Is Gaspar alive?" Jack asked as he munched on the biscuits.

"Aye, sir," Tyler answered. "He is recuperating at the camp. Probably feelin' ornery 'cause he wants to be with us. He's ready to kill that reverend."

"Aye, my little friend. He probably still has a bad headache." Jack stood. "Thank you, men, for freeing me of my prison." Jack moved to the edge of the porch and sat down. His legs hung down. "Is the reverend in chains?"

One of the men flipped his head toward the far end of the street. "Aye, sir. Mr. Dailey and his people are holding all the renegades prisoner. Reverend is being a bit rancorous," the man said, and he smiled as he turned and followed his friends away.

Colonel Thompson and Sergeant Turner came up to the porch. "I do not want to deal with all those prisoners," Thompson said. "Have not the room or supplies. If I were a tyrant, I would bury all those bastards. They are good people though. Loyal to the crown but hard workers, and they are all searchin' for something better—as we all are. Just followed the wrong minister. I will order Dailey to send them to their families and farms. Dealing with that reverend, they have had sufficient punishment."

"What will be the fate of the reverend and his henchmen?" asked Jack.

"The man is a murderer," Thompson answered. "We will have to deal with him. The hunchback—the oafish fellow called Bork—is harmless. With a proper master, he can be contained and of some use, but he will take looking after."

"Not apprehending that damn deserter has displeased Captain Morris," Jack said. "He might enjoy being able to hang someone from a yardarm."

"Capital idea," Thompson responded. "A trial and hanging aboard a Continental navy vessel would keep things proper. Satisfy the officiaries. Captain Morris is an officer in the Continental navy. Our country's commander in chief, George Washington, legally appointed him." He clapped his hands together, released several gratifying sighs, and continued. "Better than a bunch of rebels such as us hangin' someone. Satisfy all manner of world treaties." The colonel inflated his chest, and a satisfied grin was on his face. He looked down at Jack. "Captain Morris has been notified. He, his executive officer, and the ship's doctor will be here momentarily. A capital plan you have suggested, Mr. Hollister."

"Thank you, sir. I am sure Captain Morris will be in agreement."

"Mr. Turner," Colonel Thompson said as he marched off the porch, "come with me, and I will notify Sergeant Dailey to release the prisoners. You and your sailors can take charge of that reprobate minister. I am going to enjoy seeing him hang."

———•◦•———

The November day seemed to have passed quickly, and winter was again making its inroad. The men did not notice, but a canopy of flat and curling pewter-colored clouds covered the sky and dropped the temperature. A cold northern breeze caused those in coats to tighten them about themselves. With the graying sky and the hidden sun dropping in the west, daylight dimmed. The smell of inland balsams scented the air.

Over an hour had passed since the militia had rescued Jack. The reverend and Bork sat bound in the middle of the street near the building where the midshipman had been held prisoner. Several militiamen and sailors stood guard over them. Tyler sat near Jack and tried to tend to his needs.

Across the street Colonel Thompson caught Jack's attention as the colonel mounted his horse and trotted away toward two approaching riders. The midshipman recognized Captain Morris and Lieutenant Whitehall. Then he noticed Dr. Voors. He was also on horseback, and he came around the far corner. The troop of Continental Marines followed the doctor. The colonel joined Captain Morris and the lieutenant. When the three came abreast of where Jack sat, they reined their horses across from him. Voors guided his horse to where Jack and Tyler rested. He dismounted, removed his bag from behind the saddle, and walked over to the midshipman.

"You look not much worse for wear," he said. "A bit emaciated perhaps. I see you have a nasty knot behind your right ear." He took hold of Jack's head and rotated it for a better look at the injury. "Aye. Considerably bruised. Much caked blood and discoloration. Can you see straight?"

"I see quite well. Though my head does hurt."

"No doubt." Voors gestured to a man nearby to approach. "I would like to borrow your canteen." The man handed the doctor his flask. "Thank you."

The doctor removed a cloth from his bag and doused it with water. He applied the dripping cloth to Jack's injury and gently cleaned the area. After he finished, Voors again reached into his satchel, removed a large vial, and poured a viscous fluid onto Jack's injury. "This might sting a bit, but it will help heal those bruises."

Jack winced and gritted his teeth but sat straight and motionless.

"You are a tolerant young man," Voors commented, and he swathed another strip of cloth around the midshipman's head. "You fared better than your master gunner. He will not have use of his left arm for some weeks. That miscreant's sword made a clean incision into his shoulder. Luckily the stab did not cut anything vital."

"It will be good to see Mr. Gaspar," Jack said.

"Soon, Mr. Hollister. He awaits at Greele Tavern. Captain Morris has secured a carriage to transport the two of you to the cutter. It should be arriving momentarily."

"By God, Mr. Hollister," Captain Morris said as he approached the porch. "You look as if you were in a battle. The enemy lost two of their men. By your hand I understand. And we captured that blackguard preacher. I believe we...you have done well, young sir."

"Thank you, Captain."

Captain Morris gestured toward the reverend and called, "Sergeant Turner, put that man in chains, and have the marines march him to the wharf. A cutter awaits to take him and all of you to the *Piper*. Colonel Thompson's militiamen will take charge of the hunchback. Treat him decently."

"By your leave, sir," Dr. Voors said, and he mounted his horse. "The midshipman will survive. I will go and look in on Mr. Gaspar. He is in the wagon being delayed for the moment up the street."

"Aye. The colonel is dismissing the prisoners. Thank you for taking care of Mr. Hollister."

Voors nodded and trotted off toward the confused excitement the reverend's men were creating. Colonel Thompson told the prisoners to go home and tend to their families and farms. The colonel mounted his horse and rode up next to the wagon. The surgeon halted and waited. He joined Thompson and the wagon when it came abreast. They all reined up near Jack. Tyler assisted the midshipman aboard.

"*Bonne journée, mon ami,*" Gaspar said as Jack got himself comfortable in the back of the wagon.

"It is a good day indeed, Mr. Gaspar. Did not expect you to be in the wagon. We were to pick you up at the tavern. I had hoped to see Kara before we sailed." Jack wrapped his arm around the master gunner. "You appear well. I was worried those renegades had killed you."

"Aye. Gaspar not easy to kill. Mlle Kara sends you her thoughts." The gunner puffed out his chest and smiled. "*Et vous*, get knock on head. *Très dangereux aussi.* Soon we be safe on ship though."

"Aye, my friend. It will be good to rest in our own hammocks."

Captain Morris mounted his horse and gave the command to get under way. "Our cutter awaits, and we have a trial and hanging in the morn. Let us be off." He turned and faced Colonel Thompson. "I will send a boat ashore at eight hundred hours to transport you and your officers to the *Piper* for our gruesome duty. Until then I bid you adieu."

Colonel Thompson nodded.

CHAPTER 13

The morning of November 26, 1775, lightened and exposed a cold mist hanging just above the water. A dark, crumpled steel-colored blanket covered the sky, and occasional flakes and weak swirls of snow tainted the atmosphere. A soft offshore breeze kept the schooner *Piper* pulling tightly against its anchors.

Jack poked his head through the forward hatchway, glanced aft along the deck, sniffed, and sighed. The salty air momentarily burned his nostrils. He brushed the back of his hand across his nose, closed the hatch doors, and returned below. "A grim day," Jack mumbled, and he tightened his jacket against the chill.

He continued aft to Captain Morris's cabin. When the midshipman knocked on the captain's door, he heard Morris's calm response. "Enter."

Upon entering, the aroma of strong coffee comforted him as did the elevated heat in the room. This was the first time Jack noticed the captain's little iron fireplace built into the cabin's stern wall. An abundant quantity of heat radiated from the small fire inside this box. Morris noticed the midshipman's curiosity. "Franklin stove," he said. "Dr. Benjamin's refinement of the old-fashioned fireplace. Ideal for a vessel. Knew it would be cold at sea, so I had them install one when we had this vessel refitted for battle. Excuse me a moment." The captain moved some papers he had scattered on his desk to the side and sat back in his chair. "Coffee, my boy? Had the cook brew up a pot from the remains of our stores. Take a seat, Midshipman."

"Aye, sir. Many thanks." Jack removed his jacket, reached back, and pulled a chair to the front of the desk.

"I summoned you to my cabin, Midshipman Hollister, first to learn how you feel and are getting along. And second to determine if a rumor being bandied about by those prisoners Thompson freed and that damned reverend is true. Hearsay has it a young woman rescued you." Captain Morris turned and reached to a table behind him, lifted the coffeepot, and poured Jack a cup. He leaned forward, pushed the cup at Jack, put his elbows on the desk, and looked into the midshipman's eyes. "When Whitehall first questioned that reverend, all he did was grunt. I suppose he figured we would eventually turn him loose because he was some sort of missioner to the Lord. Arrogant bastard. When he realized we would not acquiesce to his bilge, he finally said one of his men had fired a shot because he had spotted a girl standing next to the cellar door—which he said was open. All the reverend would own up to is that he saw someone tumble through the doorway after the musket was fired. Then he said, 'If that damn fool had not fired that shot, we would never have been caught.' The militia found only two male bodies but no other living person in that cellar when they came to rescue you. Was there anyone else in the prison with you, Mr. Hollister?"

Jack sat back in his chair, rubbed his eyes, and scratched his head. He looked up at the captain and then lowered his head in thought. He relaxed his hands, grabbed his knees, and rocked back. "Aye. There was an Indian girl who unlocked and opened the door. I did not learn her name, but she told me an old woman who lived in a nearby cottage had said she saw three men drag another into the basement of that abandoned warehouse some nights ago. When they exited only three came out. The old woman said she recognized the reverend and knew the scoundrel was up to no good again. She told the Indian girl to go look. The Indian girl brought me some biscuits and water and was about to come down the stairs when the shooting started." Jack sipped his coffee.

"Was this Indian girl injured?"

"Slightly. A bruised shoulder. From a fall."

"Where did she disappear to?"

"The girl seemed to know the basements of many of the old buildings. She had been hiding and living in them on her own to avoid the reverend. He had kidnapped her some time before, she said, from a distant inland tribe, but she had escaped his camp. The old woman had befriended her and provided occasional food and comfort." Jack sighed and rubbed his right arm.

"Where did the musket you had come from?" the captain asked, and he raised his cup, clasped it, and contemplated it. He raised his eyebrows. "I am sure your captors did not provide it."

"It came from the renegade who tripped on my trap and killed himself when he fell on the hoe's blade. Dropped his weapon. Also he carried bags of shot and powder."

"Aye. Of course." Morris glanced to the side of his desk and pushed the edge of a sheet of paper back into the pile.

"I knew as soon as the shooting stopped, either the renegades or militiamen would come into the basement. I told the girl she might be in some danger. Perhaps she would be interrogated or even shot. I told her to hide."

"Ah, yes," Captain Morris said, and he relaxed back into his chair. "That renegade reverend mentioned the Indian girl had helped our deserter escape that loyalist nest of miscreants. Did she say anything about Seaman Holder?"

Jack glanced across the room to a small porthole and shook his head. "Nay, sir."

Captain Morris placed his hands on the edge of the desk, nodded, and stood. "Thank you, Midshipman. The questions have ended. We need to get our present affairs under way. Mr. Gaspar will remain in your gun group. Though you know he will not be able to take any physical duties. However, he is an expert gunner, so he will function as your counsel."

"Thank you, Captain. That will make Mr. Gaspar happy."

"Aye. A good man he is." Morris moved to the porthole and glanced out. "It is snowing." He stepped away from the porthole. "We have a trial and hanging to attend to. Go on deck, Midshipman, and launch a boat and crew to collect Colonel Thompson and his crew. We will need witnesses. Besides they want to see that scoundrel hang as much as I do. I would like to have these proceedings completed by the noon hour. After, we can make ready to sail on the high tide."

———•—•—•———

"Cutter returning," the *Piper*'s boatswain yelled.

Jack's jacket was secured tightly around him and his collar turned up, and he stood in the chains. He liked to stand on this little platform off the starboard side near the bow from where their leadsman threw his line to measure the water's depth. His breath clouded in front of his face, and he watched the longboat approach. Stokes, Widget, Marvel, and another seaman shipped their oars on command and allowed the vessel to drift toward the *Piper*. The coxswain pushed the rudder to larboard, turned the cutter's bow around to starboard, and brought its hull parallel with the schooner. A seaman sitting forward stood caught a line thrown from the mother ship and secured it to the tender's bow. The coxswain snatched a stern line tossed to him and pulled the longboat against the schooner's hull. Several of the *Piper*'s crew removed an amidships section of gunwale that closed off the gangway, and then they released a rope ladder over the side. Captain Morris and Lieutenant Whitehall stood militarily at the entrance to greet the passengers. The light snowfall had ceased.

Colonel Thompson supported himself by holding onto the cutter's rail, rose, grabbed onto the ladder, and stepped onto its first rung. Sergeant Dailey, a minister, and three militiamen moved about and readied themselves to board the schooner. Midshipman Jack Hollister moved next to the lieutenant and became part of the greeting party.

Colonel Thompson grabbed the *Piper*'s rail, released his left foot from the rope ladder, and pulled himself onto the schooner's deck. He moved forward to face Captain Morris.

"Welcome aboard, Colonel," Morris said, and he extended his right hand. "I wish this was more of a social visit, but we have a grim task before us."

"Aye, Captain." Thompson clasped the captain's hand and accepted the welcome. "I should mention I am not comfortable aboard a vessel. Its movement bothers me."

"Though the *Piper*'s movement at anchor today is insignificant," Morris said, "we will proceed quickly."

When the colonel's other people arranged themselves on the schooner's deck, the captain motioned for Jack to approach him. He then whispered something in Jack's ear.

"Aye, sir," Jack said, and he snapped to attention, rotated on the ball of his left foot, and stepped toward the after deckhouse.

Morris nodded, turned to his guests, and said, "Please follow me below to my cabin. We will discuss the proceedings there." When Thompson and he reached the lower deck, the captain used his right arm to gesture to the side. "I have had my people prepare space down here to hold the trial."

Morris, Thompson, Whitehall, and the minister proceeded to the captain's cabin.

"Though Dr. Voors is the ship's surgeon," Captain Morris continued, "he was educated at Harvard and says he knows a smattering of the law. So I appointed him to represent the reverend. You, Colonel, Lieutenant Whitehall, and I will arbitrate the case. By the way that scoundrel's real name is Enoch Wrack. I have heard of a person by the name Jacob Wrack. Colonel, you most likely have as well. The barmaid Kara Balch and Mr. Hollister mentioned him to me. The redcoats have issued a writ for his capture. Seems that fellow murdered one of their own in Halifax back in the spring and escaped. Perhaps we are dealing with a relative of this Jacob Wrack."

"Ah," answered Colonel Thompson. "I have heard of this fellow, but I do not believe his shadow has ever fallen upon our soil."

"Perhaps not, but we will deal with the one we have. Unfortunately, except for Mr. Hollister, we do not have any other witnesses to his deeds."

Colonel Thompson entered the captain's cabin, removed his tricorne, and scratched his head. He seated himself near the captain's desk. "There is that hunchbacked accomplice of his, but I do not believe him reliable." Then he rapidly nodded, threw up his arms, and stood. "Treason! That scoundrel led a subversion. We can try him for treason."

A smile crossed Captain Morris's face, and he chuckled. "In our opinion that might be correct." He paused for a moment. "Except we are not a sovereign power. That scoundrel, as well as we, are all members of Great Britain.

True to fact we are the traitors and revolutionaries. We are rebelling against King George and his cronies."

"Nevertheless we are at war with those damn redcoats. They destroyed our village, and that blackguard attacked your man." The colonel pounded his fist on the captain's desk. "We need to be rid of him." Thompson closed his eyes, slouched back in his chair, and then snapped forward. "Aha! We do have a witness. He is a prisoner in my camp. Lieutenant, your people captured the bastard at the reverend's camp. Name is McLeod. Wounded but alive. We could use him if need be. What say you, Captain?"

"He is the redcoat deserter Mr. Gaspar shot," Lieutenant Whitehall said. "I do not know if he would be of much use. He had been in the reverend's camp for only a day or two." Whitehall scratched his chin. "It would take some hours to fetch him, and I believe our evidence will still only be circumstantial."

"The lieutenant is correct, Colonel," Captain Morris said. "And I do not want to delay sailing any longer than necessary. Let us try this son of a bitch with what we do have. I believe we will be successful. What say you, Mr. Whitehall?"

"I agree with both of you. Though our evidence is scant, we are quite sure he led the people that left Mr. Gaspar for dead, kidnapped Mr. Hollister, and killed at least one of those redcoat deserters. He is not a loyalist or a patriot. He deals only for his own pleasure." The lieutenant slouched back, lowered his head, and grabbed his chin as if pondering. Then his arm snapped up. "Sergeant Turner mentioned the Abenaki helping in the search for

Mr. Hollister. They found a footprint around the body of the renegade who had his throat cut. They found the same footprint where Mr. Hollister and Gaspar were attacked."

"I am sure there were many footprints in the area," Captain Morris said. "What is so outstanding about this particular footprint those savages found?"

"The sole of the right boot has a damaged edge. It is as if some animal took a bite out of it."

"Was that print seen somewhere else, Lieutenant?"

"Aye. Turner said he also saw a similar image in the dirt on the street where we captured the reverend's people."

Captain Morris scratched his head. "Aye. It is a piece of evidence." He sighed and shook his head. "But if we cannot find who was wearing the boot, it will not help us hang that son of a bitch."

Colonel Thompson tightly pursed his lips. A furrow crossed his forehead. He grunted. "If need be we can use this footprint evidence as a ploy."

The minister shuffled nervously in his chair. He closed his eyes and shook his head. "Fabrication," he mumbled. "This trial is a farce."

Colonel Thompson glanced at the man of the cloth he had brought with him and said, "You have sat quietly, my friend. Now you are mumbling. Praying are you?"

"A disciple of the devil the prisoner is. Most accept this, but I am not sure I should be involved in his conviction." The minister barely choked out the words, took a deep breath, and then said more clearly, "I will pray for him and accept penitence if he has any. That is what you brought me here for, Colonel Thompson." The minister straightened in his chair. "I will also pray for your souls, for I do not believe in taking any life. But in this case, I feel I must look the other way. The earth and our colonies have no place for such an onerous despot." The minister bowed his head.

"That is all I ask," Colonel Thompson said. He looked up at Captain Morris. "I believe we have our case, Captain. Shall we proceed with the trial? I am getting a bit uneasy aboard your vessel. The air is tight, and the smell, it does not agree with my digestion."

"As you wish, Colonel," Captain Morris said. "Let us make way to our court."

———•◦•———

Midshipman Hollister entered the crew's galley with his jacket slung over his shoulder. He found Sergeants Turner and Dailey sitting at the table and having cups of coffee.

"The last of our coffee supply," Turner said.

"Captain poured me a cup earlier," answered Jack. "I can do without. Mr. Turner, the captain wants you to have a detail string up the gallows from the yardarm of the fore-mast. Says the trial will be short. Wants the hanging over before the end of the forenoon watch."

"We should get on to it then," the sergeant said. "Swig your cup, Dailey. You can help. A landlubber such as you can learn that we marines know as much as sailors do." He chuckled. "Nothing hard. You will enjoy it."

Sergeant Dailey wriggled away from the bench and picked up his coffee cup. "Aye. Something I have always wanted to do. Test my sea legs. Mind if I take my coffee?"

"Nay. But keep a tight grip on your mug. Your legs should do fine. There is not enough chop on the water to bob a cork."

The two started for the ladder that led to the deck. "You going to join us, Mr. Hollister?"

Jack nodded, slipped on his jacket, and buttoned it. He followed Turner and Dailey to the deck.

"We will only need two or three swabs to rig the gallows. Simple process," Sergeant Turner said as he climbed the ladder. "We will enlist whomever we can catch on the deck to climb into the rigging. For the gallows all we need are a block and a length of sturdy rope. Sergeant Dailey, do you know how to tie a hangman's noose?"

"Never had to do that," Dailey said.

"You, Midshipman Hollister?"

"Aye, Mr. Turner," Jack said. "Used to make them with pieces of string when I was a boy." He paused and looked around. "While you are selecting the tackle, I will find a couple able-bodied seamen to climb the rigging."

"Many thanks, Mr. Hollister. I will teach this landlubber." Turner walked to a rack along the starboard rail where several unused blocks hung. He pointed to a six-inch pulley with a single sheave. "Mr. Dailey, take this one. A seamen can hang it from the yardarm after a line is threaded through it." Turner then removed a coil of line hanging nearby. "There is about one hundred feet here. It will do."

Dailey held the pulley, and Turner passed one end of the rope between the chocks, and he laid the rope into the sheave's groove. Jack returned with two seamen. When the sergeant had threaded about twenty feet of line through the pulley, he handed the simple block and tackle to one of the sailors. The lanky young man tied the block to his belt, jumped onto the starboard rail, and climbed up the ratlines. Turner held one end of the line, and the sailor's partner followed behind his buddy into the rigging to ensure the loose, trailing portion of the rope did not tangle. At the yardarm the sailor slid out along the boom and secured the pulley midway between the foremast and shrouds. The two men finished and climbed back down to the deck.

Turner secured the strand of rope hanging nearest the foremast to a belaying pin. He took the other end and pulled down the slack. He took the free end in his right hand and flaked about three feet of rope onto the deck in a tight S. With his left hand, he grabbed the middle of the S and crimped the three strands to produce a large bow tie. With his right hand, he then took hold of the rope a few inches from its end and started securely winding the line. He did so in a linear series of single loops around the pinched strands he held in his left hand.

"Now take note of this fact, Mr. Dailey," Turner said with a snicker. "A hangman's noose meant for a person has to have thirteen loops. The unlucky number—for the convicted...the devil's number."

"Aye," Dailey said. He and Jack grinned.

Turner continued to loop the rope around the strands. Now watch what I do."

He spread the left bow of the tie open, and he pushed the remaining piece held in his right hand through the bow. He gripped the stub down with his left with which he continued to clutch the loops and the strands they surrounded. He then took hold of the bow on the right side of the tie, and he cinched the left side tight by pulling the piece of line forming the right side of the noose. He opened the bow sufficiently so it could easily be put over the victim's head by pulling the line on the left side of the noose.

"Finished," he said. He lifted the noose and dangled it in front of him. "Either of you want to try it on for size?"

Jack and Dailey grimaced and shook their heads.

Turner grabbed the strand of rope tied to the belaying pin, loosened it, and pulled it down to raise the noose to about a foot above a tall man's height. He ordered one of the sailors to bring a stepping stool. When the sailor did, the sergeant tied a separate line to its legs, ran it out on deck, pulled it, and said, "When the hangman pulls, the victim dances."

The stool tumbled toward him. Jack scratched and shook his head.

Sergeant Turner replaced the stool. "Mr. Hollister, you can go tell the captain we have constructed his gallows."

"Aye. Thank you, Sergeant," Jack said.

He walked to the after gangway and descended to the lower deck.

The space belowdecks in the amidships area of the Continental navy schooner *Piper* was normally used for meetings, as a crew's mess, or as a hospital when necessary. It was converted now into a makeshift courtroom. A medium table was placed near the forward bulkhead. To make the scene official, a crewman hung the white flag embossed with the image of a fir tree on the bulkhead. Between the flag and table, three chairs provided seating for the court's magistrates. Chairs were placed in front of the table for the defendant, his attorney, and Colonel Thompson's minister. Extra tables were moved against the side bulkheads. The benches where crewmen sat filled the middle of this cramped space. Since no room remained for an aisle, the tribunal had to enter the court through the forward hatchway. The after hatchway provided access to the courtroom for the audience and any witnesses. These men could sit on the benches in the middle of the room or on the tables along the sides.

When Jack dropped down off the ladder from the deck, he walked the short distance to the amidships courtroom. He recognized Gaspar by the sling that crossed his back. The master gunner, Widget, and Midshipman Robert Jones were sitting together on the front bench. Jack made his way between several crewmen seated in the back, and Jack stepped over the next two benches. He touched Gaspar's right shoulder. The master gunner snapped his head around.

"Mind if I join you?" Jack said.

The Frenchman shifted his bottom. This pushed Widget a bit to the left. "Nay, Midshipman Hollister," he said. "Do not mind."

Before Jack could say a word, little Tyler nudged between Jack and Robert Jones. Then Stokes and Marvel sat in the remaining space on the front bench.

"*C'est bonne*," Gaspar said. "We are together again."

"Nay. The Iroquois, Nightjar, is missing," Stokes said.

"In his hammock," Tyler piped in. "Said 'e not like formal meetings. Rather smoke his pipe and stare at the bulkhead."

"As he wishes." Gaspar adjusted the sling supporting his left arm. "Mr. Hollister, it is good you are well. I am ready to convict *cette pourri meurtier*."

Sergeant Turner came through the forward hatchway, snapped to attention, and interrupted the gunner's rant. He faced the courtroom and said, "This tribunal is ready to begin. Everyone stand as the magistrates enter."

He then stepped aside, and Captain Morris, Colonel Thompson, and Lieutenant Whitehall entered the room. They took their seats at the head table. Captain Morris was in the middle, Colonel Thompson was on his right, and Lieutenant Whitehall was on the left.

"Seat yourselves," the sergeant announced.

"As you said, Mr. Gaspar, now we shall convict that rotten murderer," Jack whispered into the gunner's ear.

A marine carrying a musket came through the forward hatchway. He looked stiff and serious, and Dr. Voors followed. With his hands tied behind his back and with leg-irons about his ankles, the reverend hobbled in. Colonel

Thompson's minister mumbled to himself with his eyes locked on an open prayer book. He slipped into the room almost unnoticed, and he seated himself on the defendant's left. Following the defendant's entourage, another armed marine entered the courtroom and took his place next to the hatchway.

Captain Morris conferred with the two other judges, turned his eyes to the audience, slapped his right hand down on the table, and said, "This court is in session and will abide by the laws the American Continental navy established." He turned his eyes on the reverend. "You, sir, are accused of murder, subterfuge, and treason. How do you plead?"

The reverend chewed on his lip and contorted his face. "You, sir, Captain, or whatever you call yourself, must have your head in a hole. I only abide by Great Britain's laws. Not those created by a group of rebels who are attempting to overthrow the sovereign government of King George III." He took a deep breath and straightened in his chair. "You have no right to accuse me of anything. I will only answer to the proper authorities."

"I accept your plea then as not guilty," Morris said.

"My dear sir, I do not recognize the colonies as a sovereign nation. Consequently I will not satisfy you by voicing a plea."

"As you wish. Let me make one thing clear, though, Mr. Enoch Wrack. You are aboard my vessel. Neither King George nor his minions have authority here or anywhere aboard this vessel. In point of fact, neither does the Continental Congress or anyone else in the American colonies. Since you allegedly attacked two men serving under my command, the jurisdiction of your case falls to the Continental navy. That is true whether you recognize it or not. You, my dear sir, are aboard the *Piper*. It's a vessel that carries the flag of the Continental navy, and I am its master. Consequently I have total sovereignty over this floating dominion."

Wrack made a couple grumbling sounds, gritted his teeth, puffed out his chest, and looked toward Colonel Thompson.

"Your judges and jury, sir," continued Captain Morris, "are Colonel Thompson, Lieutenant Whitehall, and myself. Sitting next to you is Dr. Voors. He's a knowledgeable man whom I have assigned as your counsel. Hopefully you have discussed your accusations with him prior to this meeting."

"Yes. Your old croaker introduced himself to me, an' I told him I did not need his representation." The chains between the reverend's ankles banged on the deck as he shifted in the chair. He flexed his shoulders. "Since I do not believe you have evidence that I have broken any of your so-called laws, this whole affair is a farce. I demand you cut me loose and send me on my way."

"That, my dear sir, is not going to happen." The captain consulted with Thompson and Whitehall. "We have witnesses to your atrocious actions." He turned and faced the courtroom. "Midshipman Hollister, will you stand and tell this court what happened three evenings ago after you departed Greele Tavern and made your way toward the patriot camp?"

"Aye," someone in the court sang out. "You tell 'em, Master Jack."

Captain Morris pounded his fist on the table. "Gentlemen, this is a courtroom. Please conduct yourself properly."

Jack stifled a chuckle and pushed himself off the bench. Starting with the confrontation with the redcoat renegades in Greele Tavern, he related the attack on himself and Mr. Gaspar and his kidnapping after the two left the tavern. He then told the judges about his imprisonment by the reverend in the basement of the old warehouse.

"What of the woman we hear tell you were with?" another person in the room questioned.

Captain Morris looked in the direction of the interrogator, nodded, and said, "The question is proper. Mr. Hollister, you may answer."

"Aye," Jack answered. "A young native woman who had escaped the clutches of the accused. She helped rescue me. I felt she was in danger, so I told her to hide until everyone left the area."

"I thank you, Mr. Hollister," the voice from the audience answered.

"I would like to say," Enoch Wrack stood and grunted, "it is not possible for Mr. Hollister to identify me as his attacker. I went to his aid the next morning. That is what actually happened. One of my people was given information on the midshipman's imprisonment and told me. So several of us went to the warehouse to help him out. When we got there, though, he refused our help. As I said earlier, you have no evidence or witnesses who can implicate me in any wrongdoing."

The chains clanked as he reseated himself, and Jack jumped up from the bench. "Not true!" he shouted. "I was tied up. You only offered to untie me to allow me to eat. Then you again attacked me when I refused the slop you brought, and you constrained my arms and legs even tighter than before. You did not come to help me out. I was your prisoner!"

Colonel Thompson raised his fist and growled at the reverend, "We did not learn of Mr. Hollister's absence until late the next morning. How did your man come by this information?"

The reverend grumbled something unintelligible under his breath. Captain Morris put both his hands on the edge of the table, straightened his arms, and glared at the reverend. "You knew about the attack and abduction, Mr. Wrack, because you were a part of it."

"An' you killed my brother," a militiaman shouted from the court audience.

"What say you, Mackie?" Colonel Thompson asked.

"My brother, Dirk, went to join that reverend's group 'bout ten days ago. He kinda was a loyalist but not a rene-gade like some of the others on the reverend's crew. Always said what was right and tried to do what was expected of him. Dirk was no criminal. Did not think the revolution for independence would survive. All he wanted was to be loyal to King George, work land, and hunt." Mackie bowed his head and covered his eyes. "Found 'im in the brush couple days ago. Throat cut."

"Never heard of this Dirk," Wrack barked.

"Sergeant Dailey," the colonel said, "can you corroborate this man's story?"

"Aye, Colonel. Mackie and several of our men were searching for the midshipman to the north of the village and found his brother's body. The Abenaki found boot prints near his body similar to those near where Mr. Hollister and the gunner were attacked."

"Yes." Captain Morris nodded and sneered. "Sergeant Turner, did not you find boot prints with a torn sole in the area where we captured Mr. Wrack's group of scoundrels on the day after Mr. Hollister and Gaspar went missing?"

"Aye, sir."

Captain Morris clasped his hands together atop the desk and relaxed back in his chair. "In their search for our missing midshipman, our Indian allies found a distinctive footprint. This print has been turning up at the sites of struggle. I do believe our culprit has made his appearance with that self-righteous bunch of villainous miscreants. Sergeant Turner, please examine the soles of the defendant's boots."

A hushed murmur of voices filled the courtroom along with scraping bench legs against the deck. Sergeant Turner stood. The two men sitting in the middle of the bench in front of him moved apart. Jack shifted toward Tyler. The marine stepped over the benches and through the space to the deck behind the prisoner. He walked around, knelt in front of the reverend, looked up at him, and said, "If you would, sir, please raise your right foot."

"The hell I will! You want to see the bottom of my foot, you will have to cut it off."

"So be it," the sergeant said, and he stood and drew his sword.

He tapped the tip to the deck several times and gently gripped the blade near its hilt. He lifted the sword, rotated it into a horizontal position, and swung it. The hilt whacked hard against Enoch's right knee and caused him to kick up his leg. Turner caught the boot's heel, held it tight, raised it to hip height, and twisted the foot back. This gave all three judges a clear view of Wrack's boot sole.

"What do you think, gentlemen?" Captain Morris asked. "Do we have our culprit?"

The boot's sole was smoothly worn except for several punctures and a torn, serrated inner edge about an inch and a half below the toe. This jagged edge appeared as if some animal had once locked its jaws on the boot.

"Goddam rabid fox," the reverend said. "Bork told me I should have thrown the damn boots away." Wrack shook his head. "Footprint proves only I was present at those places you say. And I was, but I was not involved in any of those deeds you accuse me of."

"Perhaps so," Captain Morris said, "but the testimony of a Mr. Rob McLeod, who is a prisoner of the Brunswick militia, added some interesting stories about you. I do believe he is trying to save his skin. His stories are quite incriminating. He mentioned he heard you cut the throat of one of his partners—a man named Cotton. He was most likely the corpse the men found near the site where you attacked Mr. Hollister and Mr. Gaspar. Then you left my gunner to die, took Mr. Hollister prisoner, and planned to sell him to your renegade brother, Jacob Wrack, for whatever reason. And you led a group of loyal people astray. You, my dear sir, are a treasonous deceiver and a murderer. The new country we are trying to create has no place for you." The captain turned away from the defendant and conferred with the colonel and lieutenant. "Mr. Enoch Wrack, we the judges have found you guilty on all accounts accused and have sentenced you to hang. Sergeants Turner and Dailey, the marines, and representative militiamen will march you to the gallows constructed on the weather deck. This trial is adjourned."

CHAPTER 14

Ben Terry fixed his shrewd brown eyes on a large plank he had finished hewing. Earlier he had cut it from the trunk of a newly fallen fir tree. He bent over, worked his muscular arms under the timber, lifted it, and carried it to three other of the reverend's men who were trying to make the *Rosebud* seaworthy again.

Anchored on the edge of a salt marsh, the tattered sloop listed slightly on its larboard side. It awaited the incoming tide to float it off the mud. When Ben dropped the board onto the deck forward of the tiller, he shook his head. "He told us to come fix this sloop enough to sail it to Halifax. It's not been an easy job," he said, "since the reverend has let this little boat rot for the last two years."

"Aye," Rob grunted. Though Rob was Ben's brother, he had softer eyes and was a few years younger, but the two men had similar builds. "Traded a barrel of rum for this hulk the rev did—with a pirate from up the coast by a name of Dunkin. Then when you told him 'twas bad luck to change a boat's name, 'e forgets the ol' tub and leaves it to ferment in the mud."

"That's it, brother. This sloop's name is recorded in Neptune's Ledger o' the Deep an' needs to be purged from that book 'fore it can be called something else. The name

'*Rosebud*' got to be removed from everything that has anything to do with this sloop. Has to be as if it never existed."

"Posh! That's an ol' superstition."

"Might be, but the reverend is very superstitious."

"We could have painted it when the ol' preacher took it over. Or sanded and scraped away the name."

"Aye. But this sloop's name has to be removed from everything on the face of this earth. An' the reverend could not get the ol' logbook. Seems that pirate kept it, and now no one knows where he can be found." Ben bent over and picked up a hammer. "We got to get those leaks fixed 'fore the reverend calls us to his aid. They allowin' that damn sea to trickle into the hull."

Nearby, Gordon, a middle-aged Scotsman, squatted on deck. He was forward of the small deckhouse. Most called him Gordo. His white beard and long, snowy hair framed a reddish face and made him resemble a seasoned seaman. Using his knees like a vice, Gordo held a bucket between them. A wiry fellow stood in front of the bucket and held a paddle.

"Abel," Gordo said, and he started to stand, "shred more rope and cloth and then toss it in."

"Aye," said Abel.

He used a knife to chop, cut, and tear pieces of hawsers and rags. Strips, threads, and chunks fell into a viscous mixture.

"Now stir that slop."

Abel groaned, and he strained to rotate the paddle in the bucket. Gordo poured in some turpentinic, syrupy resin and tar.

"This old tub leaked when that pirate pawned it off. The caulk we mixing should seal the leaks," Gordo commented as he stretched. He bent over and lifted the bucket of caulk. "Water in the hold has been pumped down, so let us get below to plug the seams and shore up this hull."

The four men started to walk aft to the belowdecks hatchway, but they heard someone yelling. They scrambled to the larboard rail. Waving his arms and slogging through the incoming tidal water, marsh mud, and beds of spartina, a plumpish little man hurried toward the *Rosebud*. The fellow tripped on something, fell forward, and jumped up. Mud dripped from his hands, but he continued running to the sloop and yelling.

Gordo scratched his head. Rob and Ben moved to the rail. They gestured for the man to slow, and Abel turned his ear to him. All four jolted when they heard the words the runner was shouting. "The rebs captured the reverend!" They saw him throw up his arms and grab the boarding ladder. They heard him yell, "They holdin' the reverend prisoner aboard their damn gunship."

"Get your ass aboard, and tell us what happened," Ben shouted.

He bent over the gunwale and extended his hand to the man below and helped him up. Abel also rolled over the rail and shot his arm down the ladder to aid the runner aboard. The man wiped sweat and dirt from his face, and he reached up and grasped Ben's hand.

"I know'd your father," the man said. Using Ben's grip to steady himself, he climbed the ladder. The runner released Ben's hand when he reach the level of the schooner's rail and grabbed it. "You Terry boys was little nippers last I saw you. You probably don't remember me. My name is Isaiah Mackey. Husband of Alma Mackey, our reverend's cook." Isaiah climbed over the rail and stomped onto the *Rosebud*'s deck. "Some fellows who was helpin' our leader returned to camp after that Colonel Thompson released them. Alma tol' me to run an' tell you. She said we might be able to rescue him."

"In this leaky hulk?" Gordo shook his head. "That rusted cannon will probably explode if we try to shoot it."

"Aye!" Rob Terry said. "If we work all night patchin' this ol' lugger and oilin' that gun, we can sail it to the harbor on the morning tide and throw a fright into those rebs."

"We be attackin' an armed vessel," Abel growled.

"Got a chance if we surprise her," Ben countered. "Now let us get to it. The reverend needs our help."

"Your loyalty to that rogue will get us killed," Abel said. "We need more men."

"There are others in camp who are steadfast," Isaiah said. "They will come by and by."

By nightfall eight more of the reverend's men found their way to the *Rosebud*. Ben welcomed them aboard. Two were experienced lumbermen and carpenters. Ben sent them to Rob and Abel to help them with planking and decking. Ben sent the other six men to Gordo. All their experience came from working the land. He put them to work refurbishing the rusted little 4-pounder, scraping, and caulking.

As midnight approached, fatigue began to slow the men. Ben kept goading, pressing, and prodding them to work harder. Some cursed him but continued to work. Two confronted him with their fists clinched.

"Hey, mate, we're tired," one said. "We're breaking our backs. And for what purpose? This wreck ain't gonna stay afloat, and that rebel navy will blow us to hell."

The other man sat down on the deck and said, "I am not going to bust my arse any longer."

Ben stomped next to him and swatted him with a piece of rope. "You lazy clodhopper! Get your ass off the deck. This boat needs to be ready to sail on the next tide."

He stepped back and prepared to swing the rope again, but Gordo caught his arm. "Calm down, Mr. Terry." Gordo's baritone voice seemed to emanate from the bottom of a barrel. "Who in the hell made you the captain? I sure as hell did not agree or vote on that issue. The reverend needs our help. We've got to work together to get this scow into the harbor."

When Gordo took a deep breath and crossed his stout arms against his chest, his muscles stretched his shirt.

"Goddamn it. That is what I am trying to do," Ben answered. He backed away and waved his arms. "These landlubbers are just pissin' away the time. And for your information I'm the only one aboard this rotten scow who has had any experience at sea. Crewed aboard a fisherman."

"A couple months at sea does not make you a captain," Gordo growled. "At the least you need to learn how to treat conscientious men." Gordo clinched his fist. "A captain might be an asshole, but he does not treat his crew like slaves—even if some are. Get a lot more work done with a little compassion." Gordo turned and glared at the men lolling in front of him and Ben. "You two have had time to relax." The Scotsman pointed toward the *Rosebud*'s bow. "Get over there. Help those carpenters build that cannon pedestal."

The men stood and stumbled to the foredeck where Abel, Rob, and their helpers were constructing a cannon grate. When placed upon this stand, the 4-pounder could be fired above the gunwale. Rob even rigged the platform upon which the cannon would be secured to slightly rotate. They did not place the gun on the platform after they finished. "Better we set the cannon in daylight," Rob told the crew.

Instead they followed Gordo and his men back into the moldy, musty, foul-smelling interior of the sloop to continue securing the hull.

"Warmer down here," Abel said. "And no breeze to blow out the candles. Too wet for anything to catch fire."

Several hours before the sun rose, Rob and Abel had replaced and reinforced what rotten and broken hull timbers they could. Their crew and most of Gordo's men finished caulking and had reduced the leaks to an ooze in that part of the hull lying above the river mud. Water still trickled into the bilge in and around the keel and the boards abutting it where the workers could not reach. Ben held a lit lantern above his head, and Rob held a candle in front of him. They examined the inner hull's seams. Where he could fit his hand between the decking, Gordo used his fingers to measure the water depth in the bilge next to the keel.

She's still sheddin' tears," Ben said.

"Aye, mate, but not many. Less than an inch in the bilge since pumped some hours ago." Gordo stood and wiped his hands on his pant legs. "Should not require pumpin' till well in the morning."

"Good. Let's let the workers get some sleep," Rob said, and he made his way to the deck ladder. When he reached the hatchway, he yelled, "You men on deck, find warm shelter. Get some sleep."

The weather deck above the three men resounded with thumps, scrapes, and grumbles. Then the only sounds they heard were those of their own boots making contact with the ladder's rungs.

The squawk of gulls and the *Rosebud*'s cracking and creaking as she righted with the rising tide woke Ben. He uncurled himself from beneath a sail crumpled against the deckhouse, and he eased to a standing position. He rubbed his eyes, blinked, and gazed toward shore. Enshrouded in a cold fog, the salt marsh disappeared a short distance away in the white mud and salty mist. He could barely discern the forest ashore of the *Rosebud*'s anchorage. The trees appeared like ghosts. They dissolved and resolved in the miasma as slight gusts of wind at mast height whipped about the river. He looked over the gunwale and knew the keel was still imbedded in the mud.

With both hands gripping the rail, Ben stretched back and straightened. He rubbed his arms, returned to the deckhouse, and removed his jacket from its roof. He slipped it on. He looked forward and saw the 4-pounder next to the pedestal Rob and Abel had built. *Four men will be needed to lift that little cannon onto the grated platform and secure it,* he thought. He walked to it. He inspected its platform and stand closer and saw a brad not completely imbedded in a joint. He picked up a hammer, struck the nail soundly, and drove it deep into the wood.

The loud bang startled several sleeping crewmen nearby. One jumped up from behind the pedestal with his dagger drawn. Ben recoiled, hit the gunwale, and stumbled, but he caught his balance.

"What in the hell is going on?" the crewman growled.

"Sorry," Ben answered, and he staggered to straighten himself.

"Now we are all awake," Gordo said. "Where is some food? Breakfast?" He wrapped a ragged fur cape around himself.

"We have none," Ben answered. "Hurried here yesterday. No one brought any food."

Several crewmen collected against the larboard rail. Two picked up a ladder and placed it over the side of the *Rosebud*. This made a gangway to a hump in the mud covered with salt grass.

"Where do you think you are going?" Ben asked. "As soon as this tide raises the boat off the bottom, we're ready to sail. No time to go for breakfast."

"I'll go!" Isaiah Mackey yelled. "Alma always has something leftover—bread, smoked meat, or fish. Only 'bout a mile. Tide will not be high enough for a couple hours. I will hurry and bring back enough food to satisfy all before we sail. What say you, Mr. Terry?"

Ben chewed his lip, narrowed his eyes, and looked around. Abel and Rob had come up next to Gordo. Ben looked at them and saw their eyes. He knew he would be outvoted. "Get over the side, and hurry up, old man." He curled his lip. "We'll sail without you if you don't make it back."

Isaiah scrambled over the side and down the ladder. The layer of incoming tidal water beginning to flow in and around and through the grass beds did not slow him. As he stumbled and splashed across the marsh to the rocky shoreline, the old man's image blended with the dark-gray curtain the forest cast onto the fog.

Gordo nodded at Ben and scanned the men around him. They were scratching, stretching, yawning, and trying to awaken. "Best way to warm up is to begin work," Gordo said. "That cannon needs to be placed on the pedestal. Sails and lines need riggin'. Have to have barricades on the foredeck to keep everyone from catching some lead. So let's get to it."

"If I'm steerin' this hulk, I want some reinforced bulwark around the helm," Ben demanded. "Rob, come help me check out the rudder to see if it will hold. Damn thing has been chewin' the mud for the last couple years."

As the morning progressed, the breeze steadied but remained slight. The fog dissipated near the shore. Clouds continued to blanket the sky, and the flooding tide began to cover the salt grass. The *Rosebud* stood about twenty-five yards from shore. The noise of hammering and sawing echoed about the anchorage as the crew constructed protective bulwarks.

Abel and several others heard a yell from the shoreline. They looked up and saw Isaiah waving from the rocks. A bundle lay next to him.

"Lower the dinghy," Abel shouted. "Mackey has returned."

However, before the men could drop the little boat into the water, Isaiah had picked up the bundle, raised it over his head, and started wading out to the vessel. Abel climbed over the side, dropped into the dinghy, squatted, and grabbed its rails to steady himself and the boat. He looked up when he heard someone above yell to Isaiah. "Wait! Abel is comin' to get ye."

"Damn fool. Water to his waist. Yet he continues to come," Abel said, and he grabbed the oars and began to pull toward Isaiah. In two strokes he was aside the older man. "Throw in the bundle," Abel shouted. He had seated himself in a forward thwart and leaned his body away from Isaiah. "Pull yourself aboard. Hurry 'fore you freeze."

When Isaiah attempted to scramble and yank himself over the dinghy's gunwale, the little boat drastically tilted and took some water over the side. Abel leaned farther to counterbalance the load, and Isaiah slid into the dinghy. He banged a shoulder against several of the dinghy's ribs. He shook his head and pulled himself onto the transom seat. Abel gritted his teeth and rowed back to the *Rosebud*.

The dinghy's bow thudded into the sloop's hull as a crewman threw down a line. Abel tossed up the oars, stood, took hold of a rope hanging over the *Rosebud*'s side, and climbed aboard. "Mackey," Abel said, "hand up the bundle of, I hope, food, and get yourself up here. We have work to do."

When Isaiah tried to follow Abel up the rope, the older man couldn't do it with the additional weight of his water-soaked clothing. Several crewmen leaned over the gunwale, grabbed his arms, and hauled him aboard. They brought the dinghy on deck and secured it to the sloop's transom.

Isaiah looked fatigued, and he shivered. He wrapped his arms about himself and jumped around to warm up. Gordo was taller than Isaiah and more robust, and he said, "I have an old shirt and pants below. You're welcome to rid yourself of that wet garb you're wearin'."

Isaiah's body shook from the cold and wet, and he nodded thanks. As he started toward the belowdecks hatchway, the *Rosebud* creaked and groaned. With a sucking whump, her bow suddenly pitched up. The sloop rocked for a moment and then settled in a disturbed halo of rising muddy foam and bubbles. The craft began to drift sideways with the tidal current. The sloop's anchor rope was tied at the bow, and it tightened and jerked the boat to a momentary stop. *Rosebud* then pivoted on the cleat. Her stern rotated upstream. The bow pointed to the salt-marsh shoals.

"Get the jib up," Ben shouted. "Got to get this boat under control. Hoist the mainsail, and boom it to starboard."

He cut the anchor line, dashed aft, grabbed the tiller, and pushed it to starboard. The *Rosebud*'s bow faced downriver, but the sloop moved backward and upstream. The incoming tidal current carried it.

Slight, contrary winds gusted along the river's narrows and caused the mainsail to flap and pop. Ben tried to gain control and set a course away from the shoals and toward the middle of the river. As soon as *Rosebud* reached a stretch of open water, the gusts diminished, and a continuous northeasterly breeze filled the mainsail.

"Winds on a larboard beam," Ben said. "Trim the sails. We are under way." The crew slackened the starboard jib sheet and allowed the sail to balloon to the right. They then tightened the sheet as Rob and Abel shoved the mainsail boom farther over the starboard rail. This brought the large sail to a thirty-degree angle with the hull's length. The sloop sailed downstream. Its sails were tight and trim. It listed slightly to starboard and glided easily over the rippling water. The crew relaxed, and Ben steered *Rosebud* along the Fore River estuary toward Casco Bay. They fed themselves on the bread, apples, and smoked fish Isaiah had bundled aboard, and they washed everything down with stale beer from an old cask Gordo had found in the hold.

The *Rosebud* cleared the headland that defined the Fore River mouth shortly after lunch and encountered a more moderate northeasterly breeze. The sloop hiked to a steeper angle, and this made it difficult for anyone to move about the deck without the aid of some handhold. Sails tightened, speed increased, and the bow smashed obliquely through a one- to two-foot sea that crashed against the larboard side as the sloop shot into Casco Bay.

Ben strained against the tiller to keep *Rosebud*'s direction on a straight heading. "Adjust the sails," he yelled, and he fought to bring the bow around to point more into the oncoming waves.

Abel and several other men worked the sails as the vessel continued seaward.

"Schooner to larboard!" Someone yelled.

"The *Piper*," Gordo shouted. "At anchor 'bout three… maybe four leagues."   Ben stared over his left shoulder. "Goddamn it. Gonna have to jibe. Stand by the sails for my command."

The sail crews loosened the jib sheets but maintained a single turn on the starboard cleat and held the rope tight. Abel released the mainsail boom.

"Jibe!" Ben yelled, and he pushed the tiller all the way to its right.

Abel and his crewmen ducked. As the bow veered sharply to the left, the crewmen tossed off the last of the starboard jib sheet turned on the cleat. They quickly scrambled to the sloop's left side and wrapped the larboard jib sheet around its cleat. When the jib swung to the left, the crew secured its lines. Simultaneously the mainsail and its boom swung to the left. Abel secured it. The *Rosebud* tacked almost into the wind. Ben aimed the sloop a bit to the left and allowed the wind to flow across the starboard bow. Sailing on the close larboard reach, the little vessel was on course toward the *Piper*.

Rob picked up his bag and removed a telescope. He sighted it on the *Piper*. "They are rigging a gallows!" he shouted. "They going to hang the reverend."

"Get that gun ready," Ben yelled.

"Mr. Terry," a crewman said, and he scratched his head. "We got powder but ain't got no shot 'cept some bags o' ballast."

"Goddamn!" Ben yelled. He yanked the tiller to the left and caused the sloop to swerve to starboard and point into the wind. "What the hell we come out here for?" he asked as the *Rosebud*'s hull vibrated with the flapping sails and slowed. "Bring up those damn bags of rocks. We can shoot them. Get your asses ready to do damage. The reverend needs us." He eased the sloop back on course. "I hope you buffoons remembered to bring your muskets, powder, and shot."

CHAPTER 15

J ack made his way to the aft gangway when the trial ended. When he emerged onto the deck, he crossed his arms about himself and rubbed his biceps. The breeze had freshened. He walked to the gallows Sergeants Turner and Dailey and he had rigged. He took hold of the rope, wrapped another loop around the belaying pin, ensured its security, and strolled aft to helm. He looked toward the harbor entrance, and for a moment he thought he had seen a vessel heading for the sea. He rubbed his eyes and blinked. *Only a wisp of thickened fog.*

The sound of scratching and clumping on the deck made him turn around. Coming out of the forward hatchway, Colonel Thompson grasped the doorframe, pulled himself onto the deck, adjusted his balance, and stumbled forward. The large man straightened as Captain Morris, Lieutenant Whitehall, Midshipman Jones, and Dr. Voors came through the opening and strolled to the helm. Jack nodded at these officers as they moved in around him.

"We will all have a good view of the proceedings," Captain Morris said, and he scanned the deck for the drummer.

Morris spotted him standing amidships near the larboard gunwale, and he gestured to signal the sailor. The drummer snapped to attention and started to beat out the death-march rhythm. To the sound of the drum's rump-pump-pump, rump-pump-pump, Sergeants Turner and Dailey emerged from the forward hatch. The marine guardsmen followed. The final pair of guards shouldered their muskets and stepped back. Two sailors aided the reverend who was bound in chains. The colonel's minister also staggered out of the hatch. The sailors positioned the reverend between these two guards. The colonel's minister moved next to the prisoner as the militia guardsmen climbed onto the deck. The marines and militia formed a double-ranked file and marched to the gallows. This rank separated and created a guarded pathway to the step stool under the noose.

Everyone waited as the remaining aboard the *Piper* emerged from the hatchways and assembled on the deck and deckhouse roof. Some climbed onto the lower portions of the ratlines.

The marine guard on the right of the reverend nudged him forward. Jack watched as the minister led the reverend between the files of guardsmen to the mast. The minister's prayer book was open, and his lips were moving. Sergeants Turner and Dailey met them.

Captain Morris walked up and faced the reverend. "Mr. Enoch Wrack, before your sentence is carried out," he said, "do you have anything to say?"

A grin crossed the reverend's face, and he closed his eyes. Opening them after a moment, he said, "I do, Captain. As I see it, you are no better than a murderer. The trial was a farce. As I mentioned earlier, I do not recognize these colonies as a sovereign nation." He paused for a moment, inflated his chest, and continued. "You are all treasonous rebels who have turned against Great Britain's king. King George's forces will win out in the end. My only wish is to be among those who will tie a rope around your neck and also around that pompous fool's neck." His eyes turned to the helm. "The one who calls himself Colonel Thompson."

Captain Morris glared at the reverend, and his mouth opened to say something. However, a yelling sailor interrupted him. "Sail off the starboard bow!"

All eyes turned forward. The fog had dissipated, and everyone clearly saw a vessel some leagues away. It was heading for the open waters of the Atlantic.

"My glass, Mr. Jones," the captain called, and he turned aft and held out his hand.

Midshipman Jones hurried forward as he removed a telescope from his belt. He handed it to the captain. As the captain walked to the starboard rail, he slid the glass open to its full extent and focused on the distant vessel. "Nothing more than an exhausted fishing smack," he said. "Would not want to be aboard her beyond the dock. She will not survive on the open sea." Morris snapped the telescope closed, and he returned to where the reverend stood. "Mr. Whitehall, send a lookout into the rigging. We need to be aware of any traffic. I do not want to be caught off guard."

Captain Morris again faced the reverend. He then looked up and sighed. He was relieved when he saw a sailor situate himself in a brace near the top of the foremast. "Is she flying any colors?" he shouted to the sentry.

"None I can see, sir," the sailor yelled down. "Though she appears to have a name, sir."

Morris and the others stared up the mast and watched as the crewman tried to focus his telescope on the sloop.

With his left arm wrapped around the mast, he twisted himself around, laid the scope in the crook of his left elbow, balanced it, and took a sighting. "Has a name on the transom," the sentry shouted. "I can make out an R. *Rose*? There's more. Name's *Rose* something, sir."

Captain Morris shrugged, but he noticed the reverend's eyes widen. "Keep your eyes on that vessel," he yelled up the mast. "Mr. Wrack, do you know something of that vessel?"

"Like a ghost. Thought it sank several years ago." The chains binding the reverend's legs clanked as he shuffled. "Cannot be the vessel I thought of, so to answer your question, no. I know nothing."

"Very well." Captain Morris stepped back and away from the prisoner. "Let us carry on and bring these proceedings to an end. The tide is flooding, and the *Piper* needs to get under way. Do you have any other words to admonish us further?"

The reverend's shoulders dropped slightly. He sighed. "The devil with your plans, sir. I do have a few words I would like to say. The God I believe in will spare me the noose. Should I die, He will provide me with rewards for aiding Him with my services in this world."

"Your God?" Captain Morris chuckled. "Your reward? Satan, your God, will provide you with an eternity of coal and a fine shovel. Enough of this diatribe. Mr. Turner, please prepare the prisoner."

Wrack grinned and said, "As you wish, Captain. Remember, though, you and all these rebels are no better than murderers if you hang me."

The captain nodded and returned to stand next to the *Piper*'s other officers.

Sergeant Turner moved next to Wrack and gestured for Sergeant Dailey and Colonel Thompson's minister to join him. Turner removed a black hood that hung on a nearby belaying pin, shook it out, and faced the reverend. Turner raised it and moved forward to place the hood over Wrack's head.

"Belay your action, Sergeant. I would like to have my eyes free to see all you as I die."

Turner looked to Captain Morris. The captain nodded agreement. Turner lowered the hood to his side and backed away from the prisoner. He loosened the hangman's rope, lowered the noose, and caught it as it slipped down. He spread it open, moved in, and flipped it over Wrack's head. Turner gripped the reverend's shoulders and urged him back. "Step up onto the stool," he said, and he bent his head around to Colonel Thompson's minister, who stood behind him. "He's yours to pray for, sir."

Turner continued to hold onto the reverend and assisted him with his balance.

"You, man of the cloth," the reverend grumbled, "be gone. I suppose you plan to take over my flock after I am gone?"

Colonel Thompson's minister continued to look down at his prayer book. "If I want. Perhaps so."

"You, sir, don't have the gall for such duty. Sergeant, I would appreciate if you removed this shepherd. His righteousness annoys me."

"Perhaps you should move away, sir," Sergeant Turner said. "This scoundrel is not interested in any God." He tightened his grip on the reverend's shoulder. "Step back and up onto the stool, sir."

As the prisoner lifted his right leg, the sentry above shouted, "Tha'! Tha'! That! Damn scow jibed! Headin' right for us! Comin' fast! Maybe a league away!"

"Goddamn it!" Captain Morris shouted. "Prepare for attack. Lash the prisoner to the mast."

Sergeant Turner helped the reverend step off the stool, removed the noose from his neck, and tied him to the mast. Captain Morris, Lieutenant Whitehall, and Midshipman Jones retreated to the helm. Dr. Voors scrambled below deck to prepare the surgery to accept any injuries. The marines and militiamen remained on deck, but they took cover behind some fortified bulwark and readied their muskets. Colonel Thompson and his minister hid near a rampart off the deckhouse. Midshipman Hollister met Stokes, Widget, Nightjar, Marvel, and Tyler—the men he and Gaspar had assigned to the gun crew and who maintained the vessel's starboard 20-pounder. Within a matter of minutes, the ship's drummer had beaten out the warning of attack. Everyone armed himself and took positions at their assigned battle stations.

"She's a comin'," the sentry yelled.

Captain Morris and Lieutenant Whitehall held their scopes locked on the approaching sloop. "Son of a bitch is beating to windward," Captain Morris yelled. "Coming directly at us."

Jack also had his telescope focused on the *Rosebud* and realized the captain's concern. The vessel had its bow pointed as close into the wind as it could possibly be without stopping forward motion. As he watched he knew the helmsman aboard the sloop had little sailing experience because the upper third of the vessel's sail was vibrating badly. *Piper's at anchor*, he thought. *Helpless. That wreck will spear our transom.* "Move the 4-pounder to the transom. Load. Prepare to fire on command," Jack yelled.

The gun crew lugged the little cannon to the stern and placed it behind the helm. As they loaded and positioned it, Captain Morris shouted, "Fire a shot at the bow. Stop that vessel."

Jack's crew secured the loaded cannon, and he pushed its barrel up fifteen degrees and jumped away. "Fire!" he yelled.

Following the blast of white smoke and a jet of flame, the 4-pounder jumped and recoiled. The shot threw up a vertical splash about twenty feet to the left of the *Rosebud's* bow.

Jack saw the sails flutter when the sloop momentarily fell off the wind, but it continued coming at the *Piper's* stern. He remembered a situation in Plymouth Harbor. While sitting at anchor, he had to swing his little sailboat out of the path of an approaching brig.

"Hoist the mizzen!" he yelled. "Boom it to starboard and hold!"

Several men rushed to raise the mizzen sail. Once up, they pushed its boom to the right and secured its starboard sheet. The northeast wind filled the sail and pushed *Piper* backward and to the left until its anchor hawsers went taut. Jack then made a slight adjustment to the rudder. With no stern anchors set and the *Piper* pulling tight against its bow anchors, it continued to rotate to the left. For the moment this maneuver took the schooner's transom out of *Rosebud*'s path and put its starboard side to the oncoming sloop.

"Ready the starboard 20-pounder," Jack yelled to his gun crew.

Heightening Jack's urgency, Gaspar shouted from the cover of the deckhouse, "To the gun, men!"

Stokes, Widget, Nightjar, Marvel, and Tyler ran the short distance from the stern to amidships. This was where the 20-pounder was located on the vessel's right side. As Widget released the cannon from its bindings, Marvel and Nightjar pushed it to the gunwales. Tyler released the cover over the gunport, but the cannon's muzzle scraped on the side of the gunport's door when it fell open.

"Got to load the damn thing, you blighters," growled Stokes, "before pushing it through the port. Did ye forget what you've been taught?"

Marvel and Nightjar jerked the cannon back.

"Secure the recoil straps," Stokes commanded, and he used the ramrod to sponge the bore. He tossed in a powder bag, ramrodded it into the cannon's breech, and then pushed in the ball. "Cannon loaded," Stokes yelled.

"Cannon secure," Marvel shouted after he finished roping the gun to the gunwale to keep it from recoiling across the deck after being fired.

Then Marvel joined Nightjar. The two put their shoulders against the gun's carriage and pushed its barrel through the gunport. Jack sighted down the barrel, raised it five degrees above horizontal, and said, "Not a moment to spare. She's…"

Suddenly masses of cracks and pops sounded from a short distance off. Whizzes filled the air over the *Piper*. Musket shots began slamming into its hull, masts, and bulwark. Wood splintered. Ropes and lines snapped. Pellets of lead whumped and thwacked through the mizzen sail.

Men screamed and fell. Marvel, Widget, Nightjar, and Stokes dived behind the gunwale. Tyler snapped back and fell onto Jack. Everyone heard the reverend yell, "Loose me from this mast. Those sons of bitches will shoot me." Then he called out, "Ben, hold your fire! I'm in the open. In the line of fire. Argh!"

"*Sacre bleu*," Gaspar shouted.

Trapped beneath Tyler, Jack glanced up and spotted Gaspar stand and pull his pistol.

"*Le prisonnier*, he be rescued," the master gunner yelled and pointed the handgun at the reverend.

Jack snapped his head around. He saw the reverend twisting about, trying to free himself, and heard him scream. Then he looked back at Gaspar, who was attempting, amid flying musket balls and splintering wood, to get a clean shot. He switched around when he heard the reverend cry out in pain, and saw the man slam back against the mast and slump. Gaspar had not fired the shot.

Killed by his rescuers. Jack grinned and rolled Tyler off him and onto the deck. He saw the boy's face grimace. The little seaman's shoulder was torn and bleeding. "Man wounded!" Jack laid the little seaman's head in his lap. "Dr. Voors, this man is bleeding badly." He saw Gaspar lower the pistol, glance toward the schooner's stern, stoop down behind he deckhouse.

"Voors is looking after Mr. Whitehall," Gaspar shouted. "I believe the lieutenant's dead."

Jack looked toward the helm. Captain Morris and Midshipman Jones crouched near Lieutenant Whitehall's body. Dr. Voors shook his head. *Piper*'s marines and Colonel Thompson's militiamen were hunkered down behind protective bulwarks and returning fire.

Stokes crawled next to Jack. He ripped off his shirt, tore it in half, and used it to bind Tyler's shoulder wound. "I take care of boy," he said. "You fire cannon. Sink that son of a bitch."

Musket shots kept zinging overhead. Jack remained low, and he slithered next to the cannon. He peered along the barrel. The *Rosebud*'s bow nearly filled his entire view. He could see musket barrels protruding over the sloop's rails. Its crew seemed able to fire about two rounds per minute. *Able to reload fast*, he thought. He looked back at Stokes and shouted, "I need your quill."

The seaman reached up to his jacket's collar and extracted a thin spike. "Slow match's hangin' on carriage. Larboard side," Stokes said, and he slid the quill across the deck to Jack.

The midshipman snatched up the spike, wormed his way around the cannon's carriage, glanced up, and saw a whisper of smoke curling upward from a thin piece of line that hung on a hook above his head. He reached up and grabbed the smoldering cord. He rose to a kneeling position, ran his fingers along the top of the cannon's breech, and felt the fire hole. He positioned the quill in his fist, slowly lifted the spike to the opening, and made a quick stab. With his other hand, he laid the smoldering end of the slow match over the fire hole. Within seconds he smelled burning gunpowder. He made a rapid twist and whirled away from the cannon's carriage.

The big gun blasted with a blinding flash. Pain shot through Jack's head from ear to ear. The cannon lurched. An acrid, white plume enveloped him. The explosive concussion tossed Jack into the bulwark still protecting the marines. Heat burned his eyes and flushed his face. As if in slow motion, his hands moved and covered his face. He lay encased in absolute silence. He took a deep breath, rubbed his eyes, and opened them. An exuberant twisting, flinging, jumping blur of colors, lines, and blobs danced above him. He closed and rubbed his eyes again. When he parted his eyelids this time, a creamy gray haze overshadowed the frolicking scene. The foggy blur moved closer and darkened. He blinked. There were two black spots.

A brown brushy mass topped each, and a visage began to resolve. He then felt pressure under his shoulder.

Jack blinked and shook his head. He felt the weight of his body shift downward. His legs locked. They stabilized with the pressures being exerted against his sides. *I'm being lifted.* A vague image now faced him. *Stokes. He's trying to speak to me.*

As if coming from a deep well miles away, Stokes's voice said, "Bit shocked 'e is. He'll be all right in a minute or two. Hold him till 'e gets 'is balance." Stokes stared directly into Jack's eyes. "You blew the bow off that wreck. Sank like a rock. Beautiful shot."

Jack looked around. Nearby and behind the bulwark, marines were shaking their muskets and yelling, "Huzzah! Huzzah!" Several came up and patted him on the back. However, their voices and the hoopla sounded as if they were miles away. Jack glanced starboard to where the *Rosebud* had once floated. All he saw were men swimming or floating, wreckage, foam, and bubbles.

A smile crossed Jack's face. Dr. Voors came forward and signaled the men holding the midshipman, to help him walk to a bench the surgeon had prepared.

After about thirty minutes of Dr. Voors's attempts at repairing what time would eventually correct, Jack became eager to return to his duties. "Thank you, Doctor," he said. "You have done what you can. Though the heat flushed my face and my ears seem plugged, I do believe I will survive. How is Mr. Tyler?"

Dr. Voors nodded, wiped his hands with a cloth, and slowly raised his arms. "A bit sore, but he will weather the storm. Though his left shoulder was damaged badly. It will probably never be of much use to him."

Jack stood. "Sorry for that, but the lad is strong. Where might I find Captain Morris?"

"He is at the helm saying his good-byes to Lieutenant Whitehall. A musket shot shattered his skull. Never knew what hit him." Dr. Voors threw the cloth he was wiping his hands with in the box containing his medical paraphernalia. He bent over, closed the box, and straightened. "The carpenter is sewing the lieutenant's body in canvas. The captain plans to have his funeral at sea."

"Thank you, Dr. Voors. I will go aft and see if I can be of any help," Jack said.

He threaded his way around the debris scattered on deck, and he proceeded to the *Piper*'s stern. His scorched face glistened with the salve the surgeon had applied. The midshipman found Captain Morris standing over the canvas burial shroud containing Mr. Whitehall's body. The carpenter was sewing in the final stitches at the head of the cloth casket. The straps were to be placed at the levels of the ankles, abdomen, and shoulders to secure the corpse. They were all that remained to be put in place.

"Good man," Captain Morris said without looking up as Jack came next to him. "Too young to die in such a ridiculous way. A bullet from a bunch of scoundrels trying to save their pernicious leader. Tomorrow we will properly bury Mr. Whitehall at sea."

"And what of this leader of scoundrels?" Jack asked. "Are we to bury him?"

"No." Captain Morris glanced toward Falmouth. "His body is being taken to shore for burial."

"They is goin' to bury him in the intertidal area, Mr. Hollister," a nearby seaman said. "Facedown. So if 'e decides to dig himself out, 'e's just goin' to dig deeper."

Jack had a quizzical expression, and he snapped his head in the seaman's direction.

"Aye, sir," another seaman said. "He is goin' to dig himself to his rightful place—Satan's palace."

Jack and Captain Morris both glanced at the two seamen. The captain uttered an "uh-huh," but Jack scratched his head and stifled a laugh.

"Aye, gentlemen," Morris said. "That will be Colonel Thompson's decision. He and his militia have ten to fifteen of the reverend's sopping rats that need cages. I'm sure the colonel will know what to do with the prisoners our men fished out. They are all in his care now. We need to get to sea." He looked to Jack. "With the loss of Lieutenant Whitehall, the *Piper* needs a new first mate. Midshipman Hollister, I would like to appoint you to that position."

Jack's jaw dropped. He hesitated "I…I am honored, sir," he said, "but I lack experience."

"You have no less than Lieutenant Whitehall had when he came aboard," the captain proclaimed. "Have to start somewhere. Now, Mr. Hollister, ready the *Piper* for the sea.

I'm going below to bring the logbook up-to-date. We sail on the tide."

Jack chewed his lip and took a deep breath. "Aye, sir," he uttered, but he was daunted as he watched Captain Morris walk forward to the hatchway.

CHAPTER 16

A few pieces of wreckage from the *Rosebud* still floated about at four o'clock in the afternoon. That was when the tide neared its peak and, with only minor damage on deck, the *Piper*'s anchors were raised. A moderate wind blew from the northwest and easily pushed the schooner into Casco Bay. Overhead and to the south, the sky remained covered in a ruffled, gray blanket of dour clouds. With its canvas filled and stretched taut, the *Piper*'s bow cut through the one-foot chop covering the harbor's surface as it rounded into the bay. Amid a percussion of hammers and saws from the crew mending minor battle damage, they rode south down Casco Bay with the outgoing waves. Nearing the village of Port Elizabeth—situated atop a headland to the west—the *Piper* began to encounter the Atlantic's swells. Some were topped by large, foamy, wind-driven whitecaps. When the schooner passed through the mouth of the bay, an occasional reflective wave ran counter to the wind and crashed against the hull starboard of the bow. This sent cold saltwater and spray above the bowsprit. Some water strewed aft down the deck and blanketed the helmsman. A mile or so beyond the surf, blasting over the rocks and up cliffsides, the ocean's waves became more orderly.

Jack stabilized himself by holding a rail that encircled the after deckhouse roof. He turned to the helmsman and said, "Set course to one hundred sixty degrees and hold." He gripped the rail and made his way forward hand over hand along the slanting deck to the mainmast where several seamen were tending the mainsail's lines. "Trim the sails as needed."

"Mr. Hollister, sir," Stokes said. He was working with another crew, and he straightened. "When I am not needed in the gun crew, I do duty as the *Piper*'s boatswain, sir. As such I keep the deck, sails, and rigging in order. Captain Morris informed me of your promotion. I am at your command. You may inform me of your needs, sir."

"Aye, Mr. Stokes. Thank you," Jack replied, and he smiled and nodded. "In a day or so, I will learn the ship's protocol."

"Midshipman Hollister," a voice behind Jack called.

He turned and saw it was Midshipman Robert Jones. "At your service, Mr. Jones."

"Captain Morris would like you in his cabin as soon as all on deck is secure."

"Thank you, Midshipman. All is well. *Piper*'s heading is one hundred sixty degrees to the south. Mr. Stokes, will you take over while I am gone?"

"Aye, sir."

Jack turned. A gust of wind rasped his cheeks. He made his way aft and descended through the hatchway. Midshipman Jones followed.

When Jack entered Captain Morris's cabin, he found it crowded. He moved to a space behind a chair in front of the captain's desk. A group of small glasses was arranged on top of the desk. Jack straightened, put his hands on the back of the chair, and nodded at the captain behind the desk. To his right and sitting on a bench next to the bulkhead were Sergeant Turner and Master Gunner Gaspar Arno. His left arm was still slung against his chest. At Jack's back Dr. Voors occupied one of a pair of chairs just inside the door. Midshipman Robert Jones had followed Jack into the cabin and had seated himself in the other chair. The captain and several others smoked their pipes and filled the cabin with a sweet tobacco aroma.

"Please sit, Mr. Hollister," Captain Morris said. "I called this meeting to inform the *Piper*'s officers that I assigned you as my first mate. For now you will continue the rank of midshipman. Perhaps an elevation in rank will come later. This change has been noted in the *Piper*'s log. Earlier I informed Bosun Stokes so he could remain on deck to supervise repairs of the damage our vessel sustained during the encounter with the *Rosebud*." Captain Morris rose from his seat and faced his officers. "Please inform your crews of Midshipman Hollister's change in duty." He turned to Jack and extended his right hand. "Congratulations, Midshipman Hollister. You are now second in command of this vessel. I know you will work with the others to keep our vessel safe and sound."

Jack stood and shook the captain's hand. For a moment he was speechless. Then he lifted his head, inflated his chest, and snapped to attention. "I will do my best, sir."

"Huzzah!" the others chorused, and each in turn congratulated Jack.

Captain Morris reached around to a cabinet behind him, opened it, and removed a bottle of Madeira. "Gentlemen, a toast to our new executive officer would be appropriate."

The captain bent forward and poured a shot of the sweet wine into each glass. Each person took a glass, raised it, and said in unison, "To Midshipman Jack Hollister."

Everyone tossed back the drink. A moment of silence followed as a tribute to Lieutenant Whitehall. As the officers returned the glasses to the desk, they began to engage in lighthearted chatter.

Captain Morris returned the bottle of Madeira to the cabinet. "I know you are enjoying Midshipman Hollister's promotion, gentlemen, and that our course is set for home, but we have a matter to take care of. Please seat yourselves, and we'll get on with it. After, you can return to your stations." The captain used his knee to push his chair away from the desk. He turned and seated himself. "On the morrow after breakfast, we will bury Lieutenant Whitehall. Mr. Hollister, I expect you to arrange the ceremony. Everyone aboard will be present. After a short period of mourning, we will set our course for the harbor in Beverly. If the winds and weather hold, we should be there in three days." He glanced up at the officers. "This meeting is adjourned. Please carry on."

While the ship's officers departed, the captain stood and moved to two small stern portholes. He unlatched them and raised the windows. Opening the portholes allowed the outside air in and freshened the interior of his smoky cabin.

Everyone at the meeting moved forward through the vessel and dissipated into its various nooks and crannies. When Jack entered the makeshift courtroom, he noticed it had been restored to its original use as the crew's mess. Though the ship's flag still hung on the wall. As he looked around, Dr. Voors, the most senior of the ship's officers, stepped next to him.

"Mr. Hollister, as you no doubt expect," the surgeon said, "my many dealings with death have given me considerable experience with the formalities of burying someone at sea. Since this is your first funeral, I would like to offer my service. Between the two of us, we can organize a quick and smooth event. Then you and the captain can set our course for home without delay."

"Thank you, Dr. Voors. I would greatly appreciate your help."

———◆◆◆———

Except for the periodic swell, the ocean remained flat and reflected the pewter sky. Patches of ripples created by the gusts of a slight northwest wind spewed across the water's surface. The *Piper* drifted slowly to the southeast well beyond the sight of any land. Her hull creaked with languid rolls and pitches. Lines slapped against the masts and bulkheads, and sails drifted slightly to and fro.

Jack met with Sergeant Turner and Dr. Voors on the deck amidships before breakfast. "Sergeant, your six marines will serve as the honor platoon," Jack said. He turned to the larboard side and swung his splayed hand over the deck. "They will make rank here. As master-at-arms you will stand in front of them. Captain Morris and you, Dr. Voors, will stand on the platoon's left. I learned Seaman Marvel is an accomplished bagpiper, and he will be positioned on the platoon's right. When I asked the seaman if he could squeeze out a dirge, he said he could."

"Aye, Mr. Hollister," Dr. Voors said. "I've listened to him play. He is good"

Jack nodded and moved nearer to the starboard gunwale. He looked things over and then shifted left toward the bow. He stopped next to a wide plank that lay atop a pair of sawhorses. "Lieutenant Whitehall's body will lie here." He placed his hand on the plank. "Three casket bearers will stand on each side of the corpse. On my command they will send the deceased to the deep." Jack turned around and pointed aft. "The firing squad will line up there along the gunwale."

"Midshipman Hollister, sir, you said my marines are the honor platoon. Are they also to stand as the firing squad?"

"No. Dr. Voors has selected six seamen who have been issued muskets. They will arrange themselves in pairs. Each pair will fire a volley on command. A formal burial ceremony calls for three volleys." Jack moved and stood at the head of the wide plank. "As the *Piper*'s executive officer, I will stand here and officiate this ceremony." He looked down the plank and out to sea. He then turned to face the sergeant and surgeon. "Is all I have arranged as it should be, Dr. Voors?"

"Aye. It is indeed," the surgeon answered. "The captain and the deceased, God bless 'im, if his spirit is still among us, will appreciate the formal burial. It is perhaps the first such ceremony in our country's naval history. You have done well, sir."

"Thank you, Dr. Voors, for your guidance. And to you, sergeant, for your help," Jack said, and he patted Turner on his back. "Let us go now below for coffee and victuals."

⸺•◦•⸺

About ten minutes before nine o'clock, Jack was back on deck. "Boatswain Stokes, have the fore and mainsails furled," he ordered. "Maintain one jib. Have the helmsman set rudder fore an' aft and secure the helm. Let the *Piper* drift."

"Aye, sir," answered Mr. Stokes.

As Stokes yelled out the commands, the crew scurried around the deck loosening and pulling sheets and lines. They lowered the large sails and furled them onto their booms. With the jib sail still catching the wind and the helm locked, the *Piper* drifted on a somewhat straight course.

Captain Morris and Dr. Voors came on deck. They took their positions. The captain nodded at Jack.

"All hands on deck to bury the dead," Jack yelled.

A scurry of boots and feet vibrated up the ladders and on the deck. Crewmen hurried to positions amidships. They avoided the file of marines Sergeant Turner led. Dr. Voors broke away from his location next to Captain Morris and walked to a group of sailors trying the arrange themselves along the starboard gunwale.

"Careful, matey, tha' musket is loaded," one said as another waved his weapon's barrel toward the crowd.

Dr. Voors grabbed the shoulder of the sailor swinging the musket, squeezed it, and pushed him against the gunwale. "Calm yourself, man," he growled, "and set the butt on the deck. The rest of you line up behind this man." When they fell into rank, he arranged the file into pairs. "On Mr. Hollister's command," he said, "I want three volleys fired into the air. One right after the other. Do you all understand?"

They all uttered a feeble response. "Aye, sir."

"Thank you, gentlemen. I am comfortable you will do your duty properly."

The surgeon returned to his place next to the captain. From his position on the right at the head of the wide plank, Jack scanned the scene. He was holding a missal in his right hand, and he saw Marvel was on his correct spot. The seaman and his bagpipe were ready. Jack nodded at him and shouted, "Attention!"

On the command the *Piper*'s crew stopped chattering.

"Parade rest," Jack commanded.

Seaman Marvel began piping a slow march. The sound of the bagpipe dampened the scrapes that momentarily ground on the deck as each man moved his feet apart, swung his arms behind him, and clasped his hands against his back.

A group of six sailors were standing in rank near the stern. At Jack's signal they bent over, lifted the canvas casket containing Lieutenant Whitehall's body, and held it between them.

"Ship's crew, come to attention," Jack commanded.

Again the sound of tramping rattled the deck. Midshipman Jones led the pallbearers, and they marched forward along the starboard side to the burial plank. Raising the casket to waist height, they placed it on the plank, stepped to the side, came to attention, and faced seaward. Midshipman Jones unfolded the ship's flag and draped it over the casket.

"Parade rest!" Jack commanded. "Bow your heads." Jack raised the missal to the level of his chest, opened it, and began to read the committal. "We are assembled here to commit the earthly remains of Lieutenant Logan Whitehall to the deep." He felt his voice crack. He paused, sighed, and continued. "We hope for the general Resurrection on the last day and the life of the earth to come through our Lord Jesus Christ. He will arrive at this second coming in his glorious majesty to judge the world, and the sea shall give up her dead." Jack paused again, glanced around at the flag-covered casket, and took a deep breath. "The corruptible bodies of those who sleep in him shall be changed and made like unto his glorious body. According to His mighty working, He is able to subdue all things unto Himself." Jack raised his head. "Amen."

Jack lowered his head and closed the missal. After a moment he looked up and glanced in Captain Morris's direction. He then returned his focus to the lieutenant's casket. "Lieutenant Whitehall was a young, honest, and responsible man. He was trying to learn his duties as I am now. Though we only had a short time to get to know each other, I believe we all respected him. His death came too soon. It ended a life of dedication, enthusiasm, and patriotism. He was an officer with considerable potential in the Continental navy. He loved the sea and his freedom. Unfortunately we will never know what his contributions to America's independence might have been. Lieutenant Whitehall will be sorely missed." After a moment of contemplation, Jack issued his command. "Ship's crew, a-ttention. Hand salute!"

With a single subdued sound, everyone straightened, stared forward, raised a right hand to a brow, and saluted.

"We commend this body to the deep," Jack said.

The two casket bearers stationed at the head of the plank took hold of the corners of the flag covering the casket closest to them. The four others turned to face the plank and moved next to it. All lifted and angled the plank to allow the canvas casket containing Lieutenant Whitehall's corpse to slide into the ocean. Sergeant Turner called out, "Firing squad, fire three volleys."

The lieutenant's body slid off the *Piper* and splashed into the sea. Simultaneously three separate, distinct musket blasts echoed across the water, and white smoke rose and curled into the starboard rigging.

As the report subsided, Seaman Marvel began piping a dirge, and Sergeant Turner ordered, "Secure the flag!"

On this command the casket bearers folded the flag and handed it to Midshipman Robert Jones.

"At ease, men," Jack called. "This ceremony is concluded. Return to your duties. Get the ship under way. Dismissed!"

Again the *Piper*'s deck rumbled with stomping, scraping, and the yelling of commands as the ship's crew members dispersed to their stations. Within fifteen minutes the foresail and mainsail were hoisted. With the wind freshening from the northwest, a small chop danced over the sea's surface. The sails filled and tightened. Boatswain Stokes ordered another jib sail hoisted. With this accomplished and all sails trimmed, the wind pushed the schooner southeasterly at a lively pace.

Captain Morris and Midshipman Jones stood on the stern as Jack walked up. Morris held a sextant in his hand. The midshipman stood next to the deckhouse, bending over its roof, tinkering with the latch on a polished rosewood box. "It has been twenty-some hours since the *Piper* quit Casco Bay last evening," the captain said. "Mr. Jones, have you opened Mr. Whitehall's instrument box?"

At that moment he heard a snap and a clack, and he saw the box lid fall open onto the deckhouse roof.

"Aye, sir," Midshipman Jones said.

The captain turned and looked at the instruments in the box. Each item was stored and protected in a velvet compartment—compass, boatswain's whistle, telescope, sextant, and a small chronometer, which registered the time as 1120 hours. He reached in, removed the sextant, and handed it to Jack. "Lieutenant Whitehall's sextant. It is yours now. The sun is overhead but will be covered within the next few minutes, and there is a need to know our position on this vast ocean. Together we will sight on the burning globe and compare each other's readings."

Jack accepted the complex navigational instrument with a nod and smile. "I am honored, sir," he said. "I will provide it with the same care Mr. Whitehall did."

Jack inspected it, carefully slid the moveable arm, looked through the eyepiece, and adjusted its focus to match his eye.

"You have done this before, have you not?"

"Aye," Jack said. He sighted on the sun and adjusted the moveable arm until a beam of light blazed through the eyepiece. Lowering the instrument and blinking his eyes to readjust, he looked at the sextant's scale and read the angle at which the sun's light had impinged on his eye. "Forty-three degrees and twenty-five minutes is the angle I read, sir," he said.

Captain Morris raised the sextant he held to his eye and took a reading. "Aye. The measure I have is only a minute off. Beverly is at forty-two degrees, fifty-five minutes latitude. Mr. Jones, please record the *Piper*'s position as forty-three degrees, twenty-five minutes. North latitude."

Midshipman Jones wrote the position in his notebook and looked down at the chronometer in the box. "I will enter the sighting in the log as taken at eleven hundred forty-eight hours."

"Good," Captain Morris said. "Mr. Hollister, have the helmsman maintain our present course. At four o'clock this afternoon, change course to two hundred twenty-five degrees. That will place us on a southwesterly course toward Beverly. If the winds hold and we maintain our present speed, we should make our destination in about two days."

———

At four o'clock in the afternoon, Jack came on deck and strolled to the stern. Boatswain Stokes tended the helm. The wind's speed had not changed. It continued to blow from the northwest and pushed the *Piper* along at about five knots through a sea of one- to two-foot waves. The sky was overcast, and the daylight dwindled.

"All appears well, Mr. Stokes?"

"Aye. It is getting colder, but the weather is holding."

Jack took hold of the safety rail behind the helm and scanned the vista forward of the bow. "The captain has ordered a course change to two hundred twenty-five degrees."

"Aye, sir. Two-two-five it is." Stokes rotated the wheel about a half turn to starboard, and the *Piper*'s bow rotated to the right.

The sails began to flap and flutter as the bow panned the horizon.

"I will take the helm while you oversee the trimming of the sails."

"As you wish, sir," Stokes said, and he released the wheel when Jack stepped up and gripped the handles.

Jack made a slight adjustment to larboard and brought the schooner onto course.

The boatswain yelled to the deck crew, "Step lively, me hearties, an' trim the mainsail and foresail. We're headin' for home."

Sailors scurried about the deck pulling and securing sheets. Within a few minutes, the sails inflated, became taut, and pushed the *Piper* ahead and into a starboard list. Waves that broadsided the hull clapped and swirled as the schooner cut through the chop.

"Sail on horizon! Off bow. To starboard," a lookout in the rigging yelled down.

"Mr. Stokes, to the wheel," Jack shouted.

The boatswain came running and took charge of steering the schooner. Jack pulled his telescope from his belt and scurried to the bow. He focused on the horizon and scanned to the right. Some miles ahead and beyond the earth's curvature, a pair of white rectangles contrasted brightly against the black and gray cloud bank on the horizon.

A large ship indeed, Jack thought. *One of the masts is flying a banner.* He knelt down onto the deck next to the gunwale. He placed the telescope on the rail and grasped it tightly to keep it from vibrating and swaying. As the bow rose and fell, the far-off sails appeared and disappeared. Jack critically adjusted the focus each time the white rectangles came into view, and he was able to discern the vessel was large and flying a red Union Jack ensign. *British transport.* He stood, collapsed the scope, and hurried below to the captain's cabin.

"Enter," Captain Morris said when Jack knocked.

"Sir, a British transport," Jack told the captain. "Perhaps five to six leagues off the starboard bow."

"Is she in convoy?"

"I saw no other sails."

The captain turned, grabbed his telescope from a shelf behind him, and stood. "Lead the way."

Jack and Captain Morris headed for the deck in haste. They reached the bow, and Jack pointed a little to the right of it and toward the horizon.

"Daylight is dropping," the captain said, and he extended his telescope and sighted where Jack was pointing. "I see nothing." For a moment more, he scanned. "Ah, there it is." He watched. "Indeed. A British brigantine. Transport no doubt. Her topsails and large sails are visible."

"Earlier I saw only topsails."

"Our speed is faster. We are gaining on her." The captain braced himself against a stanchion and kept his glass locked on the distant vessel. "She is surely for Boston. Our courses are the same. We'll follow through the night. Have the helmsman maintain course. Send two lookouts into the foremast rigging. By morning we will be ahead and to the west. Those sails and any others will flare in the rising sun. That will make a good prize. If she's alone we'll heave to and she'll come to us." The captain closed his scope and turned to Jack. "She'll have food stores aboard for her crew and to trade. Surely a cargo of importance to our cause as well. Aye. She'll make a good prize."

Jack nodded in agreement, and the captain turned and headed back to his cabin. The midshipman made his way aft. "Mr. Stokes," he said upon reaching the helm, "maintain our present course. Ahead is a British transport the captain wants to stalk through the night. I'll send two lookouts into the foremast rigging. Keep them alert."

"'Tis good," Boatswain Stokes said. "The crew will enjoy a jolly skirmish."

"And our meals might improve. She'll be having unspoiled food aboard," Jack said with a smile. "Carry on, Mr. Stokes. If you need me, I'll be below."

———— •◦• ————

The overcast sky held the darkness. Though a streak of silver defined the horizon to the east when Jack came on deck. He stood against the larboard rail and scanned the sea. The cold breeze urged him to tighten his coat and scarf. He patted his arms to stimulate warmth, and he shouted into the rigging. "Stay alert up there!"

Within five minutes the bright sliver in the horizon dimmed, but its center grew and formed a stretched dome. Edges that curled down from the overhead blanket resolved to ragged streaks of light. Across the cloud layer, the illumination splayed from whitish to smoky black overhead. Again Jack yelled into the rigging. "Be aware of sails to north and east."

"Aye, sir. Sails," one of the lookouts called down. "Sails behind and to larboard, sir! Two…maybe three leagues."

"Keep watch." The midshipman turned to a nearby seaman. "Go! Inform the captain. British transport in sight on the horizon."

"Aye, sir," the sailor said, and he scampered toward the after hatchway.

In a few minutes, Captain Morris came on deck and headed to the helm. As he walked, he motioned for Jack to follow him. A seaman stood at the ship's wheel, and Boatswain Stokes watched him steer.

"Boatswain, man the helm," Captain Morris commanded. "Point the bow into the wind and heave to. We'll wait for that Britisher to come nearer. Mr. Hollister, call general quarters. Inform Master Gunner Gaspar to ready his team on the larboard 20-pounder."

Jack nodded. "Aye, aye, sir." He headed below to the crew's mess, and he found Gaspar and several others, including the drummer, at breakfast. "Master Gunner, Captain asks you take charge of the gun crews and ready the larboard cannon. Drummer, beat to quarters."

"Ah!" Gaspar beamed. He slid back his bench, jumped up, and slapped Nightjar and Widget on their shoulders. They were sitting near the bulkhead, and they slurped their coffees, stood, and followed Mr. Gaspar and the ship's drummer.

"Aye, mates," Widget said as all hurried forward to their stations. "I will alert Marvel and Tyler an' meet you on deck."

Jack caught the edge of a table and held it tight. He balanced himself as the schooner pitched to starboard and pointed into the wind. Within a few minutes, he heard the familiar series of tap-tap-taps followed by a rapid rumble on the drum resonate through the schooner. He scampered back on deck and joined Captain Morris at the helm. Wind blew directly in his face as the *Piper*'s bow pointed to the northeast. With the sails taut but unnaturally back-filled, the schooner drifted slightly forward and back. It remained somewhat fixed in its position as it bobbed and rocked in the waves.

Captain Morris held his glass on the approaching vessel. "About two leagues off," he said.

"Changing course to south, sir," a lookout yelled down from the rigging.

"We've been seen," the captain grunted. "Trying to make an escape." Keeping his scope glued against his eye, he continued to watch the transport. "Bosun, give chase!"

Stokes yelled the commands to bring the *Piper* back to life. Sailors scampered about the deck. They pulled lines and pushed booms. The helmsman brought the schooner's bow to the southeast. The sails filled. The hull groaned, and the water against it slushed and slurred as the vessel recaptured forward speed. Stokes took the ship's wheel, adjusted it, and aimed the bowsprit like a lance directly at the transport's starboard side. When all stations signaled their readiness, the drummer ended the call to general quarters.

"She's the *Olive*," Captain Morris said when he focused on the vessel's stern. "Out of Plymouth I believe."

Being lighter and more streamlined, *Piper* closed on the larger vessel.

"Armament, lookout?" Captain Morris yelled. "Is she armed?"

"Two large cannons amidships, sir," the lookout shouted. "Small cannon on quarterdeck. Crew not at quarters. See five or six carrying muskets. No one at cannons."

"Mr. Stokes, come alongside," the captain commanded. "Master Gunner, send a ball across her bow. Sergeant Turner, have your marine prepare to board."

Lines rattled and twanged when the *Piper*'s 20-pounder blasted and spit fire, smoke, and a cannonball. The cannonball splashed about thirty feet from the starboard side of the *Olive*'s bow.

From his position atop the deckhouse roof, Jack watched six seamen. Swords swung from their belts, and they lined the *Piper*'s larboard rail. Each held a coil of rope in the left hand and the end of a grappling hook in the right. The hook was attached to the end of the line. As Stokes eased the *Piper* next to the *Olive*, the *Piper*'s seamen along the rail began whooping and hollering. The *Piper*'s marines answered a couple musket shots from the *Olive* with a barrage of shots. When about four feet separated the two vessels, Jack yelled, "Throw grapples!"

Along with more whooping and yelling, the clawed iron shafts, each trailing a line, looped and sailed over the gap between the vessels. They clunked when they hit the *Olive*'s starboard gunwale and rolled over it. A couple clanked as they landed on the deck and skittered across it. Immediately the *Piper*'s sailors hauled in the ropes, pulled them taut, and ensnared the brigantine. They tugged tighter, and they closed the space to the *Olive*. Sporadic musket and pistol fire continued as *Piper*'s marines and sailors climbed, crawled, or swung onboard the transport. Swords clanked, and men screamed when the opposing forces connected. A crewman was shot in the rigging and fell a short distance to the *Olive*'s deck. Another was wounded amidships, and he stumbled against a ladder to the quarterdeck. Two of *Piper*'s seamen fell back onto the deck bleeding. Obverse crewmen continued to clash.

A blast of the 4-pounder and a shout "End this useless carnage!"

Jack swung his head around and saw a small rotund man. He was wearing a tattered bicorn and dressed in a red and white uniform. *The captain?* Jack reasoned. *Perhaps.*

The man stood on the brig's quarterdeck swinging a white flag. "The cargo we carry is not worth the spilling of blood," he yelled.

"These are goddamn rebels," a larger, younger uniformed man shouted as he stepped off the ladder onto the quarterdeck. He stood in front of the other. "How dare you give this vessel to the enemy?"

When the younger man lifted his right hand from the ladder's rail, Jack noticed he was clutching a pistol. The man raised the weapon and fired it at the captain. The older rotund man swung his hand to his face and fell back.

"Tha' mutinous son of a whore shot Captain Dugan," one of the *Olive*'s crew members yelled.

Jack grabbed a musket from a nearby marine, aimed, and fired. The captain's killer swung around and crumpled. Gasps and cheers could be heard from the *Olive*'s crew.

"Surrender your weapons," a voice shouted. "Captain was right. We need not lose any more of our crew."

Jack jumped aboard the *Olive*. A man near his own age broke from a group of sailors amidships and dashed up the quarterdeck ladder to where the captain lay. The young man knelt and lifted the captain's head. "He breathes! Come quickly."

"Dr. Voors!" Jack cried, and he ran across the deck and bounded up the ladder. "Follow me. You're needed." Sprawled in front of him were the legs of the injured captain and the back of a young man dressed in seaman's clothing. The young man was bent over and cuddling the officer's head. "Dr. Voors, quickly!"

"Aye, Mr. Hollister. Behind you," Voors answered.

"Help is coming, Uncle," the young man mumbled. He remained on his knees, twisted, and faced Jack. "Thank you," he said as he looked up. Tears glistened in his eyes.

Jack stared at him and gasped. "Andrew? Andrew Graham?"

"Aye, Mr. Hollister. It is I," Andrew said. He was holding the injured man's head and blood oozed between his fingers. "My uncle. Please help him."

As Sergeant Turner supervised the disarming and containment of the *Olive*'s crew, Dr. Voors stooped next to the *Olive*'s captain and took charge. He touched the captain's neck, and he felt no pulse. "This man's dead," he said.

Jack offered his hand to Andrew. The young seaman took it, pulled himself up, and momentarily choked. Andrew wiped his eyes and faced Jack. "He was a good man. Taught me seamanship after you left Plymouth. Counseled me in the ways of the sea. He was not really my uncle. I just called him that. We were close. He was like the father I lost. I loved him."

"Aye," said Jack. "You told me of him when we explored Plymouth Harbor together, but you never introduced him."

"He was always at sea, Mr. Hollister." Andrew wiped his eyes again. "That horrible Mr. Petty should not have shot the captain. Uncle made him his mate when the first mate died a week after we sailed." He shook his head. "I do not know why he did that. Uncle said he was a good sailor and knew his way around ships, but they always argued. Petty had in his own mind how things should be. He considered the captain weak and a lover of colonials. Accused him of disloyalty. Treason. Wanted the captain to step down. Mr. Petty wanted to be captain. Killing Uncle was not the answer."

"Is this one of the prisoners?" Captain Morris said as he stepped next to Jack. He held a black, leather-bound book in his hand. "Sergeant Turner and his marines have the crew of the *Olive* detained at the bow. This seaman must join them."

"Aye, Captain," Jack said. "This is Seaman Andrew Graham of the *Olive*. He is in my charge. He and I met on the wharves while I was still in England. We became friends. He also enjoyed listening to the adventures sailors told of their travels on the high sea. Captain Dugan..." Jack pointed to the captain's body. "He took Andrew in hand and became his mentor."

"Aye," Morris said. "Several of the *Olive*'s crew mentioned the captain and the man you shot had been quarreling for the past week. Though the killer had a few followers, they have surrendered. Most of the *Olive*'s crew found him a disobedient lout. Mr. Hollister, by killing him you might have saved us from more bloodshed."

"Perhaps, Captain, but thank you."

Captain Morris raised his hand holding the book and gestured. "The deceased master of this vessel recorded his fear of an imminent mutiny in the ship's log several days ago. He did not name any instigators. Just noted his concern." He turned and looked about the deck. "Have Mr. Graham join the prisoners. You and he can converse later. For now I want you to secure this prize vessel. Inventory the cargo and transfer some provisions this vessel carries to the *Piper*. Have the crew throw that evildoer over the side." Morris turned to Andrew. "We'll give your uncle, Captain Dugan, a proper burial."

"Thank you, sir," Andrew said.

Jack nodded at Andrew as a marine walked toward him. "I will talk with you later."

The marine took the young man by the shoulder, led him to the starboard rail, and from there to the bow.

———•◦•———

By noon the wind had subsided to a casual breeze. The two vessels drifted as a unit to the southeast on an almost-flat sea surface. The clouds smoothened, but the sky remained overcast. Though the air warmed slightly and humidity increased, an occasional wisp of forest tinged the salty atmosphere surrounding the vessels. This foreshadowed a front rolling seaward off the continent.

Jack sat at the table with Captain Morris, Midshipman Jones, Sergeant Turner, Boatswain Stokes, and Master Gunner Gaspar. The men had completed examining the inventory of the *Olive*'s cargo—lumber, sundry building materials, candles, various pieces of furniture, crates of everyday china, barrels of salt pork, tea, bundles of wool cloth, four hogsheads of Scotch whiskey, and ten boxes of muskets. Each box held twenty weapons. Also on the list were ten casks of gunpowder and ten of lead shot.

Several crew members commented on finding the Scotch whiskey. Captain Morris ordered several gallons transferred to a smaller cask and brought aboard the *Piper*. "But most important to our cause," he said, "are the weapons, powder, and shot. These will remain aboard. General Glover will take charge of all the cargo, military and commercial, when the *Olive* is docked in Beverly. Mr. Stokes, what provisions for the crew does the vessel carry?"

"She is well supplied, sir," Stokes answered. "Besides the usual victuals, the *Olive* has a hold that contains four cages of live chickens, three loose hogs, and two stabled steers—the usual amount one would find at the beginning of a voyage. This is unusual, sir. I would have expected, since the *Olive* has crossed the Atlantic and is only five days from Boston, her food supply to be down to bare essentials. It appears the crew was not being well fed."

Captain Morris sat back in his chair and leafed through the pages of its logbook. "I do not see any entries corresponding to the crew's feeding or what might be construed as a menu. Perhaps someone other than the captain handled this responsibility. His mate perhaps."

"I will question Seaman Andrew Graham, sir," Jack said. "I trust he will answer truthfully."

"Aye, Mr. Hollister," Captain Morris said. "Do take care of that. In the meantime, Mr. Stokes, have the cook and your men transfer part of this food to the *Piper*. I would like a couple days of supplies. The balance will remain aboard the *Olive*."

"Aye, sir," Stokes answered. "The crew is at it now. I expected that was what you wanted."

"Very well," the captain said. "Mr. Hollister, I am appointing you as master of the schooner *Piper*. It is simpler to sail, faster, and only requires a crew of four. From here you should make Beverly in two days. The *Olive* will no doubt take four or five days. Being square-rigged it requires more men to tend her sails. Mr. Hollister, you will have several days to prepare with Colonel Glover and his people to welcome the *Olive*, take charge of its cargo and the prisoners when we finally arrive, and administer the disposition of this vessel as a prize." The captain rose from his chair, placed his hands on the table, and stood straight. "Gentlemen, you are dismissed. Let us get on with our tasks." He turned to Jack. "Mr. Hollister, I am ordering Seaman Widget to serve as your boatswain and navigator.

He's a competent sailor and has worked with Mr. Stokes sufficiently to be of use to you. You will need three others to serve as crew. Select them from the *Piper*'s company."

"Sir?" Jack shifted in his chair, stood, and took a deep breath. "I appreciate your faith in my abilities, but I am uncertain of them."

"I have watched your development, Midshipman, and feel confident you will be able to do what is necessary to complete your mission. You are a quick thinker and a knowledgeable seaman. I watched you handled several dire situations with considerable success. You have the makings of an officer. Now get on with your work."

"Aye, sir," Jack said, and he rubbed his hands together. "I will not disappoint you." He moved around to leave the captain's cabin, but he paused, turned, and faced Morris. "Sir, I have a request."

"Aye, Mr. Hollister? And what might that be?"

"I would like to take the prisoner Andrew Graham with me. As I mentioned before, I trust him. I do believe he's a good seaman and will join us in our quest for independence once this journey is over." Jack ran his hand through his hair and rubbed the back of his neck. "He might have information about what is happening in Plymouth—or of my family." He waited for the captain's response.

Captain Morris moved to the side of his table and lingered while the others at the meeting shifted about and tried to leave. "Midshipman Jones, please stand by." Turning and facing Jack, the captain said, "Your request is not unusual but sensitive. You may take Mr. Graham with you, but I am assigning a marine to go along also. Though the *Olive*'s seaman is your friend, he is our prisoner. I would be remiss if I did not send a guard."

Jack nodded. "As you wish, sir."

Captain Morris focused his attention on Midshipman Jones. "Mr. Jones, I am appointing you as second mate aboard the *Olive*. You will now assist me. Though your responsibilities will not be as demanding as those of a typical first mate."

Captain Morris watched Jones take a deep breath, open his mouth as if to gasp, and lower his head. Someone passing out of the cabin door chuckled. Another mumbled, "He is so young."

"Sir, I am not sure I am ready for such authority," the midshipman stated.

Jack smiled and raised his right hand to the midshipman. "Congratulations, Mr. Jones."

"Have confidence, young man," Captain Morris interjected. "You will do well. Though I believe at first the men will probably not take you seriously. You are a midshipman, however, and I believe the experience will do you well. We, too, will be returning to Beverly forthwith. Your term of authority will be short-lived, but this baptism will be long lasting. I expect to anchor in Beverly Harbor shortly behind the *Piper*."

"Aye, sir. I...I will do my duty," Jones mumbled.

"Yes. You will do as I command, Mr. Jones," Captain Morris said, and he straightened. He stared at Jones, stretched his arms onto the table, and fisted his hands. "Now, gentlemen, let us adjourn to the deck and provide Captain Dugan with a proper but informal burial. After, Mr. Hollister, you will take command of the *Piper* and be on your way to Beverly."

CHAPTER 17

With Andrew Graham at the *Piper*'s wheel, Jack sat on the stern rail and faced forward. Seaman Widget stood behind the deckhouse and talked to the marine guard, who was leaning against the structure's side. The slight wind across the starboard beam pushed the schooner at what seemed a good speed.

"Mr. Widget, would you measure our speed?" Jack asked.

"Aye," the seaman answered. "'Tis but a simple process, Mr. Hollister." Widget bent over, opened a cabinet attached to the rear side of the deckhouse, and removed a wooden box. After setting it on the deckhouse roof, he turned the latch, raised the cover, and took out a large brass reel and an hourglass. Wound onto the reel was a thin cord with a triangular chip of wood tied on its end. "Just got to drop the log chip over the side and count the knots that slip by my fingers while all the sand passes through the hourglass."

"That is a small glass," Jack commented.

"The time for the sand to fall is supposed to be twenty-eight seconds, sir."

Widget walked to the starboard rail, set the timer in a safe place, and released enough line to allow the log chip to hit and bounce along the water's surface. He squeezed the line to hold it in place. His left hand rotated the hourglass. Almost simultaneously the fingers on his right hand eased the tension on the line. He counted as the knots slipped through his fingers. "Eight. An' a bit more line. *Piper*'s movin' a little faster than eight knots, sir." Widget repeated the measurement three times. When he finished, his chest puffed out, and a smile of accomplishment crossed his face. "We're cruisin' at about nine knots, sir."

To the west the cloud blanket split from the horizon and exposed about two-thirds of the setting sun. The bright ball shot an eerie reddish-orange blaze across the water's surface. Jack turned to look behind him. Trailing the *Piper* at some distance, the *Olive* floated like a celestial image surrounded by a brilliant aureole. Her large, square, and billowed sails radiated in the evening luminescence. As Jack watched, the glowing brigantine dimmed as the sun sank below the horizon. Beyond the twilight the *Olive* was lost in darkness. "At this speed, tomorrow we should be enjoying a proper dinner in Beverly. If all goes right with the *Olive*, it will be at the wharf in two days. Thank you, Mr. Widget. Please relieve Andrew at the helm. He and I will go below for a bite to eat."

"Aye, sir." Widget reeled in the line and placed the timing instruments back in the box. He returned it to the cabinet and moved next to the helm. "Course, Mr. Hollister?" he asked as he took hold of the ship's wheel.

"Continue southwest about two hundred twenty-eight degrees. We should make landfall by sunrise."

"Aye. Sout'west it is, sir."

Jack and Andrew headed down the after hatchway, and the marine guard followed.

———•◦•———

When Jack and Andrew entered the galley, they saw a table laid out with plates. Each contained some combination of meat, smoked fish, smashed potatoes, onions, beans, and carrots. Centrally located sat a bowl of biscuits. A small cask of beer stood on a nearby counter. Steam from a coffeepot sitting on the little iron stove added another flavor to the air.

A grinning, young, dark-skinned West African lad stood in the corner. "Thank ye, Mr. Jack," he said, "for askin' me to accompany you."

"You're welcome, Amadi," Jack said. "You seem to have a talent for making shipboard victuals edible. Cook could spare you. And I needed someone who could feed my crew. Besides, I know you are the better cook."

"I learn from my Ibo gran'mama. She still in Nigeria."

Jack smiled, walked around the table, lifted a fork, and stabbed a chunk of roasted meat. "What do you think, Andrew? Should we partake of this lovely buffet?"

"By all means," answered Andrew. "The cook aboard the *Olive* was stingy. He doled out meager portions. Said we had to save our food for the soldiers in Boston. I felt good being able to do my part for the British Army, but now I'm feeling bad. This food lying on this table was to go to our soldiers."

"Aye." Jack nodded and pursed his lips. "Let us make ourselves a plate and retire aft to the captain's cabin. There we can talk in private. Perhaps you and I can reminisce of our days in Plymouth. I do miss the place."

———•◆•———

Jack tossed some kindling into the Franklin stove. When the fire got going, he put in a chunk of coal. "We'll have some heat while we eat." He chuckled and returned to his plate of food. "Have you seen any of my family? I'm particularly interested in knowing if Ian and his party returned safely. They departed Boston in mid-September."

Andrew swallowed what he had been chewing and sipped his coffee. "Shortly after you and Ian left Portsmouth in 1774, I joined the service. Since then I have spent little time in Portsmouth. As luck would have it, the freighter I worked on returned to Liverpool last summer. Being away for almost a year, I gave up my position and made my way home to Plymouth. After some months on dry land, I became anxious to be back at sea." Andrew tapped his fork on the plate in front of him and then maneuvered it into a mound of mashed potatoes. Collecting a small glob on the tip of the tines, he pushed the fork into a chunk of smoked cod and shoved the mass into his mouth. He chewed and swallowed. "Got hired as a seaman on the *Olive*. We hauled her anchors on the twenty-second of October. As the *Olive* moved through Plymouth Roads, we passed the incoming *Clara H*. One of our crew said she was the Hollister's newest brigantine. That is as much as I've heard of the Hollister name—until you and your rebels attacked us."

"Thank you, Andrew," Jack said. "Now I know Ian, Uncle Edgar, my cousins, and everyone who left Boston are safe in England. They were aboard the *Clara H*." Jack took a swig of his coffee, straightened, and looked directly at his friend. "Andrew, I am not going to apologize for the attack on the *Olive*. Great Britain and the American colonies are at war. War can make friends of enemies—and it can also cause friends to become enemies. I'm sorry your captain was killed. He seemed to have been a good man, but one of your own shot him. His killer was the mutinous contagion within your crew."

"Uncle…rather, Captain Dugan," Andrew said, "irritated some of the crew. He did not agree with King George's or parliament's attitudes toward the American colonies. Though he was a staunch and loyal Englishman. In Uncle's opinion the colonials should be given their independence. He did not like the way Great Britain is trying to subjugate the colonials—first by taxing them and now by force. Uncle's opinions angered a few of the crew, but First Mate Petty had no call to shoot him. Petty was an antagonizing bastard who wanted command of the *Olive*. I am not sorry he was killed."

"Yes. It is no good to have your man Petty, a first mate, able to influence a crew of a few easily led men. Most of your crew seemed loyal to your captain. Had that not been the case, your captain would have lost to a mutiny well before we came upon you." Jack stood, took the coffeepot off the stove, and refilled his mug. "Would you care for more?"

Andrew shook his head. "All the sailors aboard the *Olive* pledged their allegiance to the king and Captain Dugan— even though some disagreed with the captain's views. I, too, am loyal to Great Britain and believe the rebellious colonists are traitors."

"Those rebels, as you consider the colonials," Jack countered, "left Great Britain to free themselves from the tyranny and oppression imposed on them by the British nobility and aristocracy. All the colonists want is to be independent. They want to own property and believe as they wish. Great Britain has imposed unreasonable taxes and has taken other hostile measures that have frustrated the colonists' rights of life. Had there been reasonable taxes and colonial representation in the British Parliament, we would not be in this unreasonable war. However, parliament is run by nobs and their minions who believe colonists, whether loyal to the crown or not, are no better than peasants. That is not a good view of decent, hardworking, independent-minded people."

"Your words are treasonous, Jack," Andrew said. He clenched his fists, shoved back on his chair, and stood. "It was those who lived the servile life that fled Britain. They are not of the station to govern."

"Where have you been living, Master Graham?" Jack asked. "Under the cloud of deception created by those who rule, I feel. In order to maintain their power, the monarch and his sniveling partisans dictate how the minions should live. Each person should determine his or her way of life—not some king." Jack pushed back his chair. He pursed his lips and glared at Andrew. "I've lived with these people for almost two years. They have accepted me. I will use what talents I have to help them fight for their independence."

"Jack, I hate that a friend I once knew is a traitor to his country." Andrew sidestepped around the table. "You know a bunch of ragtag rebels are no match for the British Army and Royal Navy. They will not win this war."

"Be that as it may, the colonials are a determined bunch." Jack nodded to the marine guard. "As far as our friendship, remember what I said earlier. War makes enemies of friends."

"I am sorry to hear you say that. I am your prisoner, and I would welcome being treated as such."

"Aye. That you are. Until we arrive in Beverly, you will be confined to quarters." Jack relaxed and backed away. He lowered and scratched his head. "Andrew, you could join us in our aspirations. The rebels will win in the end because they are resolute. When they do, Great Britain will lose the war and also the friendship of a country of unfathomable opportunity."

"Perhaps so. A traitor I am not. I would like to rejoin the crew of the *Olive*, who are also prisoners of this ludicrous endeavor."

"So be it. When Captain Morris and the *Olive* arrive in Beverly, I am sure the *Olive*'s crew will also be given the opportunity to join the Continental army or Continental navy. Since there are no facilities to maintain prisoners of war, those who don't join us will be returned to your compatriots—perhaps in Boston or New York. As of now, Mr. Graham, you are a prisoner, but do consider this. Upon your return to the redcoats, they will most likely impress you and the others into His Majesty's service." Jack reached for his jacket and slipped it on. "Guard, confine this man to his quarters. I am going on deck to relieve Widget at the helm. He needs to eat and warm himself."

———•◦•———

During the early morning hours, the breeze slackened and shifted to the south-southwest. This required the sails to be readjusted. Jack and two seamen reset the foresail, mainsail, and little mizzen to starboard because the wind blowing onto the *Piper* was now coming from the left. After the modifications the vessel sailed over the rippling, oncoming, lead-colored swells and bucked through the occasional foaming chop. It cruised at about four to five knots.

Jack replaced Widget at the helm. "Go below. Warm and rest yourself," he said. "You've been at the wheel since midnight. Amadi has coffee and victuals."

"Aye, sir. That would be good," Widget said, and he released the wheel's handles. "Course has returned to two-two-eight degrees." He ambled to the after hatchway, turned, and said, "We're nearing landmasses. You might want to assign a lookout to the bow."

The night had lightened into a dreary, featureless gray morning. A slight but continuous snowfall had reduced visibility to about two miles.

"Aye," Jack said, and he saw a yawning seaman come through the after hatchway, step around Widget, and stretch.

"Can I be of service?" he said while rubbing his eyes.

"Aye," Jack said. "Scamper into the rigging and watch for landmasses and other hindrances."

The sailor tightened his jacket, pulled his knit cap down over his ears, and headed off to the foremast's ratlines. He grabbed hold of one of the lines like a monkey, swung onto the lower rungs, and climbed the taut rope ladder to the mast's topsail yardarm. He situated himself safely among the lines.

Just before the noon hour, the falling snow quit. The sky remained overcast, but visibility improved. To starboard a flock of gulls paralleled the *Piper*'s course. After a few high-pitched squawks, the flock turned away.

"Land off starboard bow," the lookout yelled down.

Jack looked to the right. Off in the distance a grayish forested mound stood out. He flipped a retaining cord over the top handle of the ship's wheel to keep it from rotating and walked forward to the after hatchway. He opened it and shouted, "Mr. Widget, on deck."

Within a few moments, the boatswain stepped onto the deck.

"Appears to be an island about three miles off the starboard," Jack said. "I am not familiar with these waters. You should take the helm."

Widget moved to the rail and cupped his hands around his eyes. "Aye, Mr. Hollister, 'tis an island indeed. Could be Kettle Island. 'Tis at the southwest entrance to Gloucester Harbor. If 'tis we're 'bout six hours from Beverly." He walked to the helm and relieved Jack at the ship's wheel. After tweaking the course, he said, "If 'tis Kettle Island and we stay on course, 'bout two hours ahead we should pass between two islands that are close together. They are only 'bout a mile and a half apart. Great Misery Island on the starboard and Bakers Island to larboard."

"Thank you, Widget." Jack craned his head upward and yelled, "Lookout, keep your eyes open. Watch for more islands ahead—and sails."

Jack adjusted his cap, locked his hands behind his back, strolled amidships, and looked in the direction of the mainland. *Today is December 2, 1775. We departed the* Olive *yesterday. I need to bring the logbook up to date.* He turned and walked back to the hatchway. Before he stepped onto the ladder's top rung, Jack turned to the helm. "I'm going below. Call me when those two islands are sighted."

Jack finished writing up the events that had occurred since the *Piper* sailed away from the *Olive*. He laid the quill on the table, closed the logbook, and consulted the ship's chronometer. *Been more than two hours since we passed that island.* As he was readying himself to return to the weather deck, he heard Widget's yell. "Islands ahead on right and left."

Jack pushed away from the table, grabbed his jacket and cap, donned them, and headed up the ladder. When he approached the helm, Widget pointed to the right and left. "Great Misery and Bakers, sir."

As if the *Piper* were cruising along a river, Widget navigated the schooner between the islands. He sailed closer to Great Misery Island. "Water's deeper on this heading," he said.

The water's edge was about halfway up the shoreline. That indicated midtide. Waves lapped partially submerged boulders, rocks, and outcrops. Stout grass beds surrounded by hillocks of sand grew above the high-tide line. Beyond stood a barrier of alder bushes that protected a robust forest of oak, maple, and pine trees. The interior emitted chirps of chickadees and caws of crows. From some hidden pool, a loon wailed. A covey of black ducks exploded skyward ahead of the bow. Two great blue herons fished near a pile of boulders. When the lookout hooted loudly, the pair took to wing, honked several times, and soared over the trees like pterodactyls.

"Lord willin', we be in Beverly by sunset," Widget said, and he added a point or two to the compass heading.

"We should fly our colors to reassure those on shore we are friend and not foe," Jack said.

"Aye, Mr. Hollister. Hopefully we'll not come upon a British man-of-war."

Jack smiled. "The most likely vessels we'll see will be fishing smacks from Gloucester. If I read the charts correctly, we are only two to three miles offshore."

"Aye," Widget said, and he rotated the ship's wheel to larboard. "Shoals, sir. Should add a mile or two to seaward lest we come to rest on one."

"I'll go below and bring the flag. I believe it was stored in the captain's cabin after Mr. Whitehall's burial."

After about thirty minutes, Jack returned. He held the nicely folded flag in his left hand and a steaming mug of coffee in his right. "For you, Mr. Widget. Warm yourself while you steer us home," he said, and he handed the mug to the helmsman.

He then walked to the mainmast and released a thin cord that hung from a pulley near the top of the mast. He secured the flag to the line, hoisted it, stepped back, saluted, and strolled to the starboard rail. He turned and looked to the top of the mast. The white flag with an image of a spruce tree stitched into it designated George Washington's new navy. It vibrated in the wind. *The* Piper *now represents the navy of a country trying to be born.* He returned his gaze toward the shoreline. *I wonder what adventures await when we reach the port.*

<hr />

Jack pored over a navigational chart in the stern cabin of the schooner. He felt the deck vibrate and heard the rudder groan as it moved. *Turning.* He looked at the chronometer. *Been almost four hours since we passed those islands.* He removed his jacket from a nearby chair, tossed it on, and scampered off to the weather deck. When Jack's head cleared the top of the hatchway, he turned and faced the bow. The view of distant wharves and piers caught his attention.

"Beverly Harbor ahead, Mr. Hollister," Widget said as he worked the ship's wheel. When the *Piper*'s bow pointed toward a tall, narrow steeple, Widget shouted to the three sailors working the sails. "Strike the foresa'l an' mizzen. Trim the main and jibs."

Jack headed to the bow, turned, and yelled to Widget, "Two longboats approaching. About a league away."

He saw a cloud of white smoke spew from a point on shore. Then came the rumble of a cannon blast.

"Not to fear," Widget called. "They sees our flag an' are welcomin' us."

Jack looked about the deck. He saw the sailors had trimmed the main and struck the other two sails. They were now standing against the starboard gunwale and scrutinizing the harbor. "You men, load powder. Fire the 4-pounder to acknowledge the welcome."

The men scrambled to the little cannon mounted at the bow, and within moments it belched a white puff followed by a loud report that echoed around the harbor.

"What of those approaching boats, Mr. Widget?"

"They to aid us to anchorage, sir."

The *Piper* and the longboats closed on each other. When the vessels were about two hundred yards apart, Widget yelled, "Strike all sails!"

As soon as the sail were dropped, the schooner slowed but continued to drift. Inertia and the incoming tide carried it. When the longboats came abreast of the *Piper*'s hull, one on each side, towropes were thrown from the schooner and attached to the sterns of the rowboats. Almost immediately the eight oarsmen in each boat pulled hard on their oars and moved ahead until the ropes became taut. The oarsmen continued to strain on the oars as they rowed for shore.

Widget stayed at the helm and kept the schooner between the longboats. "These Marbleheaders knows how to pull a vessel," he said. He stood proud and puffed out his chest. "Cod fishermen they are. Good seamen."

"You're a Marbleheader, are you not, Mr. Widget?" Jack said.

"Aye, sir. That I am."

Jack smiled and nodded. "I'll be in my cabin. Inform me when the *Piper* is at the dock."

———•◦•———

Jack checked his pocket watch and recorded the time in the logbook. *Four hours past noon plus forty minutes. Two December in the year of our Lord, 1775. The* Piper *arrived in Beverly.* He laid the quill on the desk and blotted what he had written. He closed the logbook, closed his eyes, and lowered his head into his hands. *Strange. Another vessel sailed from this continent at almost the same time some months ago. I was to be on it—going home. Much has happened since. I wonder what the future is to bring me.* He released his head, shook it, and slapped his hands on the desk. "Perhaps Andrew Graham has had a change of heart," he mumbled. "He and his guard need to be informed we're in port."

Jack shoved back the chair and stood. He walked out of the cabin door, through the mess, and to the crew's quarters.

"Marine, wake that man," Jack said. "In a short time, the *Piper* will be docked in Beverly. Prepare him to go ashore."

"I'm only dozing," Andrew said. He turned on his back and sat up. "I'm tethered to this bunk."

A sudden jolt knocked Jack off-balance for a moment. "I believe we are at the dock," he said. "Have you given any thought of joining us and staying in the colonies?"

"I am not a traitor. I wish to be held as a prisoner of war or sent home."

"As you wish." Jack turned and gripped the forward deck ladder but paused. "You will be turned over to the Massachusetts militia along with other crewmen of the *Olive* when she makes port."

He climbed up to the weather deck.

———•◦•———

Daylight had dwindled by the time the *Piper* was secured to a wharf. However, before lanterns and wharf lights had to be ignited, enough twilight remained for Jack to observe the activity on the dock and deck of the schooner. He walked aft to the helm where Widget was tying the ship's wheel's king spoke in its top location, locking the rudder in a fore and aft position. "Mr. Widget, when you have finished, have the crew hang some lanterns on the deck. I'm sure we will have visitors soon."

"Aye, sir."

Just as the boatswain started to round up the sailors and set them to their tasks, Andrew Graham came through the forward hatchway. A rope strung behind his back and tied to his wrists gave him limited use of his hands. The marine guard exited the hatchway after Andrew. As soon as the marine came onto the deck and stabilized himself, he pointed his musket barrel at the prisoner's lower back and followed him to the mainmast. The marine pointed to a cask and said, "Sit."

"I'm sorry our friendship had to end this way," Jack said as he approached Andrew.

"It would not if you returned to England as you should," Andrew said, and he laid his hands on his thighs. "Staying in the colonies and aiding the rebels. You are the turncoat. Not I."

"Perhaps so." Jack extended his right hand to the prisoner. "If there remains a semblance of our relationship, maybe you could do me a favor when you return to Plymouth. Should you come upon any of my family, I would appreciate it if you could tell them I am in good health and content with my decision to remain in America."

"Better you should tell them yourself, Mr. Hollister."

Jack nodded, but several loud thumps and scrapes by the starboard rail caught his attention. He glanced to his right and saw that Widget and a couple of sailors had dropped the gangplank over the side. Moments after it was secured, the dock rattled, banged, and creaked from the clomping of several horse-drawn wagons. These vehicles rambled to a stop next to the *Piper*. They raised dust and bounced debris off the dock. Each wagon carried several men holding muskets. Jack recognized the robust fellow leading the convoy, by the beaver fur tricorne he was wearing. "Colonel John Glover," he mumbled.

Quickly returning his attention to Andrew, Jack said, "Perhaps one day I will, when I return to Plymouth, but for now I have more pressing matters."

Jack turned and walked to the head of the gangway.

Colonel Glover started up and bellowed, "Midshipman Hollister, where is Captain Morris?" He stomped up the plank, stood facing Jack, and then glanced around. "Only three men on deck? And a marine pointing a musket at another? What is going on?"

"Captain Morris is perhaps a day or two behind the *Piper*," Jack said. "He and most of the *Piper*'s crew are returning aboard a prize vessel we captured two days ago. A brigantine by the name *Olive* that was transporting supplies, weapons, and ammunition to the redcoats in Boston."

"Ol' Morris put you in charge of the *Piper*? Why not Whitehall?"

"Lieutenant Whitehall was killed in an earlier encounter, sir." Jack stepped to the side to allow the colonel to come on deck.

"Oh my God. Sorry about the lieutenant. Did not know him well. A young man. Good sailor. Anyone else injured or killed during the capture of the *Olive*?" Colonel Glover shook his head and then looked up at Jack. "You must have impressed your captain."

"The captain and first officer of the Britisher were killed. One of our men, Mr. Tyler, was injured. Let us go below, and I will fully inform you of the encounter and our voyage."

"Aye, Mr. Hollister," Colonel Glover said, and he took hold of the rail and started to gesture to the others who had accompanied him in the wagons. "Few of the Marblehead militia. They can help secure the *Piper* and stand guard."

"Aye, Colonel," Jack said. "I have one prisoner your militia can take charge of. Mr. Andrew Graham. Seaman aboard the *Olive*. He and I went about together when I was in Plymouth. We were friends then, but that relationship has ended. He is an avowed loyalist."

"Very well. I will have my men take him in tow."

After Colonel Glover instructed his men, he and Jack went below to the captain's cabin.

While Amadi served the two men coffee, Jack found the cupboard where Captain Morris stored his cache of liquors. "A tot of rum or brandy, Colonel?"

"Aye. Either. I feel we'll be here for a while."

When Jack finished informing Glover about the *Piper*'s voyage and the events that had transpired in Falmouth, the two had polished off all of Captain Morris's rum and brandy, and two pots of Amadi's weak coffee. It was well after ten o'clock in the evening.

"We should eat something," Jack said and called Amadi.

"Aye." Colonel Glover stood and stretched. He reached into his coat pocket and pulled out a rolled parchment. "A communiqué from General Washington. It concerns you."

The Nigerian cook entered the cabin.

"We have not eaten," Jack said. "Bring us what food you have available."

The cook nodded and slipped out the door.

Colonel Glover untied and unrolled the parchment, and he laid it on the table in front of him. He scanned the general's communication. "First is an answer to your concern about a Lieutenant Arian Brace. Seemed his loyalty was in question. The general held a secret inquiry with several of his trusted officers, but no evidence was found to support the suspicion. Only hearsay.

"Few trusted the man, so General Washington reassigned Brace to a post in Philadelphia. The lieutenant left Cambridge about a week after you had departed for Beverly." The colonel raised his head, took a breath, and continued. "Brace never arrived in Philadelphia. He hasn't been seen or heard of since. Washington wrote that he sent word to other military and commercial people who travel the route to Philadelphia to be on the lookout for the lieutenant. The only report of a sighting the general received was from some Rhode Island militiamen. They saw Brace at an inn outside Providence several days after he left Cambridge. Beyond that he has disappeared." Glover again raised his eyes from the document. "He might have encountered highwaymen or secreted himself across to Long Island where there are many loyalists and several redcoat garrisons. He might turn up again one day. Who knows? The search for Lieutenant Brace is over."

The colonel returned his eyes to the communiqué. "General Washington also informed us he had accepted some bookseller's proposal, a Mr. Henry Knox, to collect and transport the cannons captured during the Battle of Fort Ticonderoga from the fort to Boston. He commissioned Knox to the rank of colonel and put him in charge of the expedition. Knox and several others left for Ticonderoga about two weeks ago." Glover shook his head. "This Knox fellow plans to use sledges to haul these cannons, a load of some tonnage, three hundred miles or more over mountains, through forest, across rivers, and through ice and snow." He gritted his teeth and continued to shake his head. "A preposterous mission, but I admire General Washington's resolve. Though I do believe he is grasping at straws."

"Except for my concern about Arian Brace, what you have just told me, Colonel, does not affect my situation. What is directly important to me in the general's communiqué?"

"Midshipman Hollister, I know little about you. I only met you the day the *Piper*'s voyage began. Captain Morris appears to think very highly of you, though, and so does His Excellency George Washington. He wants you to return to Cambridge posthaste. The communiqué states he has an important assignment for you. He gives no indication of what this task might be." The colonel looked up from the document. "I suspect a promotion is on the horizon. You have well satisfied your apprenticeship." He sat back in his chair. "Your old friend, Captain Diaz, is in Beverly with his men. I sent a message to him when I learned of the *Piper*'s arrival to come take you to Cambridge. He will be here at sunup."

Jack slowly sat back in his chair and for a moment stared at the ceiling. "I do not know what General Washington has in mind, but I am certain my future will be different from what I expected. I will be ready. However, I do regret not being able to say farewell to Captain Morris and my friends from the *Piper*. I would appreciate it if you tell the captain I enjoyed serving under him and hope to do so again one day. Please give my good-byes to the crew. They are a dedicated bunch of men."

www.ingramcontent.com/pod-product-compliance
Lightning Source LLC
Chambersburg PA
CBHW030551180626
46816CB00005B/1492